Moon Blest

Books By Jay Lynn

Moon Blest

The Dragon Marked Chronicles

The Dragon Sage

Prince of Dragons

Mission Stone: Quest of the Five Flames

Moon Blest

Jay Lynn

First print edition 2022
ISBN-13: 978-0-9993073-6-4

Book cover design by: Inkwolf Designs
Editing by: H.B.

For my two little wolves

Chapter 1

Racing through the woods, a form darted between thick evergreens and easily leapt over shrubs. Chest heaving, her lungs and calves were starting to burn, but the girl didn't dare to slow her pace. Her long honey-colored hair flew behind her like strands of gold.

Faster, a voice whispered urgently to her as the sound of pounding footsteps grew closer.

Pumping her arms, the girl pushed her aching body to its limit. Traveling another five hundred yards, she burst through the underbrush and into a clearing surrounding a small lake. Lifting her arms into the air, the girl excitedly jumped up and down just as two teenagers broke into the open space behind her.

"Yippee!" she squealed. "I won!"

"Argh," groaned Jonas as he collapsed onto the ground.

"How do you always beat us?" whined Matt while releasing a deep huff.

"Because you guys are a bunch of slow-pokes," teased a tall, brown-haired girl with bright blue eyes as she stepped out of the woods. "That was great, Ella. I think you've gotten even faster."

"Thanks Kaylee, but it was just luck," Ella said with a wink.

Smiling brightly, Ella turned and walked to the edge of Fire Lake with her three best friends. In the early morning, the sun's rays would shine off the surrounding mist, causing the water to appear ablaze. Rumors claimed that bizarre things happened here during the darkness of night, yet Ella found a strange peace whenever she stood near the shore. After the deaths of her parents during a rogue attack ten years ago, Fire Lake had become her sanctuary.

"So," Kaylee began, stretching out her limbs. "Are you going to the bonfire tonight? There will be a lot of cute boys there."

Ella giggled. Since she lived in the pack house as an orphan, kitchen duty was part of her chores. Normally, that meant nightly dishes and cooking three times a week. However, during special occasions, like this weekend's bonfire, it was her job to help cook and serve the food. Ella didn't have a choice other than to attend. At least she would have off for her birthday in three days.

"I'm not sure how much socializing I'll be doing. You know I have work."

Kaylee waved a hand dismissively. "It's not like Alpha Jack is going to have you serving all night. Come on, don't you want to start hunting for your mate?" Kaylee sighed and began tossing pebbles into the lake. "I wish that I could find my mate."

Ella smiled. Kaylee was only three weeks younger than herself, yet she had been talking about finding her mate for as long as she could remember. A mate was the name commonly used among werewolves for their spouse or soulmate. Each wolf had a mate chosen for them by the Moon Goddess herself. Although werewolves couldn't shift into their wolf form until they reached their sixteenth birthday, and in turn find their soul's other half, their inner wolf was able to speak to them from a young age. Crystal, Ella's wolf, had been her confidant since before the passing of her parents. In fact, Ella couldn't remember a time when she didn't hear her wolf's strong soothing voice. Sometimes, she wondered if it was Kaylee or her wolf that was more eager to find a mate.

"Mates are overrated," scoffed Matt, Kaylee's brother. He was a year older than them and had yet to find his mate. "I've seen enough warriors turn to mush because of *some she-wolf* and I'm not about to let that happen to me."

He crossed his arms over his chest and lifted his chin into the air as if he could defy the Moon Goddess's will with his words.

Smirking, Jonas walked up to Matt's other side. "Who wants to bet that 'some she-wolf' turns him into the biggest bowl of mush that there is?" he questioned while making air quotes with his fingers.

Growling, Matt dropped his arms and tackled the other boy.

Ella and Kaylee shook their heads as Matt tried to pin his friend and make him take back the words. Jonas managed to wiggle himself free and took off into the forest, laughing while he threw taunts over his shoulder.

Balling up his fists, Matt quickly stripped down to his compression boxers and shifted into his wolf. The magic of their blood allowed tight clothing to morph with their bodies as they grew and changed into their wolves. As such, werewolves almost always wore form-fitting underwear. With a howl, the dark brown wolf took off into the woods.

Shaking her head, Kaylee picked up her brother's discarded clothing. "Boys," she muttered, rolling her eyes. "He's just showing off since he can shift."

Fighting a smile, Ella placed a hand on her friend's shoulder. "Don't worry. Soon, it will be our turn. Then, both those boys are going to be in a world of trouble."

With a laugh, the girls started to make their way back towards the forest. A shiver traced its way down Ella's spine.

The grin dropping from her lips, she quickly glanced over her shoulder. Her brown eyes searched the trees surrounding the lake, but saw nothing out of the ordinary.

Did you see anything? she asked Crystal.

No... her voice trailed off as if she wanted to add something.

Ella bit her lip, not caring for the tension she could feel coming from her wolf. *It could have been the wind.*

Crystal didn't reply, causing Ella to shift her weight back and forth. "We should get back to the jeep," Ella told her friend, picking up her pace. "After all, the party starts in just a few hours."

Whisk in hand, Ella briskly mixed a bowl of batter for the onion rings. Something about the repetitive action helped to soothe the tension in her muscles. Crystal was uneasy and nothing seemed to calm her, causing Ella's stomach to turn sour. Eyeing the towering platters being carried outside to the tables, only made her groan inwardly. Some of her favorite foods were being served during the BBQ-style party and she wasn't sure that she would be able to keep any of it down.

"Ella," called Lisa, one of the full-time kitchen staff members. "Could you take these plates out to the tables?"

Dipping her head in a nod, Ella set the bowl of batter on the counter.

"Sure."

Grabbing a large tray holding plates of buffalo wing dip, she made her way out of the back of the kitchen and towards a set of sliding doors left open for the servers. Ella paused at the sight before her. It was dusk, and the entire pack was spread out across the grounds of the pack house. A large bonfire was on the edge of the celebration with colored lanterns strung between the lampposts for additional light. Rows of tables were spread across the space, with warming tables for a buffet-style meal set up over by the grills.

Children ran playfully through the grass and laughter filled the air mixed with music from the DJ station.

A smile pulled at the corners of Ella's mouth. The vibrant excitement was contagious, ridding earlier stress from her mind. The moment Ella placed the tray down on the nearest table, a pair of arms circled around her.

"There you are," giggled Kaylee as she quickly let go and started bouncing in place. "I was starting to think that you would never escape the kitchen and I definitely need my bestie. I saw several hot wolves already who could be potential mates. It's almost as exciting as the Moonlight Celebration that King Alpha Magnus holds at the castle every year."

"Somehow, I think our party will pale in comparison," Ella enlightened, though she had no way of knowing for sure.

Every year during the first full moon after the summer solstice, unmated werewolves from each pack, aged eighteen and older, were invited to the gathering in hopes of finding their mates. It was a long-held tradition which had grown into a week-long festival.

I wonder what it will be like.

Crystal chuckled. *Give it a few more years and we will see.*

Her words made Ella smirk. Their birthday might not have arrived, but both of them seemed to believe that their mate wasn't any of the wolves who were already of age.

"Ella," hollered the well-known voice of her self-chosen tormentor. "Ella, why are you just standing there? I'm starving. Bring me some food."

"Coming, Courtney," Ella replied, fighting an eye-roll.

Picking up one of the bowls of dip, she strode over to the other girl and placed it in front of her.

Courtney brushed back a lock of her short, dirty blonde hair with a sneer. "Well, it's about time. You should know better than to let your Luna starve."

"You're not Luna yet," Kaylee informed her. "Carrel hasn't even marked you."

Something vile flashed in the older girl's eyes. "You dare speak to me with such disrespect, Omega? Remember, I can have you thrown out of the pack!"

Someone needs to put her in her place! snapped Crystal, urging Ella to let her out.

You know we can't shift yet, she reluctantly reminded her wolf.

Privately, she agreed with her. As the longtime girlfriend and mate to the alpha's son, Courtney had taken it upon herself to treat everyone like her servants. Even as kids, she and Ella had never gotten along and it was getting more difficult to hide her dislike for her future leader.

"She meant no disrespect, Lady Courtney," Ella soothed, trying to draw attention away from her friend before the spiteful girl had her punished. "Is there anything else I can get you?"

Shifting her narrowed eyes to Ella, Courtney raised her chin, then looked out at the party dismissively. "Sparkling water, on ice, and make it quick."

Declining to comment, Ella turned away, taking a red-faced Kaylee with her. Once they were out of earshot, her friend stomped her foot.

"Why did you let her get away with that? She's not the Queen Luna, even if she thinks she is."

Ella sighed. "Believe me, I know. I live with her, remember?" Putting a hand on her hip, Ella continued, "Besides, Courtney *is* going to be our Luna one day and she doesn't take losing well. Have you forgotten what she did to Amber?"

"No," Kaylee quietly relented.

Ella knew she wouldn't. The beautiful brunette had arrived at the winter formal in a gorgeous gown that her mother had made her. The entire night she was surrounded by wolves vying for her attention, leaving Courtney forgotten by their peers. Courtney didn't take well to being outshone. The following week, Amber was accused of cheating on her exams. As punishment, her head was shaved in front of the whole school. After that, most of the pack wouldn't even speak to her, stating that they wanted nothing to do with a cheat. Ella was one of the few who still kept the poor girl company. There was no way that Amber had cheated, of this Ella was certain. The only crime she had ever committed was unknowingly getting on a malicious girl's bad side.

"Don't worry," Ella whispered, giving her friend a quick hug. "I won't let that happen to you.

Stepping back into the kitchen, Ella fetched Courtney her drink and returned to her without incident. Thankfully, the she-wolf was too engrossed with her conversation to even notice Ella's presence. Peering around for Kaylee, Ella slowly made her way through the tables. A soft smile touched her lips as she gazed happily around at all of the excitement. Suddenly, she stiffened. A strange spark warmed her chest before it flowed out to each of her limbs.

What is this? she wondered.

It wasn't a bad feeling, but the odd sensation caused her to frown and grab the front of her shirt. It was then that Ella felt the pair of eyes leering at her darkly. Searching her surroundings, her eyes connected with none other than Carrel Stanford, the future alpha of the pack.

Crystal, what's going on?

I'm not sure, her wolf answered uneasily.

If the feeling hadn't left her legs, Ella would have fled. She didn't have many dealings with Carrel, but those she did were not pleasant. It was no secret that he found her to be a nuisance. There was a time when he actually told Ella that such a low member of the pack shouldn't be living there in the pack house, which was usually for higher ranking members and their families only. His precious Courtney was the daughter of the gamma after all.

As Carrel took a step in her direction, Ella finally re-found her strength. Turning on her heel, she took off towards the pack house. Ella was nearly there when a hand grasped her upper arm. Forcefully spun around, she came face to face with the man she had been trying to avoid. Carrel's normally hazel eyes were completely black. A thread of fear traced its way through Ella's body. Why was his wolf in the forefront? None of the reasons she could think of were good. Without a word, he pulled her into the house and up the stairs towards his father's office. Once inside, he forced Ella into the nearest chair and quickly locked the door.

Raking his fingers through his mud brown hair, Carrel fought a growl. He didn't understand how this could have happened. He was happy with Courtney and so was his wolf, Drex. Yet, when he finally found his mate, it wasn't someone who could even compare to the beauty who had been warming his bed. In his mind, Courtney was a goddess, tall with a full bust, long legs and all too kissable lips.

Ella Welsh, on the other hand…he peered at her with a frown. Ella's long blonde hair was pulled back in a ponytail with loose strands framing her freckled face. Her velvet brown eyes were a pleasant enough color, but that was it. She was too skinny with tiny breasts and still boyish hips. The girl didn't look anywhere near the sixteen years she would soon be.

It's like we've been mated to a child, he scornfully said to Drex.

All I smell is fear. Get rid of her, Drex scoffed.

Carrel could smell the fear emanating from her as well. It was *not* a trait that a luna should have. There was no way that he would be trapped with this girl for the rest of his life. She would bring his pack down. Carrel could not abide weakness. His pack would be the strongest in the kingdom and those who didn't make the cut, he would discard. No one, not even his supposed mate, would stop him. As an alpha, the goddess would simply grant him another. Ella must have been a mistake.

Don't worry my friend, he told his wolf confidently. *No one will ever know about this.*

Lifting his chin, Carrel stormed over to Ella's side. Towering above her, he watched her with sharp, blazing eyes that bore not a single speck of kindness.

"What is your middle name?" he suddenly snapped.

Eyes widening to large pools, Ella couldn't form a single cohesive thought. Leaning as far back in the plush leather as she could, she stuttered, "Lou-louise."

Carrel grunted in response. "I, Carrel Liam Stanford, reject you, Ella Louise Welsh, as my mate."

A gasp escaped Ella's lips as a pain tore through her chest, causing her wolf to whimper. He was her mate? So that was the strange feeling coursing through her from the moment he appeared tonight. It was the mate pull? Somehow it felt more like a foreboding than the happiness she expected. What about Courtney? Was their relationship a lie? Tears started to shine in Ella's eyes despite her best efforts to keep them at bay.

"Why?" she whispered.

Her mate was supposed to love her, cherish her. Yet, Carrel hadn't even given her a chance. The moment he recognized what she was, he had tossed her aside like a pile of trash.

"Why?" he mocked coldly. "As if you need to even ask. I will not be trapped by an ugly, weak, and pathetic mate like you. You are not fit to be my Luna."

Ella's mouth gaped. Her arms instinctively curled up over her chest protectively as Carrel bent down over her.

"Now listen well, girl," he commanded in his best alpha voice. "You will *never* speak of this to anyone. In fact, you will leave this pack tonight and *never* return. I want you out of my sight for good."

Heart racing, Ella absently shook her head. This couldn't be happening. She must be hearing him wrong. How could he despise her so greatly that he would not only reject her on the spot, but banish her from the only home she had as well.

"Please, don't do this," she pleaded, her body beginning to shake as tears started to run down her cheeks. "I have nowhere else to go."

For the briefest moment, Carrel almost relented. He didn't really want to throw a fifteen-year-old orphan out of the pack.

You know what would happen if your father ever found out, Drex reminded him.

Carrel pressed his lips together in a thin line. Yes, he knew, and he wasn't about to let that happen. His father believed in taking care of all pack members and valued the connection he shared with his mate, Carrel's mother, Karen. The consequences of rejecting his own mate would be severe. Alpha Jack might even deny him his right as the next alpha.

"You heard me," Carrel growled, his brief moment of empathy having vanished. "Pack a bag and get out or I will kill you."

Moving away from the chair, Carrel unlocked the door and held it open.

On shaky limbs, Ella slowly rose and darted out of the space. There was no talking to Carrel. At that moment, she wanted to be as far away from him as possible. Her small room was on the opposite side of the manor. Traveling towards it, her mind whirled. Where would she go? What would she do? Ella had no money and few skills apart from cooking and cleaning. The woods were home to rogues like those who had already killed her family. Unable to shift, how was she going to protect herself? Ella's steps faltered. Rogues. That's right, if Carrel banished her from the pack, then she would be a rogue as well.

We can't let him do this, Crystal insisted.

There had to be something they could do. Alpha Jack! That's right. He was the only one who could override Carrel's commands. She doubted that Carrel could hate her more than he already did, but if she spoke to the alpha, then perhaps he could aid her in relocating to another pack.

Changing course, Ella made her way outside. Keeping her head down, she quickly circled around, seeking the alpha. Finally, she spotted him near the edge of the party by the bonfire. He was talking with his beta, Steven. Ella flew to his side, dropping into a deep bow.

"Alpha, pl-please. I need to speak with you," she said shakily, the tears already flowing once again.

Both men peered at her pale, wet cheeks with surprise.

"Ella dear, what is it?" Steven questioned.

"Al-alpha—" Now that she was standing before him, Ella was at a loss as to what to say. How did you tell your leader that his son was trying to get rid of you because he found out that you are his mate? Perhaps it would best just to blurt it out. There couldn't be any easy way to tell him what was happening, right?

"Whatever it is, you know you can tell us," Jack said, his brows furrowing worriedly.

Trying to swallow the lump forming in her throat, Ella nodded faintly.

Here it goes, she told Crystal.

You can do this, her wolf encouraged.

"Sir, it's about Carrel. He—"

"There you are!" thundered a voice she had come to dread.

He was close. Too close. How had he found her so quickly? Ella backed away from him without even realizing it, almost as if her body was screaming at her to run.

"How dare you speak to the Alpha, my father, after what you have done?" Carrel continued, coming to stand dangerously close to her.

Lips parting, Ella's mind went blank. What did he just say? After what *she* did? She hadn't done anything. In fact, she had hardly spoken the entire time they were in the alpha's office.

"What?" she whispered dumbfounded.

"Don't try and play innocent. I caught you red-handed in the Alpha's office. You even dropped this when you ran," Carrel added, lifting a valuable gold pocket watch that had belonged to Alpha Jack's grandfather.

Shaking her head violently, Ella prayed to the goddess that this was all some twisted dream. "I didn't take that." She turned to gaze at Jack. Though he hadn't spent much time around her, she had lived in his house for almost ten years. He should know that Ella wasn't a thief. "I didn't take anything," she repeated sincerely.

"First a thief, now a liar," Carrel spat venomously, cutting off what his father was about to say.

"N-no," Ella cried, unable to do more than shake her head.

"Go ahead then," he taunted with a smirk. "Tell my father that you weren't just in his office. He'll know you're lying. Your scent is all over the room."

"Is this true, Ella?" Jack questioned with a deep frown. "Were you in my office?"

A crowd had gathered around the space, watching her with mixes of confusion and scorn. Among them was Kaylee, who after glancing at Ella for a few seconds with a scowl, turned and disappeared from view. In that moment, Ella knew that it didn't matter what she said. Her scent and Carrel's word were all the proof needed to find her guilty. It would be like Amber all over, but this time worse. Carrel had already commanded for her to leave and he would see to it one way or another. If she tried to stay, no one would aid her once she was branded a thief. In a few short minutes, he had successfully destroyed whatever chance Ella had of living in the Red Moon Pack.

Stepping closer, Carrel leaned in and whispered so that only Ella could hear him. "This is your last chance to leave, or you *will* die."

Gasping, Ella stiffened, her eyes never leaving Carrel's face as he withdrew from her personal space. The evil glint shining in his gaze told Ella all she needed to know. He wasn't just trying to scare her off. She had no doubt that Carrel *would* hold true to his word and kill her as he promised.

Fear and a desire to survive, coursed through every part of Ella's body. Spinning on her heel, she ran as fast as she could into the forest, never once daring to look back.

The bright, gleaming light of the bonfire had long since faded into a new day. Still, there was no sign of Ella.

Releasing a sigh, Jack continued to stare at the woods where she had disappeared. The girl was still too young to be out on her own. So, when morning came and she hadn't returned, he sent a group of warriors to find her.

This doesn't feel right, Ace, his wolf, stated firmly.

Crossing his arms over his broad chest, he privately agreed. Just then, Steven strode up to join him.

"Any sign of her?" Jack questioned without turning.

"No, Alpha," he informed his leader and friend. "I searched your office as requested. There doesn't appear to be any signs of a break in, however, the girl's scent was in the room."

"Where?"

"In the front area and on a leather chair by the desk."

"Anything behind the desk or rear bookshelf?"

Steven paused briefly before shaking his head. "Not that I could find. She never went back there."

I told you the pup isn't a thief, Ace insisted.

Then why was she in our office? Carrel could have walked in just as she started.

Ace scoffed in his mind. *Really? Where do you keep that watch?*

"Steven."

"Yes, Alpha?"

Jack shook his head. "I'm not going to ask this as your Alpha, Steven. I want your opinion as my friend."

Frowning, Steven nodded. "Anything."

"Do you believe him?"

A long sigh sounded beside him. Peering at the treeline, the middle-aged man didn't answer at first. "No," he said at last. "I don't think Ella is a thief, however something did happen in that office, Jack."

Jack froze. "She isn't Carrel's type."

Steven bobbed his head in agreement. "True, but something terrified her. All my wolf could smell was her fear." He turned to gaze at his friend. "Ella wasn't just scared; it was more than that. My wolf commented that she smelled

13

like our prey before they die. That girl thought she was going to die."

Chapter 2

Feet flying behind her, Ella ran as fast as she could through the forest. After three hours, she finally slowed her pace to a jog. The power of Carrel's all too real threat gave her strength that she didn't know she had. Ella raced faster and for longer than she ever did before. Normally, it took half a day for her to reach the edge of Red Moon's territory, but at the rate she was going, Ella would cross over to the free lands by morning. There were a few miles of unclaimed land in-between each of the packs so that rogues, either by choice or not, could have a place to live peacefully without infringing on an alpha's territory. These lands would now be Ella's new home.

It was neutral territory, for not all rogues were violent. The majority were smaller family packs that wanted to remain separate from the seven larger packs that existed in King Magnus's domain. Other species lived in these lands as well. However, every place had its villains. The free lands were more so. A rogue was still an outcast, forced to defend himself on his own.

The thought stopped Ella in her tracks. *I'm a rogue,* she sobbed bitterly. She had no family, no friends, no one at all. Not one person stepped forward to defend her when Carrel spouted his ridiculous lies. How could everyone believe that she would take something that didn't belong to her? Watching Kaylee turn away from her had been the most terrible thing to happen since the death of her parents. Even her best friend didn't believe she was innocent.

Tears streamed down Ella's face to the point that it blinded her. Leaning against the trunk of a tree, she released a heart-shattering cry. The adrenaline from her fear-induced trek left her body numb to everything, but the never-ending pain. Ella sobbed until there were no more tears to be cried and her legs gave out. Sitting on the forest floor, she was too drained to even raise an arm and wipe away the moisture on her cheeks.

Come on, get it together, Crystal urged sympathetically. *This isn't the end. We are not the weakling he thinks we are. We are beautiful and strong!*

I don't know, Ella countered sadly. *He might be right. How are going to survive out here on our own?*

We will never know until we try.

Ella knew Crystal was right. There had to be something she could do. Ella was young. However, she wasn't the first wolf to be run out of her pack. Slowly getting to her feet, she used the hem of her shirt to dry her face. Taking a few deep breaths, Ella peered around at the dark woods. Without the constant fear of Carrel appearing to slay her, she recognized the area that she was in. It was close to Fire Lake. Wrapping her arms protectively around herself, Ella began to walk in the water's direction. Placing one foot in front of the other, Ella concentrated on going forward and nothing else. In a few minutes, she stepped out of an opening in the trees and into the meadow encompassing the lake.

Well, we got this far, Ella said softly to Crystal, taking in the luminous glow of the water.

Strolling towards the edge, she peered out at the mist swirling just above the surface of the lake. It rolled in graceful waves, covering the area from the moon's light. Taking a seat on the damp grass, Ella hugged her knees to her chest.

"Please, Goddess," she begged quietly, "tell me what I should do."

Just as she expected, no reply came to her. With a sigh, Ella rested her chin on the top of her legs. After a few minutes, a playful wind swirled around her, lifting up the ends of her hair and drawing her eye back to the lake. Straightening, Ella studied the misty surface. The wind continued to shift through the earth-bound clouds until they parted as if by command. Getting to her feet, Ella gazed down at the moon's refection on the water.

"Oh," Ella uttered with poorly hidden disappointment. "It's just the crescent moon."

She watched the gleaming white shape dance over the lake with a strange longing. Why did she feel as if the moon was calling out of her?

Wait, the moon, Crystal said drawing her attention.

What about it? Ella asked her wolf. *All I see is the white moon's reflection.*

Exactly, came a smug reply. *A white crescent moon.*

There were a few seconds of silence before Ella's eyes widened and a smile pulled at her lips. "Of course!" she whispered excitedly. "The White Crescent Pack. I've heard Alpha Jack speak of them. They are known for taking in homeless rogues!" Gazing up at the sky, Ella clasped her hands together. "Thank you, Goddess."

For the first time tonight, Ella felt a small thread of hope. Blackwood was their neighboring pack, but the White Crescent pack was on their other side. If she could make it through the central free lands surrounding King Alpha Magnus's territory, then she would be able to reach it without crossing into any other pack's lands. All she had to do was survive the journey through unknown rogue territory.

We can do this, Crystal told her confidently.

17

Yes, we can, Ella agreed. Taking a deep breath, she turned north and began walking the only way she knew how, forward.

A knock sounded on Jack's door. Setting down the papers in his hand, he called for his visitor to enter. Carrel strode confidently into the space and settled himself into one of the leather chairs.

"You asked to see me, Father."

"Yes," Jack nodded with a neutral expression on his face. "I wanted to talk to you about Ella."

His son released a long, exaggerated sigh. "Why? We've been over this already."

"Humor me," the alpha commanded in a tone that left no room to refuse. "What happened last night?"

Carrel draped an arm over the side of the chair and fought the urge to roll his eyes.

Careful, Drex warned him. *The old man doesn't believe your story.*

He's just fishing, Carrel countered. *If he had any proof, then we wouldn't be sitting in here having a chat.*

"There isn't much to tell, sir," Carrel began calmly. "I came upstairs to get something and saw a light on in your office. I decided to check it out, since I had seen you outside, and found Ella going through your stuff."

"When did you find my watch?"

"She dropped it when I came in. Must have startled her," he added off-handedly.

Thrusting out his bottom lip, Jack nodded his head. "Strange thing about this watch," he told his son, rising from behind his desk. "For the last three years, I've kept it hidden in a book all the way over here," Jack said, pointing to the very back of his office. "There are only three people who know about that hiding place. And if that isn't strange enough," Jack continued, stopping in front of his son. "Then tell me, Carrel, why isn't Ella's scent on the watch or anywhere near the back half of the room?"

Shit, Drex muttered.

Carrel shrugged his shoulders, declining to answer.

"What...happened?" Jack stressed, growling low.

I smell fear, Ace told him needlessly.

The alpha could scent it as well. Carrel had lied about Ella stealing. That knowledge alone was enough to bring his wolf to the forefront. No one tricked this alpha and got away with it.

"Don't make me repeat myself, boy. Did she get on your snobby mate's bad side? Or decline your advances? I know how you are with some of the she-wolves."

Eyes widening, Carrel had to press his lips together to keep from bursting out laughing. His father really thought that he had interest in that tomboy? It was too much. Confident that this interrogation was now going in his favor, Carrel shook his head.

"I'm sorry, Father, but I can only tell you what I know. I *did* see Ella in here, and no, I've *never* touched her."

He seems to be speaking the truth...for the moment, Ace conceded.

Jack leaned back and rubbed his face, feeling some of the tension leaving his shoulders. At least his son hadn't tried to attack some innocent girl. For a moment there, he was beginning to fear the worst. At the same time, he was right back at the start with no answers. Crossing his arms, Jack watched his son intently.

"I might not know exactly what happened, Carrel, but know this: if anything happens to that girl, I'm holding you personally responsible. I've already called Alpha Isaiah of Blackwood to keep an eye out for her. Hopefully, we can find her before the rogues do."

Jack moved forward to tower over his son. "I will be keeping a *very* close eye on you from now on. If you put one toe out of line, I promise that you will *not* inherit Red Moon from me. Am I understood?"

Carrel had to use every ounce of his strength to rein in Drex. His wolf was clawing to the surface wanting to rip his father's throat out.

How dare he threaten us!

Cool it, Drex. We will get Red Moon one way or another, but we aren't ready to kill him yet.

When Carrel finally had control of his wolf, he answered crisply, "Yes, sir."

Moaning softly, Ella pressed a hand against her growling stomach. She hadn't eaten anything besides the few nuts and berries that she was able to scavenge as she continued to walk through the never-ending forest. Every snap of a twig or rustle of the long, dry grass had her sensitive hearing on alert. Daytime was the safest time to travel, for werewolves were not the only creatures lurking in the woods. This also meant that she was easier to spot. With the constant threat of detection, Ella didn't stop for more than a few minutes at a time to rest or grab a quick drink from a stream.

Two days had passed in a blur. Everything looked and smelled the same. Ella knew that she was still in the free lands, but not much else. She didn't have a map to tell her where exactly. Unfortunately, there weren't any signs either. Not even on the two roads she crossed. From what she could remember, she needed to find a river. The White Crescent Pack's territory was to the right of it.

Another mile passed and Ella scrunched up her nose. The faint smell of running water reached her senses. She was getting closer to her goal. Picking up her pace, Ella started to jog through the trees. A small flowing river came into view up ahead. Smiling, Ella ran even faster at the sight. Nothing else seemed to register in her mind other than the fact that she would be within White Crescent's lands before dark.

We're not alone, Crystal suddenly warned her from the depths of her mind.

Glancing to each side, Ella could make out the forms of three large brown-colored wolves. There were two on the right and one on the left.

Stay calm, Ella told her wolf. *If we can make it to the pack's territory, they shouldn't follow us.*

Time to run.

Ella agreed. The only advantage on her side was her speed. She doubted that they would expect a wolf to be so fast in human form. Even as a wolf, Matt wasn't able to outrun her. Digging her feet into the ground, Ella lunged forward, withholding nothing as she sped away from the wolves tracking her. Veering to the right, she aimed for White Crescent. The sound of a loud howl broke the silence of the woods. Heart pounding in her chest, Ella tried not to think about what that meant. Keeping her gaze forward, she focused on pushing her body to its limit.

Bounding out of the trees, a grey wolf leapt into her path.

Ella twisted at the last second, kicking off a tree trunk to switch directions. Her agility didn't deter the hunter staying close on her tail. When Ella tried to cut back to the right, another wolf appeared in her sight line.

Crap.

These rogues knew what they were doing. As long as she couldn't shift, there was no plausible way to get to the pack's territory now. At best, she could circle around later. All that mattered was getting them off her tail. Reaching the river, Ella skidded to a stop. The rushing water churned before her. Heading downstream, Ella scanned the surface, searching for some way across. Up ahead, some large rocks reached out into the water. There was an open space in the center. However, close by were a few logs crammed against another set of rocks. It wasn't the best bridge she had ever seen, but Ella was willing to take the risk.

Diving into the water, Ella pulled herself up onto one of the stones. A large splash at her back told her that at least one of the wolves followed. She leapt to the next rock and the one after. Pausing, Ella was now faced with the gap in her makeshift bridge. It appeared so much larger up close. Glancing behind her, she saw two wolves swimming nearer.

"You can do this," she muttered encouragingly.

Bending her knees, the she-wolf sprung off the rock and landed on the edge of the first log. Ella's foot slipped, causing her to crash down on her hands and knees as she tried to keep from being swept away. As she went to take a step, her one foot jerked back. Peering down at her shoe, Ella spotted her laces tangled on a broken branch. Tugging forcefully, she yanked her foot free just as the first wolf reached her. Screaming, Ella swatted a hand at her foe as she attempted to back away. A wave suddenly rose from the current, enveloping the wolf and washing him downstream.

Move! Crystal ordered, giving life once more to Ella's momentarily frozen body.

The second wolf was closing in upon her and the last three had already jumped into the water. Scurrying over the logs, Ella managed to clear the river and make it safely to the other side. It brought her little comfort since her hunters were still zeroing in.

Taking off, Ella put every ounce of strength into her speed. She had no idea how long she was running before a brown wolf suddenly appeared and head-butted her square in the chest. Ella's body flew through the air as she was thrown backwards. The air was forced from her body, causing her to gasp painfully as she tried to catch her breath. Chest heaving, Ella rose unsteadily to her feet. She knew some basic combat skills, but nothing that would aid her in a battle against four shifted wolves. Eyes darting around, she looked for some opening in which she could escape.

A low, almost humorous sound came from the grey beast currently circling her.

Thanks for staying with me, Crystal, Ella thought, bidding her friend a final farewell.

It's not over yet.

Ella didn't see how she would get out of this. None of the wolves had attacked yet, leading her to believe that something far worse was about to come. A flash zipped past some of the trees to her left. Had the rogue from the river survived and caught up to them? No, Ella didn't think that was it. The ones surrounding her didn't seem to notice the other presence.

Rushing forward, another group of wolves unexpectedly attacked from the underbrush. Ella didn't know where to look first. There were at least a dozen of them in total coming from all sides. Hoping that she might be able to escape during the chaos, Ella turned and fled. She pulled to a stop, sliding on the ground as two wolves bit into one of the hunters—right where she would have been! Scooting backwards, Ella scrambled to her feet, only to find herself face to face with a pair of bright blue eyes.

The new wolf's tan fur was covered in blood on his face and paws. Teeth bared in a growl, he watched Ella intently.

Eyes darting around the space, Ella noted that her original foes were all dead and she was now surrounded by a new, even more dangerous set of captors. The wolves drew close enough to keep her in place, but refrained from attacking. By the tilt of the tan one's head, she guessed that they were mind-linking each other.

We need to do something, Crystal shouted in her mind.

What can we do? You know I can't fight! Ella just about screeched in return.

Let me out, Crystal insisted. *Let me out. Let me out!*

With Crystal's voice chanting over and over in her head, Ella couldn't focus on anything that was going on around her. An intense pain suddenly raced through her limbs. A scream escaped her lips as Ella dropped to her knees. Curling up into a ball, she felt like her very bones were on fire. One by one, each bone snapped and reshaped itself. A muzzle grew from her face and long thick fur covered every inch of her body. Just like that, the pain vanished. Gasping, Ella peered down at the ground only to see a set of pale blue paws.

What in the world?

She must be delusional. No wolf had blue fur. Shifting her focus to the wolves around her, Ella's vision blurred. Her body swayed, causing her to collapse onto the dirt floor. As she struggled to stay awake, two of the werewolves shifted back to human form.

"Crap, I didn't think she was old enough to shift," a tall young man with spiky black hair observed. He peered over at his leader. "Looks like it was her first time shifting, Beta."

"Happy birthday," the beta muttered sardonically. Releasing a sigh, he ran a hand through his dark brown hair. "Let's get her back to the pack house. It's gonna be alright, kid."

With a whimper, Ella's head dropped to the ground and everything around her faded to black.

Sitting at his private table in the massive dining room, Alpha Nicholas scanned the kingdom's weekly report for anything of interest. Setting a plate of food in front of him, his mate, Amanda, kissed his cheek before taking her place by his side.

"What has you so captivated this morning?" she asked in a teasing tone as she took in his messy black hair laced with silver.

Smiling, Nick folded the paper and moved it aside. "Nothing much in here, love," he admitted, gesturing to the packet next to him. "Our new visitor, on the other hand, has me puzzled. What was a pup who couldn't shift doing in the rogue lands?"

Amanda sighed, lifting her shoulders. "She seems awful young to be a spy."

Nick nodded his agreement. "Kyle informed me that Yvette thinks she was on the run for days."

"Days?" his luna repeated incredulously, her green eyes widening.

"She was severely dehydrated and half-starved."

"The poor dear."

Nick chuckled. "Now don't get too sympathetic until we know *why* she was running. The girl could be a criminal."

Amanda pressed her lips together to fight the smirk threatening to show itself. She didn't need to say a word. Nick knew that she found the idea ridiculous the moment he had voiced it. Chuckling, he leaned over and gave her a kiss. Approaching footsteps drew him back quicker than he would have liked.

"Forgive the interruption," Kyle apologized with a bow. "I can come back later."

The alpha waved off his apology as he watched his second in command. A towering six foot five inches, Kyle's short brown hair and stubble-like beard were a direct reflection of his efficiency and strength. Nick knew he wouldn't have sought him out if it wasn't important. "That's alright, Kyle. What do you have for me?"

Glancing around the bustling dining room, his beta simply informed him, "She's awake."

Nick stiffened briefly. Quickly wiping his mouth, he slid back in his chair. "I will see you later, love. I need to see to this."

Purposefully rising, Amanda strode over towards the beta and clasped her hands in front of her. "What are we waiting for?"

Her husband's light grey eyes narrowed. *I don't want you seeing her until I know it's safe,* he told her through their shared mental link.

What's the matter, afraid she'll bite? Violet, Amanda's wolf, questioned smugly.

You're not going to win, Nick's wolf, Maddox, said with a laugh.

"Kyle, lead the way if you will," the alpha conceded.

Lightly grasping Amanda's hand, he tucked her fingers in the crook of his arm. Making their way out of the dining hall, Kyle led them outside the manor and down a nearby path to the pack hospital. Due to their visitor's unusual circumstances, she had been placed in an isolated room and away from prying eyes. The beta posted two of his team outside her door at all times. Other than the hospital's head doctor, Yvette, and two nurses, no one was allowed near her room.

Entering through the rear security door, Nick was almost immediately confronted by Kyle's spunky mate. Chart in hand, she bowed quickly before getting down to business.

"Thank you for coming, Alpha."

"Not at all, Doctor, what can you tell me?"

"She's stable. Her glucose, sodium and potassium levels were low. Her glucose returned to normal last night. And we have been correcting the severe dehydration with plenty of fluids. I've confirmed that the she-wolf is an adolescent, but I'm afraid that's all I can tell you with her in her current state."

Nick frowned, crossing his arms. "What do you mean, her 'current state'?"

Yvette and Kyle shared a quick uneasy glance which the alpha did not miss.

"You should take a look," his beta advised, pointing to the small window in the room's private door.

Growling faintly, Nick peered through the opening.

What could they possibly want us to see? he thought to Maddox.

His eyes first traveled to the empty bed before scanning the rest of room. It didn't take him long to see a large mound near the back wall. The figure was completely covered in a blanket except for the end of a muzzle and two paws. Jerking back, Nick peered at Kyle and Yvette with a frown.

"Why is she still in her wolf form?"

"She been like that since the Beta's team brought her here yesterday. I used a small IV so that she wouldn't blow a vein when she shifted back, yet..." Yvette shrugged helplessly. "The girl's been awake for about half an hour. Every time we try to enter the room, she hides in the corner. I was hoping that your alpha dominance would be able to get through to her."

Nick bobbed his head in agreement. Even though she wasn't part of his pack, an alpha's power should force her to submit and change back. "Has she shown any signs of aggression?"

"No, no," Yvette quickly dismissed any such thoughts. "She just curls up in a ball and shakes. Nick, the girl is terrified."

Terrified of what?

Or who? Maddox interjected.

Whatever was causing this behavior had to be from more than the rogues who chased her onto their lands. Turning about, Nick placed his hand on the door.

Sure enough, the moment the entry began to creak open, the she-wolf leapt up, accidently flinging off her blanket as she pressed herself into the corner. Keeping her head bowed in submission, she visibly shook.

Having only taken a few steps into the space, the alpha froze. Kyle had mentioned the girl possessing an unusual colored fur. However, he had disregarded it as a strange pattern or his beta's poor attempt at a sense of humor. Neither was the case. Nick almost didn't believe his own eyes. Covering every inch of the she-wolf was pale blue fur, like tinted snow. Recovering from his shock, Nick moved a little closer.

"I am Nicholas Carlson, Alpha of the Swift Wind Pack. My staff is here to help you. Now shift!" he commanded in his best alpha voice.

Ella whimpered, keeping her gaze downcast. The Alpha of Swift Wind? Oh no, she must have accidently entered their lands when she crossed the river. She was in the wrong pack's territory!

What are we going to do? she asked her wolf frantically.

Ella had heard of this pack before. They were the strongest, second only to King Magnus's pack, Silver Fang. Alpha Jack once mentioned that Alpha Nicholas and the king were close friends. Heart racing, she fought the urge to puke on the floor. This was not a man that she wanted to anger.

Stay calm, Crystal soothed.

Watching the she-wolf show no signs of changing, Nick frowned. He couldn't sense any defiance in her, so why wasn't she obeying his command?

"No one is going to hurt you," he said, trying again. "But they can't help you in your wolf form, now I said shift!"

Whining, the blue wolf lowered herself to the ground with her belly on the cool tiles. Nick could swear that he could see the glimmer of moisture in her eyes.

What do you think, Maddox? Is she under a spell? It would explain the color of her fur. Before his wolf could answer, Nick felt the warmth of his mate's hand on his arm.

Let us try, Amanda requested.

I don't think that's a good idea, Nick protested through their link. He distinctly heard his mate snort.

If she was going to attack, it would have happened by now. Violet senses no danger. Please.

Exhaling with a long breath, the alpha finally relented. *As you wish, but I'm staying close by.*

Amanda smiled. *I wouldn't have it any other way.*

Taking her time, Amanda walked within a few feet of Ella and knelt down on the floor. Her mate grunted unhappily behind her, but she ignored him.

"Welcome to Swift Wind, little one, my name is Luna Amanda. I promise, we aren't going to hurt you. Our Beta tells us that this may be your first shift. Is that true?"

Ella's gaze darted in her direction, then quickly away. A moment later, she whimpered softly.

"I see."

So, it's as we thought, Violet commented.

"Do you know how to change back?"

This time, Ella peered up at her for a few seconds. Dropping her gaze, she stayed on her belly and crawled towards the woman until her nose touched her knee. She then whined sadly as if saying 'help me'.

"It's alright," Amanda told her, gently petting her fur. "The first time can be a little scary. Now, I want you to close your eyes. Imagine your fur disappearing and your body starting to shrink back to a human's. I want you to picture every detail that you can, the color of your hair, eyes and skin. See it in your mind over and over until the shift is complete."

Doing as the luna said, Ella shut her eyes. She thought of her long blonde hair and her pale, furless skin. A strange sensation began to warm her core prior to traveling the length of her limbs. It wasn't painful, as the shift had been, more like a tingling feeling. Focusing on the luna's words, Ella kept her eyes squeezed tight until she felt the cool tiles beneath her skin. Sitting back on her heels, she stared at her long fingers, turning them over as she studied them intently.

We did it, Ella told Crystal with an inward sigh.

Ella hugged her body tightly. Without her fur, she was suddenly cold.

"Thank you," she whispered to Amanda.

Retrieving the discarded blanket, the older she-wolf wrapped it around the girl's shoulders.

"You're welcome. What is your name?"

The red-haired woman in front of her reminded Ella of her mother, with her kind smile and gentle voice. Though she was sure that the luna could be as strong as steel when she wanted.

"Ella," came the quiet reply.

If it wasn't for her heightened hearing, Amanda would never have caught it.

"Ella, can you tell us what pack you're from?"

Ella froze, her eyes widening to dark pools. She couldn't tell them that she was from Red Moon. If Carrel found out where she was, then who could say if he would bring her back just to carry out his threat. The evil glint in his gaze told Ella that he would happily slay her as he promised. The man wasn't a wolf, he was a demon. Of all the mates she could have been given…

Calm down, Crystal soothed. *He's not going to get you here.*

Ella wanted to listen to her wolf, but she was too panicked to do so. Even giving her real name had been a mistake. The moment Carrel banished her from the pack, she had become a rogue. That was all she was now.

"I'm...I'm a rogue," Ella told them with tears streaming down her cheeks.

Biting her lip, she pulled her knees up to her chest and buried her face in the prison of her arms. Sobbing quietly, she didn't dare look at anyone in the room again.

She's a rogue? Maddox scoffed. *And I'm a fuzzy cat.*

Don't let her tears sway you. We don't know anything about this girl. She could have been born a rogue.

Then the pup would know how to fight.

Nick didn't want to admit it, but his wolf had a point. Dealing with a few wolves would be nothing for someone who grew up in the free lands. He should know. Two of his warriors had been adopted into his pack from there when they were fourteen. At the time, they had fought better than some of his trained men.

"Well, I'd like to thank you for stopping by, but this visit is over," Yvette stated, walking into the room and standing between the alpha and her patient while making a shooing motion. Nick narrowed his eyes, but the she-wolf didn't back down. "Forgive me, Alpha, but Ella doesn't have the strength for an interrogation right now. At least allow me to give her a proper exam and get her changed into some warmer clothing. The poor girl is in her underwear."

Frowning, Nick looked at Ella, actually *looked* at her for the first time since she was able to shift back into her human form. Her long blonde hair hung down in tangled clumps, and her skin was covered in patches of dirt. Releasing a sigh, he nodded. If anyone else had spoken to him as Yvette did, they would have been quickly reminded of their place. She seemed well aware of what she could get away with. Though if truth be told, Nick never could say no to his baby sister. His best friend and beta was the one he should really feel sorry for.

"Very well, Doctor. We will speak later, Ella." *Have Kyle bring her to my office as soon as she is discharged,* he told Yvette.

30

Of course, Brother, she replied with a grin. *Thank you.*

Shaking his head, Nick held out his arm for his wife. She bid the girl a quick farewell, promising to check on her later before wrapping her arm around his.

"Will you be joining us for lunch, Yvette?" Amanda questioned as they walked together towards the door.

Glancing back at the she-wolf, now completely covered by the massive blanket, she shook her head. "I should make it for dinner as long as I'm able to finish my rounds on time."

"The others can cover them," Kyle interrupted with a grunt.

"He's right," Nick agreed. "You need to take care of yourself as well, little sis."

"I will," she promised.

Nick watched as two nurses entered the space with arms full of towels, clothing and hygiene bottles. The door closed quietly behind them. Standing in the hallway, the alpha pressed his lips together.

"What are your orders, Alpha?" Kyle asked.

"I'm placing you in charge of her security. For the time being, no one is to speak a word of what they saw. Make sure your men know this as well." Crossing his arms, Nick rubbed his chin. "We need more information. Her being a rogue just doesn't make sense and my wolf agrees. Amanda, can you have someone trusted discretely look into any missing she-wolves from the other packs? I don't want it to be known where she is yet."

"Consider it done."

"I have a few meetings this afternoon. Then, I'll speak with Silvia."

"Good idea," his beta said thoughtfully. "There has to be something to explain her unusual...coloring."

Nick couldn't have said it better himself. Maddox sensed no malice from their new guest, only fear. Whatever she was hiding, he was going to find out. There could be away to help her if she was in trouble. However, if she proved a threat to his pack, then Nick would not hesitate to throw her back into the wilderness from whence she came.

Chapter 3

Rubbing his temples, Nick leaned back in his chair and closed his eyes. His meetings had run much longer than he expected. Lunch came and went, but he still hadn't been able to steal away to speak with the pack elder about Ella.

Alpha, came Kyle's voice through the mind-link.

Yes, Beta?

Yvette is discharging her. Do you want me to bring her now?

Yes, Beta, Nick answered.

Perhaps they could clear up some of the questions nagging in the back of his mind. After a moment, he linked his wife to let her know that Ella was being brought to his office. There were no doubts that she would desire to hear what the girl had to say as well.

Once Amanda arrived, the alpha moved to a group of chairs in the center of space. He figured the more casual setting might put the girl at ease. It didn't take long for Kyle's firm knock to sound on the solid wood door.

"Come in," Nick called out.

His beta entered with a freshly scrubbed Ella. Her hair was pulled back in a loose braid revealing brown eyes and a light path of freckles across the bridge of her nose. She was wearing a dark blue long-sleeved t-shirt, sweatpants and sneakers, most likely borrowed from Yvette's daughter.

"Have a seat," the alpha requested politely.

Ella placed herself on the edge of the nearest chair while Kyle leaned back comfortably in the other vacant seat. Keeping from making eye contact, Ella bowed to each of the leaders as she said softly, "Thank you for saving me from those rogues. I'm sorry, I…um…should have said so earlier."

"There is nothing for you to be sorry about, dear. Anyone would have been upset in the same situation," Amanda told her kindly.

"Yes," Nick agreed. "And how you came to find yourself in such a situation is why we are here." He watched as Ella tensed. "The safety of my pack comes first, Ella. If you are to have any future here, then there are a few things I need to know. Understand that I will not tolerate lies."

Blinking, Ella's head snapped up. Gazing at Nick, a spark of hope flashed in her eyes.

Did I just hear him right, Crystal?

I believe so, her wolf answered.

"You would let me stay here, Alpha?"

"It is a possibility," he confirmed. "I do require a probationary period before allowing any new members to join my pack."

"I'll do anything," Ella said sincerely, inching closer to the edge of her chair. "I can cook and clean."

Someone her age should be in school, Amanda said crossly to Nick through their bond.

He glanced at her while raising a brow. *Don't our boys do chores?*

What does that have to do with anything? she returned with more than a hint of Violet in her luna tone.

"Before we discuss any chores you might be assigned, first things first, Ella. What brought you to our territory?"

Her shoulders lifted with a sigh. "I was actually trying to get to the White Crescent Pack. I had heard that they were known for taking in rogues. Before I could reach their lands, I was attacked by those wolves and crossed the river while trying to escape from them."

"How did you cross?" Kyle interrupted. "The water around there is pretty swift."

Ella nodded, glancing up at him. "I used some rocks in the water and then jumped onto a few logs on the other side."

Resourceful, Maddox muttered approvingly.

Nick, Amanda called, seeking his attention, *Alicia has some news.*

The alpha nodded solemnly while he and the luna conversed through their mind-link. After a moment, he turned to look at Ella again.

"You claim to be rogue," Nick started at last. "Were you born one?"

Ella shook her head. "No, sir."

"Then how long have you been a rogue?"

"A few days, sir."

Nick and Amanda shared a glance.

Shifting in his seat, Nick loosely linked his fingers together. "Tell me, Ella. What pack are you from?"

Ella's fingers dug into the fabric of her pants. She couldn't tell him. If he knew where she came from, then it would be far too easy for him to discover why she was kicked out. No pack would want a thief. Ella would lose any chance she had of joining Swift Wind.

"I—I was banished, Alpha."

"You seem awfully young to have been banished. Still, you didn't answer my question. What is the name of your pack?" he repeated, using his alpha dominance.

Biting her lip, Ella fought back the tears stinging her eyes. She wouldn't cry. Crying could not solve her problems.

Stay strong, Crystal encouraged. *We are strong. I feel it.*

Ella wasn't sure about that, but she didn't question her wolf since she needed every bit of her reassurance.

"I can't go back," Ella insisted desperately while staring at the floor. "I can't."

Interesting, his wolf said.

Nick wasn't sure that was the word he would use. He couldn't be sure, but Ella didn't seem to realize that she just defied the order of an alpha. A truly submissive wolf would never have been able to do so. For whatever reason, Nick believed she was indeed scared of going home. Since asking straight out was getting him nowhere, he decided to try a different route.

"Ella, did you know that it is very unusual for a pup to go missing from a pack?" Nick watched as every one of her muscles seemed to tense. "In fact, the first one I've heard of in a long time was reported a few days ago from the Red Moon Pack. It seems that a fifteen-year-old girl with blonde hair and brown eyes ran away Saturday night. Sounds familiar, doesn't it?"

Oh no! Ella cried out in her mind. Unable to say a word, she clenched her hands and continued to look at the floor with a new intensity.

"Here's my question, Ella," Nick started, keeping a close eye on her every move. "Why would your Alpha report you as a runaway, yet you are telling us that you were banished?"

Her throat suddenly dry, Ella tried to swallow the lump settling there. "He...Alpha Jack wasn't the one to banish me."

A frown pulled at Nick's lips. "Then who gave the order?"

You need to tell them, Crystal insisted.

Don't you remember what Carrel said? He will kill us!

They can protect you from that coward. If you don't tell the Alpha what happened, then he will never let us stay.

"Ok, ok," Ella whispered, not realizing that she had answered her wolf out loud. Taking a few deep breaths, she raised her eyes to look at both the alpha and luna. "Please don't tell anyone," she begged.

Taking their silence as encouragement, Ella finally let out the words holding her heart a prisoner of fear.

"The Alpha's son, Carrel, was the one to order me to leave."

The three wolves watching her showed various degrees of surprise.

"Why would the future Alpha give such a command?"

"I guess because he doesn't want anyone to know. He doesn't want his *girlfriend* to know…that I'm his mate."

A stunned silence filled the space. Nick, Amanda, and Kyle could hear their wolves growling in their minds. They couldn't possibly have heard right. A wolf's mate was supposed to be treasured. Why would a future alpha banish his luna? Was she lying?

It would explain why your dominance had no effect, Maddox reasoned.

He was right. Even at a young age, a wolf deemed worthy by the goddess of a luna's rank would not be easily controlled. Ella could have been showing signs of submission at the hospital due to confusion and fear.

Yet, if she was Red Moon's future luna, why would the alpha's son be foolish enough to reject her? Was he not aware of the damage it could do to his pack?

"I know it sounds crazy," Ella conceded. "Your mate is supposed to love you, cherish you."

Despite her best efforts, two drops fell from her cheeks onto her clenched fists. Sniffly, Ella wiped her face briskly. Building up from among the fear and sadness was a justified anger. Having started her story, the rest of the words flowed freely. Ella couldn't have stopped them even if she tried.

"He—he didn't even give me a chance. I know I'm not beautiful like Courtney, but he called me ugly and weak. That wasn't even the worse part," Ella continued with a frown as she stared at a point on the floor. "He told me to leave, to leave or he would kill me. How could he do that? We've barely spoken in all the years that I've lived in the pack house. I never thought Carrel would be so cruel as to banish me from my home."

Ella lifted her gaze to meet Nick's. Her cheeks were wet and flushed, but there was a blaze in her eyes for the first time since they had met.

She has some fire, he heard Maddox observe approvingly.

"You know what he did when I tried to talk to Alpha Jack?" Ella questioned. Not waiting for an answer, the she-wolf continued with an almost hysterical laugh. "Carrel told his father that he caught me stealing from his office. I've *never* taken anything in my life, but no one believed me. Not even my best friend. I knew that if I tried to stay, Carrel would make my life hell before he chose to end it, so I ran."

After Ella finished telling her story, no one said a word. She waited, her stomach churning unpleasantly. How could she have been so foolish? The alpha of her pack hadn't believed her. Why would a complete stranger? Shoulders sagging, Ella slowly rose to her feet.

"Thank you for helping me with the rogues, but I think it's time for me to go."

Amanda's eyes widened, her lips parting. "Wait a moment, dear. Why do you want to leave so soon?"

Ella unconsciously twisted her fingers. "Well I...I thought you would want me to."

The luna blinked. She peered at both the alpha and beta, her eyes clouding slightly as she spoke telepathically.

"No one wants you to leave," Amanda reassured at last. "Though your mate's treatment is surprising, none of us doubt your words."

Giving them an incredulous stare, her mouth moved wordlessly. Her lower lip began to quiver. Sniffing, Ella gave them a watery smile.

"Thank you."

Someone believed her! The knowledge was enough to warm her heart. Perhaps there was hope for her to have a future here after all.

Gracefully, Amanda rose and wrapped an arm around the girl's shoulders. "Come, after all this excitement, I think it's time for you to get some rest. We can talk more about this later."

Nodding, Ella allowed herself to be steered out of the office while Nick and Kyle remained behind.

Exhaling deeply, Nick placed both hands on the arms of his chair and leaned his head back. He then closed his eyes.

"I do wonder why the future Alpha rejected his mate as soon as he found her," his beta muttered.

"Difficult to say," Nick said, keeping his eyes closed. "Ella did mention a girlfriend. He could believe that the Goddess might grant his chosen she-wolf as a second chance mate."

He did seem like an arrogant little prick, Maddox recalled, thinking of the last time they had met.

While Nick had pleasant dealings with Jack, he never did care for the alpha's only child.

"What do you want to do?" Kyle inquired.

"I'm not sure yet," Nick admitted, lifting his head. "Though I doubt the girl is lying, there is still the matter of her strange fur."

"What did Silvia say about it?"

Nick groaned, rubbing his temples. "I haven't been over to see her yet. All of my meetings ran much longer than planned. I'll go now. Stay here and watch over my Luna."

"Of course," Kyle agreed immediately as they both rose to their feet. "You can count on me."

"I always do."

Strolling down the sidewalk, Nick made his way towards the pack's school. A massive library was attached to the one side, filled not only with the pack's history, but the one person who knew more about werewolves than anyone he had ever met.

Silvia was a Swift Wind elder. She had been charged with keeping the pack's history since before Nick was even born. There was no one else he would trust with researching Ella's blue fur. Silvia not only had vast knowledge of the pack and kingdom's history, but werewolf lore, the strength and weakness of other supernatural creatures, and some of the oldest legends long forgotten by the world. Her three apprentices combined, only knew a fraction of what she did.

Striding through the towering shelves of books, Nick was hit with a sense of nostalgia. When he was younger, he spent many hours paging through the seemingly endless books. Nick briefly stopped one of the library aids who directed him towards the file room. Entering the dim space, the alpha spotted a short woman with snow white hair pinned back and a pair of glasses hanging around her neck on a delicate chain. She was climbing up a narrow ladder to replace some old refinance books which were no longer on the main floor. Silvia never could throw a book out. 'One day you might need it,' she would say.

"Shouldn't one of your assistants be doing this?" Nick inquired, helping her down the thin rails.

Silvia chuckled. "Really, Nicholas," she chided, while still accepting his aid. "I'm quite capable of putting away a few books."

"I never said otherwise," he countered with a grin.

"As much as I enjoy our visits," Silvia told him, patting his hand. "What brings you to this old grey wolf?"

"Silvia, you are timeless," Nick laughed.

"Flattery will get you nowhere," she teased.

Knowing that the lightness of their conversation couldn't last, Nick's smile slipped from his face. "There is a matter that I wanted to discuss with you…privately."

Silvia studied the sudden seriousness of his face. Gesturing for him to follow her, she stepped out of the room and padded down the hallway towards her office. Closing the door softly, Silvia turned the lock.

"No one will disturb us in here, Alpha."

Nick nodded, unsure of how to proceed. She may very well think that he was mad.

"What I'm about to inquire does not leave this room, and it may sound a little…strange."

"Well, I would think that would be obvious," she replied crisply. "Come, Nick. This isn't like you. There's no need to beat around the bush, I've heard just about everything."

Raising a brow, he questioned, "Have you ever heard of a wolf with blue fur?"

The woman just stared at him. The seconds ticked by, but she still didn't move a muscle. Nick was starting to worry when she finally blinked.

"Why would you ask me that?"

"The Beta and his men, along with my son, James, found a teenage girl being attacked by rogues. After they saved her, she shifted into a blue wolf."

"What color blue?"

"A pale, light blue."

Picking up her glasses, Silvia purposely set them on her face and passed through a doorway into a small private library. She began digging through the packed shelves one at a time while mumbling to herself.

"Have you heard of this before?"

Silvia's movements stilled. "Many years ago, when I was still an apprentice for the previous keeper, he told me a legend about a wolf, whose fur was the color of a pale blue moon. It was not until years later that I came across a record of this type of creature. I've always found it fascinating for some reason. Now, I know why."

The she-wolf continued to shuffle through her library.

"And why would that be?" Nick questioned, following after her as Silvia moved to another bookshelf.

Smiling, the small woman removed a thick, dusty, leather-bound book with several page markers sticking out of it.

"Because, I believe the Goddess may have sent her here."

Jerking back, the alpha frowned.

Do you think Silvia is getting a little too old? he asked Maddox.

I don't know. There are stories of the Moon Goddess intervening.

While he had been having a private side conversation, Silvia began flipping quickly through the worn pages. Suddenly, her fingers stopped and she slowly peered up at her alpha.

"You may find it difficult to believe, but after all my years in this world, I know that everything happens for a reason," the history keeper stated, turning the book so that Nick could see its contents. "If she's what I think, she's going to need to be protected."

Brows furrowing, Nick looked down at the page she placed before him. Covering the top half was an old black and white painting of a pale wolf with the moon's light shining upon it. 'Moon Blest' the caption read.

"What does it mean?"

"I'm afraid my memory isn't what it used to be. This will require some more research and most likely a trip to the king's archives." Removing her glasses with a sigh, Silvia slowly pressed the temples into the frame. "A Moon Blest wolf is extremely rare. From what I recall, there is only one born every few centuries. They are...very powerful. Enhanced strength, speed...some records mention elemental abilities. There is no way to know for sure. Werewolves desire them for the power they bring to a pack. Witches covet them for their fur and even some vampires seek them for their personal collections."

His brows lowered darkly. "I've never heard of such a wolf. Are you sure?"

Silvia gave him a humorless laugh. "Of course I'm certain, Nicholas. Do you really think that a rare wolf, blessed by the Goddess would go around advertising itself? Wars have been waged as packs have fought for its power. Although..."

"What?"

"I must admit, this is the first time I've heard of a female being Moon Blest."

"I suppose if her mate found out what she is, he wouldn't let her go," Nick mumbled to himself.

The she-wolf chuckled. "Considering wolves are possessive of their mates in the first place, hers is bound to be extremely so. You might have to sedate him when they meet, just so she can use the bathroom."

If only you knew, he thought sardonically. Carrel already rejected Ella, but if he found out that she had rare powers… Nick was certain that the boy would come after her.

He had his chance, his wolf practically hissed. *If he dares to touch her now, we'll rip his hands off.*

Nick wanted to agree. The boy didn't deserve Ella after what he put her through. However, this was about more than just himself. As alpha, it was his responsibility to care for his pack first and foremost, and Ella was not technically part of his pack.

"I'll allow her to stay for now," Nick said quietly. "But this is more complicated than simply adopting a rogue. If this girl will be as coveted as you say, how can I ask my wolves to put their lives on the line for a stranger? I won't make that decision for them."

Silvia didn't comment right away. "Then ask the pack to decide for themselves if they are willing to protect her. The outcome may surprise you."

Three days had passed since Nick learned about the meaning of Ella's blue fur. Amanda, Kyle and his gamma, Caleb, were the only ones he had told. Nick wanted the chance to mull a few things over before he shared the truth with Ella. In the meantime, the she-wolf's confidence was returning and she seemed to have blossomed overnight. Ella and Roxy, Kyle's seventeen-year-old daughter, were inseparable. Nick's three sons were already treating her like their little sister. A few times, Nick caught them growling at a wolf who stared at her for too long. James, the oldest at eighteen, was especially protective. The warrior-in-training had been with Kyle the day Ella was found. Simon and Henry were both a few months older than Ella. The red-headed twins looked like their mother, and even had her more humorous nature. Needless to say, Amanda was thrilled to have another girl to dress up and spend time with since Roxy was the only one between all the leading members of the pack.

Seeing that Ella was already wiggling her way into their hearts, Nick knew he best sit down with her and have a talk. Deciding for a change of scenery, the alpha invited Ella for a walk around the grounds. Leaving the pack house, Nick took the path to a small nearby lake. There would be less chances of listening ears without the confines of walls. Several minutes of silence passed before Ella couldn't keep the question burning in her mind at bay any longer.

"Is something wrong, Alpha?"

A gentle smile touched his lips. Chuckling, Nick shook his head. "Nothing that you have done, I assure you." Deciding that there was no easy way to approach the subject, he got straight to the point. "Have you ever heard of a Moon Blest wolf?"

As expected, Ella shook her head no.

"It's a very rare type of wolf born every few hundred years. They are said to be extremely powerful and in turn, are coveted by other supernatural creatures. The most significant way to tell a Moon Blest wolf apart from other wolves is by their fur."

Eyes locked on the alpha's face, Ella scarcely dared to breathe. Some intangible feeling told her from the moment Nick began speaking, that he was talking about her, but she didn't want to believe it.

Then, he told her, "They have a distinctive blue fur."

Ella's face paled. With everything else that happened since she woke up in the pack hospital, Ella didn't have the chance to wonder about her strange fur. This certainly couldn't be it. Her parents were murdered by rogues. For the past ten years, she was practically invisible. Then, when she was almost of age, her mate…there was no need to think of that again.

"There must be some kind of mistake, Alpha Nick," Ella rejected, shaking her head. "I'm not blessed. There isn't anything special about me at all. I'm just an omega."

Scratching the side of his face, a smile pulled at the corner of his mouth. "I'm afraid I'll have to disagree with you. My Beta told me about your speed and on more than one occasion, you've shown signs of a powerful aura. Let's not forget you were mated to *him*. Which would have made you a future Luna. There is great strength hidden within you, Ella. Whether you want it or not, it will always be there and you will have to learn to master it."

He's right you know, her wolf agreed, causing Ella's heart to fill with dread. *Haven't you felt it? Ever since our birthday, sounds are louder, distant images clearer. We are getting stronger every day.*

Waving her hands in front of her, Ella admitted defeat. "Okay, okay," she told both Nick and her wolf. "Say I accept what you both are saying, then what? This sounds really dangerous, Alpha. You mentioned other supernatural creatures. Am I going to be hunted?" she questioned, her voice rising in pitch.

"It is possible," Nick informed her. Lying about the possible danger would do more harm than good. Moving closer, he placed a hand lightly on her shoulder. "I know this is a little overwhelming, Ella. Amanda and I have already discussed it and we want to help you."

"You do?" she almost stuttered.

He nodded. "We would like to offer you a place in our pack. As a member, you will be protected and we will help to train whatever powers you may have. However—"

Ella's body drooped, the light of hope dimming in her eyes. She should have known that it was too good to be true.

"However," Nick continued, making sure that he didn't break contact. "I first want to speak with the rest of my pack." He watched as Ella's gaze snapped back to his face. The girl was far too easy to read. He would have to work on her poker face. "Understand that I must put the lives of my people first. They need to know about you and everything that accepting you into our pack will entail, since it will be their lives on the line."

Ella slowly nodded. He was a kind man. She did understand what he was saying. If she remained here, it could put his pack in danger. Thinking it over, Ella wasn't sure that she could burden him with her problems. Opening her mouth to speak, Nick's eyes narrowed.

"Don't even think about it," he stated in his alpha voice, cutting her off. "No one thinks of you as a burden, Ella. A wise woman recently said to me that she believes you were meant to come here. And you know what? I believe that to be true."

Unable to control herself, Ella launched forward and wrapped her arms around the alpha in a tight hug. The man released a throaty chuckle as he returned her embrace.

"Now don't thank me just yet," he said. "I've called for a pack meeting at the school's auditorium tonight. Amanda will make sure that you have the proper clothing, since it will mean that you're going to have to shift in front of the pack."

The thought of standing before hundreds of people and showing off her true form was terrifying. However, if it meant that she might be able to stay in Swift Wind, then she would brave anything. Ella didn't realize until that moment just how much she wanted to be a part of this pack.

Pacing back and forth, Ella stopped before the thick maroon curtains and peeked out into the auditorium. Most of the pack were already seated. The last few members were filing in and guards sealed off the doors. It was almost time. Quickly jerking back, Ella took several deep breaths and vigorously shook her hands as she attempted to calm her nerves.

I can do this. I can do this. I can do this, she chanted soundlessly.

It will be fine, Crystal promised. *Everyone loves you.*

I don't know. How can I ask them to put their families in danger for me?

A true pack protects its own, Crystal insisted.

Ella was about to reply that she wasn't one of them yet, but just then, Nick and Amanda joined her.

"Don't worry," he said, giving her a warm smile. "You will do fine."

"Thanks," she whispered in return.

Amanda squeezed her hand before she and the alpha walked through the curtain and onto the brightly lit stage with Ella trailing behind. Roxy, as well as James, Simon and Henry, gave her a 'thumbs up' from the front row.

Here goes nothing.

"Thank you for joining me tonight," Nick said into the microphone, causing his voice to echo around the large space. "I've asked you here because I believe in honesty. I do not keep secrets from my pack. Some of you have had the pleasure of meeting our newest prospective member."

A few younger wolves yelled 'yeah' from the audience, earning both a couple of chuckles as well as a few glares from James and the twins.

"Due to her…unique circumstances, I've decided that the decision to allow her to join Swift Wind will not be mine alone, but one made by the pack as a whole." Nick let his words sink in for a few moments prior to continuing. "I doubt it needs saying," he told them in his alpha voice, "but what you are about to see and hear does NOT leave this chamber, no matter the outcome."

Satisfied that he had made his point, Nick held out an arm, welcoming Ella to move closer to him.

Keeping a strained smile in place, Ella took center stage. She gave the pack a small tentative wave.

"This is Ella. After her mate rejected her a few days before her sixteenth birthday, she was forced to leave her pack. A few rogues from the free lands attacked her and chased her into our territory where she was saved by Beta Kyle, my son James and the Beta's team of warriors." Nick said with pride.

His gaze found Silvia's and held for a second. "A wise she-wolf once told me that everything happens for a reason. I believe that Ella was meant to find us, so that the brave and honorable members of Swift Wind can help protect her."

The alpha turned to look at the younger wolf. "Ella, if you would be so kind," he said with a nod.

Taking a deep breath, Ella toed off her shoes, then removed her sweatshirt and sweatpants. Amanda had purchased a black sports bra and a pair of skin-tight bike shorts for her to wear for the meeting. Closing her eyes, Ella focused on allowing Crystal to take over her body, just like they practiced. Her legs lengthened, a tail sprouted from her back and her face changed shape into the muzzle of a wolf. Opening her now deep blue eyes, Ella stood on the stage as a baby blue wolf. Amanda moved to her side, gently patting her fur as startled murmurs traveled throughout the crowd.

"Quiet!" the alpha commanded.

Everyone immediately complied.

"As you can see, Ella is no ordinary wolf. With Silvia's aid, we have discovered that she is a rare wolf blest by the Goddess herself. This is known as 'Moon Blest'. Only one is born every few centuries. Ella…" he peered at her with a soft smile, "is a blessing from our Goddess. However, because of her power, she will also become a target of not only wolves, but for other creatures as well."

Nick gave another nod, signaling for her to shift back into her human form. Taking her clothes from the luna, Ella quickly dressed.

"I ask you now, members of Swift Wind, will you accept her into our pack, to be cared for and protected as one of our own?"

For a few painful seconds, no one moved. Then, Yvette stood up.

"I don't know about anyone else, but I for one, am not about to let a young wolf fend for herself. I say yes."

Caleb, the pack's gamma, rose next. "A gift from the Goddess or not, I'm not turning my back on someone in need. Let her join."

One after another, members of the pack stood up and showed their encouragement. Hands covering the bottom half of her face, tears fell from Ella's wide eyes. The luna wrapped her arms around her.

"See Ella, you are one of us."

Lifting his hands. Nick motioned for the pack to once again take their seats.

"Your kindness and support fills me with pride. I have never known a more noble group of wolves than my beloved Swift Wind."

A tall thin woman with jet black hair stepped out from behind the curtain with a gold chalice and a jeweled dagger. Alice stopped beside the alpha and bowed respectfully.

"Come, Ella," Nick called, motioning for her to stand before him. "Your blood must join with mine in order to link you with the pack."

Ella had seen this ceremony performed once many years ago at Red Moon. This would be the final tie to cut her from her old pack, her old life. Once she swore her loyalty to Swift Wind, Alpha Jack and Carrel would have no power over her. With the dream of a fresh start coming true, Ella knew there was one more thing she wanted to be rid of…her name. She wanted no reminders of who she once was or from where she had come. They were all in the past now. Ella desired to begin over.

"Can I…" she began quietly. "Can I pick a new name?"

"Of course," the man before her agreed. "What would you like to be called?"

Ella grew quiet for a second. Her mind went back to the peaceful water of Fire Lake. She had always loved the way the water rippled in the light. She had felt a strange bond with water since she was a child. The perfect name suddenly appeared in her thoughts.

"River," she answered with certainty. "I'd like to be called River."

After all, crossing a river brought her to her new home. She could think of no other name that would better honor that.

"Very well."

Taking the thin blade, Nick swiftly sliced the tip of her extended finger.

"Just a few drops is all I need," he instructed.

Ella complied and watched as the alpha cut his own finger next.

"River, do you swear your loyalty to Swift Wind? To obey your Alpha and the laws of this pack? And to protect your pack members with your life?"

"Yes, I swear it," she answered without hesitation.

Nick held his finger over the cup, squeezing several drops of blood to mix with Ella's.

Can you hear me? Nick's voice rang out in her mind.

Ella blinked, a slow smile stretching across her face. *Yes, I can, Alpha.*

Good. Turning out to the crowd, he spoke through the link, so that not one person would miss his words. *I happily present to you the newest member of Swift Wind, who from this day forward, shall be known as River Carlson, my adopted daughter.*

A round of cheers broke out among the crowd. Mouth gaping, Ella couldn't utter a word. *Did he say 'his daughter'?*

Amanda squealed as she embraced Ella tightly.

"I love my boys, but I've always wanted a daughter. Welcome home, River."

Beaming, Ella offered up a few words of thanks to the goddess. For the first time since her parents died, she really did feel like she was home.

Chapter 4

Stepping out of the back seat of a large SUV, Nick raised a hand to shield his eyes from the sudden glare. He instantly regretted leaving his sunglasses in the well-tinted vehicle. Gazing at the Red Moon Pack house, his beta strode up beside him with a poorly hidden frown.

"Are you sure about this, Alpha?" Kyle asked needlessly.

They both knew this was necessary to help protect Ella, or rather *River*. A missing pup would not be easily forgotten. Alpha Jack had to know that she was safe. The fewer wolves looking for her, the better.

"Stay alert," Nick ordered the six warriors surrounding the two vehicles. "I'll call if you are needed."

His men nodded obediently as their alpha headed for the main building. Nick just wanted to get this over with so that they could return home before nightfall. King Magnus graciously allowed them to travel through Silver Fang's territory, saving him time and the hassle of making the entire journey through the free lands. Though hostile rogues were few in number, Nick didn't want to be bothered with a fight. There was already more than enough on his mind.

"Welcome," boomed a strong voice as the Red Moon's Alpha appeared in the doorway.

"Thank you for agreeing to meet with me," Nick politely returned. He would not allow Carrel's uncalled-for behavior ruin years of friendship with the other leader.

Shaking hands with both Nick and Kyle, Jack led the men into the depths of the house towards his study.

"I must say, I was surprised by your insistence to travel all the way to Red Moon and speak in person. I do hope Amanda and the boys are well."

Nick smiled, recalling why he had always gotten along with the other man. "Yes, they are fine. I trust Karen is as well?"

"Yes, yes," Jack confined, sitting behind his desk. "Watching my diet like a hawk."

The men shared a few light chuckles before Jack cleared his throat. Interlacing his fingers, he shifted into an all business manner.

"Now, Alpha Nicholas, for what purpose have you arranged this meeting?"

Arms resting lightly on the sides of the chair, Nick wiggled into a more comfortable position. He had been playing over and over in his mind what he would say throughout the entire journey. Now that he was finally here, Nick wished he had more time.

Let's get this over with, Maddox advised. *I don't want to be away from Violet for longer than I must.*

Listening to his wolf whine for their mate was just the push he needed.

"We've been friends for many years, Jack. Because of this friendship, I wanted to extend the courtesy of telling you that the young former pack member you were searching for is safe."

Bolting upright, the other alpha's eyes widened. "You've seen Ella? Where is the girl? Is she alright?"

Nick and Kyle exchanged a glance. "She is fine. My Luna is watching over her."

Exhaling, Jack leaned back and raked a hand through his greying brown hair. His movements paused as Ace murmured in his mind, *What did he mean, 'former pack member'?*

Stiffening, Jack's eyes narrowed slightly. "If you are aware that she is a member of my pack, then why did you not return her home?"

"Ella was initiated into my pack two days ago. Therefore, she is no longer a member of Red Moon. I came here as a curtesy simply to let you know that the girl is alive and well."

Holding Nick's unwavering gaze, Jack's face darkened to a deep crimson. His eyes flashed black as his wolf fought for control. How dare he come here and calmly inform another alpha that he has stolen one of his members? This wasn't a bunch of wildflowers they were talking about. It was taking everything in his power to keep from pouncing on the other man.

Kyle sat on the edge of his chair, watching Jack closely.

Easy Kyle, Nick advised. *We both knew he was going to be upset. The last thing we want is a fight.*

A battle over the she-wolf would involve an investigation from King Alpha Magnus and a much closer look at River. He needed Jack to understand why he took her in. For it was not meant as an insult.

"How dare you!" Jack roared. "I demand that you return her at once!"

"Even if I was willing to consider it, Ella would be too terrified to come willingly," Nick informed him, never once breaking eye contact.

Just then, Steven burst into the room. His gaze quickly passed between the visiting alpha and beta, and his own alpha. "I heard you roar through the link, Alpha, is everything alright?"

Jaw clenching, Jack continued to watch Nick. "That remains to be seen. Explain that remark, Alpha Nicholas."

"I will tell you what I can, but the future Alpha will be able to better clarify, than I can."

This time it was Jack and Steven's turn to quickly glance at each other. Body tense, the Red Moon Alpha crossed his arms.

"I'm listening."

"Last week, my Beta and his warriors found a young she-wolf being chased into our territory by a group of rogues. She was in rough shape and our head doctor informed me that she had been on the run for days. At first, all she would tell us was that she was a rogue." Nick watched as Jack's frown deepened.

That seems like news to him, commented Maddox.

Agreed, but we can't be too careful. I doubt Carrel will ever tell him about River being his mate and we certainly don't want to share that.

"After my Luna and I began to earn her trust," Nick continued, "she confessed that the son of her former alpha had unjustly accused her of stealing and banished her from the pack. If I remember correctly, his words were 'leave or I will kill you'." His grim words hung in the air for a moment. "Therefore, Ella was approved to join Swift Wind."

"I don't understand," Jack growled, running his hands down his face. "Even if she did ask to join, you can't simply steal another pack's member. For all you know, she could be lying or a criminal."

The alpha's protest was losing heart. Nick could hear it in his tone and smell the smallest trace of fear.

He doesn't believe River lied, said Maddox with ironclad certainty.

Nick trusted his wolf's instinct, so he pressed on.

"I, of course, had Ella checked into prior to allowing her into my pack. She was reported as a runaway, not a criminal. There are no living family or relatives. Not to mention, her level of fear was not cohesive with an adolescent outburst or attention attempt. She spent several hours hiding in a corner of her hospital room under a blanket." As Jack's gaze dropped to the floor, his long-time friend rested his elbows on his knees.

"Ella's original goal was White Crescent. Do you know why? She said that they are known for taking in rogues. Whatever happened between Carrel and Ella convinced a wolf, unable to defend herself, that she was now a rogue. She ran through the free lands for days, alone. You should be glad that I found her first. Alpha Logan would not have bothered with the curtesy of telling you that he had her."

What Nick didn't say, was that since the White Crescent Alpha was unmated, he possibly would have taken the girl as his mistress in exchange for her protection. This supposedly, had already occurred once before, though he couldn't say how true the rumor was.

Rising to his feet, Nick dipped his head politely.

"I will show myself out."

As he made his way to the door, Jack's voice caused him to delay his departure.

"She was never going to come back, was she?"

Peering over his shoulder, Nick's gaze locked with the other man's. Sadly, he shook his head. "No, Jack. Even if I brought her by force, she would have fled the moment she was given a chance."

The Red Moon's Alpha closed his eyes tightly with a sigh. *What have I done? A pup should never fear her own pack. I failed this girl under my own roof.*

"It's not your fault, my friend," Nick reassured.

Jack lowered his head. "My son's actions are my responsibility. So yes, it is my fault. Take good care of her."

Nick agreed easily, "I promise."

Exiting the office with Kyle, he quickly made his way to the front door. Passing a large living room, he spotted Carrel with a sparsely dressed she-wolf making out on one of the couches. Footsteps slowing, he eyed the fresh marks declaring them mates on each of their necks.

That must be the girlfriend he rejected River for, he said to Kyle through their link.

As if feeling the two powerful men's eyes upon him, Carrel looked up with a frown.

Nick's gaze narrowed and darkened to black, causing the future alpha to lean back with a glare.

We should leave, Alpha, Kyle advised.

Placing a hand on Nick's shoulder, he gave him a gentle squeeze. The 'spell' of death stares broke. Allowing nothing else to keep him, Nick strode out of the manor and into the sun. At that moment, one thing became very certain. The instant Carrel took over as Alpha of Red Moon, Nick would have nothing to do with this pack again.

Amanda paced back and forth at the front of the manor. Nick called when they were on their way back to Swift Wind, so he should be arriving soon. Peeking out the window again, she saw a light coming from the tree lined road. Rushing out the door, Amanda stood on the porch as two cars grew ever closer.

Nick didn't even wait for the car to park before pushing open the door and leaping from the vehicle. He could feel the tension coming off his mate in waves.

"Amanda, what's wrong?" he questioned, encompassing her in his arms.

The luna relaxed, her body sinking into the comfortable warmth of his body.

"Sweetheart," Nick said, rubbing her back. "Tell me what's wrong. Maddox doesn't like to see you in distress."

Amanda pushed back slightly. Her gaze passed over the warriors on high alert surrounding them.

It's River, she told him through their link. *Silvia just returned from the castle. She needs to see you immediately.*

Dismissing his men, Nick interlaced his fingers with his luna and ordered Kyle to follow him. He strode briskly down the path leading towards the school. The main building was dark. However, the lights shone brightly from the bottom level of the library. Not daring to guess what news awaited, should the fates deem it so, Nick made his way to the history keeper's study.

"Enter," Silvia called out before he even raised his hand to knock.

The older she-wolf wasn't in the main space as he thought. The normally clear and organized office was scattered with countless pieces of literature. The inside of her small private library was even worse. The skinny table positioned in the center of the room held a map, stacks of books and scrolls. Hunched over in a chair, Silvia was taking notes from one of the multiple open manuscripts spread out before her.

"Well, don't just stand there," she said with a huff. "Come in, come in."

Dark circles colored the skin under her eyes and the woman's normally sharp gaze was dull from a lack of sleep.

"Silvia," Nick exclaimed, rushing to her side. "What in the world is going on?"

Taking a sip of coffee, she waved off his concern. "Tsk," she clicked her tongue disapprovingly. "It's nothing a little sleep won't cure. I've been busy combing through the royal archives. Perk of being a keeper of history," she added more to herself. "And I was able to find some more information about Moon Blest wolves."

Amanda, Nick and Kyle gathered around the table, listening closely as she spoke. "The last record of a blue wolf was nearly six hundred years ago. His name was Alexei Cooper of the former Blue Ridge Pack. Their territory is now ruled by Blue Lake," Silvia informed them, pointing to an aged book. "During his rather short lifetime, he rose through the ranks to become the King Alpha's Beta. At which point, his power was used to wage a bloody war with the vampires."

"I've heard of that," Kyle muttered. "It was known as the Dark Moon War, since the fighting only lasted a single cycle of the moon."

"Correct," Silvia agreed. "However, thousands of vampires and wolves were killed in that short amount of time.

The war only ended because both King Roark and Alexei died. I once read a journal entry about a wolf who wiped out an entire valley of vampires with a sea of flames. It would seem that the record is indeed correct, since Moon Blest wolves have power over the elements. Usually just one though."

"This doesn't bode well for River," Nick pointed out. "Vampires are not very forgiving. Having already fought a Moon Blest, they may seek to get rid of her before her powers fully develop."

"They may be only the beginning of our troubles."

Brows narrowing, Nick peered back at the she-wolf. He didn't like the sound of that. The list of possible enemies was continuously growing.

"Thus far, between the records, rumors and legends I managed to shift through, I have found what I believe to be four separate Moon Blest wolves. The strength and number of powers appears to increase with the creation of each new one." Unrolling a scroll, Silvia gently tapped the decaying material under her fingers.

"This is the reason for my hasty return. This scroll is over a thousand years old, dating back to the time of the third wolf. It was written by a powerful witch known for her premonitions. In this, she speaks of the Moon Blest wolves. It says that if ever a female were to be born with fur blessed by the moon's light, her power shall be greater than any who have walked before her. Her voice shall cut through mountains and her eyes shall see beyond the hands of time. Nature itself shall obey her whim. All shall feel her power and bow down before her. Yet, no wolf, nor spell, shall bend her will to them. She alone shall possess the power to conquer Cerberus and cure the curse of night."

Taking off her glasses, Silvia rubbed her eyes. The others just stared at her, unable to process what she read. The record keeper wasn't surprised. It took her three times to make sure she had not misread the ancient text.

"This can't possibly be right," Amanda refuted.

Cerberus was their fiercest of enemies. King of the Hellhounds, he once rose up in an attempt to destroy all those in the living world. The supernatural creatures were only able to push him back to his abyss by joining forces. Weakened, he returned to the depths, gathering strength as he waits in the shadows, sending his soldiers out to attack when least expected. The day he returns to the surface is long feared.

"Surely you don't think this is talking about River." The luna gave a hollow laugh. "She's not a warrior. The girl only just learned how to shift. Nick," she said, turning to her husband. "Please, tell me you don't believe this. River can't fight Cerberus."

His gaze never leaving Silvia, the alpha exhaled through his nose. If there was any chance at all of this being true, then he wanted to be prepared. There were too many lives at stake to ignore a witch's words.

"Amanda, have Alice arrange a meeting with Malinda. The cost doesn't matter." Hopefully, the witch could shed more light on the future. "Kyle, increase the patrols around our territory. If Cerberus is planning to resurface, he will slowly begin increasing the number of attacks to test our strength. I'll inform King Magnus about this possibility. Knowing that a witch foresaw his return should stay any questions for the moment. I trust Magnus, but I don't want anyone outside the pack to know of her power. The past has proved this knowledge alone to be dangerous."

"Are you sure about this?" Amanda questioned, touching his arm.

His warmth instantly began to soothe her racing heart.

Nick showed no signs of uncertainty. "Yes, love. Magnus can't be caught off guard any more than we can. I just hope Malinda can give us a better idea of what we will be dealing with." Nick paused, looking at the scroll, thoughtful. "Starting tomorrow, River begins training with our warriors. Kyle, have Caleb see to it personally. She may not be a warrior, but she's about to become one. Her life may depend on it."

Sitting in the soft grass, River stretched out her legs. She held for a ten count prior to changing position. Never one for much exercise, River wanted to make sure she warmed up before she began her first lesson with the pack's gamma. The last thing she wanted was to get a cramp part way through. Following Roxy's lead, the she-wolf brought her one knee to her chest and leaned back, stretching muscles she didn't even know she had. River was glad that her new friend would be in the same training session.

Roxy's black hair with red streaks was pulled back in a high ponytail. She wore a deep red sports bra and matching compression shorts, since they would be shifting at some point during the exercise. River smiled as she glanced at her new hot pink tankini and shorts. Amanda insisted on taking her shopping for clothes after her initiation. The vast amount of money spent had made River uneasy, but the luna dismissed her protest. Considering that she came with nothing but the clothes on her back, which tore during her first shift, she was in desperate need of a new wardrobe.

"Morning, girls," Caleb called brightly.

Dressed in a t-shirt and shorts, the gamma walked towards them with Henry, Simon and two other teens that River didn't know.

Jumping to their feet, River and Roxy gave Caleb a respectful bow.

"Good morning, Gamma."

"River, I'd like you to meet my sons, Luka," he said pointing to the first seventeen-year-old wolf with shoulder-length sandy hair tied back from his face. "And Tye."

His other son smiled brightly as he waved. Tye was about five foot eleven and the shortest among the males present. He looked just like his brother with the same hazel eyes.

However, his brown hair was trimmed close to his scalp instead of longer.

"They are going to help me gauge your skill level. Due to the sensitive nature of your training, Alpha Nicholas has set aside a private section of the forest and added a guard around the perimeter to ensure your safety during the exercise."

"And that's why we're here," Henry bragged as he and Simon crossed their arms proudly with matching grins.

Caleb raised a brow. "You're both here because you *need* extra training."

"Hey!" they protested simultaneously.

Roxy snickered and River was forced to duck her head to hide her own smirk.

Insisting that they get started, Caleb led the teens into the woods. They walked for about ten minutes before finding themselves by a small clearing. Towering maple, spruce and fir trees surrounded the secluded area. At the back side was a twelve foot rock face with a wide flowing stream gliding over the edge and weaving its way off through the woods. The creek was a modest size, at no more than two feet in its deepest parts. It was the perfect place to hide River's fur from unwanted eyes.

"Alright," Caleb began clapping his hands loudly to gather the younger wolves' attention. "Everyone pair up. Roxy, I want you to go with River to start."

"Yes, sir," she clipped off happily.

River mimicked her friend's movements; bring her arms up in front of her chest in a defensive stance while keeping her palms open. Gaze darting to her teacher, she waited for some kind of instruction.

"Begin," Caleb ordered.

Wait, River puzzled. *Isn't he going to show us anything first?*

Roxy's hand shot out like lightning, striking River square in the chest with her open palm. She watched as River stumbled back a few steps with wide eyes.

Come on, the dark-haired girl told her friend through the pack's mind-link while playfully wiggling her eyebrows. *Defend yourself.*

River scrunched up her face, fighting a giggle. *It's so on,* she returned.

She couldn't remember Kaylee ever talking to her through the link. No one ever did. Even if she was standing there in the room, few people took notice of her at Red Moon. Each day in her new home showed River just how different this pack was. The rumors were true. Swift Wind was tough, but they were also incredibly loyal.

Trying to remember something from the little training she was given, River was knocked down again and again. Each time, she got back on her feet with a set, determined expression on her face.

Watching the she-wolf closely, Caleb didn't see one drop of tears, or hear one whimper of complaint as Roxy kept pushing her on her butt.

See, his wolf, Chase, said approvingly. *The pup is strong-willed. She will make a fine warrior.*

"Alright, take a break," Caleb ordered, striding over to his newest student. "River, get into a defensive stance. At six foot five, the gamma towered over her as he watched her raise her hands once again. "Keep your arms close to the body," he instructed pushing her elbows in. "You always want to protect your major organs and your core in a fight. If you can't breathe, then the odds are you will lose."

River nodded as he moved to her other side and shifted her right leg back in a wider stance.

"Now bend your knees slightly. This will give you better balance." Getting into his own defensive position, Caleb showed her what to do. "If you stay on the balls of your feet, it will increase your speed and improve your reaction time in battle."

Over the next hour, Caleb began from the ground up, teaching River basic self-defense techniques. After giving his students another short break, the gamma called them back into line.

"For the second half of your class, we're going to spar in your wolf forms. Tye, you're with River."

She watched as the teen shifted into a large dark brown wolf with black front legs and paws. He was tall to begin with, yet in his wolf form he was massive compared to her. River was certain that she could ride him like a horse. The top of Tye's head easily reached her shoulder. One by one the other students changed shape.

Lips parting, River smiled as she gazed at Roxy. Her friend's black and red hair was the same coloring as her lush fur. Her fur was mostly black, marking her as a powerful wolf in her own right. However, there were vibrant red streaks around her neck and laced through her tail.

Come on! Crystal yelled excitedly in her mind.

Closing her eyes, River allowed her wolf to the front of her thoughts. Each time they morphed into a wolf was less painful than the last. Now, River felt nothing more than a tingling sensation course through her body. When she opened her blue wolf eyes, everyone was watching her.

I still can't believe it, Roxy said through the mind-link. *Your fur is so cool looking.*

River could feel Crystal hum happily at the compliment. *Thanks. I really like yours. The red is incredible. It makes you look dangerous,* River told her playfully as she wagged her tail.

Both girls turned their heads as Henry snorted.

Can we start already? he complained to the gamma. *Otherwise, they might start braiding each others' fur.*

Roxy growled at her cousin, her lip curling back to show a hint of her sharp teeth.

"That's enough," Caleb ordered firmly. "Roxy, you're with Luka. I don't need a blood bath from you two right now."

The two wolves turned their heads away with matching huffs before moving towards their partners. River gazed at Tye, suddenly realizing that in this form their heights were much more even. *How are we so tall?* River wondered.

It must have something to do with our power. Higher ranking wolves are always bigger and stronger, Crystal told her proudly.

River wasn't so sure. Her blue fur was difficult to ignore, but she found it unbelievable that she was some specially blest creature. There wasn't anything special about her during her entire life. Why would she magically be special now?

We have always been special, her wolf insisted. *There just wasn't anyone smart enough to see it after our parents died.*

Frowning, River forced her attention back on the start of her next lesson. She couldn't afford to get distracted. Caleb would not be pleased either if he knew that her mind was wandering. Taking in her teacher's every word, River listened as the gamma spoke of the similarities and differences between fighting as a human and as a wolf. There were less differences than she would have thought. Everything basically centered around protecting your own vital points while attacking your enemy's weak spots. Though werewolves possessed extraordinary healing abilities, Caleb stressed the importance of refraining from any serious attacks.

"I want you to focus on speed and control," the gamma instructed. "A good warrior doesn't attack wildly. He looks for an opening and uses it to his advantage." Glancing at Tye, he privately reminded his son, *don't take it easy on her, but let her get at least one or two hits.* Watching the brown wolf nod his head, Caleb ordered everyone to begin.

Tye and River circled each other near the edge of the stream. Darting forward, the deep brown wolf nipped at River's front leg.

She jumped back out of range and quickly rushed in from the side towards his hind legs.

Turning at the last moment, Tye avoided her attack, using his head to push the blue wolf onto her side.

Rolling over, River sprung to her feet.

Tye dashed in once more, aiming for a paw.

Ears turned back and tail erect, River pushed off the ground with her front legs, twisting her body as her jaws lightly clamped around the scruff of his neck before he had time to react. Letting go, she pounced away, then came at him from another direction.

She's quick!

Tye barely had time to intercept the pale mass zeroing in on him. The two wolves crashed together in a tangle of legs as they rolled onto the ground. Tye managed to right himself quickly and gazed around for his sparring partner.

River, on the other hand, wasn't as agile with her newfound speed. Having moved closer to the stream than either of them realized, when they rolled onto the ground, River fell over the edge. Shutting her eyes, the blue wolf waited for the resulting splash of cold water. A distinctive chill rested beneath her paws, but nothing else. Frowning, River opened first one eye, then the other.

What in the world…?

River held her legs stiffly as she peered down into the flowing stream under her paws. She could feel the current's movement. She could see the water moving gently on its way as if she wasn't even there. It was as if the thinnest sheet of glass lay between her paws and the liquid of the stream.

Caleb raced to the edge of the water followed by the four other wolves. Roxy shifted back immediately, her mouth gaping.

"Holy crap, River!" she exclaimed. "You're walking on water!"

Oh…my…goddess, she's right! River said to Crystal. *We can walk on water.*

Tail wagging, the blue she-wolf tentatively moved her paws on the water's surface. After a few seconds, she let out a happy yip and began to stride up and down the stream.

Let me try something, Crystal requested, bringing their movements to a halt.

Stretching out her muzzle, River blew a long breath over the surface of the water. A line of ice formed along the creek. It held for a split second before breaking apart as the current carried it downriver. Ears standing straight up, she bounced on her paws.

Did you see that? River questioned the others excitedly.

Suddenly, River plunged, legs first, into the water. The resulting splash soaked her fur as she rose from the shallow stream. The other teens shifted back, roaring with laughter as River climbed out of the creek bed with a large grin. Shaking her fur, she sent a shower raining down on her classmates.

Still laughing, River changed back into her human form.

"I can't believe I just did that."

Puffing out his lower lip, Henry put on a fake frown. "Neither can I, now I smell like wet wolf."

Glancing at each other conspiringly, Roxy and River reached out at the same time to push him into the water. A second later, they both hopped in after him, giggling loudly as Simon and Tye followed.

Standing beside his father, Luka watched the younger wolves for a few seconds.

"I guess this confirms the Alpha's theory about her."

Caleb nodded. "Yes, I have no doubts that she is Moon Blest. Did you see her speed with your brother? She doesn't seem to know how much faster she is than a normal wolf and her birthday was only a little over a week ago."

"It's incredible. I just..." his voice trailed off as her watched the others' water battle.

"Just what?" Caleb encouraged. He had found Luka to be quite insightful for his age.

The younger wolf shifted his weight from side to side. "I guess I just wonder why the Goddess would grant a wolf these kinds of powers. In time, no wolf will be a match for her."

The gamma's brows furrowed. Luka had a point, yet if her abilities weren't meant to protect her from other wolves, who was she supposed to fight?

Cutting the engine, the captain of their small boat steered the vessel expertly into the dock. It had been a few years since Nick crossed the fjord to the north of his territory. Convincing his luna that she was needed by the pack, only Kyle accompanied him into Malinda's valley of mist. Hand resting by the hilt of his knife, Nick studied his surroundings closely. You could never be too careful when dealing with witches. Walking down the short pier, the two wolves peered into the rolling mist permanently covering the ancient forest. Nick couldn't say if it was naturally occurring or a spell. The thick fog had been a part of the forest for as long as anyone could remember.

Now what? Kyle asked, one hand gripping his blade while the other held onto the handle of a small square case.

Patience, she's sending a car.

The wind howled and shadows moved among the trees. The seconds slowly ticked by like an eternity. Nick's own patience was beginning to wear thin when a sleek black car rolled to a stop before them. The windows were tinted completely black, obstructing the view of inside. The rear door opened automatically. Glancing at each other, the wolves cautiously entered the vehicle. Once seated, the door shut and the car drove steadily up the road.

Shifting in his seat, Kyle froze, his eyes locked on the front driver area.

Do you see something? his alpha questioned, peering about.

No, Kyle replied. *I don't see anything Nick, there's no one driving this car.*

Instead of looking alarmed, Nick leaned back with a grin. *Yes, I found it strange my first time here, too. It's an enchantment. Witches use them a lot.*

His beta didn't seem to find this information amusing. Back stiff, his gaze continuously scanned the inside of the car was well as the woods as they made the journey in a tense silence. After about fifteen minutes, a cottage appeared through the mist. Two lamp posts glowed at the edge of the path leading to the house. The car came to a gentle stop right between the posts. Nick and Kyle exited the vehicle and strode forward through the veil. Stepping onto the porch, the front door swung open on its hinges to welcome them.

"Alpha Nicholas," greeted a woman with curly black hair swept away from her face and gleaming green eyes. Her flawless skin spoke of youth, yet he knew her to be at least a few hundred years old. "What a pleasure it is to see you again. I must say, I found your request for my services to be most intriguing."

Nick took her outstretched hand and gave it a quick kiss.

"You are as radiant as ever, Malinda. It's as if time itself has bent to your will."

A slow smile spread across her beautiful face. "You flatter me," she purred with a knowing glint. "You must want something great indeed."

Spinning around, she strode through an open doorway into a darkly lit room. Snapping her fingers, the lights flashed on, revealing shelves of potions, books and exotic ingredients—the likes many witches could only dream to get their hands on. A small wide-rimmed pot sat in the very center of the round table. A blue flame flickered mysteriously beneath it. Lowering herself gracefully into a high-backed velvet chair, Malinda smirked.

"Payment first."

Nick nodded to his beta.

Kyle strode forward and placed the small box on top of the table and unlatched it. Opening the lid, he turned the box and pushed it towards the witch.

Leaning forward, Malinda peered inside at half a dozen carefully packaged vials. She gradually pulled one out, examining the dark red contents in the light.

"Well now," she drawled happily. "How can I be of service?"

Nick motioned for his beta to join him at the table. "First, I have a condition."

"Go on."

"You cannot use my payment or the knowledge gained from this transaction to harm my King or my pack."

Malinda's eyes narrowed shrewdly. *He always was a smart man, for a wolf. Hmm…his Luna isn't here, and this must be the Beta. What could be so important that he would come all the way to me?*

"Agreed," Malinda told him. "Now, what do you seek to know?"

Nick and Kyle glanced at each other briefly before the alpha spoke. "I have reason to believe that Cerberus will rise again. I want to know when, and anything you can tell me about how to defeat him."

Malinda's soft ivory skin paled. "You must be joking."

The wolf before her firmly held her gaze. One of the witch's powers was the ability to detect lies. She could feel no deceit coming from the proud man. If that beast did come to walk the earth again, it would mean death for them all. Pushing away from the table, Malinda started grabbing various bottles from the shelves. Once she finished collecting the ingredients, she began pouring the required contents into the miniature cauldron one by one without a word. Gently stirring the mixture, Malinda muttered a spell in the ancient tongue. Sweeping her hands over the steam, she inhaled deeply. Malinda dropped into her chair, her eyes misting over to a pure, dull white. Placing her palms flat on the table's surface, a strange smile crept onto her face.

"Hmm…" the witch hummed in a husky tone. "Before the full rise of the next Blood Moon, in less than three years hence, the king of Hell's fire beasts shall once more ravage our lands. His power is great, and left unchallenged, the rivers will run red. River…" she paused. Tilting her head to the side, the twisted grin widened. "Nicholas, you naughty boy."

The alpha shifted, his jaw clenching. He should have known, but this was a risk he had to take.

"Young, strong and true, with fur kissed blue by moonlight, only one wolf will have the power to land a killing blow. Evil cannot be vanquished permanently, but destroy his mortal body and this form will be banished back to hell." Inhaling deeply, the witch twisted her head to a strange angle before turning back towards the wolves. "A word of caution.

No mortal creature can face an army of fire alone. Allies will even the field. However, the girl's soul must be whole for any chance of victory."

"Her soul?" Nick questioned with a frown. Understanding filled him. "She doesn't have a mate. He rejected her."

"Hmm…" was all the reply he received as Malinda continued to watch him with her strange smile. "The Goddess always has a plan. Protect the girl, Nicholas. Your family was chosen."

Eyes fluttering closed, the smoke suddenly dispelled. When Malinda peered at her guests again, her eyes had returned to normal. Her back plopped against the soft material of her chair. *So, his rise will indeed come to pass.*

"What are we going to do?" Kyle muttered, not realizing he had spoken out loud.

Running his knuckles along the side of his jaw, Nick sighed. "What we planned," he answered simply. "We have less than three years, correct Malinda?"

The woman nodded slowly. "Correct, it will happen before the Blood moon. I'm afraid his power blocks mine from seeing any more clearly. It could be tomorrow or three years to the day."

"You did the best that you could."

Kyle frowned. Glancing at the witch, he told his alpha, "I meant about her mate. That *boy* already rejected her."

Nick's eyes narrowed. "He was never worthy of her. It no longer matters if he was her mate or not, the bond has been broken. We have no control over such things. Preparing her for battle and strengthening our allies will be the best thing we can do."

As the two men spoke, Malinda watched them carefully. *Should I tell him? No,* she decided. Rejecting the idea just as quickly. The wolf already had enough on his plate.

"I offer my friendship and support in this fight, as well as that of my coven," Malinda told them, drawing both their gazes. "Congratulations Alpha Nicholas, you have your first ally."

Chapter 5
2 years later

The sun glistening off her pale blue fur, River sprinted through the Swift Wind western forest. She had been running for a good half hour, yet her breathing was steady and her legs free of any aches or pains. The countless hours of strict drills had paid off. The land around her shifted into a sharp incline as the she-wolf ventured into the more mountainous parts of the territory. Eyeing a short cliff face, River leapt onto the rock and propelled herself upward onto the peak.

Gazing around at the forest below, she searched for any signs of movement through the trees. There was nothing. The lack of chirping birds and chattering squirrels told her otherwise. Eyes narrowing, River caught a flash of fur through the canopy. Backing away from the edge, she crouched down and waited.

A large wolf with black fur and vibrant red streaks quietly slipped into the clearing below the cliff. Roxy was followed by a familiar brown wolf with black paws. Two others entered shortly after.

Sniffing the ground, Roxy lifted her nose to the air, taking a few steps in one direction, then another. A low growl escaped her lips.

Her scent has vanished, she told Tye through the pack's mind-link. *How can she disguise it so well?*

It's part of her powers, he replied matter-of-factly. *Where do you think she went?*

To the east, another group of wolves appeared. There were five total. At the head of the squad were two cinnamon-colored wolves with thick black stripes.

Roxy? they puzzled simultaneously. *What are you doing here?*

Rolling her eyes, the she-wolf pawed at the ground. *What does it look like we're doing, Henry? Tracking River.*

Did you find her? his brother questioned.

Roxy shook her head. *Her scent vanished before we reached this clearing.*

We still haven't been able to pick anything up, so I doubt she went the way we came. Why don't we... His voice trailed off as a mist began to quickly cover the earthen floor.

From her perch, River blew a cooling breath, twisting some ice with her recently gained ability to control the air. The resulting mist rapidly encased the trees and brush.

Stiffening, the wolves perked up their ears as they scanned the area for the slightest sound.

Got you! Roxy shouted in her mind, spinning around as she felt a breeze swiftly pass behind her. Lowering her head, the fiery wolf rammed her skull into a large mass and quickly picked up her muzzle, sending her opponent crashing onto the ground.

Ouch, groaned a distinctive male voice in her mind. *What did you do that for?*

Before she could reply, a series of growls, then whimpers erupted from Roxy's other side.

Tye was thrown onto his side, a set of glowing sapphire eyes hovering above him as River gently tugged at his scruff.

Without a word, the blue wolf vanished back into the thick haze.

You're not winning this time! Roxy shouted through the pack bond, secretly impressed by her friend's skill.

Roxy might have been the stronger opponent when River first started training, but it hadn't lasted long. By the time the younger wolf turned seventeen, she was already joining the warriors on border patrols and training missions against rogues. Today's session wasn't technically for River, it was for them. Their task was to land a single blow on the female warrior, something that was becoming far and few between. In a few more months, Roxy doubted she would be able to touch her at all.

Leaping out of a tree, River appeared on the edge of Henry's team. Gripping the closest wolf's back leg, she tugged him backwards and out of sight. Like a phantom, the she-wolf darted forward from another location, picking off the team members one by one.

Knowing that he had to do something, Henry ordered the remaining members of his team to move out. Roxy and her last wolf joined him as they raced through the forest. A group of falls lay to the east. With River's ability to control water, they headed south instead.

We can't run away, Roxy complained. *We are supposed to be tracking her, not the other way around.*

If we stayed in that mist, she would have defeated all of us and you know it, Simon replied curtly.

The twins weren't any more pleased with the situation than she was. They had to think of another way to turn the tables on River, and quickly. A thick wall of ice appeared in their path. Skidding to a stop, by the time Henry and Simon spun around, only Roxy was left from either team.

Engaged in combat, the black wolf lunged for one of River's paws. The blue beast arched back, tucking her legs into her chest as she moved out of the way. Striking with a paw, River countered with an attack to Roxy's muzzle, pushing her head in the other direction to reveal her throat.

Lightly gripping her friend to signal her defeat, River turned to face her last two foes.

The remaining three opponents circled each other with their ivory teeth gleaming in the sunlight. The defeated team members stood off to the side, watching the final match unfold. River's brothers charged at her from opposite sides. Waiting until the last moment, the blue wolf sprung up into the air, her back feet landed on the tops of their heads as she slipped out of their reach. Identical cinnamon and black wolves growled softly as they stood shoulder to shoulder.

We're going to get you for that, Henry declared, his tail briefly wagging before he tucked it securely between his legs. A wise warrior kept his tail out of reach during a fight.

Sticks and stones, River teased back, referencing an old childhood rhyme.

All at once the fighting commenced, resulting in a blur of claws and fur. With each strike, River used her enhanced speed to block and counter her foes. Henry and Simon were tough opponents. Even without the pack's mind-link they fought as one, reading each other as no one else could. Keeping the use of her powers to a minimum, River flowed between them, causing the two wolves to nip each other instead of her. Leaping over them, she gripped Simon's back leg, jerking it out from under him. The she-wolf then aimed for her downed opponent. As Henry came to his brother's aid, River changed course at the last moment, tackling the other twin to the ground.

With his twin defeated, Simon released an irritated snarl. The two large wolves circled each other once more. The battle played out like a dance, with the fighters smoothly avoiding their foe's attack. When Simon lunged forward, River inched back, like the push and pull of the tide.

Quickening her pace, River made a feint to Simon's paw. When the wolf jerked back, he turned his head to the side as if to nip at his sister, but River swiftly twisted her body and aimed for the subtle opening instead.

Pawing the ground, Simon shook his body, unable to hide a grin despite his frustration.

You've gotten really fast, little sis. Good job.

It's all thanks to our amazing teaching skills, Henry interjected walking up from the other side.

River had to fight a snort. *I think our brother has lost his mind,* Crystal observed with a chuckle. She was about to agree with her wolf when a strange feeling filled her senses. Her body took on a weightlessness and the image of a black wolf tackling her from behind flashed in her mind. Suddenly tense, River's ears turned back as she gazed around the forest. Just as her vision showed her, Roxy pounced from her blind spot. Rolling onto the ground, River allowed her friend to jump right over her before leaping to her feet. Darting in, she knocked the other she-wolf onto the ground and pinned her.

Okay, okay, I give, Roxy exclaimed, showing her neck in submission.

Tails rod straight, the twins approached the still prone wolf with low growls.

What are you doing? Henry demanded. *You already lost, Roxy. That's against the rules.*

I gave the order, said a voice in their minds as a large tan wolf slowly moved from the shadows with Caleb's dark brown one.

You can shift back, their teacher instructed. *The exercise is over.*

All ten warriors morphed back into their human forms before the beta and gamma changed as well.

"Good job, everyone," Caleb praised. "Your tracking was spot on, and most importantly you stayed together as a team. That was a good call to move out of the mist, Henry."

"But we failed," Simon pointed out with a frown.

Kyle nodded. "Failure is a tough, but useful teacher. No wolf you battle will be like River. However, there are other creatures out there that you need to train to fight. Don't focus so much on tracking her scent that you forget to use your other senses. Always look and listen for a threat that could be hiding in the shadows."

The warriors nodded as they listened closely to the beta's advice.

Crossing his arms, Henry frowned slightly. "How come you had Roxy attack River after the battle was over?"

"It was a test," River answered for her leader.

Giving a rare smile, Kyle nodded. "Correct. True battles are not clearly marked with a beginning or an end. You must be prepared to defend yourself at all times." Shifting his gaze to the alpha's daughter he added, "Impressive work in sensing Roxy's attack."

River's brows furrowed. Could she take credit for what took place? She hadn't really felt Roxy sneaking up on her. In fact, if it wasn't for the vision, the other girl would have defeated her.

"I didn't sense her," River admitted, glancing at her friend. "You had me, Roxy. I had no idea that you were behind me."

It was her teacher's turn to frown. "How did you block her attack?"

River shrugged. "I'm not sure. I felt really strange for a moment, then I could see a quick image of a black wolf jumping on me seconds before it happened. I can't explain it, but somehow I *knew* she was going to attack."

There were a few seconds of silence before Kyle exhaled, rubbing the short scruff on his face. "It can't be," he said, more to himself.

Roxy walked to his side, her arm linked protectively with River's. "What's the matter, Dad?"

"I believe that I can explain what you saw, but I didn't know that it was possible for a wolf."

"What do you mean?"

Kyle smiled sardonically. "You seem to have a new power, River. It's known as a premonition—a vision into the future. I've only heard of powerful witches being able to use this gift."

River blinked several times, her brows raising towards her hairline. "Wait, are you saying that I can see the future?"

"Why not?" Roxy shrugged. "You control wind and water already. Oh, can you see who my mate is? Is he good looking? What pack is he from?"

"Roxy," Kyle drawled, bringing her rant to a halt. She might be turning nineteen this year, yet he didn't want to think of his baby girl with a mate. Especially since it would mean that she would be leaving the pack to join whichever one he belonged to. "We should inform the Alpha. Malinda is the best person who can determine if that is what you are experiencing."

"You're right," River agreed. "If it's alright, Gamma, I'll return and speak with him."

"Not on your own," Caleb said protectively. "This session is over anyway." Raising his voice, he waved the other warriors back towards him. "Return to the pack house and take a lunch break. I'll send you further instructions this afternoon."

"Yes, Gamma," they replied in unison.

Shifting into their wolves, the warriors set off into the forest together. Standing beside Roxy, River paused. Crystal sniffed the air, her body tensing as her sharp blue canine eyes searched their surroundings.

What's wrong? Roxy questioned, turning to peer around the forest. Her wolf, Rose, was also on alert.

I'm not sure. It feels like we're being watched.

Growling softly, Roxy nudged her friend on the side. *Let's go. If there is something out there, we're safer with the team.*

River privately agreed, but for some reason, she didn't feel the urge to run from this presence. It felt oddly familiar. There were times when she visited Fire Lake years ago that this same strange sense would strike her. Even now, with her growing abilities, she felt no threat from it. Slowly spinning around, River took off into the woods with Roxy to rejoin the rest of their pack members who were waiting close by. As she disappeared from view, a pair of blazing red eyes peered out of the brush.

"Soon, Moon Blest," whispered a deep voice like a promise. "Soon."

The short heels of his leather combat boots tapped on the polished surface of the marble floors as a tall man strode down the castle's corridor. Blood streaked his short chocolate-colored hair, traveling down his neck and arm to disappear beneath his tight-fitting black tank top embroidered with the crest of Silver Fang. No one dared to block his path as he marched straight for the king's study. The solid mahogany doors were immediately pulled open by the warriors stationed there before he was within reach.

"Adrian," King Alpha Magnus greeted, waving his eldest son forward. "I'm glad you've returned. There is an urgent matter I wish to discuss with you and your brother."

"What a coincidence," Adrian stated, striding towards the desk. "I, too, have an urgent matter to discuss."

Both Magnus and Blake's eyes widened as they took in their visitor's appearance. Spying the blood smeared over the top half of Adrian's body, Blake jumped up from his chair while their father quickly sped around the desk.

"What happened?" the king exclaimed, visually checking his son for injuries. "Were you hurt?"

Adrian shook his head, his normally calm blue-green eyes painted dark with anger. "My warriors were attacked on the way back from Blue Lake. I lost some good men." His fists clenched by his sides. "Father, we were attacked by hellhounds."

Magnus's skin paled for a moment before his face darkened. "Damn it!" Raking his fingers through his steel-grey hair, the man paced the plush rug for a few seconds. "These attacks are getting worse. How many were there?"

"Three," Adrian answered taking a seat next to his younger brother.

Blake's blue eyes were clouded as he stared thoughtfully at the floor. Interlinking his fingers, he managed to keep his hands from combing his permanently messy brown hair.

None of the men needed to voice the depths of their concern. Hellhounds were vile creatures of darkness. They were larger, faster and stronger than a normal werewolf. It took three wolves to defeat a single beast. Only an alpha had the power to face them one on one.

Releasing a sigh, Magnus lowered himself into the chair behind his desk. "I would like to think that these events are a coincidence, but I know that there is no such thing."

Adrian's frown deepened. "What do you mean?"

Magnus shifted his gaze to his son. "Lord Belozersky is requesting a meeting with Alpha Nicholas at his castle Velladona."

The prince stiffened. "Why would he want that?"

Pavel Belozersky was one of the most powerful vampire lords in the world. Vampires didn't follow the rule of a king as they had done in the past. For the last millennia, territories were ruled by lords who governed their lands as they wished. A council of elders consisting of the oldest and strongest five vampires oversaw the other lords to keep balance and maintain order. Pavel was the head of this council. In the vampire world, his word was law. Rumor told that he was the one to slay both King Roark and his beta during the Dark Moon War.

"He has declined to share his reasons," Magnus told them honestly. "With the rise in hellhound attacks in all of our lands, his request may have to do with Nick's initial discovery of Cerberus's return."

Adrian leaned forward, watching his father closely. "Are you going to allow it?"

The older man pressed his lips together thoughtfully. "What do you think? Would you allow it?"

Exhaling, his son didn't answer right away, a fact that pleased the king. Such decisions shouldn't be made with haste.

"We've been on good terms with Lord Belozersky since Grandfather took the throne. To refuse outright would be an insult. At the same time…Alpha Nicholas's life and safety are of greater importance. Did he give any indication that he would guarantee the Alpha's safety?"

Magnus smiled and nodded. "He swore a blood oath."

A brow lifted at this news. Vampires rarely gave such a promise. A blood oath was their most sacred vow. To break it brought them physical harm, which could mean their life, depending on the oath taken.

"Well, this is interesting," Blake muttered, voicing Adrian's own thoughts.

Interesting indeed, Adrian mentally agreed.

He must really want to see Nick, but why? I don't recall him having any particular relationship with him in the past, his wolf, Cole, observed.

Something deeper must be going on here.

"If he is willing to guarantee Alpha Nicholas's safety with a blood oath, then I see no reason to deny the request. Given that it will be the Alpha who is traveling to vampire territory, I would offer him the option to decline or accept the request and would support whichever he decided upon."

Fingers tapping the polished surface of his desk, Magnus watched him for a moment. "Spoken like a strong, but fair king. I agree completely with you. Explain to me again why you still refuse to officially take the throne? You are clearly ready, Adrian. For the past year, you have already taken over dealings with Blue Lake, Shadow Claw and Red Moon. It is high time you accepted your place as the next King Alpha."

Plopping against the back of the chair, Adrian ran his fingers through his hair, accidently forgetting about the blood caked within the short strands. The number of times they had this conversation seemed to be growing. Werewolf law allowed for an alpha to pass on his title when his heir reached the age of twenty-one. Many wolves didn't find their mates until eighteen or older, so this extra time allowed not only for the young alpha to learn his duties and mature, but to find his other half, his luna. Without her, both the alpha and his pack were incomplete. Adrian was twenty-three. Still, he had yet to find his mate. For two years he had managed to push off his father's growing eagerness for him to take his place as the next king. With his birthday coming up at the end of the year, he knew that he was running out of time to complete his search.

Closing his eyes, Adrian sighed. There was no point in delaying the inevitable anymore, he had spent years looking for her. Perhaps it wasn't meant to be. He could feel Cole whimper, as if all hope was gone.

Gazing at his father, Adrian told him, "At the end of the year, after my birthday has passed, I will formally accept my duties, Father."

A large grin spread across the older man's face. "Well, that's the best news that I have heard in a while." The smile slipped away. "What of your Luna? You will need a bride."

The prince fought a sour taste that attacked his senses. Cole growled softly, knowing what he was about to say. *We don't have a choice, my friend,* he soothed. *Father's right, we do need a Luna. We'll find someone like us, a she-wolf who cannot find her mate or has lost hers.* His wolf said nothing, so Adrian took his silence as agreement.

"Once I'm king, I will choose a Luna to rule by my side."

Remaining in his father's study for a few more minutes, Adrian excused himself to get cleaned up. Blake meandered down the long corridor by his side. It had been quite some time since the brothers were able to talk leisurely in such a way with the growing attacks on the werewolf kingdom.

"Are you sure you don't want to come with father and me to Swift Wind? It's been awhile since you visited."

Adrian shook his head. Though what Blake said was true, he still had several things to catch up on. For now, Magnus and his brother took care of matters in the other three packs: Swift Wind, White Crescent, and Blackwood. Soon, these responsibilities would be his as well. Thankfully, with Blake's help as his beta.

Blake gave him a sideways look. "Come on, Adrian," he insisted, nudging his brother with his elbow. "Roxy and River are both really hot, maybe you should take one of them as your mate."

The older prince gave a humorless laugh. "I'm not ready to claim a mate that isn't mine. Besides, Roxy…" Adrian was about to say that Roxy was a little too strong-willed for him, but thought better of it. That girl could be as fiery as the streaks in her hair, not that it was bad thing. Adrian had no doubt that she was a born leader. With seven wolf packs to keep in line, he was privately hoping for a mate that was less wild.

There is nothing wrong with a spirited mate, Cole interjected. *Sometimes you act too old for your age. She might be good for you.*

Don't you start on me, Adrian mildly complained while shaking his head with a laugh.

Studying the expressions crossing his brother's face as he spoke with his wolf, Blake burst out laughing.

"Let me guess," he said with a smirk. "Cole agrees with me, doesn't he?"

The younger prince was rewarded with a glare.

"If you're not interested in Roxy, then what about River? It's been about two years since you've seen her. I wish she was my mate, the girl's grown into a goddess."

Adrian raised a brow, but said nothing. He wouldn't call the brief glimpse he got of the alpha's new daughter as 'seeing' her. River was only living with the pack for a few weeks and was extremely wary of strangers. The moment he caught sight of the she-wolf standing at the top of the main stairs, she had bolted. Adrian wasn't able to so much as get a whiff of her, let alone a proper introduction. From what he saw, she appeared fairly young. Even given two years, she couldn't possibly be more than sixteen.

"Sorry to ruin your dreams, but she may be too young for me."

An almost eight-year age gap would be a bit of a stretch for a werewolf. No matter what his brother thought, there was no way that he was going to marry a child. Smirking slightly, Adrian decided to change the subject.

"And what of your own mate? As my Beta, father is sure to see to it that you're married next."

Blake threw his hands up in the air. "Like I haven't tried! I visit the other packs and attend the Moonlight Celebration every year. If only I could get a small trace of her scent," he groaned longingly.

Adrian knew just how he felt. "Don't worry, you still have time to find her. You only just turned twenty-one. Look at Logan, he was twenty-two before he found his mate."

Blake nodded absently as he thought about their friend. There were times when he first became Alpha of White Crescent that some fairly unfavorable rumors had spread about him. Unmated at the time, a she-wolf from another pack requested to join Logan's pack after surviving a violent rogue attack. Her former alpha thought a change of scenery might help her.

A couple of months later, Logan took her as his mistress. Blake told him it was a mistake, but his friend didn't heed his warning about the woman. The loneliness had gotten to be too much for the man. He wanted a luna and thought that the Moon Goddess might have sent this woman to him. It didn't take long for the truth to come out. The real reason she was ejected from her pack was because she had been sleeping around and the alpha, her uncle, was embarrassed by her conduct.

Logan quickly ended their relationship and sent her back in a rage. However, the damage her short time in White Crescent caused was already done. A year later, Logan discovered why it had taken so long to find his mate. She was a human.

Looking at Danelle, you would never know it. She fit into her role of luna so well that not a single member of his pack questioned his choice to keep his mate. A wolf being mated to a human was rare, but not unheard of. Since the werewolf gene was dominate, all children born from a human parent were wolves.

Seeing what his older brother and close friend had gone through while searching for their mates, Blake knew the second he was blessed with his, he wouldn't let her out of his sight. If she allowed him, he would mark her on the spot. Only a fool would willingly let his soulmate slip through his fingers.

Chapter 6

Standing near the tree line on the western part of Red Moon's territory, Jack crossed his arms over his chest with a scowl. Blood spotted the grass in growing pools as it traveled out of the woods. The bodies of the slain rogues were already disposed of, yet the hard lump settling in Jack's stomach would not dissipate. Two of their warriors were badly injured. One had not survived.

In the two months since he had passed the alpha title to his son, Carrel, the number of attacks had increased drastically. There were more threats coming at his pack now than Jack had seen in decades. His warriors were exhausted with the increased patrols and numerous battles. Yet, it was more than that. Jack could feel that something wasn't right with his people. Their strength seemed to be fading and he couldn't understand why. The entire pack was tested for all kinds of viruses, poisons and gas leaks.

Perhaps it is a spell, Ace ventured thoughtfully.

It is possible, Jack replied. *But there are few who would be able to cast something powerful enough to affect the entire pack. The greater question would be why? I don't see any reason someone would be trying to wipe us out. I have always had good relations with the other packs and the local covens.*

He distinctively heard Ace scoff. ***You've** had good relations with the other packs. You are no longer the Alpha. These issues did not begin until after **he** took over. That is no coincidence and you know it.*

Exhaling with a long huff, Jack declined to answer, so Ace pressed on. His wolf knew that he needed to hear the truth, whether he liked it or not.

You are a good man, Jack. It has been an honor being your wolf, but Carrel is not you. He has never been and never will be.

He is my only child, Ace. He is my only heir.

Jack could feel his wolf pacing in the back of his mind. *I know. His darkness is not your doing.*

Shaking his head, Jack ran his hand over his face. No, Carrel had changed. Over the last few years, he had become a good student, a great warrior, and had not once put a toe out of place. His son finally earned the right to be the next alpha. Jack was proud of him.

You have seen what you wished to see. Now open your eyes, Alpha of Red Moon! Ace commanded, urging his other half to gaze once more at the blood staining the ground around them. *We are responsible for the lives of this pack. If he will not protect them, then you must.*

Hands curling into fists, Jack stood staring at the ground with such intensity that someone might think he was expecting it to rise up and pounce on him. Finally turning away, he took off across the grass towards the pack house. Ace was right. Deep down, Jack had always known what his wolf was telling him. One way or another, he had to make things right for his pack.

Entering the manor, Jack strode up the stairs without a word to anyone and headed towards his old study. Luckily, Carrel's new beta and gamma were leaving as he walked into the room. Taking a seat, Jack studied the younger man with a frown.

Carrel's skin was paler than usual and dark circles rested under his eyes. He didn't look well at all. Courtney was newly with pup so perhaps her morning sickness was keeping him awake. Forcing himself to harden his heart, Jack said the words he came to say.

"What did you do, Carrel?"

The new alpha stiffened at the firm tone in his father's voice.

"What are you talking about?" he snapped in return.

"The pack is weakening. I'm sure you can feel it too. That is why the rogues are attacking us more frequently. They can sense it and are trying to take advantage."

Placing his hands on the top of the desk, Carrel leered at his father. His eyes narrowed to slits and a tendon pressed against the skin on his neck.

"How dare you," he growled with more than a hint of Drex in his voice. "*I* am the Alpha of Red Moon, not you. And no one will dare speak to me with disrespect if they want to keep their head."

Jack's eyes darken. "And I thought you had rid yourself of such foolish arrogance. It would seem we are both wrong. Being alpha does not put you above everyone, Carrel. You should know this by now. Your responsibility is *to* your pack, not the other way around. Something is wrong with our people. You cannot deny this."

Pushing off the desk, Carrel spun away with a hiss.

I don't have the energy for this fool, he thought with a groan.

Maybe we can use him, Drex suggested. *Your father might be able to find out what is hurting us. I know you feel it too. We grow weaker by the day.*

Yes, they were. For some reason, his father felt as strong as ever. This illness wasn't affecting him. Carrel released a sigh. If this continued for much longer, his pack was in serious danger. He couldn't complete any of his plans without his warriors. Slowly, he spun back around to face Jack.

"Do you know what is causing this?"

"Ace and I believe it may be a witch's spell. Has anything happened to cause a rift between Red Moon and the covens or neighboring packs? I can't help unless you're honest with me."

Carrel's frown deepened. For once, he really hadn't done anything...yet. The rogue assaults were keeping him far too busy protecting his own lands to commence with striking out against his neighbors like he originally planned.

"No. There's been nothing," he told Jack. "There really hasn't, Father."

Jack held his gaze for a few seconds before nodding. He seemed to be telling the truth. So where did that leave them now? Fingers drumming the arm of the chair, the former alpha peered at the floor. First, they needed to find out if it was a witch. Jack knew just the person he could go to.

"I need to consult an old friend of mine. I won't be gone for long. A few days at the most. Call me if there is another attack."

Pressing his lips together, Carrel bit back a retort. His father seemed to have forgotten who was in charge.

"Fine." Crossing his arms, he puffed out his chest. "And *you* call me if you find anything out about *my* pack."

Little punk, Ace growled in Jack's mind.

Ignoring both of them, the old alpha left the room to find his mate. The sooner his journey began, the better.

Thick trees lined both sides of the narrow dirt road as Jack traveled deeper into the mountains. After another mile of driving in the darkness, he turned up a sharp incline. The curving path took him to a cabin built into the rock face as it overlooked the valley. Jack had known the witch who lived here for many years. For as long as he could remember, Raven enjoyed a bird's eye view of her surroundings.

Stepping out of the car, the wolf was greeted by a voice from the shadows of the long porch stretching out over the mountainside.

"Alpha Jack," she purred leisurely. "To what do I owe this pleasure?"

"Lady Raven," Jack replied with a short bow. "I am in need of a favor."

A short woman with silver hair to her waist and unnaturally youthful features stepped into the light of one of the large windows. Arms crossed loosely across her front, she studied the unexpected visitor. Protective spells surrounding her mountain had alerted her the moment he entered her territory. Knowing Jack, he would not have come here without good reason. Raven quietly studied him for a few seconds before replying.

"Well, this is a surprise. Favors don't run cheap, but seeing as I am still in your debt, I will make an exception. Follow me."

Jack didn't say a word as he trailed behind the petite figure. Raven took the former alpha through the main living space and into the carved rock towards the heart of the house. Entering a small room, she quickly closed the door behind them. Waving a hand, a wall of candles lit themselves on both sides of the space. Raven passed several shelves of herbs and various ingredients before taking a seat at her reading table. Opening a gold inlayed box, she pulled out a worn set of cards.

Energy was very important to a witch, and the magic flowing from the earth to this part of the mountain was strong. Transferring some of that mana to the cards in her hand, Raven peered at the man sitting across from her.

"Ask your question," she instructed softly.

Jack's brows furrowed as he took a deep breath. "Ever since my son, Carrel, has taken over as alpha, the pack has weakened. If we can't find a solution, then my pack...my family, will be wiped out. I want to know why. Why is Red Moon weakening?"

Slowly closing her eyes, Raven inhaled deeply. She shuffled the cards three times, her hands moving as if by their own accord. Opening her eyes once again, she laid them out in a well-practiced pattern. A frown was etched upon her face as she studied the pictures in front of her.

"Cursed," she whispered strangely, her gaze never leaving the cards. "Punished…banished."

Brows lifting, Jack's lips parted. "What do you see?"

"A great wrong has been committed for which Red Moon must now suffer. Its warriors lose strength because their Alpha is incomplete. He has rejected his mate."

Jack's head jerked back. "That can't be right. Carrel is mated to Courtney. He even has a pup on the way."

Raven shook her long glistening mane. "No," she refuted. "The cards do not lie. The girl is not his true mate. Your son has rejected the one chosen for him by the Goddess." Gaze narrowing darkly, Raven continued. "But he did not simply refuse her. He insulted her…threatened her…and then banished her from your pack."

Breath catching in his throat, Jack was sure his heart skipped a few beats. There was only one she-wolf that the witch could possibly be speaking about.

"Ella."

I knew there was something strange about what happened with her, Ace growled in his mind.

Jack had felt the same. He could recall Alpha Nicholas's visit like it was yesterday. He had described her as terrified and stated that Ella was convinced she was a rogue. Suddenly, it all made sense. Carrel *had* banished the girl to hide the fact that she was his true mate. He banished the rightful luna of his pack!

Raven's voice drew him back from his near murderous thoughts.

"His treatment of his mate angered the Goddess," she was saying.

She's not the only one, Ace practically spat.

"She has cursed him for his crime so that as long as he reigns as Alpha, his pack will never prosper."

Clenching his jaw, Jack forced himself to remain calm. Throwing the table across the room wouldn't solve anything. He needed Raven to aid him, not to piss her off as well as the goddess.

"How do I break the curse?"

Raven finally lifted her gaze to peer at him. "*You* cannot, my friend." Waiting a moment for her words to sink in, she added, "If the one who broke the bond can repair what has been done, then there is a chance that the curse will lift. He must sincerely earn his rejected mate's forgiveness. If not…"

The witch didn't need to finish her words. If the goddess wasn't appeased, then Red Moon would crumble under Carrel's rule. There was no other option.

"I am sorry, Jack," Raven said, folding her hands gracefully in front of her. "I see dark times ahead."

Exhaling slowly, the man shook his head. "There must be a way to fix this. I can't fail my people. They don't deserve to suffer for Carrel's mistakes. Or for my mistake in making him Alpha."

"*You* did not fail them. Why do you think that you and your mate are unaffected?"

Jack didn't seem to hear her. "I must go," he muttered rising to his feet. "There is no time to waste. We have to find Ella."

Quickly thanking his old friend, Jack rushed from the room and headed straight for his car. Raven followed behind like a shadow. Standing on the porch, her words caused him to pause.

"Remember, Alpha of Red Moon, a curse from the Moon Goddess cannot be broken unless the heart behind it is true. Hollow words may only deepen her anger."

"I understand. Thank you, Lady Raven."

Pulling away, Jack disappeared back down the road and into the same heavy darkness. The situation surrounding his pack could not be worse, if Carrel didn't beg Ella's forgiveness and right his wrong, then Red Moon had no chance to survive.

A heavy rain had begun to fall the day before with no signs of stopping. The meadows were already becoming muddy swamps. Carrel didn't want to think about what it would do to local crops if it continued for much longer. His scouts reported mudslides in the eastern part of his territory and warnings for flash flooding were already sent out to all the pack.

"Damn it," Carrel muttered as he leaned his head against the back of his chair. "What am I going to do?"

If he had been hoping that the emptiness would magically answer him, then he was disappointed. Conditions in Red Moon were not improving and his father hadn't returned from his journey. Carrel didn't know what was taking him so long.

He better get his butt back here soon, he thought sourly.

Patience, Drex soothed. *If he went to see a witch as we believe, then it will take a little time. Witches are not easily swayed to aid wolves.*

Carrel scoffed, but didn't reply. Moving his hands to his temples, he began to massage the sides of his head. As if there wasn't enough going on, he now had a headache on top of it. A soft knock sounded on the door.

"Come in," Carrel snapped, annoyed by the tentative noise.

Pushing open the door, Courtney appeared at the threshold. Her short hair was expertly styled and the low-cut dress she wore clung to her hips and swollen chest from her pregnancy. She flashed Carrel a bright smile as she sauntered into the chamber.

The alpha didn't return her grin. Inwardly, he groaned. While he liked what he saw, his mate's morning sickness tended to leave a constant lingering smell of vomit that he couldn't abide. Recently, Carrel had taken to avoiding her when he could. He was considering taking a mistress on the side. Once Courtney lost her curves as their unborn pup continued to grow, he doubted that he would find her even the least bit attractive. Just the thought of her with a rounded stomach made him want to gag. Carrel stiffened as he felt his mate's arms wrap around his shoulders.

"What's the matter, honey?"

"I have a headache," he told her tartly, hoping she would leave. However, this seemed to have the opposite effect.

"You poor thing," she cooed, pressing herself against his back. "How about I give you a nice massage to help with some of your stress?"

With a soft growl, Carrel quickly rose to his feet. "Not now," he snapped. "I need to see to the border patrols."

Eyes narrowing, Courtney chased after him as Carrel stormed across the study.

"Wait!" she cried. Her irises flashed black for a moment before returning to normal. "What is wrong with you? I've hardly seen you since we found out about the pup. I'm starting to feel like you're avoiding me. I'm your mate, your *Luna*, you're supposed to take care of me, Carrel!"

Carrel's steps instantly halted. Spinning around, he grabbed her firmly under the chin as he towered over her. "You and I both know that you are *not* my true mate," he reminded her darkly in a frighteningly quiet tone. "You are what I say you are. If I choose to ignore you because I am dealing with issues in the pack, then I will do so. If I choose to take a mistress while you birth my heirs, then I will do so. If I get bored with you completely and decide to toss you aside, then I will do so," he finished with venom as he gazed straight into her eyes. "Do not forget your place."

Eyes widening, Courtney couldn't move for a second. The effect of his words vanished as the heat of her anger bubbled to the surface. How dare he treat her this way after all she had done? Courtney had been cleaning up his messes since their youth. The only reason he was able to hide his temper from his father was due to her aid. If it wasn't for her, Carrel wouldn't have become alpha.

"How dare you speak to me like this?" she hissed in return. "Have you forgotten everything I've done for you? I'm not one of your pawns, Carrel."

Jaw clenching, the alpha's next words were cut short by his beta's voice announcing his father's return through the mind-link. Peering at the woman still in his grasp, Carrel pushed her away forcefully.

"I'll deal with you later," he promised like a curse.

Leaving without a backward glance, the alpha traveled down to the main floor. Jack appeared through the front door just as he entered the foyer.

"Welcome back, Father. What news do you bring?"

A distinctive snarl met his ears right before the older man leapt at him.

Jack's clenched fist met his son's cheek with a satisfying crunch. He gave Carrel no time to recover from the fearsome attack before striking again. The two men locked in a grappling match. Yet, Jack was stronger, more experienced, and fueled by possibly the greatest anger of his life. Twisting Carrel's arm, he picked his son clear off the ground and threw him out the front window.

"You traitorous welp!" Jack shouted as he stepped through the broken window frame to follow Carrel out into the rain. "How dare you lie to me?"

Eyes flashing black, Carrel rose to his feet. Drex was clawing in his mind, demanding that he let him out so that they could taste their attacker's blood. First, Courtney spoke back to him, now his own father assaulted him. He wouldn't stand for this. Someone was going to pay.

"You dare to attack your Alpha!"

Gaze narrowed dangerously in the still falling rain, Jack growled, "You don't deserve to be Alpha, boy."

With a loud snarl, Carrel raced forward, shifting into a large black and grey wolf. His massive paws pounded the ground, splattering mud everywhere. He opened his jaw to reveal rows of pointed teeth.

Remaining in his human form, Jack dodged the first strike. Allowing Carrel to slip past, he wrapped his arms around the wolf's neck, squeezing tightly. Pulling the wolf up off his front legs, the former alpha slammed his son into the mud.

"You think that you can fight me?" Jack sneered, eyeing the wolf with disgust. "Every day you grow weaker. Your actions have cursed this pack."

Carrel leapt to his feet, growling low in the back of his throat as he faced his father once more.

"That's right. I found out what's wrong with our warriors, our pack. The Moon Goddess has placed a curse upon Red Moon because of you, Carrel Liam Stanford! She was angered by what you did to Ella."

At the mention of the girl's name, the alpha jerked back. Turning to gaze at the growing number of pack members listening to his father's every word, he quickly ordered them to disperse.

He can't possibly know, Carrel said to his wolf.

The beast inside of him disagreed. *He knows.*

Shifting back into a human, Carrel crossed his arms. "I don't know what your source told you, but you are being misled."

Jack's eyes shone black and remained that way. Ace's deep gravelly voice came forward with a hiss. "You still dare to deny it? We know what she is. What she was. I could execute you for your deeds on the spot."

Skin paling, the younger man took a step back. He wasn't foolish enough to realize that he stood no chance against the former alpha right now. In fact, he felt weaker now than he did after Ella's banishment when he first considered taking Red Moon by force.

With difficulty, Jack managed to calm Ace somewhat. They needed Carrel alive if he had any chance in lifting the curse from his people. When it was done, then he could consider his options on how to remove his son as alpha.

"My source is without question," Jack stated firmly in his normal tone. "But you have much explaining to do. Why would you banish your true mate from our pack? Why would you treat the girl, meant to be your Luna, so harshly?"

There was no refuting anymore. His father did know the truth about Ella. A strange weight lifted from Carrel's chest. There was nothing left to hide any longer. He hadn't realized that part of him was waiting for the last two years for the truth to come to light. Now that it finally had, he was pleased. A smile slowly spread across his face.

"Because she was ugly," he told his father smugly, watching with satisfaction as Jack's eyes widened and his mouth temporarily gaped. "Ella wasn't worthy of being my mate. So, I rejected her and ordered her to leave that night. It wasn't my fault that she tried to tell you what happened. I guess the foolish girl thought that it might save her from banishment." Shrugging, Carrel wiped some of the water away from his face. "She got more than she bargained for in disobeying me."

Watching the delight shining in his son's eyes at the memory of his mate's misery caused bile to build up in Jack's throat. Who was this man? He couldn't possibly be his son. He was so filled with hate, with a cruel enjoyment of other people's pain. When had he changed from his sweet little boy into this monster?

"Do you have any idea what you have done?" Jack questioned, the fury igniting once again. "You've insulted the Moon Goddess!"

Carrel shrugged. "So what."

Striding forward, Jack grabbed the alpha by the shoulders. "Have you not heard what I've been saying? She cursed you, Carrel. She cursed Red Moon because of you. Your actions are going to get everyone killed!"

For perhaps the first time, Carrel appeared worried. Pushing his father's hands away, he rubbed his face. "She can't take this pack away from me. There has to be something that we can do."

Jack's face dropped as he studied the other man. "There is, but I'm no longer sure that you are able to do it."

Sighing dramatically, Carrel glared at him. "And why would you think that?"

"Because it requires for you to be sincere," Jack told him bluntly. There was no longer any point in being diplomatic. It would be wasted on him. "The only way to break the curse is to earn Ella's forgiveness. And I mean truly earn it. Her being forced to say 'I forgive you' will not be enough."

Growling, Carrel turned his head away. He was starting to think that the rain was matching his mood as the cool water dripped down on his body. He didn't care for his father's solution. Begging wasn't his style. Lowering himself to that ugly girl would be insulting on every level. Gazing around at the various buildings of the pack, Carrel sighed. He worked too hard to give up everything that he fought for. *He* was the Alpha of Red Moon and he wouldn't lose it over some worthless girl.

"I will go and speak to her," he announced sourly. When Jack didn't say anything, Carrel raised a brow. "What? I thought you would be thrilled to hear this."

Jack shook his head. "It won't be that simple. She is part of the Swift Wind Pack now."

"And your point?"

"Alpha Nicholas protects his pack members fiercely. A few days after he came to tell me about Ella, I took her belongings to her. Nick wouldn't allow me to so much as see her. I doubt he would do so now either."

Carrel growled. "Then how am I to break this stupid curse?"

Running his fingers through his hair, Jack was quiet again. "The Moonlight Celebration," he mumbled. "In a few weeks, King Magnus will be holding the Moonlight Celebration in Silver Fang. Since Ella is of age, she should be there."

"We don't have a few weeks to wait. The rogues are going to continue attacking us. Hell, they could strike again at any moment."

"Do you have a better idea?"

Grumbling, Carrel didn't answer. Turning on his heel, he made his way back towards the pack house.

Watching the alpha nearing the building, Courtney quickly slipped out of the room and headed towards the back of the house. Once Carrel's heavy footsteps stomped upstairs, she let out a sigh of relief. She couldn't believe what she overheard. Ella was Carrel's true mate! Her face reddened at the thought. That skinny, freckled-faced tomboy was supposed to be the luna? What had the goddess been thinking? Courtney was pleased that Carrel chose her instead. However, she didn't want to think about him going to see the girl that he was supposed to be mated with. Telling her racing heart to calm, Courtney shook off her unease. If it helped save the pack from this curse, then she would have to deal with it. It wasn't like Carrel would have any feelings for the ugly little pup after all this time anyway. There was nothing for her to worry about.

Chapter 7

Sitting in front of her vanity, River was brushing out her long golden locks. She had just finished drying her hair after a warm shower. All that remained was applying some light makeup and she would be ready for dinner. Setting down the brush, River picked up a framed photo of her parents. It was one of the few pictures she had of them. Luckily, Alpha Jack had brought it to her after she settled into her new home. She didn't have the courage to face him at the time. How different things were not so long ago. A soft smile touched her lips. River wondered what her parents would think of her now. Would they be proud of the person she had become?

Of course they would, Crystal insisted, breaking into her wayward thoughts. *There is no questioning our awesomeness.*

River giggled. Her wolf certainly was sure of herself. While there were times when River still had her doubts, Crystal didn't seem to have the same affliction. She could always count on her other half to guide her.

Suddenly, River's reflection blurred. The room swayed despite her being seated. Grabbing ahold of the sides of the vanity, she closed her eyes to help fight the strange sensation. The walls of her bedroom faded away. Thick grey stone came to surround her in a massive chamber. The tall windows were tinted to block out the harshness of the sun, while giant chandeliers hung from the arched ceiling. The remnants of a spell faded from the polished marble beneath her feet. River peered around to see that she wasn't alone. Alpha Nicholas, Luna Amanda, Beta Kyle, Roxy, her brother James and the witch, Malinda stood around her within the circle of the spell. There was also a strange ash-blonde girl and a tall man with dark shoulder-length hair hanging in his face to shade a set of red eyes.

Vampires! she mentally shrieked. Why were they in a place with vampires?

The vision grew stranger yet as they moved towards a grand set of stairs. A tall man with ash-blond hair, like the girl next to them, stood on the landing with his arms out in welcome. River got a strange feeling from him, as if they had somehow met before. He was elegantly dressed, like an aristocrat of old.

The images sped forward, pulling them into a dark and dreary dungeon. Their host walked over towards a large sheet blocking something from their view. Snarls were coming from behind the covering. Pulling it aside, he revealed a dark creature, the likes River had never seen before. Its short black fur was almost non-existent. Plates of armor covered parts of the leather-like skin. The claws on each of its toes shone sharply like razors and instead of eyes, there were dancing flames in both eye sockets and on the end of the beast's thick tail.

There was only one possible identity for the creature before her eyes that River could think of: hellhound. This had to be one of the creatures of darkness that she was destined to fight. Why was it in the keep of a vampire? The list of questions without answers grew in her mind. Just as quickly, the vision faded away and River was once again sitting in her room as if nothing happened.

Head swimming slightly, she shut her eyelids for a few seconds and took several slow deep breaths like Malinda had instructed her. River was glad that the witch was staying in the manor to help her learn to control her new power. She would need someone to aid her in figuring out the meaning of her latest vision.

As soon as she felt steadier on her feet, River made her way downstairs to the main floor. With dinner ready to be served, it was the best possible place to find the spellcaster. She would ask to see her once the meal was completed. Thoughts of Malinda temporarily left her mind as River entered the living room.

"Uncle Magnus!" she heard Roxy shriek happily as the girl threw herself at the king.

Chuckling, he embraced the she-wolf fondly before she turned to tackle Blake next. After coming to live in Swift Wind, River learned that not only were Nick and Magnus close friends, the two men were distantly related as well. From the moment they met, he insisted that River call him 'uncle' since she was part of the family.

Face lighting up with a grin, River gracefully strode towards their guests. "Uncle Magnus, what a pleasant surprise this is."

Giving her a quick hug, Magnus held the young woman back a few steps so that he could get a better look at her. Glancing between River and Roxy, he smiled.

"I know it's only been a few months, but I can't believe how grown up you both are. Blake," he started, nudging his son on the shoulder, "why can't you find a stunning mate like one of these ladies?"

Blake's brows drew together briefly. "Believe me, I pray to the Goddess for that all the time." His scowl lifted with a mischievous smirk. "Hey, if either of you decide that you want to choose your own mate, I would be honored to be your chosen. All you need to do is say the word. There's no need to worry about Father accepting you. He'd be thrilled."

"That, I would be," Magnus agreed. "One of you needs to start giving me some grandchildren," he muttered as he strode over towards Nick.

"Father!" Blake stressed, his cheeks turning a pale crimson.

After everyone finished exchanging pleasantries, Nick led the way into the dining room. The three leading members of the pack and their families were all present. That included Yvette, whom Kyle at times had to personally remove from the hospital to make sure that she ate. If she wasn't working to help welcome new pups into the world, then she would experiment on cures for various supernatural aliments. Thanks to Yvette, the pack had an almost perfected antitoxin for wolfsbane.

Once the kitchen staff had begun to serve dessert, Nick took a long sip of his coffee.

"Alright my friend," he said gazing at the king. "As much as I enjoy having you and Blake show up here unannounced, why don't you enlighten us as to why you are here?"

"You always were straight on target," Magnus noted approvingly. Watching the last omega leave the room, he took a deep breath. "I wish I had more pleasant news. Although I wouldn't say it's a bad thing, the request I bring is bizarre."

Frowning, the alpha set down his cup and waited.

"Lord Belozersky would like you to join him at Castle Velladona for a special meeting."

Silence filled the space.

"I beg your pardon?" Amanda questioned.

"I wish I were joking, but I'm not. Given the increasing issues we are having with the hellhounds, I don't need a battle with the vampires as well. He has given a blood oath that you and anyone who joins you, will not be harmed. I would like you to seriously consider accepting his invitation."

Nick's brows furrowed. "You want me to consider it? This isn't an order then?"

Magnus shook his head. "No, it is a request. Adrian thought the final decision should be left to you and I agree with him."

Nodding, Nick's fingers curled around the lower part of his face thoughtfully. "Why me?" he asked more to himself. "Blue Lake is closer to the vampire territory than Swift Wind if he desires to meet with the werewolves."

This time it was Magnus who frowned. Gaze locking on his friend, he told him, "Because Lord Belozersky requested you by name. He said that he would be 'blest' at have Alpha Nicholas and his family visit him at his castle as soon as possible."

Everyone at the table stiffened.

Do you think Pavel knows about River? he asked Maddox.

It is possible, his wolf answered. *Pavel is old and Silvia confirmed that the historic reports of the Dark Moon War name him as the one to defeat the last Moon Blest. It can't be a coincidence that he used that word. He could be using this as a way to quietly dispatch her.*

There was no way that Nick would allow that to happen.

"Please thank Lord Belozersky for me, but it isn't possible for me to leave my pack at this time."

Magnus slowly nodded. "Very well. I will see to it."

"If I may, Father," River interjected. "I think that we should see what this vampire lord has to say."

All eyes turned to her, but River didn't take back the words. She was given the vision for a reason. Though she could not discuss it in front of the king, she had to let those present know that more might be going on here.

"River, you don't know what you are saying," Nick insisted.

"I understand your concern, but should we not at least think about his offer. Who knows," River added peering at Malinda, "maybe there is something he needs to show us."

Brushing back her hair, the witch spoke next. "I could mediate on the subject and see what the spirits can tell me. Turning down such an opportunity, out of hand, might not be in our best interest. I have known Pavel for many years. He never does anything without reason."

Nick set a closed fist on the table. "I'm fairly certain that I know what Pavel's interests are. If he only wanted to share some knowledge with our kind, then he would not have specifically asked for me as he did. That vampire is not going to be in the same room as my daughter!"

"Really, Nick," Amanda drawled, glancing at Magnus.

You messed that up, Maddox added.

He didn't need the reminder. For a moment there, Nick had forgotten that there was someone present who didn't know about River. Thinking about her being near that wolf killer caused him to be careless.

"Nick," Magnus growled softly. "What is going on here? Has Pavel tried to harm your daughter in the past?"

With a long sigh, the alpha shook his head. "No. It's not what you think, Magnus. You see…well," Nick scratched the back of his neck. There was no way he was going to be able to get out of not telling his king at least part of the truth. "River is not like most wolves. She was born with special powers that are rare to our kind. No one outside the pack knows for her own protection. If others found out what she can do, I fear that there are some who may try to take her and use her for her gifts."

Eyes widening, Magnus didn't say anything for a moment. "Well, this is certainly a surprise," he said, glancing at all those seated at the table. "Do these 'powers' have anything to do with why you think your father should meet with Lord Belozersky?"

River slowly nodded. "Yes, it does. You see, I have premonitions."

Magnus blinked at her. Then, to everyone's surprise, he started to laugh. "That is not what I thought you were going to say. My word, Nick!" he exclaimed leaning against the back of his chair. "I can see why you would be extra protective of her, but you could have at least told me. It's not like I would lock her up. Though the offer of being Blake's mate still stands."

Setting an elbow on the table, the younger prince wiggled his brows. "What do you say, River? If we start a fire you can always put it out."

"Really, Blake," Roxy scoffed, rolling her eyes as River burst out laughing.

"I think that was the corniest pick-up line I've ever heard," Amanda murmured, hiding her smile.

If only he knew what I could really do. He might run for it, River said to her wolf.

Yes, Crystal whispered conspiringly. *Let's tell him and watch as he runs with his tail between his legs.*

You are so mean.

You were thinking it too, her wolf pouted. *We are much stronger than we once were.*

Yes, they were. Blake wasn't an enemy who deserved the full force of their newly made skills. He was their friend and River would not hurt her friends.

River's brothers had taken it upon themselves to join in the conversation as well.

"Who said you could flirt with our sister?" Simon questioned, his eyes narrowing.

"Yeah, we'll fight for her honor," Henry added, his fork from eating a piece of cake still sticking out of his mouth.

"Take it easy, you two," James scolded, giving Blake a look of sympathy. "He was just kidding."

Nick looked at them and growled softly, ending the twin's mischief. Pinching the bridge of his nose, he shook his head. "What am I going to do with you two?"

"If they're bad now, Uncle Nick, wait until River finds her mate. I doubt they will even let him near her," Roxy laughed, earning her a few cross looks.

River's gaze dropped to the table, her smile vanishing.

Don't you dare waste a single thought on him, her wolf advised.

"Perhaps we should focus on the issue at hand," River suggested, changing the conversation in a more productive direction. "I want to accept this Lord Belozersky's invitation and my wolf agrees."

"It's dangerous," Nick countered. "We could be playing right into his hands."

"Not necessarily. If Pavel is offering us an olive branch, we should take it. He would be a very powerful ally against Cerberus," Malinda advised.

Lips pressing into a thin line, Nick lowered his gaze to the table with a thoughtful frown. Part of him wanted River as far from this lethal vampire as she could get, but he seemed to be the only one. If the she-wolf was insisting that they go, then he would at least hear what she had seen. Ignoring her visions would not serve them well.

"What did you see?"

River flashed him a grateful smile. She then described every detail which she could recall from her premonition. She remembered the light glowing around them, who was there, and most importantly, the beast locked away in the depths of the vampire's castle. As River told them about the hellhound, she heard her family gasp.

"That isn't possible," Kyle refuted firmly.

Yvette shook her head. "In theory, it could be possible. It would require some powerful magic."

"I've never heard of someone taking one alive before, though," Caleb added.

"Neither have I," the king admitted. "When hellhounds die, their bodies burst into ash. It's impossible to study them. If Pavel does indeed have a living hellhound in his keep, then we may learn important facts on how better to defeat them." He turned to look at River. "Was there anything else?"

She shook her head. "I'm afraid not. It's the longest vision I've had so far. I don't know how to control when I get them or what I see."

"Seeing into the future is tricky. You may never be able to. We can focus your strength so that the transition is easier and less draining on your body. When I first developed my gift, I would pass out afterwards."

River nodded as she listened to Malinda's words. Her mentor was right. She would rather not be weakened by this gift. At the moment, she had enough abilities to keep control of.

"It would seem that we don't have much of a choice," Nick muttered sardonically. "Magnus, if Pavel is serious about extending his blood oath to include everyone joining me at his castle, then we will go."

The king raised his brows. Knowing how stubborn the alpha could be, he hadn't expected him to be willing to change his decision so quickly. He seemed to hold a great deal of faith in his daughter's vision. Magnus shifted his gaze to River briefly. He could always feel a strange energy coming from her. What other secrets were they hiding about this she-wolf?

"Very well," he agreed. "I will convey your message. I will advise you once I receive his answer."

River glanced down at her untouched food. She knew what Pavel's reply would be. Soon, they would be traveling to his castle. It was too late to change her mind, but River hoped that their visit would be as harmless as it appeared.

Darkness was descending upon the woods surrounding Swift Wind's Pack house like a thick cloak. The day following Magnus's visit, he called to inform them that Lord Belozersky accepted Alpha Nick's condition. Soon, he would be sending someone to deliver them to Velladona. River wrapped her arms around her body protectively and waited. They were close.

A car pulled up to the bottom of the driveway's gates. Grabbing her overnight bag, River left her room and gradually made her way down to the foyer. At the top of the stairs, she took a deep breath.

We can do this, Crystal encouraged.

Nick and Amanda were already greeting their guests. River knew whom she would be seeing, yet meeting the two vampires in real life was somehow different than from her vision. The first one she could identify as she reached the bottom step, was the man with long dark hair hiding half his face. His eyes were an equally deep brown instead of the red she recalled. Beside him, was a small girl who appeared to be around her age. Her ash-blonde hair appeared similar to lord Pavel's.

"River, there you are," Nick said with a smile. "I would like you to meet Princess Marina Belozersky and her bodyguard Count Babanin. They will be transporting us to Lord Belozersky's castle."

"It's a pleasure to meet you," River greeted with a small curtsy. "Though I do wonder, how are we going to travel there? I doubt we will all fit in the car I saw arriving."

A slow, mysterious grin appeared on the pale girl's face, revealing her pointed fangs. "We won't be making the journey by car," Marina informed them. "I have been given the honor of taking you to my father."

River's brows furrowed. What did she mean? Did this have to do with the fading light River foresaw? That didn't make sense. Malinda hadn't mentioned using her magic to transport them all.

Just then, Malinda appeared through the wide threshold in her long traveling cloak. Pushing her hair back from the side of her face, her eyes sparkled.

"Marina happens to be a talented sorceress," she said clearing up the mystery. "It is a unique gift for vampires, but she has spent the last few centuries mastering it. We had the pleasure of studying with the same enchanter together."

"Yes," the vampire drawled, the hint of a true grin touching her lips. "Tell me, how is Master Thorn these days? I have not seen him for a few centuries."

"Doing well, last I've heard. It's been a while since I've seen him myself. He is currently studying the effects of mystical energies up north."

"Interesting."

"Yes," Malinda agreed. Peering at each of them in turn, she informed them, "Marina is a trustworthy friend. Her spells are second to none. There is no reason to fret."

I don't like this, Kyle mentally said to Nick. *Wouldn't it be better to take a car or a plane even? At this rate, we will be at the vampires' mercy to return to the kingdom.*

While Blue Lake had three squads of warriors standing by should they require aid, Nick wasn't pleased with this development either. Malinda was the only one among them capable of using magic. Should something happen to her, they would be trapped.

"If I may," the female vampire said softly. "The mountains separating our territories are too hazardous to make by vehicle. To do so would require traveling several hours out of the way to the nearest usable crossing." Her gaze shifted to Kyle. "My father also does not allow aircraft anywhere near the castle. We do not have a landing field big enough to accommodate you. Using the vortex spell is the most efficient means."

Brows raised; the two men shared a telling glance.

"What's the vortex spell?" Roxy questioned, defusing some of the building tension.

An apt teacher, Malinda gladly explained. "It's a trans-dimensional enchantment which can move objects across great distances. Once it's cast, we shall be in Velladona in the blink of an eye."

"Whoa, that sounds amazing!" Frowning, Roxy tapped a finger against the side of her cheek. She looked at the pale woman across from her. "Why didn't you just use that spell to come here in the first place? Why drive? Sounds like a waste of time."

"A powerful enchantment such as this can only be cast once a day and requires a full day to recover."

"Yes," Count Babanin added. "King Alpha Magnus supplied the car once we entered his lands, so that the Princess could conserve her strength."

"It's time," Marina informed them. Spinning on her heel, the mysterious woman exited the manor and went to stand in the grass outside with her guard.

Taking a few deep breaths, River followed the others outside. Alpha Nick, his luna and Roxy stood on River's right while Kyle, James and Malinda took her left side. River's grip tightened on the handle of her bag as the vampire's voice quietly began the enchantment in a language she could not understand. A magic circle appeared beneath their feet. The complex design of shapes and symbols was like nothing she had ever seen before. It was beautiful and wonderous.

Then, just as she saw in her vision, the trees of the forest began to fade and the soft grass under her feet was replaced with the solid stone of Lord Belozersky's castle. They did it. They had arrived in the vampire's territory.

In front of them, Marina opened her eyes. The light dissipated and she stumbled slightly. Her guard immediately wrapped his arms about her and lifted her into the air.

"Come," he told the princess with glowing irises. "You need to rest."

The woman in his arms did not reply. Raising a hand to touch his cheek, she merely nodded. In a flash, they vanished from the space.

"Welcome, Alpha Nicholas. I'm honored that you and your family could join me here," rang out a voice at the front of the chamber.

Peering at the stairs, the she-wolf could easily make out the vampire ruler. His hair, the same color as his daughter's, was tied at the base of his neck and he was dressed from head to foot in elegant clothing. Holding out his arms, Pavel levitated down the steps and strode towards them.

Nick bowed slightly as he approached. The rest of the pack followed suit while Malinda dropped into a curtsy.

"Thank you for inviting us, Lord Belozersky," Nick stated without any real feeling. "My king informed me that you have something you wish to show us."

The vampire blinked for a moment. His face suddenly broke out into a surprisingly charming grin. "Right to business is it, Nicholas?" he laughed. "You act as if this is the first time we've met. Come, old friend, there is no need to be so formal."

"Old friend?" the alpha growled. *Like hell.*

"Wait, the two of you know each other?" Kyle questioned, studying the vampire intently.

"Yes."

"No."

The two men answered at the same time.

Pavel quirked a brow. Casually, he waved a hand dismissively. "Don't tell me that you are still holding a grudge over our little misunderstanding?" he asked with a humorous gleam in his eye. "That was years ago, my friend."

"Misunderstanding?" Nick returned incredulously. "You tried to rip my head off. Literally."

"All in the past. Though, as I recall, you did bite me first."

"I'm not here to play games with you, Lord Belozersky," the alpha hissed. "Show us the hellhound or we are leaving."

The ease disappeared from the vampire's expression immediately. "I do wonder how you know about that?" he drawled watching River. "You have a lovely daughter, Nicholas. Aren't you going to introduce everyone to me?"

Don't let him bait you, Maddox warned, helping Nick to get his warring emotions under control. He had known that coming here was a bad idea. Nick should never have allowed them to convince him otherwise. *It's a little late now.*

The feel of Amanda's warm hand upon his arm aided Nick in regaining his equilibrium. Eyes fixed like daggers on the man across from them, he gestured towards his wife.

"This is my Luna, Amanda."

"Lord Belozersky," she greeted carefully.

"Please, call me Pavel."

Nick ignored his once again smiling eyes. "My eldest son, James. My Beta, Kyle. His daughter, Roxy and our friend and ally, Malinda, whom I believe you already know."

Pavel bowed to the witch before his gaze settled on the one woman that Nick did not introduce.

When their sights connected, River felt that strange familiarity once more. Something told her that this wasn't the first time he had seen her. She tried to think of a time when he might have been to Red Moon, but nothing came to mind. Alpha Jack had never been one to entertain vampires.

"Nicholas," Pavel scolded softly. "You forgot to mention Ella, or should I say River?" He watched carefully as her lips parted with a gasp and her face paled. Chuckling, Pavel started to turn away while saying, "I do believe River suits you better. Now come, I would say that I have a surprise, but you seem to have already figured out who my other guest is."

The walk to the depths of Pavel's dungeon seemed to take forever. An underground tunnel led them out of the main castle and into a subterranean structure. There was no telling how deep the secret building went. The ceilings of the room they were taken into were easily three stories tall. There were no windows. The lights came from candles lining the walls and a few chandeliers. Some pieces of equipment were set up to one side with a large curtain strung around what River knew was the hellhound's cage.

The snarls coming from behind the sheet grew louder as Pavel strode towards it. With a dramatic wave of his hand, he pulled the curtain away to reveal the creature of darkness and flame.

Snapping its jaws, the beast growled in the back of its throat. Reaching a clawed paw between the bars, it tried to strike the vampire.

"Now, now," Pavel chided darkly. "It's best for you to behave."

Everyone's eyes remained locked on the hellhound, yet Pavel only watched one of his guests and one alone.

"How in the world did you capture it alive?" Amanda wondered.

The vampire shrugged his shoulders casually, as if this feat was nothing unusual for him. "Marina's magic was of great help. It was foolish enough to break into my castle. I've heard the werewolves are having similar issues. We've managed to study it for the past week."

"I assume you found something of importance," Nick stated. "Otherwise, you wouldn't have brought us here."

Pavel didn't answer him. His gaze remained on River. The hellhound had ceased its growling and was watching her solely. The beast's eyes were following her every move and every breath. The vampire didn't miss the intensity which it was stalking its prey.

"River, come closer for a moment," he requested.

Nick growled and blocked his daughter's path.

Pavel's eyes narrowed sharply. "There is no need to be rude," he told the alpha frostily. "Do you want the information you came for or not?"

"It's alright, Father." Placing a hand on his arm, she moved to the front of the group. "I want to see the beasts we are meant to fight."

Stepping aside, Nick let her walk forward towards the vampire. As he went to follow, his instincts had him darting backwards as something shot upwards out of the floor. Steel spikes narrowly missed the members of his pack. A second set lowered from the ceiling, effectively cutting the space in half with River, Pavel and the hellhound on one side and the rest of them on the other.

"What is the meaning of this?" Nick demanded, his eyes blazing black. "Malinda, can you break through it?"

The witch gently placed a palm on the metal surface. A magic circle came to life, rejecting her energy and knocking her away. Kyle darted forward to catch her before her body hit the ground. Malinda's eyes narrowed sharply as she peered at her palm. The burn on her skin was already disappearing as she healed herself.

"It's been enchanted," she told the alpha. "I can't break this without my potions, forgive me."

"Damn it," Nick growled loudly. "Pavel, what are you doing? Release her at once!"

The vampire said nothing as he stalked towards the cage. Holding out a hand, he used his power to rip the door from its hinges, releasing the creature of fire anxiously waiting inside.

Racing forward, River grabbed the steel, pushing and pulling as she fought to slip through.

Nick's hand curled around her own. "Remember what we taught you, River. You can defeat it. You must," her father said encouragingly.

I'm not ready, she whispered through their link, privately pleading for someone to come to her aid. This wasn't one of the rogues she had battled with her pack members. Training was one thing, but River had never fought a battle all on her own. Warriors were a team. There was always someone to stand beside you if you fell. Here, no one would be able to save her and a hellhound was unlike any enemy she had ever faced before.

Twisting away from the bars, River gasped as the beast slowly exited its cage. The creature didn't pounce upon her as she thought it would. It seemed to know that she was trapped and was enjoying taking its time with her demise.

Don't panic, Crystal advised, pacing in the front of her mind. *We have to go for its weak spots. Focus on the underbelly and the throat.*

Understood. Wait for my signal.

Hearing the voice of her wolf helped to steady River's racing heartbeat. As long as she had her wolf's support, then they could get through this. Pavel wasn't going to get rid of her that easily. Sooner or later, she would have to defeat one of these fire beasts. It was time to show this vampire who he was messing with.

River moved away from the steel wall purposely. Stretching out her fingers, she waited for her foe to make the first move.

The beast launched forward with incredible speed. River darted out of the way, barely missing the snapping fangs seeking her flesh. When it came at her again, she dove.

Rolling to her feet, the she-wolf tried to attack the hellhound's flank, yet it twisted away, leaving her clawed hand to strike nothing but air.

As the dangerous dance continued, Nick fought to keep Maddox from taking over. If Malinda couldn't lower the barrier, then his wolf wouldn't be able to either. His black eyes locked on the vampire hovering in the air high above the slaughter.

"Damn it, Pavel!" he roared, vying for the other man's attention. "You swore a blood oath that you would not harm her!"

The man's cold eyes darted briefly to the wolf. "I'm not harming her."

"Like hell you're not. You have her trapped with a hellhound! Lower this barrier at once or I swear I will tear you apart the moment I get in there."

"Calm yourself," Pavel instructed mildly. "Your daughter is more levelheaded than you are at this time."

Growling, Nick shifted his sights back to River. While still in her human form, she was holding her own fairly well. She gained a few cuts which healed instantly. Yet, Nick knew just dodging her enemy's attacks wouldn't be enough.

The next time the beast leapt at her, River raced towards it, sliding under the creature instead of jumping out of the way.

Now! she hollered to her wolf.

Crystal burst forward, taking control of their body. Skin shifted to fur, bones lengthened and claws formed from her fingers, cutting into the underside of the hellhound as it passed by her. Ears pressed against the sides of her head, River growled deeply as she stood proudly on all fours.

Blood dripped from the hellhound's stomach, but its fiery eyes showed no notice of it. It raced towards River once again. The two collided with snapping jaws and sharpened claws as they competed to do the most damage.

Breaking away, River's chest heaved as she gave herself a moment to heal. None of her attacks seemed to do enough damage.

"Stop holding back," Pavel said from above her. "If you hope to defeat Cerberus you will need more than just strength and speed. Hellhounds are made of ash and flame. Did the Goddess not give you power? Then use it."

Ash and flame, River echoed in her mind.

Pavel seemed to already know what she was, so why was she still hiding it? Habit, she supposed. Ever since she found out about her powers, River fought to not only control them, but to keep others outside her fellow warriors from seeing them. A blessing could easily be a curse instead.

No more hiding, Crystal encouraged. *It's time to show just how strong we are.*

River couldn't agree more.

Like a broken record, the hellhound charged. This time, River didn't race out to meet it. Taking a deep breath, she blasted it with ice. The force of her attack knocked it backwards. The frozen water quickly dissipated as it regained its feet, but the she-wolf was far from finished. Ice shot across the floor from her feet in a wide circle. Dancing gracefully upon the frozen sheet, she rounded the hellhound, attacking from the side with a controlled burst of water. When the beast was thrown off its feet, she raced in, using the ice to wrap around it while she pounced. Claws encased in her ice, River dug into its chest and tore at its throat. She didn't stop until the hellhound's body went limp and faded to ash in her mouth. Stepping back, her eyes widened as she watched the large creature's entire form smolder and vanish. The second it disappeared, the steel spikes began to lower.

"Not bad," announced a voice frighteningly close to her.

River flinched involuntarily, causing her to frown. Turning, a younger man stood behind her with a striking resemblance to Pavel. *Why didn't we sense him?*

"You must be the new Moon Blest Wolf I've heard about," he drawled somberly.

His serious expression didn't soften as he spoke. Was this man friend or foe?

"Who are you?" Roxy demanded, suddenly by River's side. "And how could you just stand there while she was getting attacked? What is wrong with you vampires?"

Her eyes blazed in a way that River hadn't seen before. If she didn't know better, she would also think that Roxy was a creature born of fire, she certainly had enough spunk within her. Roxy and the new vampire glared invisible daggers at each other.

"How dare you speak this way to me? Do you have any idea who I am, wolf?"

Roxy snorted. "All I see is a coward who lets people get attacked without lifting a finger to help."

Scowling, the man's pale blue eyes flashed red and his face contorted with a snarl. Inches away from Roxy, he spoke in a dangerously quiet voice, "You dare insult my honor, mutt?"

"I'm not afraid of you, bloodsucker."

Two fathers simultaneously pulled their children back.

"That's enough, Dimitri," Pavel warned. "There is no reason for you to antagonize our guests. Forgive my son, he can be quite passionate about upholding our family's honor."

"It's a little too late for apologies," Nick snarled, leaping at the vampire. "You tried to kill my daughter."

Pavel dodged, not looking worried in the least. "Kill her? Now, why would I do that? Only a Moon Blest can send Cerberus to the abyss where he belongs."

Not fully listening to Pavel's words, Nick continued with his attacks. Maddox had already taken over, shifting them into their wolf form.

"Calm yourself, old friend," Pavel urged. "We both know that facing a hellhound is very different than a normal werewolf. I wanted to see her skills for myself. She's not bad. However, it will take more than the level she is at to face a monster of fire. Besides, Dimitri and I were both watching should we have needed to intervene."

Pavel's words made sense to Nick, yet his wolf didn't want to hear it. Attacking his pup, for whatever reason, was unforgivable. He wasn't going to stop until he felt the vampire's flesh between his teeth.

"Could you all stop acting as if I'm not even here?" River demanded, drawing their attention. "I'm not the weak, frightened girl I was when I came to Swift Wind." she sighed, gazing at the ancient vampire who was peering at her with an amused expression. "If Lord Pavel wanted me dead, he could have done it years ago. Am I right?"

Watching him closely, River didn't break eye contact. She knew she was correct. Feeling his eyes upon her during her battle confirmed her earlier suspicion. River knew in her very bones that Pavel was the one watching her from the shadows all her life. She felt the same essence while playing at Fire Lake as a child and even in her new home.

"I know I am," River continued confidently. "You've been watching me for years. Why don't you just tell us the real reason you brought us here?"

No one moved a muscle as a slow smile appeared on the vampire lord's face. "It was a test, my dear. One, I am happy to say, that you have passed." Watching the alpha shift back into his human form, Pavel directed his gaze upon him. "She certainly acts like your daughter, Nicholas. I must say, I'm looking forward to this new alliance. Consider me at your disposal."

Chapter 8

River couldn't believe everything she was learning in Pavel's company. Their overnight stay had already stretched out to a week. The beast she fought wasn't the only one the lord had managed to capture with the aid of witches. Several more were locked way within his specialized dungeon. Each of the wolves were teamed up with another wolf or vampire to practice defeating them. Marina and Malinda were currently using their magic to hinder any killing blows upon the hellhounds, since such a beast wasn't easy to come by. Once defeated, they returned the creature to its cage to await another practice session.

Strangely enough, Roxy and Dimitri, Pavel's oldest son, seemed to be paired together most often. Storming across the gardens, they were once again arguing. River wasn't close enough to hear what the issue was this time. She learned early on to avoid getting involved if she could help it. Their fire and ice personalities could be a hazard to bystanders.

"I hope you get a sunburn and catch on fire!" Roxy finally shouted as she made her way towards River.

River had to bite her lip to keep from laughing. "You do know that sunlight being a weakness is a myth, right?" she asked needlessly, considering they were all standing in the exposed light of the formal gardens.

Lesser vampires had an aversion to extended time in sunlight, almost like an allergy, but purer bloodlines felt nothing at all. There was no chance that Dimitri would suddenly self-combust as Roxy wished. Vampires usually hunted at night because there were less enemies to compete with, not that it mattered much these days. The lord of each clan was extremely wealthy and owned their own blood bank. So, donated blood and a line of volunteers willingly giving it, made hunting no longer necessary for the majority of their kind.

"I can always hope," her friend muttered, pulling her legs up to her chest as she sat in the grass.

River joined her while twirling a rose between her fingers. "I know he wasn't overly friendly when we first met, but why do the two of you detest each other so?"

"I don't know," Roxy admitted with a sigh. "Every time he comes near me, he just gets under my skin. He doesn't even have to say anything."

River's brows furrowed. *I wish there was a way we could help,* she said to Crystal.

This isn't something we can help with, her wolf chuckled.

What do you mean?

Don't worry about it. Why don't we try cheering her up?

Something about her wolf's words unsettled her. What could she know that River didn't? Shrugging, she focused on how to bring back Roxy's smile. There was just one thing sure to do so.

"Can you tell me about the Moonlight Celebration again? It's next week, isn't it?"

Visibly brightening, a large smile dominated the she-wolf's face. "Yes, it is," she just about squealed. "Next Saturday will be the opening night at Lockwood Castle in Silver Fang. The official beginning ceremony, where King Magnus welcomes all the packs, starts at sundown. However, wolves start arriving hours beforehand. Last year was my first time, and I promise, you will never forget it!" Roxy told her with gleaming eyes.

As River continued to listen to her friend describe the various food stands and activities for the celebration, her heart began to ache. She was glad Roxy's troubles had vanished from her thoughts.

Then what is troubling you?

I guess I'm a little jealous, River admitted sadly. *I know we have to attend now that I'm of age, but it seems so pointless.* It would be years before River could pick a chosen mate. After a certain age, unmated wolves who couldn't find their mates were allowed to choose their own companion. Unless she would happen to meet a wolf rejected like herself, River had no chance of meeting anyone.

A party is never pointless, Crystal said, interrupting her wayward thoughts. *This is the only time all the packs will be together at once. It doesn't hurt to help strengthen the bonds that father has been building with the other Alphas. Who knows when you will meet your next ally? We have to go,* her wolf insisted.

River already knew this, yet was it her imagination or was Crystal becoming even more eager to attend? Too bad she couldn't switch places and go in her wolf form. That way she wouldn't have to worry about running into someone she didn't want to. Good thing *he* had no reason to seek her out.

"Are you sure you don't want me to join you?" Jack questioned, studying Carrel's jerky movements with a frown.

His son was throwing the last of his clothing in his suitcase with a look of disgust. Courtney was staying with her parents for the week, so there wasn't any reason why he shouldn't go. Perhaps it would be better to keep an eye on Carrel after all.

"That's not necessary," his son snapped, closing the lid with a huff. "You know the pack needs you here. If there is another attack, my warriors will need Steven and your strength to back them up."

The thought caused him to clench his jaw. It wasn't just his father who was unaffected by the curse. Those he immediately replaced once Carrel took over the pack, the beta and gamma, showed no signs of weakness either. Carrel didn't want to believe his father's story about a curse, but it didn't seem like he had a choice. The old leaders were fine while the new ones, appointed by him, were falling apart. If the frequent attacks weren't enough to prove he was being punished, then that clearly showed him the truth. All Carrel had to do was find his pathetic former mate. He didn't need his father watching over him as he begged her forgiveness, especially since she wasn't worth the effort he was making to find her.

Unfortunately, there wasn't any other way. What Jack didn't know was that Carrel had already tried to set up a meeting with Ella and was refused by Alpha Nick. He knew the older wolf didn't care for him since the day Nick visited their pack house two years ago. The knowledge of the powerful man's dislike was reenforced by his lack of interest since Carrel was initiated as alpha. The man had the gall to refuse his invitation to even attend!

"If you need anything, don't hesitate to call me," Jack instructed, unable to rid himself of his fatherly concern, despite Carrel's vile personality.

Sighing dramatically, Carrel picked up his bag and exited the room. "Yes, I know."

Can we just go already? Drex questioned irritably. *The sooner we get this over with, the better.*

Carrel couldn't agree more. Now all he had to do was find the girl.

Sitting on a large rock, River skipped a few pebbles across the surface of the pond. Watching the ripples dance their way over the inky water, she let out a sigh. Tomorrow they were leaving for Silver Fang and the Moonlight Celebration. Tilting her head back, River stared at the not quite full moon. How had this day come so quickly?

"I thought I might find you here," chuckled her father's strong voice.

A slow smile spread over her lips.

"Oh? And how did you know I would be here?"

River scooted to the side to make room for him to join her.

"Because, my daughter, you are very much like your name. You're always somewhere near the water."

Giggling, River knew she couldn't argue with that.

"So, what are you doing out so late? We're leaving early in the morning."

River's gaze lowered to the ground. "I know," she said quietly, her smile disappearing.

Nick studied her profile for a moment. With so much happening lately between hellhound attacks and training with Pavel, he hadn't realized how forlorn she seemed. Was she worried about running into Carrel? As the new Alpha of Red Moon, he was sure to be there. As much as Nick would like to, there was no conceivable way to keep him from attending.

"I won't let him harm you, River. You do know that, don't you?"

River blinked. Looking at her father, her brows furrowed. It took her a moment to realize to whom he was referring. A shadow of a grin touched her features.

"Thank you. I know none of you would allow that. I haven't thought about him in a long time, actually."

This time Nick frowned. "Then what's the trouble?"

River sighed and twisted her fingers together.

How can I explain this without sounding silly? she asked Crystal.

Don't worry, he's not going to laugh at you. It's understandable, considering what happened to our mate.

Licking her lips, River focused on the water. The words might come easier to her if she was peering away from him.

"I guess, part of me wishes that I didn't have to go," she confessed with a sigh. "It sounds like a lot of fun and I don't want to sound like a brat, but what's the point of going if I'm not going to find a mate?"

His mouth forming a silent 'o', Nick nodded his head.

Biting into her lower lip, River continued. "I just wonder what the future's going to be like when everyone else has their mates and I'm all alone. James has his future Luna, Tye and Luka both found theirs. Roxy, I doubt will be unmated for long and the twins…" River laughed softly. "Well, I'm sure they will eventually find she-wolves who will put up with them."

Beside her, Nick smirked for a moment. There were days he didn't know what to do with them either. Stretching his shoulders, the alpha peered up at the stars.

"I wish I could tell you that I know everything will work out for the best, but only the Goddess knows what tomorrow will bring. I do know that you should never give up hope." Nick rubbed his face for a moment and sighed. "Did I ever tell you that I wasn't first in line to become Alpha of Swift Wind?"

Eyes widening, River's head pulled back. "You weren't? Why? You're a great Alpha."

A humorless smile touched his face. "Thanks, it took me a little while to get the hang of it. You see, my brother was the Alpha before me."

River never knew that Nick had an older brother. Now that he said it, it did make sense. There were a few pictures with a similar looking man in the living room. The subject of who he was never came up, so River didn't ask. She merely thought he was a relative of some kind.

"What happened to him?"

Her father's eyes clouded. "He was killed, many years ago. His name was Conner. He was a few years older than me, but we were still close. His Luna, Laraine and their daughter, Ava, didn't survive the attack either." Nick paused for a second to swallow the lump in his throat. "One of the darkest days in my life was when I had to bury my brother. I lost my best friend and my leader that day."

Wrapping his arm around River's shoulders, he pulled her close. "I'm not going to tell you that things are going to be easy. But, if you take it one day at a time and believe in yourself, you may be surprised by all the good things that will happen. After all, it brought us you. Amanda and I wouldn't change that for the world."

Tears welling up in her eyes, River gripped him in a tight embrace.

"Thank you," she whispered. "I love you."

"I love you too, kiddo," he told her, hugging River back. "Come now," Nick ordered softly, pulling her to her feet and wiping her eyes. "We have a big day tomorrow. Let's see what it brings us."

A bright smile on her face, River didn't know where to look first. Lights were strung throughout the castle, gardens and surrounding town of Carlisle. All higher-ranking pack members were staying at the castle in the center of the activity. From the look of things, River wasn't sure that a week would be enough time to take everything in. There were so many foods she'd never tasted before and Crystal's heightened sense of smell was going into overdrive, demanding that she go to this stand, only to catch the whiff of something else and beg to go there first.

Her belly aching from eating too much too quickly, River began to wander to a quieter section of the festival. There was a large pond in a small park with walking trails and boats to row upon the calm water's surface. River passed several humans, witches and even a few vampires as she made her way down the nearest path.

I can't believe how many different races live here in Silver Fang.

Father did once tell us that it is the heart of trade in the kingdom. It would make sense for all types of beings to dwell here.

That's true, River agreed. *I'm surprised Uncle Magnus has been able to keep the village so cozy.*

While by no means small, Carlisle was kept with a limited population to control its growth and size as well as crime. Non-pack members had to apply at the castle in order to move there for an extended period. This way, Magnus could also make sure that his own people were never outnumbered by those who may wish to bring them harm.

Having circled back to the beginning of the trail, River paused. Her eyes narrowed as she caught sight of some of Courtney's minions. Had it really been two whole years since she saw anyone from Red Moon? *I guess it was going to happen sooner or later.* The trail went right past where they were standing. Moving towards the town, she pulled her shoulders back and lifted her chin proudly. As she strode closer, it wasn't River who the snarky girls were gazing at.

Another woman was sitting on the bench with her head bowed. Her brown shoulder-length hair was shielding her face, but River could smell the hint of tears that she was fighting to hide. There was something else about her that seemed so familiar.

"I can't believe that you would bother to show your face here," one of the women said, giggling behind her hand.

"Yeah," another agreed. "Haven't you done enough damage? No one wants a cheat for a mate."

River stiffened. Amber? Were they really trying to ruin her chances at finding a mate? Someone needed to put these wenches in their place. Eyes narrowed to slits, River gracefully strode over to them without a second thought.

A small crowd was already growing around the scene, with people whispering as they blatantly stared at Amber's crumbling form. Rising shakily, she tried to leave, but two of the women blocked her path.

"Where do you think you're going, cheat?"

Her trembling fingers gripping the sides of her pants, Amber looked her abusers right in the eye.

"You know I'm no cheat, Emma. Why won't you just leave me alone?"

"And let you sully another pack's name? That would be careless of us," the other girl sneered.

"The only ones tarnishing their pack's name would be you four," River stated in a firm tone. Her voice drew everyone's attention as her body radiated power. "I've heard of the incident to which you refer and there was never a single piece of proof. Only the accusation of one spiteful girl. To condemn someone with no supporting facts is foolish."

Faces reddening, the women gaped at her. "Who do you think you are to speak to us like this?"

River considered them for a moment. She had known each one of them, had gone to class with them, seen them on a regular basis as she did her chores. Did they really not recognize her?

I've told you before, Crystal hummed. *We've changed a lot.*

Crossing her arms, River peered at each one of them in turn before answering.

"I am River Carlson, daughter of Alpha Nicholas of Swift Wind. If you would like, we can take this matter directly to King Alpha Magnus. I'm sure he would be *pleased* to hear that there are she-wolves causing issues at his *favorite* celebration."

Knowing that was the last thing they wanted to do, the women couldn't seem to gather their thoughts. Holding up their hands, they quickly backed away. River didn't think their faces could get any paler.

"No. No. That won't be necessary."

"Then I suggest you behave yourselves for the remainder of your visit."

Nodding, they bumped into each other as the four she-wolves rushed away as quickly as they could. River watched as the crowd, too, seemed to dissipate, now that there wasn't anything left to see.

Exhaling with a long breath, Amber slumped back down on the bench. She rubbed her palms across the top of her pants as she tried to ease her shakiness. A soft thump next to her drew her attention. Looking at River, she flashed her a grateful smile.

"Thank you," Amber said sincerely. "Not many people would do what you did."

River waved off her thanks. "It was nothing. No one likes a bully."

Blinking, Amber tilted her head to the side as she studied the woman beside her more closely.

"Ella?" she whispered so quietly that River almost didn't catch it.

Blushing, Amber pressed her lips together and shook her head. She must have been seeing things. It had been years since Ella disappeared, but this woman was the alpha's daughter. There was no possible way that they could be the same person. To her surprise, River let out a low laugh.

"It's been a long time since I heard that name," she admitted quietly. "How are you, Amber?"

Not once had the she-wolves from Red Moon said her name during their verbal assault. Mouth gaping, she leaned forward without thinking and wrapped her old friend in a hug.

"It *is* you. What happened? Where have you been?"

Returning the embrace, River sighed, "It's a long story. And best left for a more private setting," she added glancing around at the people casually walking around the park.

"So, you go by 'River' now?"

River nodded.

"I like it. It must be nice to have a fresh start. I've thought about it too. I just wouldn't know where to go."

"You'd be welcomed at Swift Wind. I'm sure my father wouldn't mind if you joined our pack."

Amber's gaze lit up. "Really? You would do that?"

River laughed. "Of course. You were always my friend. The only true one I had there, it would seem."

Gaze dropping, unwanted memories couldn't help but bubble up to the surface. No matter how long she lived, she would never forget that day. She would never forget the betrayal of watching her supposed best friend turn away from her when she needed her most.

We have Roxy now, Crystal reminded her kindly.

Yes, they did. Roxy would never betray her. If anything, River would have to hold her back from ripping the offending person's head off. The thought caused her to smile. Suddenly, River was overcome with a dizzy sensation. Knowing what was about to happen, she lowered her head and used a hand to cover her face. Images flashed before her and when the vision passed, the grin was still on her face.

"Are you alright?" Amber questioned, reaching out to touch her arm.

River nodded. "Yes, thank you. Just a dizzy spell. I get them from time to time. Why don't you come by my room at the castle when you get the chance? I'm staying in the east wing and will let the guards know to expect you."

Amber's hazel eyes sparkled. "I would love that."

River rose to her feet. "The beginning ceremony is about to start, so I have to go. Why don't you try the food stall over there on the edge of the park? I promise, it will be worth it."

Gaze following the direction River was pointing, Amber forced a smile. "I was thinking of just heading back to my room."

"That's no way to celebrate," River teased. "If you want to go afterwards, I won't stop you, but consider it a friend's request."

With everything that River had just done for her, Amber knew it would be rude to refuse. If trying one stall would please her, then who was she to complain? Nodding, Amber wished her friend goodbye, hoping that they would see each other soon. And just like that, she was alone again. Amber knew she should be used to it by now, with even her parents remaining distant. Wolves were social creatures and the loneliness was slowly ripping her heart to shreds.

Courtney's dislike of her had slowly caused the whole pack to shun her. Whether they believed her claim of innocence or not, no one wanted to get on their new Luna's bad side. It could be gruesome indeed.

As Amber stepped into the light of the street, she heard the crash of glass. A man with messy brown hair and piercing blue eyes stared at her. The food in his hand dropped from limp fingers to join his broken purchase on the ground. Nothing else around him seemed to move. Amber's breath caught in her throat. The scent attacking her was intoxicating, causing her wolf to scream inside her mind.

"Mate!" the man shouted rushing at her.

Picking Amber clear off her feet, Blake swung her in a circle shouting 'mate' over and over again. Once he allowed her feet to touch the ground, he began planting a kiss on one cheek, then the other before burying his nose in her hair.

"Thank the Goddess I've finally found you!" Pulling back, he gazed happily into her wide startled eyes. "You're so beautiful. I will love you forever! Please, please, tell me your name," Blake pleaded.

If the man before her was in wolf form, his tail would have been going a mile a minute. Amber, on the other hand, couldn't believe it. She had found her mate! The initial joy bursting in her heart froze with dread. The poisonous words Emma spoke rang in her mind. 'No one wants a cheat for a mate.' The moment he realized who she was, he was bound to reject her. Swallowing the lump in her throat, Amber fought back the tears trying to break through.

"I'm...I'm Amber Brown of Red Moon," she whispered, almost wishing she didn't have to tell him and ruin this moment.

"Amber," he repeated excitedly. "You're mine now, Amber. I'm Blake Elrod, second Prince of Silver Fang," he told her, puffing out his chest.

Instead of a happy squeal or even a kiss, the she-wolf still in his arms paled. Her bottom lip quivered and tears were visible in her eyes. His wolf could smell her fear and it displeased him greatly.

"What's wrong?" he asked worriedly. "You don't have to be afraid. I would never hurt you. You are my mate, my love."

Shaking her head slowly, Amber couldn't seem to form any words. At last, she whispered, "You're not going to reject me?"

Blake's head jerked back. "Why would I reject you? I've been searching the entire kingdom trying to find you. You are mine!"

"But...but...you must have heard the rumors about me. My pack shuns me as a cheat."

Blake's eyes darkened as he watched Amber's arms wrap protectively around herself.

"What do you mean a cheat? Like you sleep around?"

"No!" she denied immediately, her gaze connecting with his. "I would never. I've never even..."

The prince smirked as her cheeks flushed and she looked at the ground. Privately, he breathed a sigh of relief. He would never tolerate his mate being unfaithful.

Her voice barely above a whisper, Amber continued, "I was accused of cheating on an exam in school years ago, but I didn't do it. Courtney just doesn't like me," she added with a mumble.

Blake snorted. He recognized that name. The she-wolf had thrown herself on him more than once when her boyfriend wasn't around.

"Your pack turned its back on you because someone *said* you cheated on a school test? That's the most ridiculous thing I've ever heard. Sounds like a pretty shitty pack," he announced not caring who heard him.

Someone had made his mate upset and his wolf didn't like seeing her tears. It didn't matter if the girl in question was now a luna. Pulling Amber to his chest, Blake cupped her chin with one hand to direct her gaze back to his face.

"You're mine now," he repeated with determination. "If anyone dares to speak ill of you again, they'll have *me* to deal with. You don't ever have to go back there for all I care. We'll send for your things."

Amber sucked in a breath as Blake lowered his head to plant a gentle kiss on her lips. She leaned into him, savoring his warmth and strength. So, this is what it felt like to be loved by your mate. Happy tears slid down the sides of her cheeks. Amber wanted to shout with excitement, but lacked her mate's courage. She let out a small yelp as Blake suddenly picked her up bridal style.

"Come, my love," he announced, straightening his shoulders and puffing out his chest. "We have a celebration to get to."

As the moon rose higher in the sky, people began to gather in the castle's courtyard. A large stage was set up at the front for the king, while several smaller stages circled around for each of the other packs. Following her parents, River walked out onto the brightly lit platform and stood beside her brothers. Alphas and their families from other packs were quickly starting to appear. River knew Red Moon's dais was somewhere to the right, so she peered at the royal platform to her left instead.

A large smile stretched across her face when she spotted Amber hugging Blake's side. He had his arm tightly around her while speaking to his father and mother. A bright grin was on both of their faces. When Amber caught sight of River, she waved shyly and mouthed, 'thank you'.

River waved back whispering, 'you're welcome'. She was glad her old friend listened to her advice. After seeing Amber and Blake meet, she knew that she would have dragged the other woman over there if she had to.

You big softy, Crystal teased.

You would do the same for her, River countered. *Amber deserves to be happy. She'll make a great Royal Beta female.*

I couldn't agree more.

River broke off her internal conversation as Magnus drew everyone's attention.

"Welcome everyone to the Moonlight Celebration!" Magnus announced stepping forward on his stage. "This honored tradition not only allows those of age to find their mates," he said glancing happily at his son, "but strengthens the bonds of our packs, our family. Tonight, my Queen Luna Kiki and I are proud to announce that our son, Second Prince Blake, has found his mate. Welcome to the family, Amber."

An excited round of applause thundered through the crowd.

Turning towards the first stage, Magnus continued. "To begin our celebration, I'm pleased to welcome Alpha Logan Donovan of White Crescent and his Luna Danelle."

There was a round of clapping as Logan and Danelle bowed.

"Next, I welcome Alpha Nicholas Carlson of Swift Wind, his Luna Amanda, their children James, Henry, Simon and River."

Another round of applause sounded in the courtyard.

The king shifted his attention to the next stage. "Please welcome Alpha Matthew Bright of Blue Lake, his Luna Katrina and their children—"

"Ella?" hollered a loud voice interrupting the king.

All eyes angrily turned to the tall man shouldering his way through the middle of the courtyard. People backed away, not wishing to be anywhere near him.

"Ella, is that you?"

"Alpha Carrel Stanford!" Magnus boomed fiercely. "You dare to disturb my ceremony?"

Carrel didn't seem to hear him. His eyes stayed glued to the graceful woman standing proudly on the stage in front of him. It couldn't be her. His vision had to be deceiving him, yet her smell told him otherwise. Gone was the awkward girl whose body hadn't caught up to her age. In two short years, Ella had grown a few inches in height. Her curves had filled out in all the right places. Her glistening honey-colored hair fell down her back in soft waves. The freckles across her nose faded to reveal high cheekbones and full, all too kiss-able lips. Carrel almost fell to his knees as he gazed upon her. She was the most beautiful woman he had ever seen.

She is ours, Drex announced hungrily. *Claim her. Claim our mate.*

Carrel couldn't agree more. Three wolves he hadn't noticed at first, pushed Ella protectively behind them.

"Stand aside, she's mine," he shouted, dashing towards the stage.

"Stay away from my daughter!" Alpha Nicholas commanded in a dangerous tone, his eyes flashing as he moved to the edge of the platform. "You already have a claimed mate."

The aura he was putting out caused the surrounding wolves to bow down and submit instantly. Alpha Logan had already jumped to the ground and came to stand in front of Swift Wind. On the other side, Alpha Matthew did the same. Were these two strong packs really siding with him so easily? Carrel could feel other powerful wolves gathering on the other side of the courtyard behind him. Even Alpha Isaiah of Blackwood was quickly approaching.

"Return to your place at once," Magnus instructed, knowing full well that he would be dealing with the young alpha later.

Carrel took a step closer. "You don't understand, she was supposed to be my mate."

"Back away, boy!" commanded an equally fearsome voice that Carrel knew well.

Striding through the main gate, Prince Adrian appeared in the courtyard. He was dressed in a polo and dress pants, having come late from a meeting outside the castle. Face set like stone, the future king alpha glared at the younger man darkly.

"What gives you the right to interfere?" Carrel demanded. "I don't care if you are the prince. She was my mate first and I want her back."

"You have a Luna. You *chose* your mate," Nick snapped coldly, managing to hold Maddox at bay. "You have no claim on my daughter. This is your last warning. Stay away from her."

Carrel opened his mouth to speak, but paused as Adrian's aura increased like a deadly storm.

"I will not say it again," he advised frostily. "Back off!"

The prince said nothing else, but his eyes dared for Carrel to disobey him. The younger alpha suppressed a shudder. To fight Adrian would be a death sentence. Unable to do anything else at the moment, the Red Moon Alpha bowed slightly, spun around, and stormed out of sight.

Adrian's gaze lifted to easily find River. His expression was one of intense determination as he slowly crossed the remainder of the courtyard towards the stage where she stood. Leaping up, he quietly stood at the edge, his gaze never leaving River's face. Her brothers gradually backed away with wide eyes as the prince took one step, then another, towards the she-wolf.

River's heart was racing so quickly she could barely catch her breath. Her legs wouldn't move and her voice felt trapped inside of her throat. Yet, she felt no desire to run. If anything, she desperately wanted him to come to her.

What is happening, Crystal?

It can't be, her wolf whispered in awe.

River didn't get the chance to question her. Adrian was towering over her. Still, she didn't feel threatened by his presence. Quite the opposite. The scent of him, like fresh rain combined with something that was all his own, made her dizzy. She wanted nothing more than to lean further into him and feel the heat of his skin beneath her palms. Their eyes locked together and River gasped as he raised a hand to gently trace the side of her cheek with his fingers.

"Mine," he whispered possessively.

Her eyes widened. How was this possible? She already was given a mate. Crystal provided no aid at the moment as she howled happily in her mind.

Mate, mate, mate, her wolf chanted over and over.

Wrapping his arm around her waist, Adrian twisted to face the crowd. Gazing at his father's slack jaw, he smiled broadly.

"Forgive my tardiness, Father," he began calmly, as if nothing unusual had happened. "Please continue with the ceremony."

Recovering, Magnus once more started welcoming the remaining alphas to the celebration. Adrian pretended to listen, but nothing seemed to get through his ecstatic mind. The girl—no, the woman beside him had to be River. All this time, she was right under his nose. Unable to keep the smile from his face, Adrian knew she was well worth the wait, and nothing, nothing was going to take his beloved mate away from him.

Chapter 9

Foot pressing down on the accelerator, Carrel ignored the incessant ringing of his cell phone. He knew who was calling, but the alpha didn't much care. The only thing occupying his thoughts was his mate. Ella, or River as she seemed to be named now, had changed so drastically that he still couldn't believe what he witnessed with his own eyes. Like a tale from an old story book, an ugly duckling had truly transformed into a swan. Drex was roaring in his mind, breaking his almost non-existent concentration on the dark road in front of him. Their bond had been broken for two years, so why was his wolf so strongly connected to the she-wolf that he had let go?

"Damn it!"

Slamming his fist on the steering wheel, Carrel pulled over to the side of the road. He picked up the phone, ready to switch it off completely when he saw the word 'urgent' written in all caps. Carrel exhaled with a hiss and pushed the call button.

"Thank the Goddess!" his father practically shouted from his end of the line. "Are you alright? Why haven't you picked up the phone?"

Carrel rolled his eyes. "In case you've forgotten, I've been trying to save my pack. You wrote that it was urgent, was there another attack?"

The younger alpha could practically feel his father seething. A smirk found its way to his face. It served Jack right for always sticking his nose in his business.

"It wasn't an attack," Jack told him darkly. "It's Courtney. She…she's had a miscarriage. The doctor did everything that he could, but he couldn't stop it. High blood pressure and too much stress on her body." There was silence on the other end of the line. "Carrel, did you hear me? You need to return as soon as you are able, Courtney needs you."

Face scrunched up with disgust, Carrel resisted the urge to throw the phone right out of the window. What a useless woman. For weeks now, he had put up with her vomiting and for what? She couldn't even produce him a proper heir. No matter.

"You call that urgent?" Carrel snapped crossly. "Even the doctor mentioned that miscarriages are common in the first trimester. From the sound of it, her life isn't in danger. So, unless there is a *real* emergency, don't bother me."

Cutting off the call, Carrel turned off his phone and tossed it onto the passenger seat. He didn't need to hear how his chosen mate was continuing to fail him.

"Damn it!" he hissed, hitting the steering wheel over and over.

Chest heaving, he leaned his head on the headrest.

Calm yourself, Drex urged. *We will fix this.*

How? How can we possibly do anything now? You saw the way Prince Adrian acted towards her, she was given another mate. She should have been ours!

Drex growled softly at the reminder of what they had lost. He was determined to take back the rejection. His body ached just from being away from her. River would be theirs one way or another.

There is still time, his wolf insisted. *She never formally rejected us, so with a little help, I'm sure we can right what has been wronged.*

Carrel's head straightened. He knew just what his wolf was referring to. Only one person could mend a broken mate bond and that was a witch. Carrel hadn't personally dealt with their kind before. His father was friends with a local coven, yet he never saw fit to take his son to any of their meetings. Shrugging, he pushed his pent up anger aside. Getting the old alpha involved in what he was about to do was the last thing he wanted. Jack had messed with enough of his plans as it was.

"I need someone father doesn't know. Someone he wouldn't have gone to for help."

Frowning, Carrel placed his chin in his open palm while he stared out the window. His eyes widened with a grin.

Agatha, he said to his wolf.

Carrel didn't know why he hadn't thought of her before. She was the old witch who lived in the free lands between Red Moon and Blackwood. His father wouldn't allow anyone in the pack near her, since rumors told of her love of black magic. She would make any potion, cast any spell, for a price.

Lips twisting into a sneer, Carrel shifted the car back into drive and raced once more down the road. He knew the area in which she lived. It would take no more than a few hours to reach her. Carrel didn't care what he had to pay to regain his mate. Soon, she would be his.

Pacing the floor of his old office, Jack pressed the call button on his phone for the umpteenth time. It went right to voicemail. Disconnecting it, he bit back a curse. Carrel hadn't answered a single call since they last spoke. His son's parting words sent a thread of anger coursing through him. There was no way that such a heartless brute was his child. Jack had been searching for some hint of humility, some touch of kindness, but the truth could no longer be denied. Carrel was a selfish beast with no redeeming qualities what-so-ever. He should *never* have made him alpha. Now, his pack was suffering because of it.

The sudden chime of his phone made Jack jerk back. Frowning, he peered down to see the name Matthew Bright. Why was the Alpha of Blue Lake calling him?

"Hello?" he said, bringing the phone up to his ear.

"Jack, is your son there with you?"

Stiffening, he immediately stopped his pacing. "No, he's not. Is something wrong?"

Jack didn't care for the sigh he heard on the other side of the line. "Yes, and his disappearance is making it worse. I'm only giving you this heads-up due to our years of friendship." There was a moment of silence, as if he was having difficulty forming the words to come. "King Magnus is issuing a disciplinary summons for Carrel."

Jack's eyes widened and he clutched the phone more firmly.

"What did he do?" he questioned with a suppressed growl.

"Nothing pleasant," Matthew replied with a hint of disgust. "He tried to claim Alpha Nicholas's daughter in the middle of the welcoming ceremony even though he has a Luna. Carrel then ignored King Magnus's commands and nearly got into a fight with Prince Adrian when he arrived, declaring that she was his first."

"Nick has a daughter?" Jack asked strangely.

There was a pause on the other side of the phone. "Yes. Don't you remember? He adopted an orphaned girl two years ago. The whole pack is very protective of her."

Ella, Ace muttered in his mind.

"But that isn't the worse part," Matthew continued. "It seems that the she-wolf is really Prince Adrian's mate. Carrel was going after the future Queen Luna."

Jack just about dropped the phone. What had he done? Carrel was supposed to apologize to her, not reclaim his rejected mate. If what the other alpha said was true, his actions could start a war.

There was an audible sigh from the other man. "I don't envy your position, Jack, but if a war does begin, no one will stand beside Red Moon against Magnus. I think we both know what you need to do and you better do it quickly. I'm sorry."

After that, the line went dead. Jack's arm fell limply to his side. Mates and pups were the most cherished parts of a pack. For a mated wolf to try to claim a second mate while his first still lives was forbidden. For an alpha to try to claim his future king's mate was unthinkable. Yes. Jack was certain of the course he had to take. If only he could find Carrel before he caused any more damage. The fate of his pack depended on it.

Carrel parked his car outside of a small cabin in the midst of the forest. The moment he killed the engine, everything was painted pitch black. The thick canopies blocked out the stars and no lights shined from within. A chill crawled down his spine. There was an eerie energy lingering in the air that he couldn't quite identify. Carrel's steps were muffled on the decaying grass as he approached the worn, warped stairs. They creaked loudly, as if they were about to snap from his weight. The front door stood open a foot by the time he reached it. Frowning, Carrel scanned the area, gazing behind him before peering into the darkness of the threshold.

I know that wasn't open before, he said to his wolf.

"Are you going to come in or are you planning on standing there all day?" questioned a voice from the shadows.

Crap! Carrel yelled in his mind, managing to keep his outward appearance unchanged.

Stepping forward, prior to walking into the small space, the werewolf slowly inched the door open further.

"Hello?" he called out. His eyes switched to night vision, but there still didn't seem to be anyone present. "I'm Carrel Stanford, Alpha of Red Moon. I'm looking for Agatha. Is she here?"

A deep chuckling echoed from the darkness. All at once, several candles lit themselves, revealing an aged woman sitting at a worn table against the wall.

"And why would the Alpha of Red Moon seek the witch, Agatha?"

Swallowing, Carrel squared his shoulders. "I require her aid," he said firmly, pulling out a bag of gold coins. "And I'm willing to pay handsomely for it."

With a high cackle, Agatha leaned back in her chair. Snapping her fingers, several more candles lit the room. A shrewd grin deepened the wrinkles marking her cheeks. Patting the table, she urged him closer.

"Gold has little meaning in the depths of the forest, but..." she said watching him intently. "Depending on the request, we might be able to strike a bargain. Tell me, what do you need, young wolf?"

Cringing at the word 'young', Carrel suppressed a growl from Drex. They couldn't risk offending the witch. She was his only hope in fixing the damage done. Taking a seat in the opposite chair, Carrel set the money on the table.

"I need to repair a broken mate bond, can you do it?"

Twirling a lock of white hair, Agatha partly turned away. The gleam in her eyes lost their luster. "Perhaps," she sighed. "Here, I thought you had a task worth my time."

Face contorting with a snarl, Carrel slammed his hand on the table. "What do you mean? I didn't travel all the way here to be turned away. Prince Adrian is trying to steal what was mine as we speak!"

Agatha's fingers paused. While still facing away from him, a smirk pulled at the one corner of her mouth. Adjusting her features to a more neutral expression, she looked back at the wolf.

"You never said she was taken from you. Details matter in the world of spells, boy. If you want my aid, then I need details," she said calmly.

His eyes flashing, Carrel fought Drex for control of his body. The thought of their mate with another wolf was enough to cause his other half to try clawing to the surface. Using all his will, the alpha was able to push him to the back of his mind. He closed his eyes for a few seconds to calm his raging beast. When it was safe to do so, Carrel opened his eyes and took a deep breath.

"My wolf is having difficulty being apart from her," he explained gruffly. When Agatha did not comment, he shifted in his chair. "I'm not sure where to begin. About two years ago, we were tricked into rejecting her. She left the pack and was taken in by Swift Wind. Since an alpha must have a Luna, I chose the daughter of the gamma as my mate. Tonight is the first time I have seen her since she left and my wolf instantly recognized her as our true mate. I don't understand. I had thought that the bond was broken. She didn't react to me at all. Then, Prince Adrian showed up and forced me to leave before I could speak with her," Carrel spat, growling as he said the royal's name.

"And you are sure that he was trying to take the she-wolf as his?"

Carrel nodded absently. "Yes," he said firmly, replaying the scene of the other man wrapping his arm around River's waist in his mind.

Agatha studied him for a moment before speaking again. "From the sounds of it, the bond was only partially severed. That would explain the pull your wolf is still feeling."

Carrel's head jerked in her direction. "Can you fix it?"

"Hmmm…"

Rising to her feet, Agatha went to the small sink and began to wash a few dishes. Keeping her back to him, her hands moved in slow, deliberate circles across a plate.

"I don't think that I can help you."

Skin paling, Carrel leapt to his feet. "What?" Rounding the table, he went to join her side. "I don't understand. I thought you were a powerful witch? I need to fix this. She is mine. I can't lose her."

Agatha didn't answer him. Head bowed, she rinsed the plate and went on to the next one as if he hadn't even spoken.

Carrel's eyes flashed black. Running his fingers through his hair, he paced the cramped space. He knew she could do this. The rumors of her power couldn't be wrong. Every minute wasted was another minute closer to Adrian taking Ella away from him. He wouldn't allow that to happen. Carrel wasn't going to lose his mate a second time. Storming back over to the witch, he tried again. If money held no interest, then there had to be something that she would desire.

"If gold holds no value to you, then what do you want?" he questioned. "Land of your own? Protection? Is there an enemy that I can dispose of for you? Just tell me and it will be yours. You can name your price as long as she becomes mine."

Agatha's hand paused on the dish. She fought a smile tugging at her lips. "There may be a way," she admitted at last. "But the price...no, it's too much to ask."

"No," Carrel snapped. "Name it. What do you want?"

Drying her hands, Agatha gradually turned to face him. "It is not so much what I want, but what I will need. Your mate has been given to another by the Moon Goddess. To undo her will, requires much power. The price for your mate will be your soul."

Carrel's eyes narrowed. "Done."

Agatha cocked her head to the side. "Are you sure? It is a high price to give."

The wolf waved off her words. "There is no price too high to get what's mine. If my soul will complete your spell, then you can have it. I have no use of it after I die anyway," he said coldly.

The witch's eyes gleamed. "Then, let us begin."

Lighting a fire in the hearth, she set out to collecting a few ingredients from her kitchen. Laying them on a chair by the flames, she instructed Carrel to wait there while she disappeared into her bedroom. When she returned, Agatha was holding two small vials. She held out a dark blue bottle to Carrel, then set a red vial next to her ingredients.

The wolf eyed the mixture with a frown. "What is this?"

Agatha peered at him with no humor in her gaze. "It binds your soul to me. Drink up," she commanded softly. "No payment, no potion for your mate."

Pulling off the cork, Carrel's sensitive nose was overwhelmed by the pungent smell. "This isn't poison, is it?" he asked crossly.

"Of course not," Agatha refuted. "I am a witch of my word. You'll die in your own time when you are meant to."

Studying her for a moment, the alpha threw his head back, swallowing the mixture in one gulp. Coughing, he nearly vomited at the foul taste.

Smiling, Agatha turned back towards the flames. Without another word, she set to her work. The brew simmered for several long moments before she removed the pot from over the hot logs. Agatha divided the potion into two separate bowls. Picking up a knife, she twisted towards the wolf.

"Hold out your hand."

"What are you going to do with that?" he questioned darkly, eyeing the silver blade.

"Your blood is needed for the potion," she said with huff.

"Does it have to be a silver knife? You should know that an injury from that, won't heal well," he returned just as crossly.

Agatha glanced at the blade and chuckled. "I suppose you're right. I'm not used to serving werewolves." She set down the thin weapon and grasped the bowls. "Cut yourself then. Just a few drops in each one will suffice."

Carrel grunted, but did as she requested.

"One more thing, what is your mate's name?"

"She goes by River Carlson."

"No, no," Agatha said shaking her head. "Her *real* name, this potion will not work correctly without the girl's true name."

"It's Ella." A smile touched his lips. His wolf liked the sound of her name. "Ella Welsh."

Returning back toward the fire, Agatha added the last of the ingredients to each mixture and quietly spoke the words of enchantment over the potion. First, she carefully poured one bowl into the red vial. With a smirk, the witch glanced at the alpha once again while holding the second bowl.

Eyeing the amusement on her face, he grimaced.

You've got to be kidding me, he complained to his wolf. *I'm not drinking that.*

As if she knew precisely what he was thinking, Agatha's twisted smile grew. "A werewolf can only be bound to one mate at a time. First, you must sever the bond you made with your chosen Luna. Only then, can we begin to repair the other."

Warily, Carrel removed the bowl from her withered fingers. He peered down at the steam swirling off the strange greenish liquid.

"Do I have to drink all of it?" he inquired, sighing when she shook her head no.

"A few sips should be enough."

Just drink it already, Drex snapped impatiently. *I want to see our mate.*

"Fine, fine," Carrel muttered out loud.

Knowing he had no choice, he took a mouthful of the brew. It had a bit of an earthy flavor, but wasn't too awful. Taking another drink, he set the bowl aside. Carrel's eyes then fell to the tiny red bottle that Agatha was now holding in her hand.

"Please tell me that I don't need to drink that, too," he almost begged.

There was a long tense pause before the witch answered him. "No, you do not. This potion is for your true mate. You can slip it in her drink or however you wish to give it to her, but she must drink the whole potion," she warned. "Once she drinks it, her body will be in a temporarily numb state for a few hours. This will be your only chance to mark her and recreate the bond between you and your mate."

Carrel rose and moved to grasp the vial, yet Agatha pulled back her arm, just out of reach.

"Listen well, Alpha of Red Moon," Agatha told him with no hint of humor in her gaze. "If she has already been marked, then it is too late. Trying to mark her a second time while a bond still stands would drive her mad and kill her."

Jaw clenching, Carrel curled his fingers into the palms of his hands. It wasn't too late. He could feel it. River would be his and his alone.

"I understand," he murmured harshly.

This time Agatha did not stop him as he took the vial and stormed out of her cabin and into the night. Slowly striding out onto the small porch, she watched as the taillights of his car were swallowed up by shadows. A twisted smirk spread across her face as a large black crow came to land on her outstretched arm.

"Well now," she whispered to the creature. "This has been a most productive night."

Never had she expected such a golden opportunity to fall into her lap. If the foolish alpha marked the she-wolf mated to Prince Adrian, a war would tear the werewolf packs apart and weaken their entire kingdom. If he failed…Agatha had the feeling he would not stand for the woman to belong to another. Either way, she could not have found a more perfect puppet.

Turning away, Agatha traveled back inside her cabin and walked into her bedroom. A long, floor-length black curtain blocked the back wall. Flinging it open, she revealed several rows of large jars filled with swirls of light. Taking her time, the witch pulled one from a shelf. Removing the lid, she inhaled deeply. A low scream sounded from inside the vessel as the light absorbed into her body. Placing the now empty jar on the shelf, Agatha gazed down at her hands. The wrinkles faded and a healthy glow colored her skin. Smiling brightly, she peered at her much younger reflection.

"Ah, youth," she murmured, patting the side of her smooth cheek. Giggling, she twirled a lock of blonde hair. Some eerie moans sounded from the jars still sitting on her shelves. "Hush, my dears. It's not your turn yet."

Chapter 10

A grin was permanently etched on Adrian's face as he sat on a couch with River. His arm was possessively draped around her, keeping her by his side while Cole yipped happily in his mind. He wanted nothing more than to be alone with her. To kiss her soft lips, to touch the silky strands of her hair and tell her how much he adored her. He had waited so long to find his other half that he was having difficulty keeping his hands off her. Luckily, years of training and a will of steel gave Adrian the ability to control his wolf no matter how much he was whining. He wasn't about to make out with her in front of both of their families.

Seated across from them was his brother, Blake. He had a blushing brunette in his lap, trapped in the circle of his arms while he snuggled against her hair. The goofy grin he wore reminded Adrian of a smitten puppy, not that he was one to talk. He was feeling pretty smitten himself.

Next to Blake were their parents and then the alpha and luna of Swift Wind. Finally, there were River's three brothers and Roxy. Some trays of tea and coffee were placed on the tables in front of them before Magnus dismissed the staff from the royal family's large living room. The entire third floor of the castle was solely for the royals, so there was no chance of being disturbed by unwanted guests.

"Well now," Kiki, the queen luna said with a smile. "I cannot believe both of my sons found their mates on the same day. We have so much to celebrate."

"We have certainly been blessed," Magnus agreed. Glancing at River, he shook his head. "All these years you were right under our noses. It is a good thing you turned down my offer for you to marry Blake, my dear," he said with a chuckle.

"What!"

Adrian's expression instantly turned into a scowl. A low growl escaped his throat as he wrapped his other arm around River protectively and glared at his brother.

"Hey, I have my mate," Blake protested.

"He was just kidding," River soothed, running a hand up and down his arm.

Adrian's body relaxed once again, but he still kept her even closer to him.

Cheeks coloring a deep red, River couldn't seem to steady her racing heart. Just the feel of his skin beneath her fingers sent exciting bolts of electricity humming through her body. It was like nothing she had ever felt before. When she removed her hand, Crystal howled in her mind for more, demanding that she get as close as possible. Interlacing her fingers, River sat stiffly beside the prince. Head bowed, she quickly glanced over at him. The moment she saw his deep blue-green eyes watching her, she looked away, her neck and ears coloring the same crimson as her cheeks.

Why do you hesitate? Crystal questioned worriedly. *He is ours. We should mark him now before another she-wolf tries to steal him.*

I don't know, River admitted. Part of her wondered if this wasn't a dream. What if she woke up to find that she was all alone again? *I can't believe this is real. I never thought we would have another chance at finding a mate. What if he rejects us too? What if I'm not good enough…again?*

Don't you dare think like that! her wolf told her. *Our mate is nothing like that jerk. Stop over-thinking things. What does your heart tell you? Can't you feel his desire? See the way he looks at us? He loves us!*

Following Crystal's urging, River glanced at the man next to her again. When their eyes met, his face beamed. Rewarding him with a shy smile, her gaze quickly returned to her lap.

Her hand linked with Nick's, Amanda studied her daughter's quiet exchange.

We should help her, Violet said.

Amanda agreed. Using the pack's mind-link, she called out to River.

He's not Carrel, sweetheart. You should give him a chance.

Head jerking up, River blinked rapidly. Her brown eyes then locked with the luna's.

What? How did you…?

Amanda's eyes twinkled softly. *I'm a mother. Mothers know things. I can understand how uneasy you must be feeling. You don't have to rush. Get to know him.*

River nodded to herself. *I suppose that wouldn't hurt.*

Brows pleating, Adrian's gaze darted between his mate and her mother. There was an underlying tension in the space that he couldn't explain. His initial surprise and overwhelming joy had kept him from noticing it earlier. Was his mate unhappy with the Goddess's choice? He didn't think so. When she let herself relax, River leaned into him. It was only when she realized what she was doing that she would stiffen and move away. Something was causing her to hold back her true feelings. His wolf could sense some sadness within her, even a hint of fear, and Cole did not like it one bit.

"What's the matter, love," he questioned softly, tilting his head, trying to get a better look at her face. "Are you not happy being my mate?"

River pressed her lips together, unsure how to answer. "It's not that," she quietly replied without looking at him. "I'm just a little overwhelmed."

Shifting on Blake's lap, Amber reached out her hand towards River. When her old friend grasped her fingers, she gently squeezed.

"I know what you mean. We sure didn't have it easy in our old pack. I still can't believe that I found my mate." She released a low laugh and gazed back at Blake. "He didn't even care about what Courtney did or how I was treated by our pack members the last few years. I was terrified that he was going to reject me, but he didn't. Maybe you would feel better if you told your mate what happened to you? The outcome may surprise you."

Adrian stiffened. Someone had hurt his mate? It took a lot a control to keep Cole in the back of his mind. A growl managed to escape his lips, causing the she-wolf next to him to inch further away.

"Stop it," Roxy snapped, swatting him as she appeared behind the couch. "You're scaring her."

All eyes focused on Roxy for a tense moment before Adrian laughed. "Sorry, River. I wasn't growling at you. My wolf doesn't like it that you were hurt."

"You certainly are a handful," Magnus observed, watching Roxy with a faint grin as Nick scolded her through the pack's mental link. "There is definitely alpha blood in you." His gaze then shifted to River. "I don't know what happened at Red Moon, but I know Nick well. He would not have adopted you into his pack, let alone his family, if you were not a good person. You have nothing to worry about."

Exhaling with a long sigh, Nick squeezed Amanda's fingers. "River is a wonderful person and daughter, but I'm afraid things are a lot more complicated than you know, my friend."

Magnus frowned for a moment. "Do you mean these powers of hers?"

"Powers?" Adrian repeated with wide eyes.

Nick shook his head. "That's only part of it." Looking at River, their gazes connected in a silent understanding. It was time for them to know the whole truth.

Taking a deep breath, River turned on the couch cushion so that she could face the man beside her. She had to see with her own eyes if he believed her words. She had learned in the past two years that trust meant a lot to her. If this wolf was really her mate, then she needed to know that he could be trusted as well.

"My birth name is Ella Welsh. Three days before my sixteenth birthday, the Alpha's son..." her words broke off. It wasn't a time she cared to remember.

He's not going to reject us, Crystal assured her. *He needs to know about us. Remember, we are strong.*

Crystal's words gave River the push she needed. Carrel had no power over her life anymore. When she saw him a few hours ago, she felt nothing. No fear, no sadness. That was what she needed to think. He was nothing and he didn't deserve any of her time fretting over the past. Squaring her shoulders, River started again, this time speaking as if she was a bystander instead of a victim.

"Three days before I turned sixteen, Carrel dragged me to his father's office and rejected me as his mate. He didn't want anyone to know. So, after threatening me to remain silent, he banished me from the pack. I tried to speak with Alpha Jack. However, Carrel appeared and accused me of stealing from the Alpha's office. Since my scent was in the space, I had no way of fighting his lies. No one believed that I didn't do it. Even my friends turned against me."

River glanced at the she-wolf across from her. "Except for Amber. Even if you had attended the party, I know you wouldn't have believed Carrel."

"Darn right," Amber muttered with a look of disgust.

Eyes returning to Adrian, she continued, "Carrel then quietly ordered me to leave or he would kill me. So, I fled. After running through the Free Lands for a few days, I was attacked by rogues and rescued by Beta Kyle's team. After hearing my story, Alpha Nick took me in."

As her words faded, River never experienced such a painful silence before. Adrian said nothing. His jaw was clenched and his fingers had curled into such tight fists that his knuckles were white. But, it was his eyes that startled her the most. Not once did he break eye contact. However, his eyes had changed to pure black.

Leaping up from the couch, a deep growl echoed off the walls. "How dare he try to claim *my* mate after what he did!" Adrian snarled with Cole's fearsome voice. "I'll kill him. I'll kill him myself!"

Everyone quickly rose to their feet as the prince spun away and strode towards the door. Blake moved to block him, yet it did no good.

"Quickly, River," Magnus instructed. "His wolf is taking over. If he shifts, Adrian won't be able to regain control of him. You need to calm him down, now!"

The power radiating off of Adrian was the strongest River had ever felt, but with Crystal yelling 'go, go, go' in her mind, she didn't think twice about racing towards him. Getting in his path, River wrapped her arms around his waist and pressed her cheek against the solid muscles of his chest. For a moment, he did nothing. It was as if his body completely froze. As Adrian raised his hand, she hoped that he wouldn't mistakenly attack her.

One hand, then another, firmly gripped River's body as the prince embraced her. With a ragged sigh, he lowered his head to rest his chin on her hair. They stood like that for several seconds as Adrian regained control of Cole's raging emotions.

River didn't mind. Part of her was thrilled to know that her touch alone could have such an effect on him and that someone could impact her so greatly as well. Having finally felt her mate's touch, River knew she could never be in the arms of another man. She was his as much as he was hers. A broad smile spread across her face and without realizing it, she snuggled deeper into his warmth.

A low chuckle sounded beneath her cheek. River's body stilled at once. Loosening her grip, she craned her head back to look up at her mate. The hooded grin dominating his face had her flushing once again.

"Does this mean you're not rejecting me?" Adrian questioned huskily.

Smirking, the teasing words slipped past her lips before she could stop them. "I haven't decided yet."

The prince's brows rose. "I suppose I will have to convince you then," he whispered, bending down to lightly press his lips against hers.

Sparks instantly ignited from the point of impact. When Adrian increased the pressure, River's fingers clutched the front of his shirt as if her life depended upon it. The sound of someone clearing their throat had the prince forcing himself to break contact.

"Until later," he murmured in her ear.

With the sound of her heart hammering in her ears, River barely caught his seductive words. What a kiss! Most girls dream of what their first kiss will be like, yet none of her imaginary encounters compared to the real thing. If Adrian hadn't stopped when he did, her knees would have buckled. It was possible that a new name would have to be created for the shade of red that her cheeks were bound to be.

Keeping River close to his side, Adrian guided them back towards the others. Thankfully, their families had the decency to begin conversing with each other instead of staring as the couple made their way across the room. Once they were seated, Nick and Magnus turned towards them.

Magnus wasn't his normal grinning self as he peered at the blonde she-wolf. "I understand that wasn't easy for you to share, River. No man who treats his mate in such a way has the right to call himself a wolf, let alone an alpha. Rest assured that he will be dealt with."

"I agree completely," Kiki stated, her blue eyes, so similar to Adrian's, sparkled with determination. "I don't understand how your birth parents allowed for this to happen."

A sad smile shadowed the younger she-wolf's lips. "Considering how protective they were of me, I know they wouldn't have. They were both killed in a rogue attack when I was six."

Kiki nodded her head sympathetically. "I'm sorry for your loss." Her brows furrowing for a moment, she half turned to Magnus. "You said your last name was Welsh? I wonder if you're related to Ginger and Rodger Welsh. Ginger was a good friend of mine. We grew up together. She moved to Red Moon after she found her mate."

Lips parting, River scooted up to the edge of the couch. Her overly sensitive hearing couldn't believe it. Kiki had known her parents. Her mother was friends with the queen! A tender smile lit her face.

"Ginger and Rodger Welsh were my parents," River told her happily. "I can't believe you knew my mother, Queen Luna."

"Tsk," Kiki said, waving off the use of her formal name. "It's Kiki, my dear. Kiki."

"Besides, my beautiful mate wasn't the only one to know them," Magnus added. "Your parents lived here, in the castle, for almost six years. I can't believe I never made that connection before. Though, if I think about it, I was never told your real name."

Eyes sparkling, River gripped Adrian's hand tighter. "Really? They lived here?"

After they were killed, no one spoke about them. River was eager to hear anything that she could about her family.

"Yes," the queen confirmed, beaming as she gazed at her husband. "My health wasn't the best when we first wed. When I became pregnant with Adrian, the doctors grew very concerned. Ginger was finishing her medical training, so I requested for her to be brought here as my personal nurse."

"Which, I easily agreed to. As my mate's best friend since childhood, it was a relief to have someone trustworthy to care for my Kiki."

"Ginger was a wonderful person," Kiki said fondly. "She helped to deliver both of my boys and helped me care for them the first few years of their lives. To think that my son is mated to my best friend's daughter…" Her gaze dropped slightly and a brief frown shadowed her features. Blinking, the she-wolf mentally shook herself. "Please let us know if there is anything you ever need. As of today, you are family, River. That goes for you as well, Amber. Welcome to Silver Fang."

As the excitement of River's family link to the royal wolves began to lessen, Nick cleared his throat. There was still another matter of great importance that needed to be discussed. He didn't want to delay the issue and risk River's powers remaining hidden.

"There is one more thing that we need to talk about before everyone disperses for the night," Nick announced, drawing everyone's attention.

"Are you sure that's a good idea?" Henry questioned, eyeing Adrian.

"Yeah," James agreed with a frown. "Remember what Silvia said about the last king who…"

Adrian's eyes narrowed sharply. "What exactly are you saying?"

Beside Magnus, Blake growled low in his throat, shifting Amber to his other side.

"Everyone just calm down," Magnus ordered, using his alpha dominance to lessen the tension. "I'm aware that River is gifted and would never use her for her abilities. As for my son," he glanced at how Adrian was holding River protectively, "he could never harm a hair on her head."

Leaning his elbows on his knees, Nick sighed. "Adrian is not the one who concerns me. There are many others who *would* try to use River's powers. She's not just gifted Magnus, she's *blest*."

The king raised a questioning brow.

Sliding out of the circle of her mate's arms, River rose to her feet. "It may be easier, Father, if I show them."

Amanda came to stand by her side. "Are you wearing the proper clothes?"

River shook her head. She hadn't believed that there would be a reason to shift. And considering her need to hide her powers, River wouldn't do so outside of her pack unless her life was in danger. She could go in the bathroom, however the doorway would be too small to accommodate her wolf form. Peering at the open space and countless windows, she couldn't see another option.

What if we hold up one of the blankets over by the corner? Roxy asked through the mind-link. *We could create a make-shift dressing area.*

Amanda agreed that it was most likely their best choice. Without a word, the she-wolves grabbed a large blanket off one of the couches and walked towards the far corner.

Frowning, Adrian strode towards the edge of the rug, not wanting his mate to be out of his sight, even for a second.

"No peeking," Amanda growled in a warning tone.

"Eww, Mom, she's our sister," Henry whined.

"Yeah, that's just gross." Simon added. "No offense, sis."

"I wasn't talking to you two," she huffed, rolling her eyes.

A few little chuckles aided in easing the strained silence which had fallen. With her mother holding one side and Roxy grasping the other, River slipped behind the blanket and proceeded to remove her clothes. Once she was completely naked, she allowed Crystal free rein over their body.

I'm ready, she told her mother through the link.

Roxy and Amanda lowered the blanket to reveal a large blue wolf. The sound of a pin dropping could have echoed in the deafening quiet that surrounded them. The royals rose with mouths gaping.

His gaze never leaving her, Adrian met the approaching wolf halfway. "You're beautiful," he declared, reaching out to pet her lush fur.

Crystal hummed in her mind while leaning into his hand. Even in her wolf form, his touch was like magic.

Because he completes us, Crystal told her. *He will make us happy.*

River knew that it wasn't quite that simple. Staying with her mate for a few more moments, River slipped back behind the blanket to change into her clothes. When she shifted back into her human form, Magnus was shaking his head.

"A blue wolf," he murmured. "What exactly have you been hiding, Nick?"

"I'm 'Moon Blest'," River announced proudly, drawing everyone's attention as she approached the couches with her friend and mother.

Adrian moved forward to pull her to his side without a second thought. Smiling softly, River gazed up at him thankfully. Knowing that he wasn't going to run from her strange abilities eased the stress of what was about to be revealed.

Kiki shook her head with a puzzled frown. "What is 'Moon Blest'? Have you ever heard of it, dear?"

"No, I haven't."

He peered at Nick, knowing that the alpha would explain further. Magnus wasn't disappointed.

"Why don't we all take a seat and I'll tell you what I know," Nick suggested as Amanda joined his side once again.

He owed his friend, his king, the truth about River. Not wishing to delay any longer, the alpha got right to the facts. "According to Silvia, a 'Moon Blest' wolf is only born once every few hundred years. They are called this because they have been blessed by the Moon Goddess herself. Their powers increase with each new wolf and they are most easily identified by their pale blue fur. The last blest wolf to be born was Beta to King Roark and his powers were used to begin the Dark Moon War."

Nick paused for a moment, his gaze shifting between Magnus and his oldest son. Adrian especially needed to understand the depth of not only River's importance, but the lengths to which others would go to take her for themselves.

The moment her powers were known to the realm, she would be in greater danger than any other luna that had ruled the kingdom.

"Swift Wind has carefully guarded this secret for the last two years for many reasons, which I'm sure you can understand. River is also who led us to discovering Cerberus's return."

"What?" Adrian questioned, his eyes narrowing. "What does my mate have to do with that monster?"

"Everything," Nick answered evenly. "Silvia found writings from the witch, Lilith, dating back over a thousand years. They predicted not only Cerberus's return, but state that if a female wolf was ever blest, she alone would have the power to defeat him. River is the key to stopping Cerberus. Malinda Ebony has confirmed this."

"No," the future king denied firmly. "I just found my mate. I'm not going to put her in danger by having her fight the King of Hellhounds. Why? Because she has beautiful blue fur and can see the future? That isn't enough to defeat him." Feeling River stiffen beside him, Adrian gently rubbed her back. "I'm not saying that you're not strong, sweetheart," he clarified when she refrained from leaning back against him. "This is Cerberus we're talking about. He is our greatest enemy."

"Do you think that I don't know that?" River asked, rising from the couch.

As she turned to face him, her eyes flashed brightly. She was not going to have another mate think that she was weak. She and Crystal had trained every single day over the past two years. They were strong and although River didn't relish the thought of having to fight a demon beast, Pavel's latest exercises against his hellhounds had showed her that she had the skill and power to do so.

"I'm much stronger than you think, *Prince* Adrian," River told him frostily. "Premonitions are not my only ability. In fact, they are my newest skill." Holding out her hand, the she-wolf encased her fingers in ice.

"Holy crap," Blake muttered, leaning forward to get a better look.

"River has enhanced speed, senses, strength and healing powers," Amanda told the men smugly. "She can also control both wind and water."

"Yeah," Roxy added, enjoying the startled looks on the royals' faces. "Malinda says that she may have more that we aren't even aware of yet. Her powers grow stronger every day."

"I don't know what to say," Magnus admitted.

He wasn't the only one. Adrian was impressed as well. A smile touched his face as he watched his mate with her chin held high as she showed off her hidden skills. Still, no matter how strong River was, he didn't want to think about her being in danger. He was supposed to protect her, not place her in the front line of a deadly battle.

"With every moment that I get to spend with you, you seem to become even more incredible, River," Adrian said sincerely. "Yet, you are still my mate. Thinking of putting you in any harm is not something that I'm able to do."

"I certainly can't fault you for that," Nick acknowledged, glancing at Amanda. "I feel the same way about my other half."

Brows lowering, River dissolved the crystals from her hand. Crossing her arms, she spoke quietly, as if conversing with herself. "I still don't see how I have another mate."

"It's not impossible, sweetheart," Amanda informed her kindly. Even though she knew the words weren't directed at anyone, it was clearly bothering the she-wolf. "Second chance mates do happen. But to be honest, I don't think Adrian *is* a second chance."

"What do you mean?" River whispered, staring at her mother.

"The prince is almost five years older. The Goddess would have chosen his mate first. I believe that the two of you may have always been mated to each other."

Head pulling back, River gazed at a smug-looking Adrian before shifting her focus back to Amanda. "I don't understand. What about Carrel? He rejected me, remember?"

The luna nodded. "There is no denying that he was mated to you. However, he broke the bond before you were old enough to recognize it. Since you are a future Luna, if he was *truly* destined to be your other half, then odds are, you would have felt a strong connection to him so close to your birthday."

"Everything does happen for a reason," Nick muttered, echoing Silvia's words.

"That's right. If Carrel wasn't a complete jerk to you, then you would never have left your old pack and come to Swift Wind."

River dropped her gaze to the floor. Joining Swift Wind *had* changed her life. She gained a family, learned to fight and met powerful allies such as Alpha Logan, Malinda and Pavel. Not only that, but it led her to Adrian. In her heart, River knew she never would have felt for Carrel what she did for the prince, even had he not rejected her. The two wolves were like night and day. Just a few hours in Adrian's company and she didn't want to let him go, ever.

"Silvia does say that she believes that the Goddess brought me to you," River said quietly. "Do you really think that the Goddess knew I would be rejected?"

"It is possible," Magnus confirmed smiling. "I've seen some strange things in my time and our Goddess always seems to have a reason for what she does. Knowing Carrel's behavior and deceit, she could have arranged this not only to guide you where you needed to go, River, but to teach the boy a lesson as well."

River frowned, tilting her head to the side.

Magnus chuckled. "As my sons can tell you, a wolf with alpha blood craves their mate. An alpha without his rightful Luna, on the other hand, weakens not just the wolf, but the entire pack. I doubt Carrel realized, until he took over Red Moon, what rejecting you cost him."

"That would explain why he was trying to reclaim her," Kiki added thoughtfully.

"That will *never* happen!" Adrian and River's brothers exclaimed simultaneously.

The four wolves looked at each other with smirks. Adrian nodded his head with thanks. At least he knew that they, too, were committed to keeping Carrel away from his mate. He didn't care if the goddess made him River's first, second or even third mate. She was *his* and she always would be until the day he died.

"The first thing we need to do is tighten security," the prince declared, gazing at his father. Carrel still hadn't been located. The moment he stepped anywhere near the castle, Adrian wanted to know about it. "Next, I would like to place Silvia in charge of our research into Cerberus. They've been combing the archives on anything pertaining to his last appearance, but they haven't discovered much. Alpha Nicholas, could you send for her right away?"

"Of course," Nick agreed easily. The more information they could get on the demon beast the better.

"Thank you." Getting to his feet, Adrian fought a yawn. "I'm sure there is much we still need to discuss, but it's been a long night." Striding over towards River, he picked her up, bridal-style, and began to walk out of the room. "We'll see you in a few hours. Right now, I want to spend some time with my mate."

Eyes wide, River let out a small yelp as the prince lifted her into the air and left the family's main living space. He strode so quickly down the hall that they were already entering another set of rooms before she could ask where they were going.

Inside was a large sitting area, dining room and kitchenette. French doors at the back of the space appeared to lead to a balcony as they did in the suite her family was staying in. A wide hallway was to the left, most likely leading to the bedrooms.

"This is my own personal suite," whispered a husky voice in her ear. "I had your things moved to one of the spare bedrooms."

"You wh-what?" River stuttered. A flash of anger that he would do such a thing without consulting her rose to the surface. "Why would you do that?"

"You were too far away," Adrian replied with a shrug, as if his reasoning was without question.

Still cradled against his chest, River was torn between wanting to smack him or kiss him. His scent was intoxicating. With him holding her so close, she was having difficulty keeping her focus.

Keeping River close to him, Adrian walked over towards the deep couch and sat down with his mate on his lap.

"Don't worry," he told her, tilting her chin so that he could gaze into her eyes. "I won't do anything you don't want me to do. I just—Cole and I both need to know that you are safe. We waited a long time to find you, River."

Unable to peer away, River felt the sincerity of his words. It was normal for a mated pair to move in with each other right away. Her reservations weren't Adrian's fault.

"Can we…take this slow?"

A wide grin brightened his features. "Of course, River," he agreed, kissing her forehead. "We have all the time in the world now."

Adrian's lips then brushed her temple, her cheek and the side of her neck. He paid special attention to the spot behind her ear where he would, one day, leave his mark.

River couldn't say how long she remained in his arms. Time might have stood still for all she knew. Each touch of his lips or brush of his fingers against her skin made her body come to life in ways that she didn't know were possible. When Adrian finally pulled away, River groaned in protest.

A deep chuckle sounded in his throat. "As much as I would love to kiss you all night love, if I don't stop now, I will no longer be able to control my wolf."

River could understand what he meant. Crystal was chattering away in her mind as well. Most of which she wouldn't dare repeat. Who would have thought that her wolf had such a dirty mind? One of Crystal's comments caused her to blush.

"I know what you mean," River admitted, avoiding eye contact.

Eyeing her expression, Adrian's smile only grew. "I think I like your wolf. What is her name?"

"Crystal."

"Well, tell Crystal that my wolf Cole is eager to meet such a beautiful she-wolf."

Crystal yipped happily in her mind. *I like him. I like him a lot. I can't wait until you mark each other and I can speak with Cole myself. Please don't make me wait too long,* she just about begged.

I won't, River promised. *I can't do it yet. We just met. Give me a little time, ok?*

Very well, Crystal grumbled. *Humans make things so complicated.*

River declined to comment. She was growing very fond of Adrian and the thought of another she-wolf so much as touching him brought forth a possessive side of her that she didn't know she had. Still, letting him mark her right away didn't feel right.

"I'll show you to your room," Adrian said, breaking into her thoughts. Rising from the couch, he strode across the floor with River still pressed against his chest.

"I can walk you know," she giggled while kicking her legs.

"It's late and you're probably tired. I don't want you to fall," he teased.

"Lamest excuse ever," River laughed back.

Grinning, the prince didn't bother to reply. He walked past several doors before going to the last bedroom next to a large master suite. The door was open and he watched as River craned her neck to get a glimpse of the inside.

"Prefer to go in there?"

She quickly shook her head, causing him to laugh. River gave him a swat on his chest. *I like his laugh,* she thought, fighting a smile.

"What are in those other rooms?" she found herself questioning as he sat with her on the bed.

"One is a bathroom for guests and the others are bedrooms with their own ensuites like this one."

"Why does your suite have so many bedrooms? Does someone else live here?"

Adrian shook his head.

He gazed at her with such intensity that River's heart started to beat rapidly in her chest.

"Those rooms are for our future pups."

River's eyes grew to the size of saucers as her mouth formed a silent 'o'. She turned her head away while pretending to fix her hair so that Adrian couldn't see the color of her cheeks. *Why can't I stop blushing!*

Admit it, Crystal teased happily. *You want him too.*

Hush.

The sound of something dropping to the floor caught her attention. There was another thunk before the bed bounced slightly. Twisting back towards her mate, River saw that Adrian had taken off his shoes and was stretched out on the bed.

"What are you doing?" she asked hesitantly.

"Resting," he replied. Patting the comforter next to him, he yawned. "I just want to hold you for a bit." When River didn't move, he smirked, "Come on, I won't bite."

Glaring at him, River toed off her shoes and scooted up to his side. "No funny business," she warned, pointing a finger at him.

A deep chuckle sounded in his throat as he reached up and pulled her down beside him. Wrapping his arms around her, Adrian held River close to his chest with a sigh. River could feel her eyes growing heavy as she soaked in his warmth. After a few minutes, the need to use the bathroom had her wiggling to get free.

"Adrian," she called, shifting against him. "I have to go to the bathroom."

He didn't answer. Tilting her head back, River's breath caught in her throat. His eyes were closed and each breath he took was deep and even. In simply a few minutes, he had fallen asleep! Carefully removing herself from his arms, River slid off the bed. Her bags were sitting on the bench at the bottom of the bed. Grabbing the one with her pajamas, she snuck into the bathroom and changed.

Rubbing her eyes, when River re-entered the bedroom, Adrian was still fast asleep. She contemplated going into one of the other rooms instead, but River couldn't get her feet to travel in that direction. The thought of being away from him made her heart ache. With a sigh, River climbed back on the bed and pulled up the blanket, folded at the bottom, to cover the two of them. Somehow this fierce alpha was already wiggling his way into her heart. The thought both thrilled and frightened her. Unlike Carrel, if Adrian rejected her, River wasn't sure that she would be able to pick up the broken pieces of her heart.

Chapter 11

Curled up in a chair by the windows, Kiki carefully held a sealed envelope. She stared at the aged paper for a long time. Gently, Kiki's fingers traced the writing penned on the front. With a sigh, she turned to look out at the morning sunshine instead.

Tucking in his shirt, Magnus walked into the room. A smile brightened his face when he spotted his mate. He strode over towards her and placed an affectionate kiss on her cheek.

"Good morning, sweetheart."

"Morning," Kiki answered absently.

Magnus paused, his gaze catching sight of the envelope in her hands. "Oh," he murmured. Sliding over a chair, he placed a hand on her arm. "Thinking about Ginger again?"

Slowly shaking her head, Kiki reached up to rub her forehead. "Seeing River brings back so many memories. There were almost seven years between the time Ginger left Silver Fang and when she died. Why didn't I go see her?" Tears glistened in her eyes as she peered at her mate. "We still kept in touch, but it wasn't the same. How could she not tell me that she had a daughter, especially after..."

A hand covered Kiki's mouth as she turned away to look out the window.

Magnus's wolf whimpered in his mind. Something was weighing heavily on his mate's thoughts. "After what? You know that you can tell me anything."

Sniffling, Kiki wiped her eyes. She nodded as she flashed Magnus a quick, grateful smile. "I know," she said quietly. "I guess it doesn't much matter now." Shifting in her chair, Kiki grasped her husband's hand. "You know that Ginger and I had been friends for pretty much our whole lives. Well, after Adrian was born, she once confided in me that she wasn't able to have children. I had our personal doctor take a look at her and he even confirmed that she was barren. I guess that's why I'm so surprised to find out that she had a daughter. River must be their little miracle."

Magnus smiled. "She certainly is." He gazed at the letter in her hand. "You can't keep blaming yourself for not being in touch with Ginger more, Kiki. It wasn't either of your faults. Life happens. Why don't you open that letter and see what she had to say? If not for you, then for your friend. Twelve years is a long time for her to wait for you to read what she wanted to tell you."

Kiki gave a humorless laugh and touched the side of Magnus's cheek. "You're right. I can't keep holding on to the past. We can look after her daughter for her now."

Magnus kissed the palm of his mate's hand and rose from the chair. He retrieved a cup of coffee and began reading over some reports to give Kiki the privacy she needed.

Staring down at the messy script, Kiki's fingers traced the letters on the front of the envelope one more time. Her hands trembling, she turned it over, ripped open the back and pulled out the paper inside. Pausing, she took a deep breath and exhaled before reading her friend's final script.

Dear Kiki,

I hope you, Magnus, and your handsome boys are well. It's been a long time since I've seen you and for that, I'm sorry. Where has the time gone? Truthfully, I don't even know where to begin. I've been hiding something from you for all these years. Someone. Not because I wanted to, Kiki, but because her protection meant more to us than anything.

On our way back to Red Moon, Rodger and I found a baby girl floating on the water of Fire Lake. A voice from the mist told us that she was 'blest' and that we had been chosen to watch over her. We named her 'Ella', and she has been a blessing like no other. Her aura is strong. We moved to the edge of the pack and have kept to ourselves, but I fear that other creatures are beginning to sense the strength within her. Rodger and I have taken her to a local witch who cast a spell to hide her aura, but the damage has been done. We have already been attacked, and the witch we hired, killed. I know more will come. Rodger and I have also transferred Ella's scent to us. I don't know if it will work, but I will do anything to protect her.

Please, my friend, I need your help. If the worst should happen, please watch over Ella. I know that I'm asking for a lot, but you are the only ones that I can trust to keep her safe. May the Goddess bless you.

Forever your friend,
Ginger

Tears streamed down Kiki's cheeks as she scanned the letter twice more. All these years she had the knowledge of

River's power in her possession. Her friend had given her life protecting her beloved daughter and she hadn't even bothered to read her final wishes. Sobbing loudly, Kiki couldn't catch her breath.

Magnus was by her side in an instant. "Kiki, what's wrong? Speak to me, sweetheart."

Unable to answer, she held out the letter for him to read.

One hand rubbing her back, Magnus scanned over the letter. Brows rising to his hairline, he reread the words more slowly.

"I don't believe it," he muttered. Sitting on the arm of Kiki's chair, his body seemed to droop. "I just don't believe it."

"Me either. First Ginger has a surprise daughter and now…" her words trailed off as she shook her head. "The attack on Red Moon all those years ago wasn't by chance. Someone was after River. Magnus, we can't let anyone harm her."

Embracing his mate, the king kissed the top of her head and willed his warmth to sooth her. "We won't, Kiki and neither will Adrian. She's safe with us."

With a sigh, Magnus glanced back at the letter. Just when he thought he had the answers to this mysterious she-wolf, everything, once more, turned on its head. Both the Welsh's and Swift Wind had known of her gifts and hid them well. It was possible that there were others who knew about this and were waiting in the shadows. More importantly, if Ginger and Rodger weren't River's real parents, then who were?

Trying to fight a smile, River sat at the breakfast table with Adrian pressed to her side. Their chairs were so close together that you couldn't slide a piece of paper between them. His long arm was casually draped across the back of her chair as he leaned into her. It was late morning, and no one else was currently in the smaller family dining room on the third floor. Impulsively, River took a fork full of eggs and held it up to Adrian's mouth. A large grin dominated his face as he willingly took a bite.

"I see you two are getting along well," chuckled Blake as he sauntered into the room while holding his mate's hand.

Unfazed, Adrian turned to look at his brother. Once they reached the table, he could clearly see the bite mark behind the wolf's ear.

"I could say the same for you," the prince teased.

He was glad that his brother had been able to find his mate, too. Adrian peered over at River. Soon, he would have the honor of marking her and of wearing her mark as well. As if she could read his thoughts already, River's eyes connected with his. They held for a moment prior to her shifting her gaze down to her plate.

She's cute when she blushes, he thought to his wolf.

We should do it more, Cole easily agreed. *Our mate should smile every day.*

She will, Adrian returned with pride.

Alarms sounding throughout the town broke the peaceful silence of the morning. Dropping his cutlery, Adrian and his brother leapt to their feet.

"Hellhounds are attacking from the forest to the west," the eldest prince informed the she-wolves before anyone could ask. "Do not leave this floor. I'll have extra guards posted to make sure you are safe."

Head jerking back, River followed after him. "Wait a minute, Adrian. I've been training with these creatures. I know how to fight them. I should come, too."

"No," he rejected firmly without slowing his stride. He hadn't waited seven years to find his mate only to lose her now to one of these beasts. Some of his best men had been injured and even killed already. To lose River would be the end of him. Spinning around, Adrian wrapped her in a tight embrace. "There is no need for you to fight. Just stay here, please."

Just as quickly, he released her and disappeared down the corridor.

River's fingers curled into her palms. Defeating the hellhounds was her duty. How could he expect her to stay locked away in the castle while others did the fighting? Her own family was sure to be in the thick of it. No, River would not run from what she was meant to do. She was ready to face her destiny. Glancing around the empty hallway, River sped after her mate. She wasn't going to allow him to keep her locked away.

We'll show him how strong we are, Crystal said confidently.

Her wolf's encouragement only strengthened River's resolve. There were a few different ways to get down to the main floor. Watching the lights on the elevator count down, River decided to take the nearby servants' stairs so that the royals wouldn't get too far ahead. Slipping through the discreet door, she came to a stop as four large men towered over her.

They bowed respectfully and offered friendly smiles.

"My lady," the closest one said. "Carlisle is under attack. Prince Adrian has requested for us to guard you. Please wait upstairs until it is safe."

River recognized the tall, dark-haired man with broad shoulders as one of Adrian's vanguard. His name was Thomas, if she recalled correctly. Lifting her chin, she pulled back her shoulders. "I am aware of the situation and have fought against hellhounds before," she told them evenly. "I have no intention of hiding while our packs are in danger."

The men exchanged surprised glances.

River guessed that they were speaking through their pack's link. None of them expected this from their future luna.

"I'm sorry, my lady," Thomas said reluctantly. "But we've been instructed to make sure that you return to the royal's suite. Please come with us."

The she-wolf's gaze narrowed. Her brown eyes shimmered and a hint of her wolf sounded in her voice as she spoke. "If Adrian wants you to guard me, then that's fine, but I'm not going back upstairs. You can either come with me or stand aside," she finished with a soft growl.

Her aura surrounded her like a mist as she addressed the warriors, River managed to keep her expression from showing her surprise as the wolves bowed their heads in submission and took a few steps back. Though she was Adrian's mate, River shouldn't be able to officially command pack members that weren't her own.

How did we do that?

Let us worry about that later, Crystal advised quickly. *There is a battle to be fought.*

Striding forward, River quickly crossed the space and made her way towards the nearest exit. Her four protectors shadowed her without a word, but River paid them no mind. She lost valuable time with the warriors' delay and had to pick up Adrian's trail as soon as possible. Hopefully, she would be able to come to her family's aid before any harm came to the ones she loved.

Once they exited the castle, Adrian and Blake shifted into their wolves. Reports were coming in through the pack link and it seemed as if only the western forest had been breached. Adrian sent an order to the other alphas to assist with both the protection of the town and strengthening the border patrols should the enemy appear in another location. He didn't want to focus too strongly on one area should it be a diversion.

When the two princes arrived on the scene, their warriors were engaged in combat with four demon dogs. Adrian could see Roxy and River's brothers, Henry and Simon, among the wolves surrounding their enemies. Two houses close to the tree line were already ablaze as the hellhounds released blasts of fire from their mouths.

Work in teams and be mindful of the flames on their tails, Adrian instructed as he quickly studied the situation. Every part of these creatures was a weapon.

Adrian, Magnus called through the mind-link. *Nick and I have four beasts contained near the southern edge of the forest with our warriors. Be careful, they're setting fire to the town. What news from the north?*

Same here, he answered as he searched for additional threats. *Our warriors have defeated one so far. I've already sent scouts to check the rest of town and our borders.*

Well done. Keep in touch.

You too.

A ring of warriors enclosed the space from the woods to hinder any further advancement of their enemies. Teams of four and five wolves engaged each of the hounds while warriors stood ready on the side lines to switch out with their comrades if they became injured or needed an extra hand. If too many wolves attacked at one time, it made it difficult to maneuver around the fire beasts' many weapons. In most cases, the number of injured rose significantly. Smaller teams working in unison had a better success rate with this type of foe.

The hellhound to the left dashed forward, slashing through a few warriors as he tried to break through the barricade. Blake immediately took off towards them, leaving Adrian to deal with the nearest foe.

Stepping beyond the outer ring, the large black royal wolf watched cautiously as Roxy and a grey wolf attacked together from the left side. Stance taunt, Adrian's silver eyes narrowed.

The hound was quick and agile. He leapt back, twisting out of reach. When the two other wolves dashed in, aiming for his back legs, the fire creature whipped his flaming tail into them with full force.

Howls sounded in the air as the warriors were thrown back with multiple burns.

Before the hellhound could move in to land a killing blow, he was assaulted on all sides. Fresh fighters jumped forward, blocking their injured comrades and driving their enemy back. At the same time, Roxy pounced. Sharp fangs exposed in the light, she snapped at his neck.

Seeing her at the last moment, the hound twisted, arching back while slashing his claws diagonally. Unable to change her momentum, Roxy closed her eyes.

A flash of black fur pushed her to the side, absorbing most of the blow as he rammed the hellhound square in the chest. Adrian's skull pounded into the beast's armor with such force that he was thrown off his feet.

Roxy, trade out with another warrior, the prince commanded.

The black and red wolf eyed the blood staining the silver patch of fur on Adrian's chest. If he hadn't stepped in, she would have been killed. Ignoring the pain radiating from her front paw, Roxy stubbornly shook her head. She wouldn't run away with her tail between her legs.

That wasn't a request, he snapped. *You're injured. Catch your breath and allow yourself to heal.*

The hellhound had immediately regained his feet and charged at the wolves. Roxy's partner, temporarily forgotten by the beast, leapt onto their towering foe's back. He chomped down hard into the hound's shoulder. The sound of flesh tearing rang in their ears. The demon dog showed no signs of feeling the pain as he bucked the grey wolf off.

Warriors from the right rushed forward as a group while Adrian lunged for his adversary's neck. Three wolves bit into his side and hind leg, almost knocking him over.

The hound ignored them, keeping his focus on Adrian. Jerking back, he narrowly escaped and managed to catch the prince down his front leg as he pushed him away. Flames ignited in his mouth as the demon beast turned to fire a blast at the wolves latched on to his back.

The warriors jumped away, avoiding the worst of the attack.

Having arrived at the edge of the battle, River's eyes widened drastically and her hands covered her mouth on their own accord. The sight of blood glistening on her mate's body rid all other thoughts from her mind. The creature that hurt him was going to pay. Running straight for them, River leapt over the ring of wolves while shifting into her wolf form. Time seemed to temporarily pause as all eyes gazed at the arrival of the gleaming blue wolf. River's focus darted from the paw Roxy was favoring to Adrian's wounds.

Clear the area, she ordered them all. *He's mine.*

The warriors gasped as their future queen luna's voice rang out in their thoughts. Unable to disobey her, they retreated back.

Roxy watched as a swirl of air began to form a funnel around her cousin's mouth. *Argue with her later,* she advised Adrian, while nudging him out of the way. *You're going to want to move.*

River's power coursed through her with an intensity that she hadn't felt before. Sparks of light flashed within the confines of her wind. Once her allies were safely back, she released the blast with a loud, ear-shattering bark.

The sound and air mixed together into a sonic burst that hit the charging hellhound. The beast was picked up and slammed into the trees at the edge of the forest with such force that the wood splintered. Blood seeped from dozens of cuts in his thick skin as the demon tried to rise to his feet.

You dare to harm my mate! River and Crystal shouted as one.

Deep blue eyes never leaving his form, River wasn't about to give the hound any opportunity to injure her family again. In a flash, she closed the distance between them. Ice covered her claws like knives and rose up her front legs to resemble armor. Slashing her right paw in a horizontal motion, the blue wolf cleaved the hellhound's head clear from his neck. Blood splattered her fur and the ground before the fire beast's corpse burst into a swirl of ash.

Piercing howls rose up from the battlegrounds. Forgetting their foes, the remaining two hellhounds turned their sights on the she-wolf. Dodging enemies, they headed straight for River.

Spinning around, the blue wolf dug her claws into the ground to race out to meet them. She was not alone. Adrian appeared by her side. His presence made her feel weightless, as if she were running on the air itself. Grinning, she gazed back at their foes with a new vigor.

The fire beasts unleashed a joint blast as soon as the two wolves were within range.

Adrian and River darted in opposite directions. Avoiding the flames, they struck from the sides, slamming into the hellhounds. River chomped down on the right one's muzzle, freezing the creatures mouth closed before sinking her claws into him.

On the left, Adrian slashed at his foe. Fangs exposed, the two fearsome creatures snarled at each other as they engaged in a dance of death. With each step, Adrian's speed increased. A powerful energy filled his blood with a strength that surpassed his understanding. Teeth sinking into the hound's throat, he bit down with all his might and jerked his head back. The beast burst into a pile of ash that was quickly carried away by the wind.

Eyes searching for River, his gaze almost immediately connected with the beautiful wolf's. Tail wagging, Adrian dashed to her side and quickly circled around her while looking for injuries. Cole yipped happily and nuzzled the side of Crystal's face. Adrian's wolf had been longing for the day he would get to meet River's wolf. Though, part of Cole was extremely upset with River for placing herself in such danger. He was having difficulty keeping his wolf from marking her on the spot just so that they would know where she was at all times. He didn't trust letting her out of his sight. The prince thought his heart might burst as the she-wolf playfully rubbed her body against his side.

Tucking her head beneath his chin, River thankfully listened to the steady beat of his heart. He was alright. His wounds had finished healing, but that didn't lessen the dread which had momentarily filled her when she saw his blood.

River would have destroyed every hellhound in the forest if it meant sparing Adrian of any more pain.

Side by side, they walked back towards the warriors quietly waiting in awe. Adrian sent a quick message through the link to his father to let him know that the threat there had been eliminated. When the prince's steps came to a halt, all the wolves present bowed respectfully. Chin lifting, Adrian glanced at his mate proudly before looking back at the warriors.

I would like to officially present to you all, your soon to be Queen Luna, River Carlson, Adrian announced happily.

River's ears turned back and she let out a noise of surprise. *Wait. Soon to be...? I didn't agree to marry you.*

A deep throaty chuckle met her weak protest. *Oh really?* he questioned smugly. *I think the entire Kingdom may have heard your claim loud and clear. 'You dare to harm my mate',* Adrian mimicked, repeating River's words to the hellhound.

If a wolf could blush, her face would have been as dark as a tomato.

Well—I... Shouldn't you be checking to make sure that the rest of them have been eliminated?

Adrian declined to answer as the she-wolf walked over to Roxy and began to converse with her. As the adrenaline of the battle and the glee of his wolf's first meeting with River's began to wane, a scowl crept across Adrian's features. Citizens of the town were returning to aid in extinguishing the remaining blazes. Sorcerers cast water spells and witches healed those injured from the attack. How many of these people saw River's power? How many were still watching her as she stood, bright as the moon, against the trees. Ordering someone to bring him a shirt, Adrian shifted back and held the baggy garment out to his mate.

"You should change back," he stated as emotionlessly as he could.

The prince had no intention of getting into an argument with his luna in front of their people.

Eyeing the crowd, River did so without protest. Slipping the shirt over her head, she offered Adrian a smile and told him 'thanks'. Even though she was wise enough to wear her normal tight attire beneath her clothing this morning, she didn't want to walk all the way back to the castle in her underwear. Adrian pulled her close to his side and quickly strode back to Lockwood Castle. On more than one occasion, she could distinctly hear the wolf growl when a male peered at her for too long.

Once the door closed soundlessly behind them, Adrian spun around and pulled River up against his chest. His lips crushed hers with a mixture of hunger and fury. The prince knew she was a well-trained warrior. He knew that River had faced hellhounds in combat before and her impressive skills shined as brightly as her 'Moon Blest' fur. No wolf had ever been so proud of his mate. Still, seeing her dive head first into battle when he specifically told her to stay in the safety of the castle, brought forth a strong animalistic protectiveness of which he didn't know he was capable. Adrian left four warriors to watch over her and what good did that do? None. Not even Thomas, the most trusted member of his personal vanguard, had carried out his command. The blasted she-wolf managed to go exactly where he asked her not to with his fiercest wolves following after like obedient pups! How was he supposed to protect her if she didn't listen to him?

Mark her, Cole demanded, his fangs extending to points. *We will show our mate who she belongs to.*

No, Adrian refused, pulling away and breaking all physical contact.

As much as he wanted to complete their bond, the prince would not do so without her consent.

Brows lifting, River watched as Adrian paced the floor with black eyes. Her heart was pounding against her ribs. Fingers brushing her bruised lips, she didn't know if she should be angry or pleased that he had stepped away from her.

"Why did you disobey me?" Adrian questioned with more than a hint of frustration. "We had everything under control."

"Excuse me?" River returned, crossing her arms. "Prince or not, you have no right to lock me away. I'm your mate, not your property."

"I'm trying to protect you!" he stressed. "What about your powers? I thought you needed to hide them? It was more than wolves who saw you just now. There will be no way to keep this quiet. Do you have any idea how much danger you put yourself in?" he practically growled.

Clenching her jaw, River suppressed a snarl of her own. In a way, Adrian was right. She should have been more careful. However, the instant she saw Roxy injured and Adrian bleeding… No other thoughts than ripping that hound apart crossed her mind. River could understand why he was upset, for she had to admit that she was finding herself to be intensely protective of him as well. That didn't mean that she was going to let him control her.

"So it's alright for you to put yourself in harm's way, but not for me?"

"This is different and you know it. You're different," Adrian countered, fighting to keep Cole in check. River standing in practically nothing but an over-sized t-shirt was fracturing the remains of his control. "Could you please put some clothes on?"

The she-wolf lifted her chin. "Yes, I am different," River told him, ignoring his last request. "My father—my pack hasn't hidden the truth from me. Instead, they have done everything in their power to prepare me for the battle to come. In two years, I have gained a family, friends and allies who have all helped me to become stronger. So why is it that my mate, my *equal,* wants to lock me away?"

Closing the distance between them, the prince firmly gripped her upper arms with just enough might that he wasn't hurting her. "Because you mean everything to me!" he cried, giving her a slight shake.

River gasped, her eyes widening at his confession. Before she could respond, he placed a passionate kiss on her lips that had her knees threatening to buckle all over again. When he slowly pulled back, Adrian's words were a husky whisper.

"Forget whatever that unworthy pup said to you all those years ago, River. This is what it means to be a mate. This is what it *feels* like. You are my other half. Without you, I would die. You can't expect me to just hand you over to that demon beast, Cerberus. Why must it be you?" he questioned.

River could barely make out his final words even with her enhanced hearing. She knew that they had not been meant for her, yet they had to be answered. Warring emotions shined in her eyes with the hint of tears. It had been less than a day and still he was having more of an effect on her than anyone else she had met in all her life. Placing her hands on the sides of Adrian's face, River encouraged him to meet her eye.

"Because this is what I was born to do. This is why I was blest."

He shook his head.

"Then who, Adrian? Who should I ask to fight my battle for me? Do you really think I would be happy to watch my family die, for anyone to die, when I could have done something to save them? I'm scared, but I'm not a coward."

Removing her hands from his skin, Adrian clenched his jaw. "I will not allow this."

River let out a sharp breath. One moment she wanted to kiss him and the next she desired to slap his cheek. Was love really this confusing?

"This is not your choice to make!"

Exhaling with a hiss, River stormed off down the corridor towards her room. She could feel the prince's gaze upon her as she grabbed her toiletries and threw them in a bag.

"What are you doing?" he questioned with concern.

"I think we need some time apart," River informed him flatly without turning in his direction. "I'm going back to my family's suite."

Adrian's brow furrowed. "What? We were just attacked! I need you close to me. Cole and I want to know that you're alright."

Zipping up the case, River spun around with determined eyes. "You should have thought of that before trying to make me feel like a prisoner."

Striding past him, the she-wolf headed straight for the door and left without another word.

The moment it closed, the prince's fist pierced the wall. "Damn it!"

How had the whole situation gotten so out of control? Adrian really felt as if River was starting to let her guard down around him, then the hellhounds appeared and ruined it all.

Hope is not lost, Cole told him, his voice much calmer now that she wasn't near. *The battle proved that our mate cares for us.*

Then care to explain why she left?

Adrian could feel Cole smile. *Because our mate is wiser than we are. My desire to mark her wasn't making either of us very rational.*

With a sigh, Adrian pressed his back against the wall and ran his fingers through his hair. He really made a mess out of this. *We'll give her a few hours to cool down before seeking her out.*

Good idea.

Adrian wasn't going to pretend that even the *thought* of River fighting Cerberus was alright with him. He would, however, do whatever it took to prove to his mate that she could trust him to always stand beside her. After all, from the moment their eyes met, his heart was hers. Slowly making his way to his bedroom to shower, Adrian paused. He sniffed the air, a frown forming on his face.

Do you smell that, Cole?

Yes, someone was in here, his wolf confirmed.

Closing his eyes, Adrian mind-linked his housekeeper. *Erica, was someone new in my suite this morning?*

He could feel her tense as she answered, *Yes, Prince Alpha. I assigned a new maid to take care of the Princess Luna. Forgive me for not informing you sooner. I did not wish to disturb you and your mate this morning.*

That's alright. Next time speak with me first before sending anyone new. My mate's safety comes first.

Yes, Prince Alpha.

Adrian sighed. Perhaps he was being too paranoid. Still, Cole couldn't help but bristle whenever he caught the faint trace of this wolf. He trusted Erica to assign someone loyal. When his unease would not lessen, Adrian decided to look into this new maid himself. Something about this scent seemed strangely familiar and he didn't like it one bit.

Chapter 12

A smile could not help but to appear at the corners of Carrel's mouth. The goddess must be watching over him. He had expected needing to wait for the cover of darkness to slip into the castle. He even managed to procure a diluted wolfbane mixture to hide his scent from detection. The poison would weaken him somewhat, yet the temporary effect would be a worthy price in seeking his mate. For the moment, the potion proved to be unnecessary.

Alarms sounded throughout the village, sending wolves from every pack running to protect the citizens and meet the invading forces. Warriors from Silver Fang strode right by Carrel without so much as a glance. Dipping his chin, a smirk briefly dominated his features. Blending in with the flow of people, Carrel carefully made his way inside the castle. The massive space was a flurry of activity. It didn't take long to make his way towards the visiting alpha's chambers.

Carrel wasn't sure which one belonged to Swift Wind. He closed his eyes and inhaled deeply. River's scent drifted towards him with its alluring simplicity. It was sweet and more natural, lacking the heavy perfumes that Courtney had always preferred to wear. Carrel grinned.

We got it.

Carefully striding down the corridor, he followed his nose, pausing whenever he sensed another presence, until it passed. The attack might have allowed him easily inside, yet that did not mean that he would remain undetected. He heard that King Alpha Magnus was looking for him. Until he was reunited with his mate, Carrel couldn't afford to be caught. As the trail led him towards the royal's level of the castle, the wolf suppressed a growl. Carrel now stood before an elegantly decorated door. The prince's scent was overwhelming as he turned the handle and peered inside. Though much lighter, he could smell River in this space. A quick search confirmed her presence in a bedroom next to the prince.

The wolf's shoulders sagged as he entered the bright room. If River was not sharing a bed with the other alpha, then he must have arrived in time. She had yet to be marked. Trailing his fingers along the comforter, Carrel spotted the shirt River wore to bed. Holding the garment, he brought it to his nose and inhaled deeply.

Soon, Drex said eagerly. *Soon she will be ours.*

Yes, Carrel agreed. *But we mustn't give ourselves away just yet. Somehow, we have to separate her from the prince before we can slip her the potion.*

Carrel just didn't know how to get her to leave Adrian's private quarters. Since he couldn't linger any longer, Carrel departed the suite, taking River's shirt with him as he made his way to Red Moon's suite. It was the perfect place to hide while planning his next step. Drex didn't like thinking about River being anywhere near the prince, but having her scent close to him helped to calm his wolf. Carrel was going to need all of his focus to figure out how best to get her alone.

Somehow the daylight hours had slipped by relatively quickly. River couldn't say whether or not she was glad that the day was finally coming to an end. Thankfully, no one questioned her return to Swift Wind's family suite. Most of the time she had spent with Roxy. Listening to her friend's chatter distracted her from her more somber thoughts. Now, she was alone. Seated at the large window of the living room that overlooked the bright lights of the festival which was once more underway. Roxy had offered to remain with her, but River wouldn't allow the she-wolf to risk a chance at meeting her mate, even if she was having problems with her own.

"River, sweetheart, why don't you come with us?" her mother asked as she strode into the room. "There is still so much to see. I would hate for you to miss it."

Tilting her head back, the she-wolf forced a smile. "Perhaps later, Mother. I have a headache, so I think I'll just stay in tonight."

Amanda dropped a kiss on her forehead. "Don't stay mad at him for too long, River. We were warned that he would be extremely possessive of you. Adrian's protective because he loves you." A smile touched her face as the younger woman's eyes widened. "Really, dear," Amanda laughed, lowering her voice. "You're not the only she-wolf who's had to deal with an overprotective mate. Luna for centuries have had to learn to deal with this issue. Even Nick and I had a good argument or two when we were first mated."

"Really?"

"Yes," Amanda confirmed with a sheepish grin. "His wolf will settle down a little once you complete the bond. Then, every male who looks at you won't be a possible threat."

River released a humorless laugh. "That is ridiculous."

"Oh? You are trying to tell me that your wolf has not insisted that other she-wolves are going to steal him from you?"

Blushing, River turned her gaze away. Crystal did tend to get difficult to control when Adrian was around. For some reason, it never occurred to her that her mate was having the same issue in her presence.

"I'm here anytime you need me," Amanda said, patting River's arm as she left to join Nick by the door. "We'll check on you later."

A small knock sounded right as the alpha and luna were about to leave. A maid stood on the other side of the door with a tray. Glancing at the wolf, she immediately dropped her gaze.

"River, did you order tea?" Nick questioned, watching the human intently.

"Oh, yes, I did. Thank you."

The alpha stood to the side as the maid placed the tray on the coffee table without a word. Curtsying, she quickly departed from the wolf's intense gaze.

Really, Nick, Amanda scolded through their bond. *You're just as bad as Adrian.*

We can't be too careful, he said. *By the end of the night, the whole kingdom will probably know of her powers. More of our enemies are sure to surface. It won't take long for those in power to know that she is 'blest'.*

I agree, Maddox added. *Perhaps we should assign some warriors to stand guard outside the room.*

You will do no such thing, Violet hissed.

River already feels overwhelmed by Adrian's possessiveness, Amanda added. *We don't want to make things worse for them. She will be perfectly safe in the castle.*

Looping her arm through her husband's, the luna led him from the chamber, leaving River still gazing out the window with her thoughts. It didn't take them long to make their way to the next floor to meet up with Magnus and Kiki.

Adrian was waiting with his parents in the main living space. When he spotted the couple, he quickly rose to his feet, craning his neck as he peered behind them. The hopeful gaze in his eyes didn't last long. The lack of her scent told the wolf what he already knew, River wasn't with them.

"She isn't coming," Nick enlightened needlessly as his gaze settled on the other man.

"I see," Adrian murmured.

Bowing his head, he sat back on the couch. He told his wolf that he would give her some time to herself, but this was torture. It had been hours since their fight. How could she still be cross with him?

"Yes, I'm afraid she has a bit of a headache, the poor dear," Amanda added looking at Magnus and Kiki. "I wish we could have stayed to look after her, but River insisted that we enjoy ourselves at the festival. She wouldn't hear of anyone missing out on the celebration."

Adrian's head jerked up. His mate wasn't feeling well? If that was the case, then he couldn't sit there wallowing in self-pity. Angry or not, if River was ill, Adrian would do whatever he could to aid in her recovery.

"I'm going to check on her," he announced, striding out of the chamber without awaiting any sort of answer.

Shoulders sagging with a long sigh, River rested her chin in her hand. Being alone never bothered her in the past. In fact, she liked to be on her own and would often sit by the water for long periods of time. Yet, here she was, craving the presence of one sexy, though impossible wolf. Her mother's words replayed in her mind. Had she been too hard on him? It was difficult to think clearly when Adrian was nearby. That's why she chose to come back to her family's room. River needed some space to breathe.

I miss him, Crystal whimpered.

River did too. *He's not going to reject us, is he?* she asked needlessly.

Never.

The she-wolf chuckled at the certainty in her wolf's voice. River was glad that Crystal felt as she did. She didn't want to let him go either. Rising from the chair, she made her way over towards the tray. A smile settled on her face as she came to a decision. When River said that she wasn't going to run away, she meant it. That also meant that she wouldn't run away from herself.

Crystal, River called, feeling her spirits lift.

Yes?

How about we enjoy our tea and then go find ourselves our mate? It's time to show him who be belongs to.

Her wolf howled happily in her mind. As mad as Adrian had made her at the time, River shared his feelings. She never wanted anyone else to even think about touching him. It was time to complete their bond. Hopefully, he wouldn't be too difficult to find before she lost her nerve.

Rising to her feet, River was overwhelmed with a sudden dizziness. Her body fell back on the couch. At first, she thought that she might be having another premonition, but something didn't feel right. Her senses dulled, her body going limp, though she didn't lose consciousness. River could see and hear what was going on in the room around her, yet she couldn't move.

What's happening? she questioned her wolf, terrified.

I don't know. I can't control our body either.

A gentle bump on the couch next to her alerted River to the presence of another. When had someone entered their suite? Everyone had departed for the night and River couldn't recall hearing the door open. A fowl scent assaulted her nose right before a hand appeared in front of her face. Thick fingers caressed the side of her cheek, turning her face to peer at the last person River dreamed she would see again: Carrel.

If River could scream, her voice would have shattered the windows with terror. As if trapped within a nightmare, her words were locked away in her mind, unable to slip past her lips.

What is he doing here! How did he get here? What did he do to us?

Nothing could stop the cold chill clawing down River's spine. A hundred questions raced through her mind, none of which she had the answers for. This wasn't the way that she wanted to die. She didn't even get the chance to fix things with Adrian, a regret she would carry on to the next world.

Calm down, Crystal urged. The shock of seeing their former mate having passed, she was easily the more rational of the two at the moment. *He's not going to kill us.*

How can you be so sure?

His creepy smile, the wolf said flatly.

Mentally taking a deep breath, River focused on the strange expression Carrel had on his face as he peered at her. It was filled with lust, desire. Internally, she gulped. Crystal was right. The evil alpha wasn't going to kill her. He had something much worse in store.

"I'm sorry that I took so long to return," Carrel told her, petting River's long silky hair. "I missed you." Leaning forward, he placed a kiss on her parted mouth. "But don't worry, sweetheart. Everything is going to be as it should have been. I found a way to fix our bond forever."

River's stomach churned. *Oh, boy.* He couldn't possibly be serious. *There was nothing that could ever make me want to be mated with him.*

"Forgive me for putting that potion in your drink. The witch said that it was the only way to recreate our bond. The effects won't last long."

Well, that isn't good, River thought sourly.

It would seem that her previous statement was being overruled. At least she knew why she couldn't move. What kind of potion had he given her? If a witch was involved, then the possibilities were endless.

Carrel drew closer still and nestled into the side of her neck. "I've been longing for this," he whispered, tilting River's head to better expose the skin behind her ear.

An angry growl fought its way up her throat. River understood what he was about to do just as Carrel exposed his fangs. Every fiber of her being seethed. She was NOT going to let this jerk mark her. No one, other than Adrian, was allowed to leave his mark on her skin.

As Carrel tried to bite down, a patch of ice formed down River's body like a shield. The alpha pulled back with raised brows. Blinking, he stared at the frost dissipating from her body and the way the she-wolf's fingers twitched against the sides of her legs.

"What the —?"

Where did this ice come from? And she shouldn't be able to move, Carrel puzzled.

Drex growled at the unexpected interruption. *We can worry about that later. If the spell isn't working, then we need to make our move now!*

He agreed with his wolf. They had been forced to delay this for long enough. Carrel wasn't about to risk losing his mate again. As he went to lean in a second time, the door on the other side of the living room flew open.

Chest heaving, Adrian stood with black eyes and a murderous glare.

Carrel smirked. He knew, just as the prince did, that Adrian wouldn't be able to cross the space in time to stop him. Once the alpha bent his head towards River's skin, everything seemed to unfold in slow motion.

Adrian bolted forward with a pained snarl.

River screamed inside her mind, tears streaming from the corners of her eyes.

Then, a shadow zipped across River's frozen line of sight. Her body slumped to the side as Carrel was suddenly ripped away from her. The next instant, he was thrown clear through the wall behind the couch.

Eyes, a deep blood red, Pavel stood with his fangs and knife-like fingernails exposed. A hiss sounded loudly in the space as he raced after the alpha. The sounds of a scuffle easily permeated the room from the other side of the wall.

Adrian quickly scooped River up and carried her to the opposite side of the space. His wild eyes searched her face, taking in her blank glassy stare with an uneasy whimper.

"River, can you hear me?" he called, checking her for injuries. Finding none, Adrian cradled her in his arms and touched her cheek. Her steady heartbeat told him she was at least alive. "River, my love, I'm so sorry. I should never have yelled at you. I should have protected you better. Forgive me. Just don't leave me, okay? Please...please Goddess, don't take her from me."

Her black hair sticking out in all directions, Malinda appeared in the doorway. Sweat glistened on her pale skin. Spotting the prince sitting on the floor with River in his lap, she immediately went to his side.

"Are we too late?" she asked, kneeling in front of him. "Did he mark her?"

Adrian shook his head. There was no bite mark on River's skin when he checked her for injuries. "What did he do to her? It's like she's dead, but her heart is beating."

I'm not dead, River told her mate in her mind. Waves of fear and sorrow were flowing off of him and she felt powerless to ease his pain. He admitted that she meant everything to him, but River didn't understand the depth of those words until this moment. If only she could show him that she was still with him. *I'm not leaving you, Adrian. This isn't your fault.*

River's fingers touched the side of Adrian's arm with a jerky pat.

Blinking, his eyes darted to her hand. When she repeated the motion, he nodded with a watery smile and squeezed her closely. Adrian remained like that for a few seconds as if by holding her, he could somehow share his strength. Little did he know that he was.

"Lay her down," Malinda instructed softly when he drew back.

She would need to examine the she-wolf more closely to figure out what magic was used. The premonition Malinda had, showed Carrel slipping a potion into River's tea and marking her, but not the preceding events. Luckily, there were only a few options that a witch could choose from. Feeling River's steady heartbeat, and studying her glassy stare,

Malinda was fairly certain she knew the magic performed on the she-wolf. Only one spell she was aware of would place her in this frozen state. Glancing at the way River was squeezing her mate's fingers, the witch also knew that it was weak.

It's a good thing Carrel didn't know her real name. Otherwise, I might not be able to help her break this, Malinda thought with a smirk.

Adrian's head suddenly snapped up as Pavel stepped through the crater in the drywall. His normally impeccable appearance was somewhat disheveled. His sleeve was torn. His hair was tousled and there were traces of blood and dirt on his clothing. Retracting his claws, the vampire began to brush off his shirt with a grimace.

Adrian's eyes narrowed as he studied the other man.

"What happened?" the prince demanded, rising to his feet. "Did you finish him?"

Pavel shook his head with a huff. "The coward's escaped into the woods. My son is trailing him with some of your wolves."

"What!" Adrian roared. His eyes flashed black as he rushed towards the balcony.

We can't let him get away! Cole growled. *He hurt our mate. We will kill him ourselves.*

"I'll find him and tear him apart!" the wolf announced as he went to jump over the rail.

"Calm yourself," Pavel advised, gripping Adrian's arm to halt his departure. "River needs you. We have no way of knowing if he was working alone. Are you really going to risk her safety by leaving her alone when she cannot defend herself?"

Pavel declined to mention that this was the primary reason he returned to the castle instead of hunting the alpha. Any number of enemies could use the she-wolf's helpless state to their advantage. Guarding her needed to be their main focus.

"Adrian," Malinda called, drawing both men's attention. "I need your help."

Eyes shifting back to their blue-green hue, the prince immediately rejoined his mate's side. Carrel would pay, but Pavel was right. River's safety came first. He would never forgive himself if more harm came to her under his own roof. River's appearance hadn't changed in the few moments that he left her side. Gripping her hand, his gaze shifted to the witch.

"What do you need?"

"Her power is greater when you are close by," Malinda began to explain as she pulled out a few vials from a satchel he hadn't noticed before. "I believe that a binding spell was placed upon her. I can weaken it further; however she will need to use her own aura to break it completely. Hold her hand and focus on lending her your strength."

Mixing the potion in a small bowl, Malinda peered back at the woman still lying as if frozen on the floor. Leaning forward, she moved into River's limited line of sight. They would have to work together if there was any chance at success.

"River," the mystical woman said softly. "I'm going to use the reversal spell now. The magic used upon you was strong. Think of the spell surrounding you as a barrier. Once I say your true name, use your power to break through it. Think of nothing else, but pushing past that invisible wall."

When River touched the side of her leg, the witch knew that she understood. Inhaling deeply, Malinda concentrated on her own task. There would be no more secrets about the she-wolf after this. She dipped her finger into the bowl next to her and used the pinkish liquid to draw a few symbols across River's forehead. Muttering words of enchantment, she activated her spell with the wolf's true name.

"Ava Carlson."

River wasn't thinking about the name Malinda used. The moment she heard the witch speak, her sole focus was on breaking the enchantment keeping her prisoner. Seeing and hearing everything that was going on around her without being able to interact was torture. River had even tried mind-linking the members of her family with zero success. Gripping Adrian's hand, she felt her aura suddenly surge. River imagined her power expanding, bursting outwards as it shattered the spell binding her.

A groan escaped her lips as she bolted upright. "I'm so sorry," River cried, wrapping her arms tightly around Adrian's neck. "I should never have gotten so mad at you. I didn't understand how possessive you were feeling, but I feel the same way. I love you, Adrian!"

Without waiting for a response, River placed a passionate kiss on his lips just as both their families raced into the suite. The she-wolf didn't notice their presence. She didn't want to regret telling Adrian how she really felt. No matter what, she would not take back these words.

Arms holding her tightly, Adrian kissed her back with everything that he was holding in his heart. Smelling the others entering the space, he managed to rein Cole back without growling loudly. Keeping one arm around her, he gently touched the side of her face.

"I love you, River. I will always love you."

Tears slipped from the corners of the she-wolf's eyes as she smiled. "Really?"

"Really," he laughed, not understanding how she could still doubt his words.

Carrel's actions left deeper scars than she seemed to know. With time, Adrian would ease her doubts. He would prove how much she meant to him even if he had to tell her several times a day for the rest of their lives. Thinking of the other alpha caused his gaze to dart to his father.

"Did you find him?"

Rising to her feet with Adrian's help, River watched the king as well.

Sadly, he shook his head. "They lost his scent in the woods. I swear to you that he will be dealt with."

"How could our best trackers lose his scent?" Adrian questioned crossly.

River frowned. She remembered the fowl smell surrounding Carrel when he was beside her. It was a difficult odor to forget.

"He was covered in wolfsbane. That's how they lost track of him," River enlightened.

Appearing by their side, Pavel nodded. "Yes, I noticed it as well. It can be very dangerous for a werewolf to use even when diluted, but effective. I doubt we will be able to locate him until it wears off."

"In that case, I'm placing the castle under lockdown. No one will enter or leave without my consent," Magnus announced. "Only our most trusted staff will be allowed on the upper levels and I'm placing warriors on all floors until further notice. This will not happen again."

"River," Malinda said, drawing her attention. "You should stay close to Adrian until your strength is restored. Your powers are affected when he is near. It will help ease any side effects that the potion may have."

Wrapping her arm around his waist with a shy grin, River bobbed her head. She didn't mind staying close to her mate. That was just what she wanted too.

Adrian on the other hand opened his mouth to ask the witch something, but paused. If River wasn't questioning the name Malinda used then she might not have realized what was said. Considering everything she was just through, it could wait for another time.

The witch smiled knowingly. "We will discuss it tomorrow," she told him quietly.

For now, there were more important matters to deal with. Their main priority was keeping the 'blest' wolf protected. Guiding River to her room, Adrian quickly helped repack the few items she took out of her still full bags. He then carried them back upstairs to his suite in silence. River glanced at him as she followed behind without a word.

What should I say? she asked Crystal.

You'll know when the time is right. Follow your heart.

Once inside the living room, her mate turned to her with a soft smile. "I'll put these in your room. If there is anything you want, just say the word."

Shadowing the wolf, River watched as he entered the same suite she was using before. Taking a deep breath, she opened the door to his master bedroom and stood in the doorway.

"Adrian," she called, hoping that her cheeks weren't turning bright red. "I believe you have the wrong room."

A frown marked his face until the prince saw where she was standing. Brows lifting, he studied her closely. "Are you sure?"

River nodded. "I want to wear your mark. Only yours."

A wide grin stretched across his face as he came to stand in front of her. "I swear, I will always cherish you. You're mine," he announced with a soft growl as his mouth connected with hers in a deep, possessive kiss that had River's heart racing.

She smiled against his lips. *You're mine, too.*

Dawn was starting to paint the darkness of the sky with color when a light rain splattered the windshield of Carrel's car. He let out a low curse and pressed down on the accelerator. The men tracking him after he escaped Pavel were relentless. Once, a few of them managed to catch up to him before he could reach his hidden vehicle. It had taken everything in Carrel's power to subdue them enough to slip away. There was even another blasted vampire. Carrel's wolfbane mixture had given him the slim chance to escape. Otherwise, he wouldn't have been able to fight them all off while healing from the injuries the first vampire inflicted. Since when had the kingdom become friends with all these blasted blood-suckers? Carrel had never expected one to show up inside of the castle.

Carrel's grip tightened on the steering wheel. What's more, the vampire interference cost him his true mate. His last hope of getting River was gone. They would pay. They would *all* pay.

Speeding through the main gate, Carrel drove straight up to the pack house. His father was waiting on the porch with a set expression he knew well.

I'm not in the mood to deal with him, Drex said with a growl.

Carrel agreed. Whatever issue his father wanted to nag him about could wait for another time.

"I don't want to hear it," Carrel dismissed as he walked towards the porch.

Arms crossed, Jack stood at the top step unmoving. "You don't have a choice," the former alpha informed him sternly. "I'm aware that you tried to claim Prince Adrian's mate. Your foolishness time and again have put the entire pack in danger. Are you trying to start a war?"

"I'm Alpha of this pack. I don't answer to you," Carrel snapped.

"Not anymore," Jack replied in a hard tone.

Carrel's head jerked back. He couldn't have heard right. The rain once more falling must have distorted his hearing. He was already feeling a bit of déjà vu. Rubbing his face, Carrel's gaze then narrowed on the other man. It struck him that his father was barefoot and dressed in a compression shirt and shorts.

The alpha's eyes turned black. He released a deep growl and his fingers tightened into fists.

"You can't take this pack from me. *I'm* Alpha of Red Moon!"

"Not anymore," Jack repeated calmly. No emotions crossed his face as he peered at his son. "It's time for you to step down, Carrel."

"Never!"

Jack's shoulders pulled back as he lifted his chin. "This is your last chance. Step down or fight."

A mighty roar sounded as Carrel allowed Drex to leap to the front of his mind. He suddenly shifted into his wolf and snarled at the man before him. There was no way that he was going to give up his pack without a battle.

Jack immediately followed, jumping off the porch to tackle his son. He knew what choice Carrel would make and there was no way that he would allow him to win. The survival of the entire pack was in the balance. If nothing else, Jack owed them for misjudging his own child so poorly. Carrel was a twisted monster.

The two wolves crashed together and rolled away from the light of the building. Carrel landed on top and lunged for his opponent's neck. Before he could tear out his father's throat, he was kicked off by the stronger alpha.

Swiftly rising to his feet, the large black wolf circled around Carrel. Jack watched as Carrel's wolf, Drex, bared his teeth and snapped his jaws like a rabid dog. Though he took no pleasure in the battle, Ace was completely calm. Jack had trained Carrel and his wolf how to fight. A warrior did not let their emotions control them. Yet another lesson Carrel had failed to learn. When Carrel bolted forward, Jack dodged to the side and slashed the other wolf's shoulder. His claws tore open flesh, leaving a trail of blood.

Weakened by both the curse and wolfsbane, the younger wolf's body wasn't healing as quickly as it should. Blinded by his rage, Drex paid his pain no mind. He twisted around, trying to bite his father's front leg.

Ace easily evaded the attack and moved several paces away. Rushing forward he rammed into Carrel as hard as he could.

The injured wolf flew across the yard and landed on the hood of his car. The windshield shattered, leaving a giant hole as Carrel's body rolled onto the ground. Several pack members gathered to watch the challenge of their alpha. Not one made any attempt to interfere, or would have, even if it was allowed. An official challenge for the leadership of the pack was one-on-one only, and many times ended in death.

Striding cautiously forward, Jack growled low in the back of his throat.

Submit, he ordered without any hint of softness.

Ears dropping back, Carrel lowered his head and whimpered.

Jack studied him for several seconds. When Carrel's manner remained the same, his shoulders sagged. The moment he glanced at the crowd, Carrel sprung up from the ground and slashed his father across the face. Pain ripped through Jack's right eye and a pair of teeth bit into his neck.

Clawing at each other, the two wolves wrestled for control of the battle. Multiple wounds covered each of them, but neither showed any signs of backing down. Cutting Carrel across the chest, Jack twisted out of his reach and dove for his foe's back leg. Clamping down with all his might, he felt the bones snap. As the young wolf's body buckled, he struck again, digging his claws into his side and tearing open a large gash across Carrel's ribs.

A piercing howl rang out from the younger alpha as Carrel collapsed in a puddle. Hatred shone in his eyes as he glared at Jack through the rain. In the time it took for the next drops of rain to fall, the older wolf had lunged forward to snap Carrel's neck in a clean motion. His body turned limp and one last breath exhaled from his lungs like a hiss.

Peering at his son's lifeless eyes, Jack staggered back against the car's grill. He shifted to his human form then slid to the muddy ground. Nothing seemed to penetrate his senses. Not the gleeful smiles among the other wolves or the cool rain pelting his skin. His gaze was only on the heap of fur transforming back into a man.

Karen, Jack's mate, raced out of the pack house with an agonizing cry. She fell to her knees, cradling the body of her son to her chest.

"What have you done?" she questioned accusingly. "You murdered our son!"

Jack did not reply. Tears fell from his uninjured eye to mix with the rain and blood still seeping from his skin. The wolfsbane covering Carrel's body had poisoned the alpha with every bite and scratch. His wounds refused to heal. With each passing moment, more of his life force was leaving him. It would not be long until he joined his son.

Jack! Steven, his former beta, yelled as he raced towards them in his wolf form.

The warriors watching the battle alerted him to the situation, but it still took time for him to return to the pack house from his patrol.

Shifting into his human form, he knelt down by his longtime friend.

"Where is the doctor?" he demanded, eyeing the bleeding wounds.

"Don't bother," Karen spat, glaring as their healer approached Jack anyway. "What kind of leader kills his own child?"

"Have you no idea what Carrel has done, Luna?" Steven asked with a hard tone. He couldn't pretend that he knew the pain of losing a child, but he would not sit by while she acted as if Carrel was an innocent victim. He had brought this fate upon himself.

"If Jack had not taken action, our entire pack would be destroyed. It may already be too late."

"What are you talking about?" she growled.

Steven's gaze darted between Jack and Karen. It would seem he had not told her of their son's darkness.

"Carrel brought forth the wrath of our Goddess after rejecting and banishing his true mate. The Moon Goddess placed a curse on Red Moon, which is why our pack has weakened so greatly. Instead of looking to break the curse, he tried to claim Prince Adrian's mate as his own. This could mean a war with Silver Fang and every other pack in the kingdom. The other Alphas have already declared that they will not side with us if a battle begins. Knowing Carrel, he most likely refused to give up his place as Alpha and forced an official challenge. Few could have made the impossible decision that Alpha Jack was forced to. We should be—"

Steven stopped as Jack suddenly reached out and gripped his arm. The alpha gently shook his head. His skin was pale and he was barely able to keep his eye open.

"It is done," he whispered. Leaning his head against the car, Jack closed his eyes. "Goddess, forgive me."

As if she heard his plea, a light in the shape of a woman appeared in front of the dying wolf. She stood there for a second before the glow surrounding her surged, sending a pulse through each member of the pack as the curse was lifted. Just as quickly, the light vanished.

"Stand aside," commanded a female voice as a woman shouldered her way through the murmuring crowd. Striding past the line of wolves, the witch, Raven, quickly gazed over the scene before rapidly moving to stand in front of Jack. She watched him with a frown. "It's even worse than I foresaw."

The alpha didn't move or reply.

Steven watched her carefully. "What business does a witch have here?"

"There will be time for introductions later, Beta," she told him evenly as she uncapped a vial and pressed it to Jack's lips. "Saving your Alpha is of greater importance."

The magic of Raven's potion was instantaneous. Jack's injuries healed immediately, leaving pale scars on the most severe wounds. Peering at the lines traveling over Jack's right eye, she knew that the wolf would never be able to see out of it again. Spells had a price. There were some things that could not be undone.

"I suppose this time you owe me," Raven said quietly. "Rest well, old friend. The worst is yet to come."

Chapter 13

Fingers intertwined, River and Adrian strolled into the dining room of the royal family's main suite. It was mid-afternoon and the smell of various dishes spread out on the buffet caused the she-wolf's stomach to growl.

"Hungry?" Adrian questioned in a low, seductive tone.

River blushed and played with the hair covering the fresh mark on her neck. Missing breakfast didn't seem to be affecting her mate one bit. Declining to answer, she moved towards the pile of plates.

We should make him pay for that remark later, Crystal suggested with a purr.

Don't you start, River scolded, fighting against the flood of images her words brought forth. The blush coloring her skin spread to her neck and ears despite her best efforts.

Adrian chuckled as he watched his mate. Leaning forward, he gave her a kiss on the cheek. Too bad they weren't alone.

Filling a plate, River took a seat beside her mother.

"Hello, sweetheart," Amanda greeted with a grin.

I'm glad those two are done fighting, she said to her wolf.

For the moment, Violet laughed. *We know how Alphas are.*

Amanda smirked. They certainly did.

Adrian took a seat on River's other side and greeted both of their parents before gazing at Silvia.

"Thank you for coming, Silvia," he welcomed kindly. "I do hope your journey was comfortable."

"Yes, thank you, Your Highness."

River blinked. She had been so preoccupied that she hadn't noticed who was in the chamber. Apart from their parents, seated at the table was Malinda and Silvia. Glancing by the fireplace, she saw Pavel sipping from a glass as well.

"Good afternoon, Elder Silvia, Malinda, Lord Pavel. It is a pleasure to see you."

Each of them smiled and nodded to the she-wolf.

"I didn't get the chance to thank you yesterday," River continued. "If not for you both, he might have... Well, I'm grateful to have friends like you."

"Yes," Adrian agreed. "You have my gratitude as well." His gaze shifted to his father. "What news of the mutt?" he asked, referring to Carrel.

Before Magnus could answer, the sound of heated voices drew their attention. Roxy and Dimitri entered the room like a thunder storm.

"How do you keep claiming to be a great warrior when you let your enemies escape? Isn't tracking supposed to be your specialty?"

The vampire practically hissed. His eyes flashed red as he stood a few inches away from her. "In case you have forgotten, wolfsbane can mask all scents. Besides, you werewolves were the ones to let him escape. Explain how your warriors were defeated by one poisoned wolf?"

Roxy growled, inching even closer. "Don't act so self-righteous. I doubt you could have done much better if you were there."

Dimitri's eyes narrowed dangerously. Before Roxy could slip away, he snaked an arm around her waist, crushing her body flat against his.

"You have no idea the fire you're playing with," he declared softly.

A tendon pressed against the side of his neck as his gaze traced her soft lips.

At first Roxy stiffened, her eyes comically wide. When her limbs finally found their strength, her fingers curled into the fabric of Dimitri's shirt. The next instant, she pushed him away. Shaking her head, she crossed her arms over her body.

"Don't touch me!"

Refusing to meet the eye of anyone in the room, Roxy turned on her heel and stomped off down the hallway.

Exhaling with a hiss, the young vampire ran his fingers through his hair. His eyes flashed red for a second as he clenched his jaw. Without a word, he took off in the opposite direction of the she-wolf.

"Let's get back to the matter at hand, shall we? I do believe we were discussing a childish werewolf," Pavel suggested, as if nothing out of the ordinary had occurred.

"So, you knew about this," Nick sighed and muttered to himself, "Kyle will not be pleased."

"There is no reason to fret, old friend," Pavel cooed, appearing next to the wolf in an instant. A smirk spread across his lips. "I doubt they will kill each other."

River, on the other hand, frowned. "I knew they didn't like each other, but I didn't realize it had gotten this bad."

Crystal chuckled in her mind. *Don't worry. They will be fine.*

River wasn't so sure, though she kept from saying so.

"What happened to Carrel?" she questioned, peering at the others in the space. "Did you ever catch him?"

She waited on edge for an answer. With hellhound attacks and her powers somewhat exposed, River didn't need anything else to worry about at the moment. She felt Adrian take one of her clenched hands and place it in his own. His warmth seeped into her skin, leaving a tingling path that soothed her as it traveled through her body. A small grateful smile touched her face. Returning her gaze to her father, River watched as Nick shook his head.

"Forgive me, River," Nick said sadly. "We were unable to locate him after he used the wolfsbane."

"As foolish as the boy was, he did appear to be somewhat clever," Pavel admitted thoughtfully. "I am more concerned as to where he procured the potion he slipped into your tea."

"I have my own agents working on that as we speak," Malinda told them. "There are few witches capable of conjuring such a spell. And even less who would risk attacking a royal wolf. It shouldn't take long to discover the culprit."

"That is good to hear," Magnus interjected. "However, I can assure you that Carrel of Red Moon will no longer be a threat."

Adrian's brows furrowed. He had found it strange that his father was being so quiet during the course of their conversation.

"I received a call from Beta Steven this morning."

He said Beta, not former Beta, Cole observed in Adrian's mind.

"What did he tell you?" the prince asked.

"Carrel returned to Red Moon around dawn. After which, Alpha Jack challenged him for control of the pack."

"No doubt Carrel refused to step down willingly," Nick added.

Magnus nodded. "From what I was told, it was not a long fight. Carrel however, was still covered in wolfsbane, leaving Jack severely injured. He has also lost the use of his right eye. A local witch named, Raven, was able to heal him and saved the Alpha's life."

"I know her," Malinda assured. "She is a trustworthy friend."

"What of Carrel?" Adrian inquired darkly.

Everyone seemed to lean in, waiting for the king's words.

"Dead. I have already ordered a team to journey there and confirm his death. They will remain in Red Moon until after the cremation." He wasn't going to take any chances that the traitorous wolf wasn't deceased.

"Poor Jack," Amanda murmured.

The others privately agreed. It could not have been an easy task to defeat his own son in such a way.

"I do not envy his situation. However," the king said gravely, "Carrel's actions could not go unanswered for. Should he have been captured, he would have been executed for his crimes."

Adrian agreed. Had River not been involved, he still would've passed the same sentence. The man wasn't a wolf, he was a snake. What kind of person tries to take a mate by force? Thinking of the events that took place last night brought Adrian back to one very important unanswered question. Lifting his gaze, the wolf's sights locked upon the dark-haired witch seated gracefully at the table.

Malinda peered at him knowingly. "Go ahead, Prince of Werewolves," she said mysteriously. "Ask me the question weighing on your mind."

Adrian rested his back against his chair. While still holding River's hand, he dipped his chin. "Very well. Last night, when you cast the spell to help free River, why did you call her by *that* name?"

"What name?" River questioned with a frown.

She didn't recall Malinda calling her anything strange. Then again, all her concentration had been directed elsewhere.

"*Ava* Carlson."

Amanda knocked over her glass, while Kiki gasped. All the color drained from Nick's face. Silvia's brows rose to her hairline and Magnus's eyes narrowed thoughtfully.

Mouth gaping, River's gaze found Pavel's as he stood calmly to the side. "You knew?" she accused. *What about you?* she asked Crystal. *Did-did you know about this?* River could feel her wolf shifting uncomfortably in her mind.

Not for sure, she admitted. *I could smell a distinct familiarity in their scents. Ever since we arrived in Swift Wind it just...it just felt like home.*

Hand rubbing her forehead, River closed her eyes tightly. Her mind was whirling. How could this be? How could she be the daughter of the former Alpha of Swift Wind? They had died. Ava died.

"How is this possible?" whispered Nick's incredulous voice.

His gaze sought River's of their own accord. This bright, shining woman was of his blood, his brother's child. He held her as a baby. How was it that he didn't know who she was?

"How did I not know?" he asked the stunned silence. "Forgive me, River. I should have—"

"No," the she-wolf interrupted. Rising to her feet, she rounded the table to embrace him. She wasn't sure that she believed any of this, yet there was one thing of which River was positive. Nick had no need to apologize. He was the only father she really remembered. They had never treated her as anything other than family.

"You have nothing to be sorry for. You took me as your daughter. Treated me like your own," River insisted, grasping a hand from both Amanda and Nick. "Swift Wind is the one place I have truly felt at home."

It was Amanda's turn to hug the younger woman. "It doesn't matter who your parents were, you will always be ours, River."

"Yes," Nick agreed easily. "Still, I need to know. What happened that day? What happened to Conner and Laraine?"

Malinda watched the wolf sadly. "I believe Pavel would be the better person to answer that question. My visions are detailed, but he is the sole person still living who was there."

All eyes shifted their focus to the vampire lord. Sipping his drink casually, Pavel raised his brows questioningly.

"Oh? So now my presence gets some attention. And here I thought you didn't want my company, Nicholas."

"Don't be ridiculous," Nick grumbled. "We spent nearly an hour conversing with you before River and Adrian arrived."

Pavel smirked briefly before his neutral mask was back in place. "And how I have cherished those moments."

Nick growled low in his throat.

River couldn't help but giggle. When her father glared at her, she bit her lip and looked away.

Are they friends or enemies? she ventured to ask her wolf.

Considering how much Pavel enjoys riling Father up, I'd say they're better friends than they will admit.

Taking another sip, Pavel set his glass down. His gaze momentarily clouded and the humor left his features. With a sigh, he peered back to those watching him intently.

"The attack had already taken place by the time I arrived," he told them evenly. "Conner and his men fought bravely. Only a witch and a few wolves remained of the enemy forces who ambushed them. I was able to dispatch them quickly."

A vampires life was long and so was his memory. The ruling lord could still clearly remember Conner's final words as he lay dying beside his mate. There had been nothing he could do to save him. *For all this power, I still lost a friend and temporarily gained an enemy,* he reflected, glancing at Nick.

"He said to me, 'Pavel...my daughter.' Conner was only concerned with your safety to the very end," Pavel told River as he looked at the she-wolf.

Tears rolled down River's cheeks as Adrian moved to hold her. Unable to say a word, she leaned into her mate, desperately needing his comfort. He might stir her anger occasionally, however, Adrian was also the only one she desired to ease her sorrow. He truly was her other half.

"Why didn't you bring her to me?" Nick quietly demanded. "If Ava was alive and you knew who she was, then why pretend she was dead? I doubt you told the Welsh's that she belonged with Swift Wind."

Pavel shrugged. "That answer is quite simple, old friend. Because your Goddess asked me to."

Nick's gaze narrowed darkly. His sights darted to Silvia who slowly nodded.

"It is possible," she confirmed. "The Moon Goddess has been known to appear in our world occasionally. I believe Pavel speaks the truth."

The alpha sighed with a frown. "I don't doubt him," Nick mumbled. "I just wonder what her reasoning might have been."

"Isn't that obvious?" the vampire countered not unkindly. "It was to protect her. Your enemies knew what the girl was. They could smell her power. Having dwelt with 'Moon Blest' wolves myself, I knew what she was the instant I first saw her."

"I am surprised that you didn't slay her yourself," Silvia said thoughtfully.

Pavel cocked his head to the side. "Oh, why is that?"

"Due to your unfavorable experience with Alexei."

"Pff," he dismissed, waving a hand carelessly. "The man was a great fool. However, I have lived for many millennia. He is not the only 'blest' wolf that I have encountered."

River's head jerked back, accidently bumping into Adrian's chest. "Really? You have known others like me?"

Pavel grinned. "Why of course, my dear. In fact, I was with Lilith when she wrote about her vision that your elder tends to reference."

"Incredible. That would explain how you knew that a blest wolf can defeat Cerberus."

The man nodded. "She was a powerful seer. Perhaps the best I have ever known."

I wonder if she knew anything else about my powers. While River had been told about the contents of the scroll, she never read the carefully guarded parchment for herself. It could be that there was more information pertaining to her gifts. River still didn't understand how she had commanded Adrian's warriors. Was it because she was the future queen luna? Or was there another reason for the odd event?

"Silvia," River questioned, glancing at the wise wolf, "did you bring the scroll with you? I would like to read it for myself, if I may."

"I wouldn't mind taking a look as well," Malinda added.

The grey wolf nodded easily. Retrieving a box from the other room, she gently placed it on the table and took off the lid. "This contains all of my research on 'blest' wolves," she informed no one in particular.

River swiftly crossed the room to join the history keeper's side. She watched as Silvia carefully removed a cylinder from the top of the box. Her heartbeat picked up speed and she had to resist the urge to yank the paper from the other woman's grasp as Silvia, ever so slowly, withdrew the scroll. Spreading it out on the table, the older she-wolf pointed to a section near the bottom.

"Here," she instructed.

Focusing on the beautifully scripted words, River began to read out loud, "If ever a female were to be born with fur 'blest' by the moon's light, her power would be greater than any who have walked before her. Her voice would cut through mountains and her eyes would see beyond the hands of time. See beyond the hands of time?"

"That refers to your premonitions," Malinda explained. "Like Lilith and myself, you can see things that have not yet come to pass."

"Of course," River murmured thoughtfully before glancing back at the scroll.

"What about the part concerning her voice? Could that be a new power?" Adrian questioned.

"What do you mean?" the witch asked.

"During her fight with the hellhounds, River barked and this... I'm not sure how to describe it. It was like a shock wave slammed one of the beasts into a tree."

Nick studied his daughter for a moment. "That does sound like a new ability. How come you didn't tell us about this?"

River shrugged. "With everything that's happened, it kind of slipped my mind. That may not be the only new power I have though." Finger tracing the paper, River continued to read. "Nature itself will obey her whim. All shall feel her power and bow down before her. Yet, no wolf, nor spell, shall bend her will to them." The she-wolf gazed at her mentor with a frown. "Before the battle, I was able to give commands to warriors of Silver Fang. Does this passage have something to do with that?"

Malinda's brows pleated. "I would say so. 'Blest' wolves cannot be compelled to obey like normal members of a pack. It is another reason why they are feared, but for you to be able to command others, not matter their pack, is something else entirely. It's possible that you may even be able to command other races as well. I would be very careful in using this power, if at all. If others know that you can control them, then they might not trust you. Or worse, try to do you harm."

Great, River thought sourly. *This news just gets better all the time.* Why did it feel like the more 'gifts' she acquired, the greater the danger she was in. What was the point of being given these powers if she couldn't use them?

Adrian frowned as he crossed his arms. *That would explain how she was able to get past the guards I had protecting her.* That thought gave light to another idea.

"I understand why River shouldn't use this particular power freely, but if she can command others as an Alpha would his pack, couldn't she use that against the hellhounds?"

Malinda shook her head. *If only it was that easy.* "Hellhounds are not of our world. The Moon Goddess has no power over the underworld, so I doubt that River would either."

"Too bad," the vampire muttered, lowering himself into a chair. "That could have ended this war rather quickly."

Nick sighed. "You know better than most that nothing is ever that easy."

River gazed back at the final sentence on the scroll. "She alone would have the power to conquer Cerberus and cure the Curse of Night."

Malinda rose so quickly that her chair flipped over. "Let me see that," she instructed River urgently.

The she-wolf passed the aged paper over without a word.

The witch's eyes scanned the document several times. All the while, her jaw tightened and her eyes narrowed with each passage. The wolves glanced at each other, but no one spoke as she studied the ancient words.

"Why was I not told of this?" Malinda finally questioned in a hard tone.

Silvia frowned deeply. "No part of Lilith's premonition has been kept from you. In fact, you were the first person Alpha Nicholas sought after this scroll was found."

Malinda's finger pointed to the very last phrase. "These words have never been mentioned to me."

"Do they not refer to the Blood Moon?"

A ragged sigh escaped from the sorceress as she bowed her head. A Curse of Night was so much more than just a natural appearance of the shadowed moon. Lunar eclipses were part of nature. This curse was not. The elements needed to bring about such a powerful spell alone did not bode well for them. If Lilith predicted this curse coming to pass, then Cerberus was not working alone.

"Malinda?" River called worriedly. "What is it?"

Straightening, the witch looked at her evenly. "A Curse of Night is a dangerous and forbidden spell. During a lunar eclipse, the flow of magic is heightened, but so is the strength of the darkness brought forth by the earth's shadow. This curse is said to have the power to lock the moon in place. Thankfully, I have never seen a successful attempt. Should this curse be cast during a Blood Moon…"

"It would give Cerberus and his army extraordinary power," Pavel supplied for her.

Leaning back in his chair, Magnus interlaced his fingers. "How do we stop it?"

Malinda's serious expression did not ease the mounting tension. "That's the problem," she confessed unhappily. "I don't know. I have no idea who would even be able to cast this spell." The witch brushed back a few of her wavy locks with her fingers. "I need to consult the other covens. If we can find out what ingredients are required for the potion, then that might narrow down our search. However, if there is indeed a witch willing to cast this spell for Cerberus, then we are in trouble."

The others agreed. Cerberus was not just any enemy. He sought to destroy all living creatures to bring about a literal hell on earth. Only someone truly dark and twisted would choose to serve him. Hopefully, they could stop this curse before it was cast, for River couldn't fathom what kind of person would desire to turn their world into a wasteland of ash.

The rain had finally stopped falling, but the mood in Red Moon did not lift with the change of weather. Every member of the pack was dressed in black for the funeral of Carrel Stanford. His body was carefully wrapped and set to rest on a bed of timber ready to be set alight. A few members spoke briefly, but the new alpha didn't hear their words. His eyes were locked on his son's motionless corpse. Carrel was dead, and Jack had been the one to deliver the killing blow.

Karen and Courtney's sobs stood out in the sudden silence. Neither woman would so much as look at him since he had awakened in the pack hospital. Instead, Steven stood on one side with Raven on the other. Her long silver hair was tucked within the confines of her black hood as she watched the fallen wolf emotionlessly.

His pack members were taking the witch's presence surprisingly well after she saved Jack's life. He didn't know why she was remaining in Red Moon, and at the moment, the wolf didn't care. Ace missed his mate's presence and Raven's support was one of the few things keeping him from completely falling apart. No matter how dark Carrel's heart, no wolf should have to choose between their pack's lives and their child's.

We had no choice, Ace told him softly. *Even Raven will tell you that he was beyond aid.*

Karen will never forgive me for this, Jack stated mournfully. *I don't know if I can forgive myself either.*

Ace whimpered in his mind, confirming that his wolf also feared that they lost their mate, too. *It was for the survival of the pack,* was all that Ace finally said.

Shoulders slumping, Jack held back a humorless laugh. He didn't know what to think of his pack. The lack of sorrow in Carrel's passing was a disturbing revelation in how little his son was cared for as their alpha. An alpha wasn't always loved, but his son didn't seem to be even liked during his very short rein. Had he ever been? How long had he been blind to his son's cruel heart?

Steven placed a hand on his shoulder, drawing the wolf from his darker thoughts. Lifting his gaze, Jack peered at the flickering torch held out before him.

"It's time, Alpha," his beta whispered.

Jack exhaled sharply. Knowing that the eyes of his pack were upon him, he carefully kept his warring emotions concealed. Gripping the torch, he slowly moved towards the timbers. Jack paused once he reached them and studied the wrapped form of his son one last time.

"May you finally find peace, Carrel," he quietly said before lowering the flame to set the wood alight.

Returning to his place, Jack heard his wolf release a mournful howl.

Gradually, members of the pack began to disperse. Jack stood there for a long time; his gaze locked on the flames until they were nothing but a flicker.

Courtney vaguely recalled the beta and the strange witch ushering the alpha inside at one point, yet she could not say how long ago it was. Little seemed to penetrate the invisible wall she had erected around herself. Courtney lost everything—her unborn child, her mate, and worse, her position as luna of the pack.

Her fingers curled into fists as she continued to stare at the smoldering ash. The tears on her cheeks had long since dried with no more able to fall. Death was a sure way to show someone's true feelings. The wolves of her pack displayed little sorrow for their fallen alpha. Carrel's mother had been the one person to come even close to feeling the depth of despair she did with his death. As for Alpha Jack…

Courtney released a breath like a hiss. She wanted to hate him. She wanted to curse every breath in his body that he should live while his son perished. Part of her did, however deep down, the she-wolf knew it wasn't completely his fault. It was Ella's fault. Just the thought of the other woman's name caused a growl to rise up in her throat. This pathetic excuse for a wolf was the reason for so much pain in her life. Ella was why Carrel and Red Moon had been cursed.

Blood seeped from between her fingers as Courtney's nails cut into her skin. Her aura began to rise, lightly swirling around her as she blankly looked at the ground ahead. The sounds of soft footsteps had her spinning around with a snarl. Who dared to interrupt her mourning?

A middle-aged woman dressed in black held up her empty hands in surrender. "I did not mean to startle you." Lowering the hood of her cloak, she revealed a thick mass of curly blonde hair. "My name is Agatha," she told Courtney, her gaze shifting sadly over to the large pile of embers. "I had come to help your Alpha, but I see that I am too late."

"Why would a witch care about helping Carrel?"

The other sorceress hadn't bothered. Her only concern had been in saving Jack. She didn't even look twice at Courtney's mate.

Agatha moved a little closer, her voice calm and strangely soothing. "I don't know what experience you've had with my kind, but not all witches are the same. I am not here to cause you more pain. I'm here because of Carrel. I was the one aiding him in breaking this curse."

Courtney's brows rose. "What? Why would he go to a witch?"

Better yet, why hadn't Carrel told her any of this? He never mentioned anything, not the curse or Ella. None of it.

For the first time, there were so many secrets between them and it was all Ella's fault.

Agatha showed no reaction to the she-wolf's snarky tone. "He was wise to come to me," she told the other woman. "How else would you break a curse placed by a witch?"

Eyes widening, a deep frown twisted Courtney's features. "What are you talking about? I overheard Carrel speaking with his father. The curse was placed by the Moon Goddess because of Ella," she spat.

The witch glided closer while shaking her head. "His source was misguided. Though…" her voice trailed off as she peered back at where Carrel's body had been.

"Though what?" Courtney questioned. "If you know something, then tell me."

Agatha sighed. "I did not come here to bring more sadness."

The she-wolf's gaze narrowed. There was something deeper going on here and she wanted to know what. If someone had dared to do this on purpose, then they would pay.

"Tell me what you know, witch," Courtney snapped.

Agatha gave her a sideways look. There was nothing outwardly disarming in the simple gesture, yet a chill raced through the she-wolf's body. Her wolf was suddenly warning her to tread carefully.

Courtney recanted, "Please, Agatha, tell me what you know about Carrel."

Watching her for a moment longer, the witch nodded. "Whatever witch your former Alpha sought was either a poor example of the craft or purposely did not speak true. Yes, a curse was placed upon your pack, but it was not the Moon Goddess who did so. It was a wolf, named Ella Welsh, or River Carlson as she goes by now."

Courtney's eyes flashed black. Ella was responsible for this curse? It was unthinkable. She couldn't seem to get her mind around the idea that such a weak and spineless omega was capable of this type of feat.

"I don't believe it. She couldn't have."

"Two years is a long time for someone to plot their revenge. There is no denying that the girl *was* Carrel's true mate. Whatever his reasons, she might not have gracefully accepted his rejection."

Agatha waited a calculated set of time for her words to sink in before speaking again.

"You *were* the Luna after all. Do you really believe that Alpha Jack would willingly attack his own son?"

The witch's past tense use of her title stung deeply. Yes, Courtney *was* the luna and Ella had taken that from her. How could the goddess allow someone so deceitful to become the next queen luna? Courtney wasn't going to let her get away with it. How dare Ella attack her pack and have her mate unjustly killed! She would speak with Jack about this at once. Courtney paused part way as she started to turn about. Agatha mentioned Jack speaking with a witch and that the sorceress may have lied to him.

"Do you know a witch named Raven?" she questioned suddenly.

For the first time, Agatha's eyes widened in surprise. She quickly hid her reaction while adjusting her cloak.

"I have heard of her. She is strong with the dark arts. Why do you ask?"

Courtney scoffed. "She is the witch who saved Alpha Jack after his battle with Carrel. She's with him, even now."

Agatha frowned. "Then nothing you say will sway him to turn against her. She well could be in the employ of the she-wolf."

"Damn it," Courtney hissed. "She can't be allowed to get away with this."

"I fear that I can't counter dark magic, but I can offer you this," Agatha said, reaching into the confines of her cloak. Slowly, she removed a thin silver dagger. "Prince Adrian has waited too long for a mate to reject her, no matter her crimes. If you want to avenge your mate, your pack, your child, then take this. Otherwise, Ella will soon have power over the entire werewolf kingdom and no one will be able to stop her."

Courtney stared at the gleaming metal lying on an ebony cloth. Her eyes flashed between black and her normal color several times. Pressing her lips into a thin line, she finally reached out and covered the weapon before clutching it close to her body.

"I *will* stop her," she promised while gazing at the witch. "It's time for her to pay."

Deep in the mountains, a thin figure covered in black stood beside a carved archway. Ancient symbols were engraved in each pillar while a warning was etched across the top. A massive stone blocked the path beyond, yet even should it not, few would be foolish enough to attempt to cross the threshold. Here, resting in the darkness, was the secret entry to the underworld.

Snapping her fingers, Agatha lit the torches she had stationed about the perimeter. The lively flames seemed to offer less light the closer they came to the archway, as if an evil force was fighting to extinguish them. Focused on her work, Agatha paid the flames little mind. She had arranged an altar in the center of the space several feet away from the gateway. Upon it, she set a wide, shallow bowl filled with water. Candles lined the edge of her table which held a small assortment of jars, the largest one was currently covered by a black cloth. The remainder of her ingredients would have to be gotten fresh.

Sprinkling a few herbs into the water, she muttered a spell. Smiling, the witch gazed down into the viewing mirror as an image rippled into focus. A mighty beast with three heads appeared. His eyes were fire, as were the lines of fur tracing down the back of each head. Plates of armor wrapped around the front of the hound's skulls, gleaming fiercely against the light of his flames.

"What news do you bring me?" Cerberus's middle head questioned in a deep tone.

Agatha bowed. "Lord Cerberus, preparations for the ceremony are almost complete. When the next full moon rises, I will be ready."

The three heads gazed at each other with brief smiles before looking back at the witch. The lead hound narrowed his eyes.

"What of the 'Moon Blest'?"

Agatha frowned. "I'm afraid my initial attempts to dispose of her have failed, though I did find other uses for the foolish young Alpha we spoke of previously. A more direct route will be necessary."

There was a distinctive growl from the other side of the viewing pool.

"I expected more from you, witch," he said with displeasure. "The 'Moon Blest' should never have been allowed to live for this long."

"Forgive me, I only recently learned that she was still alive, my lord."

"I don't want your excuses," his right head snapped.

"You are to kill her before our rise. Is that clear?" demanded the left head.

Agatha flinched at the hard sound of his tone.

"Enough," the lead head ordered. The three looked at each other in silence as a message seemed to pass between them.

"We will send our own agents to get rid of her. Witch, you are to focus your energy on completing the curse. Uphold your part of our bargain, and everything you desire shall be yours under my new domain."

The hint of a smile appeared on her lips. "I live to serve you, Lord Cerberus."

The mighty hellhound grunted in reply. "Keep me informed of your progress."

In the next instant, the water rippled once again and the image vanished. Agatha pushed the hair back from her face.

Glancing at the row of jars on the altar, she gently laid a palm on the one still covered.

"Soon," she whispered with a twisted grin, patting the object. "Soon, darkness will cover this world just as it always should have."

Chapter 14

Between the hellhound attacks, Carrel's crazed attempt to mark her, and finding out the truth about her parents, River desperately needed a change of scenery. Reports of rogue wolves and dark witches coming after her had kept Lockwood Castle on lockdown, effectively ending the Moonlight Celebration. Being trapped on the royal's floor of the castle was wearing her patience thin. River didn't like to be cooped up. No matter how much she protested, Adrian would not change his mind. One enemy had gotten into the castle, causing his already excessively overprotective wolf to be pushed to the max. Either a trusted family member or one of her handpicked guards followed her everywhere. Only Adrian himself was allowed to escort her outside of the castle. River knew she could ignore his overbearing rules, but the strength of their growing bond meant too much to her and Crystal. There would be other battles to pick with her mate.

A few days after her arrival, the she-wolf was pacing the length of the prince's living room.

"What do you mean I can't go home tomorrow?" she questioned crossly, fighting the urge to glare at Adrian.

A frown etched on his face, the prince's resolve didn't soften.

"Since other creatures have already found out about your powers, it isn't safe. We've had two attacks on our borders, and I'm not going to put you at unnecessary risk."

River's pacing stopped. Crossing her arms over her chest, she gave him a searching look. "Adrian, we've been through this. You can't keep me locked away in the castle. Taking Cerberus out of the equation, I still have family, friends, and a life. I will never be happy staying trapped within these walls. I won't live like this forever."

Clenching his jaw, the prince didn't answer. He knew she was right. It seemed like they just kept going around in circles over his desire to protect her ever since their first meeting.

She does have a point, Adrian conceded to Cole. *We can't keep our mate like a prisoner.*

Cole growled unhappily. *Her very life is in danger. I won't approve of her not being watched over. Look what happened with Carrel when she was out of our sight.*

I agree, Adrian stated. He wasn't pleased with that particular failure on their part either. His main regret was not being able to deal with the traitorous wolf himself. *Don't forget, it's also our duty to make our mate happy.*

Hearing no protest from Cole, Adrian looked into River's deep brown eyes. He sighed. "If you wish to visit your pack, then we will accompany you."

Smiling brightly, River impulsively moved forward to give him a quick kiss.

Eyes widening for a moment, the wolf released a low chuckle. *I must say, I do like this more than our arguing,* he told her playfully through their bond.

Don't get too used to it, she teased back.

Oh, really?" Adrian returned with a smirk.

Slowly rising, he suddenly lunged at the she-wolf.

River giggled and leapt out of the way. *Too slow,* Crystal mocked. The moment her wolf said that, River knew what was going to happen. Letting out a shriek, she ran from the room with a grinning alpha on her tail.

The moment the long caravan of vehicles came to a stop, a door flung open and a blur with black and red hair raced forward to divebomb the awaiting beta. A rare smile appeared on Kyle's face. Embracing his daughter, he looked up to greet his alpha and their guests.

"Welcome back, Alpha," he said bowing as deeply as he could with his daughter still clinging to his side.

Nick grinned. "Thank you, Kyle. It's good to be back. Any news?"

Kyle shook his head. The two men spoke every morning and then once in the evening, so there wasn't anything his alpha hadn't already been told. A familiar scent drew the beta's attention just as Roxy stiffened at his side. Her heartbeat quickly picked up speed and there was the faintest trace of excitement in her scent as she moved away from her father to glare at the blond vampire by her side.

Don't tell me...

A frown pulled at the corners of Kyle's mouth as he watched the two of them.

Roxy crossed her arms, her gaze locked with the young immortal's. Neither said a word. Clenching her jaw, Roxy jerked her head in the other direction to peer at the werewolves who were climbing the steps to enter the manor. She waited until River and Amber drew closer with their mates before storming off inside.

The vampire's eyes tracked the she-wolf with an intensity that Kyle knew too well. Once she was out of sight, Dimitri shifted his sights to the other man. He bowed respectfully, his gaze filled with a strong confidence that Kyle's wolf, Rex, even acknowledged before trailing after the beta's daughter.

Tell me that I'm imagining things, he almost pleaded to Rex.

His wolf sighed. *We both know that's not true.*

"Don't worry," a deep voice said from his other side. Pavel had taken Nick's place on the steps while the wolf was watching the younger vampire. "I promise my son will accept whichever choice she makes, but she better do it quickly before he grows any more attached."

Kyle didn't reply as the vampire lord glided past him. He stood out on the porch for a few moments longer. Closing his eyes, the wolf asked his goddess why she had chosen a vampire for his daughter's mate. Vampires were rarely paired with other races since their bond was eternal. They tended not to reject their mates, for doing so wouldn't sever the pull for their other half. It was there, forever, until one of them perished. No matter what, Dimitri would always long for the she-wolf.

Why is this happening?

Not even his wolf answered him. Exhaling with a huff, Kyle traveled inside to rejoin the others. Inside the large living room he found River, Adrian, Amber and Blake seated on the couches. Nick and Amanda were standing to the right with Kyle's wife and daughter, while Dimitri lingered on the opposite side of the space near his father.

As soon as the beta entered the room, he could hear Yvette and Roxy talking.

"Don't give up, sweetheart," Yvette encouraged, giving the younger she-wolf a hug. "There will be plenty of other chances to find your mate."

Kyle groaned inwardly as Roxy's gaze shifted to stare invisible daggers at the man watching her from across the space.

"Well, I might have found him if it wasn't for someone's constant interference," she growled in a low voice. "Every time I even tried to talk to someone *he* would pop up and scare them off."

Seriously, why does he keep following me? I don't need protection, Roxy complained to her wolf.

Rose sighed. *That's not what's going on and you know it. What are you talking about?*

Stop lying to yourself, Rose grumbled.

"How long are you going to keep lying to yourself?" Dimitri questioned darkly, echoing her wolf's words.

Roxy's fingers curled into her palms. "I'm not lying to myself! I just want to know why you keep shadowing me. It's driving me nuts."

The vampire lifted his chin as his brows furrowed. "Your Goddess has a twisted sense of humor," he stated flatly.

"Stop talking in riddles."

Dimitri suddenly appeared directly in front of the she-wolf. Vampires were faster than werewolves, however the man before her was so quick that she hadn't even seen him move.

"I don't want another male near you," Dimitri announced in a husky tone.

Roxy's mouth parted and her eyes grew wide. Without warning, the vampire pulled her close and crushed her lips with his own. Rolling waves of electricity flowed through her body, bringing every cell to life. Roxy's eyes closed and a groan sounded in her throat.

Mate! Mate, mate, mate, Rose howled happily in her mind.

Stiffening, Roxy pulled out of his arms. Her hands flew to her lips as a deep blush spread across her cheeks. Unable to tear her gaze away, Roxy stared at Dimitri's blazing red eyes. Her heart was pounding, but it wasn't with fear.

"No, no, no, no," she denied, shaking her head. "Are you crazy? Why would you kiss me?"

Face still etched with a frown, Kyle moved closer to his daughter. "Because he's your mate, Roxy," he told her, unsure if he wanted to admit the truth himself. This wasn't just any wolf, it was his little girl.

"Dimitri is your mate," Pavel confirmed. "Trying to convince yourself otherwise isn't going to change that."

Eyes widening, Roxy's face paled. Her gaze searched the room before locking on the alpha. "Uncle Nick?" she questioned, wrapping her arms around herself.

Someone please tell me that I'm hearing things, Roxy privately pleaded. She couldn't be matched with Dimitri. Since the moment they met, all they did was argue. He hated her, didn't he? His presence made her uneasy, but it wasn't the jolt of electricity she heard about so often from other she-wolves.

Isn't it? Rose countered. *It sure felt like it when he kissed us.*

"Roxy," Nick called, drawing her attention away from her wolf. "I know this is a bit of a shock for you—for all of us, but they are correct. We noticed the way you two were interacting back in Silver Fang," he said glancing at the luna. "No one is asking you to choose right now, but you will have to make a choice on whether or not to accept Dimitri as your mate."

The younger woman could feel her mother place a hand on her shoulder, but the reassuring contact didn't lessen the turmoil of her warring emotions. They had to be mistaken. The Moon Goddess had to be mistaken.

"But he's a vampire!" Roxy blurted incredulously.

Nick nodded. "Yes, he is. You know well that wolves are sometimes mated with other races. I've known a few other werewolves who have had to make a similar decision."

"Yes," Pavel drawled coming to stand by his old friend. "And there is another difficult decision the two of you must make since my son is immortal."

Threading her fingers in her hair, Roxy violently shook her head. "This is too much. I don't believe it. I just can't!"

Turning on her heel, the she-wolf raced out of the space.

Dimitri made to go after her, yet his father halted his steps.

"You best give her some time," the older vampire advised.

His eyes fading back to their normal pale blue, Dimitri nodded his head. Without a word, he strode out of the house and headed towards the woods. The atmosphere left behind from the pair's departure was depressing.

"What are we going to do?" Kyle muttered to no one in particular.

His wife sighed. "There is nothing that we can do. The choice is theirs."

The beta grunted in reply while Adrian studied his mate. "What's wrong, River?"

Blinking, the she-wolf shook her head. She had been so lost in thought that she didn't realize that a deep frown was dominating her features. Having listened to Roxy complain about Dimitri before, she knew that her friend had to be torn with this news. Roxy seemed convinced that the vampire hated her.

Everything will work out, Crystal told her with certainty.

I hope so, River returned. *We should go talk to her as soon as we can get away.*

Crystal agreed, yet there was one other thing that River didn't understand. "Pavel," she said gazing at the old vampire. "What did you mean by 'they have another decision to make'?"

The lord's normally amicable features seemed to have turned permanently serious since their arrival at the pack house. Lowering himself into a chair, the man leaned back with a frown.

"As her family, I suppose it wouldn't hurt for you to know," the vampire, said more to himself. Glancing at those present, he looked at each wolf in turn. "Nicholas is aware of this, however I would ask you to keep this knowledge to yourself."

When everyone nodded, Pavel continued, "If Roxy chooses not to reject my son, then the fact will remain that he is immortal and she is not. The two of them must decide if Dimitri is going to renounce his immortality or…"

"Or what?" Kyle questioned. The knots forming in his stomach told him that he already knew the answer.

"Or…if Dimitri will turn her into an immortal."

The beta's eyes darted to Nick. "Is that even possible?"

There was a moment before the alpha responded. "Yes," he told them slowly. "From my understanding, this can only be done with a vampire's true mate."

"Correct," Pavel confirmed. "If a vampire injects some of his blood into his mortal mate, their bond will transform her into an immortal like him."

"So Roxy would be a vampire?" Yvette asked, gripping the back of the couch.

Pavel shook his head. "No. There have been four werewolves to my knowledge that chose this path. Each of them has retained both their inner wolf and the ability to shift. However, drinking a small amount of blood is still necessary."

"And if Roxy wants to stay mortal?"

"There is a potion, one of which only the council knows the ingredients, that would turn Dimitri mortal. He would retain his powers and still need to drink blood, but he would age as you do."

"Wow," River whispered. "That is a tough choice to make."

Her words needed no response. Either way, this unlikely pair would have to make sacrifices. Crystal whimpered for their friend. No matter what, she would be there to support her. Only Roxy could make this decision, but that didn't mean that she was alone.

"What do you mean that she's gone?" Jack demanded as he gazed at the warrior in front of him.

"Forgive me, Alpha," the man said with a bow. "We've searched everywhere, but no one's even seen Courtney since Alpha Carrel's funeral."

"Very well. Alert me immediately the moment anyone sees her."

"Yes, Alpha," the wolf answered with determination before departing the office.

Exhaling with a hiss, he turned towards the window and raked a hand over his increasingly grey hair. Not much of the brown remained anymore. So much for retirement. There was a lot of work to complete to get his pack back in order before he could even consider a candidate for the future alpha. Though in all likelihood, it would one day go to Steven's oldest son.

Where could she have gone?

Jack could feel his wolf sigh. *Who can say? She might have been chosen, but she was still Carrel's mate. Perhaps she just needed some time away from the pack.*

Perhaps, he replied as his fingers tapped against his side.

The alpha's body wouldn't remain still. His wolf seemed strangely antsy as well. Something intangible was telling him that he shouldn't be standing there. He was needed elsewhere, but where? Focusing his good eye on the forest, Jack could swear that he heard a soft voice telling him to hurry.

"How can you just stand there like a fool while Courtney is missing?" questioned Karen crossly. "Did you despise our son that much? She is all that we have left of him."

Jack twisted away from the window with a frown. "I never despised our son," he told her in a hard tone. "As for Courtney, I've had wolves searching for her from the moment I knew she was gone. It is difficult to find someone who does not wish to be found."

"Why don't you ask your precious witch?" the luna spat, pointing to Raven who was quietly nestled on a chair in the corner. "Or is such a task beyond her black magic? She didn't even try to save Carrel."

The wolf's brows furrowed. His mate had been verbally attacking everyone she could for the past week. Jack understood the grief she felt. Heck, he delivered the final blow, but as the leaders of the pack, they had to set an example, not punish innocent wolves for Carrel's twisted behavior.

"There is no need to target Raven with your hostility," Jack stated. "I understand what you are going through, Karen, but we have to stay strong for our pack. Snapping at everyone isn't going to solve anything."

"You understand what I'm going through?" the she-wolf repeated with venom. "Jack, you can never understand. You *murdered* our son."

Ace whimpered in his mind. The desire to take away his mate's pain was overwhelming. Jack took a step towards her, yet Karen simply held up her hands.

"Don't you dare touch me!"

The wolf froze. She might as well have stabbed him in the chest. Clenching his jaw, Jack forced himself to stay where he was.

"Karen, do you really think that I wanted to harm him? I gave Carrel several chances to fix things. I gave him the choice to step down as the Alpha and he refused. He *attacked* the future Queen Luna and was bringing a war upon us. If I hadn't retaken control of the pack, then everyone here would have been killed."

Tears slipping down her cheeks, Karen's lower lip trembled. "Then they should have died instead of betraying their Alpha," she announced without a hint of softness. "I can't stand looking at any of you anymore." Wiping her face with determination, she squared her shoulders prior to glaring at the man across from her. "I'm returning to my pack and I don't *ever* want to see you again, Jack. I hope you suffer for what you have done."

Taking a deep breath, she practically shouted at him, "I, Karen Stanford, reject you, *Alpha* Jack Stanford, as my mate forever!"

Spinning on her heel, Karen stormed out of the room.

A sharp pain tore through Jack's body. Its intensity was worse than anything that he had felt during his battle with Carrel. Ace howled in his mind. The sorrow of his cry brought the alpha to his knees.

Karen! he called out through their mind-link, but there was nothing. He could no longer hear her thoughts or feel her presence. Their bond had been broken.

A soothing hand on his back had Jack's head jerking up. Raven was beside him, her gaze gleaming with sympathy. She said nothing, for which the proud wolf was grateful. It was bad enough that someone was seeing him in such a depressing state. Forcing himself to rise, Jack took a seat at his desk.

"You did warn me that the worst was yet to come," he muttered halfheartedly while gripping the front of his shirt. "I suppose that I earned this punishment."

Studying the wolf, Raven glided across the floor to his side. Placing her fingers beneath his chin, she lifted his gaze to meet hers.

"What makes you believe that you deserve to be punished?" she questioned softly. "Jack, you saved your pack. You broke a curse placed by the Moon Goddess herself, but your strength was never hindered because you did not earn her wrath. If you were meant to be punished, then you would have been weakened as the others were."

Jack simply stared at the witch. Could she be right? Was the only sentence bestowed upon him the one that he gave himself? It sure didn't feel like it. He had not only taken his son's life, but now he lost his mate, his soul's other half. A second chance mate way a dream he couldn't even hope for.

A knock on the door drew both of their attentions. Raven lowered her hand and took a step back as the alpha called for their visitor to enter.

His beta quickly strode into the room and dropped into a bow. "I'm sorry to disrupt you, Alpha."

Jack shook his head. "Your presence is never a disruption, Steven. Did you find Courtney?"

"No, I did find something new, however."

"Oh?"

"Yes," he nodded with a frown. "I interviewed the manor's staff again and it seems that a strange woman was talking to Courtney long after the funeral. The maid didn't get a clear view of her, but she was certain that the woman wasn't from our pack or a wolf at all. Apparently, she gave something to Courtney before disappearing."

"Strange," Jack murmured. "Did anyone else see this woman?"

"Not that I know of."

"May I?" Raven questioned, pointing to the alpha's desk.

Without a word, Jack slid back his chair and offered it to the spellcaster.

Raven settled behind the desk and pulled out her worn reading cards. Closing her eyes, she shuffled the deck three times and laid them on the polished surface. When she opened her eyes, a frown marred her features.

"A witch," Raven announced simply.

Jack's gaze snapped up to meet his beta's. "How did we not know that there was another witch in our territory?"

The other man didn't have an answer.

Raven's eyes narrowed as she continued to look at the cards. "Malinda Ebony sent word that a potion was used when River was attacked. They believe that a witch was aiding Carrel."

Jack's mouth pressed into a thin line. "I don't think any of your witches would have been willing to help Carrel do something so foolish. However, these two events may be related. Lady Raven, you lead the strongest coven in the south. Do you know anyone who he might have hired?"

With a sigh, Raven folded her hands in front of her. "My coven has been looking into this since the moment I received word of it. So far, we have no leads. Not just any witch would be able to cast the spell used upon the she-wolf. This required strong magic."

"Strong magic," Jack repeated quietly. "Like black magic?"

Raven peered at him questioningly.

"There was a witch living in the Free Lands between us and Blackwood during my grandfather's time as Alpha. She was said to possess strong black magic and was very dangerous. Rumors spoke of her love of the forbidden arts. My grandfather forbade anyone in the pack from going near her dwelling and my family has upheld his command ever since. I don't know if she would still be alive, but her name was Agatha, I believe."

Raven's hands smacked the desk as she bolted to her feet. "That necromancer lives near your pack?" she demanded.

Jack thought that he saw a blaze light in Raven's gaze as she looked back at her cards.

"What the hell is a necromancer?" Steven inquired.

The witch didn't answer at first. Tilting his head to the side, Jack peered at her set face. If they had indeed uncovered another dangerous enemy, then he wanted to know as well.

"Raven?"

The sorceress sighed. "Agatha was banished from my coven and then stripped of her power by the previous High Priestess. She had a vile liking for torturing other creatures and then reviving them to complete her twisted experiments. If she found a way to regain her magic, then toying with your pack would be far too easy."

Shit, that doesn't sound good, Ace growled.

"There is only one way to find out. Steven, gather two squads of warriors. We are going to pay this witch a visit."

"I'm coming with you," Raven advised at she headed for the door. "If it is Agatha, she may have her grounds protected to keep out intruders."

"Very well," Jack agreed.

He wasn't going to stop Raven if she wanted to join them. If this witch was as dangerous and sinister as she believed, then they just might need her help.

Jack and the other warriors took a few cars to the edge of Red Moon's territory closest to Agatha's last known location. From there, they would be going on foot so that they didn't alert the witch to their presence. A few miles in and Raven was practically cussing under her breath. The sorceress wasn't used to trekking for hours through the rough terrain. Taking a knee, Jack put his arms behind his back and silently motioned for her to hold onto him. The witch paused for a few seconds before allowing the wolf to carry her.

Two more miles passed when the witch stiffened. Leaning forward, she whispered for Jack to have his warriors halt. A dark aura swirled around the forest. His men stood on edge, ready to shift in an instant. Lowering Raven to the ground, Jack stayed close beside her as she inched her way forward. Pulling out a handful of powder, he watched as she blew it into the air. The mixture ignited into sparks as it hit an invisible barrier several feet away.

"Just as I thought," Raven murmured.

Grabbing a stick, the witch etched a set of symbols into the dirt. Sprinkling more of the powder, she cast a spell to remove Agatha's barrier. The magic shimmered and faded away to reveal a small cabin in the midst of a group of evergreens.

"Be careful," Raven warned the werewolves. "There might be other traps."

Jack instructed Steven and his men to watch the perimeter while the alpha and his warriors approached the cabin. Nothing sounded from within. Climbing the stairs, Jack caught the faint scent of his son.

"Carrel was here," he told Raven.

With a growl, the alpha kicked open the door. The warriors swiftly moved inside and searched the cramped space. The dark witch's smell was fading, telling them that she had not been there for at least a few days.

"She's not here," Jack informed the petite woman by his side.

Holding up a hand Raven used her magic to scan the area as well. "I'm not sensing any other enchantments. She seemed to think that this place was well hidden. Foolish arrogance," Raven muttered.

"Alpha, Lady Raven, you might want to see this," one of his warriors called out from the bedroom doorway.

Exchanging a glance, the wolf and the witch strode across the space to enter the smaller chamber. As they did, the man who summoned them pulled back a curtain on the far wall.

"What the…" Jack exclaimed as several shelves of jars were revealed.

Brows lowering, Raven gazed at three glowing vessels sitting on the middle shelf.

"We seem to be in the right place," she said darkly while continuing to peer at the gleaming swirls.

"What are they?" Jack asked, unsure if he truly wanted to know.

The witch exhaled unhappily. "Souls of the dead."

Candlelight bathed dusty shelves of books and scrolls with a warm glow. Hours had passed by, but still, the answers to countless questions seemed forever out of reach. Silvia sighed as she removed her glasses to pinch the bridge of her nose.

Malinda glanced up to study the elder. There were dark circles under her eyes and a distinctive slump to her shoulders.

"We should take a break," the witch suggested, rising to her feet.

Silvia flashed her a grateful smile. "I wouldn't be opposed to that."

Leaving the depths of the archives, the two women made their way out to a nearby sitting area close to the main library. After ringing for some refreshments, they settled into a pair of comfortable chairs. Silence lingered in the room even after the maid departed.

"I should not be surprised that we haven't found anything yet," the she-wolf finally said as she began to sip her tea. "Though, I was more optimistic when this endeavor first began. Forbidden spells shouldn't be easy to locate. However, I was hoping that we would be able to find a way to counter this curse at the very least."

Malinda ran her fingers through her hair as she brushed it from her face. "I can't say that I'm surprised that we've come up empty-handed. I only learned of it from my mentor. She insisted that we know what spells to never cast. My girls are combing through my entire collection for protective enchantments, but I fear that we might not be able to stop it."

Lips pressed into a thin line, Silvia's cup stopped part way to her mouth. Lowering her tea cup, she frowned. "I never thought I'd hear you sound so defeated. Premonitions, prophecies, seeing into the future...call it what you will, but it is still only a piece of what may come. Nothing is ever truly clear until we have the entire picture. We can't give up until every breath has left our bodies."

A slow, humorless grin stretched across the other woman's face. "If I didn't know better, I would think that you were immortal, Silvia. You have wisdom that few are able to achieve."

"We all age in our own time," the she-wolf countered with a chuckle.

"That is so true."

Silvia's movements stilled and a glassy look shadowed her eyes. After a few seconds, she blinked repeatedly. "King Magnus is requesting us in his study."

Malinda's brows rose. "Perhaps he found something."

Neither woman needed any further encouragement. Leaving their drinks, they traveled through the castle towards the king's office. When they entered, Magnus was not alone. Malinda grinned when she spotted a petite woman with silver hair standing beside Alpha Jack.

"Lady Raven," Malinda greeted fondly. "It has been too long."

The graceful woman turned to meet the other witch. "Yes, it has Lady Malinda," she agreed with a smile. "I dare say, you have not aged a day."

"We both know that is not quite true," she returned with a twinkle in her eyes. "What brings you to Silver Fang?"

The casual atmosphere immediately darkened. Raven's expression turned serious as she glanced at the tall man still by her side.

Malinda didn't recognize him, but she knew a wolf when she saw one.

"Allow me to introduce everyone properly," Magnus interjected, motioning for his guests to be seated. Once everyone was settled, he shifted his gaze to the person closest to him.

"This is Alpha Jack of Red Moon," the king said, gesturing towards the other wolf. "Next is Lady Raven, High Priestess of the Starlight Coven. Lady Malinda, High Priestess of the Misty Valley Coven and Elder Silvia of Swift Wind, who is my kingdom's best historian."

A round of greetings passed between the four of them after the introductions.

"Now then," Magnus continued as he leaned on his desk. "Since we finished with the pleasantries, let us get down to business. Lady Raven and Alpha Jack have discovered the witch who was aiding Carrel. Unfortunately, she was no longer at her cabin, however... Well, I will let you explain Lady Raven."

The witch dipped her head in a nod. "The culprit is a necromancer named Agatha. I'm appalled to say that she was once a part of the same coven as me long ago. We found evidence that Carrel visited her cabin. However, the witch was not present when we arrived." Raven paused as her expression twisted into a scowl. The surrounding air practically sparked with the tension. "Malinda, she was storing souls."

The fellow sorceress stiffened. "You are certain?" she asked, already knowing that the other woman would not have said so unless she was positive.

"Yes," Raven confirmed. "There were three remaining. I have since released them from her hold."

"Unforgivable," Malinda muttered like a curse. "We must contact the other covens to have her located at once."

"That won't be easy," Jack interjected. "Even my best trackers weren't able to pick up her scent."

The two witches shared a glance.

"If this Agatha was responsible for creating the potion Carrel used, what are the odds that she is the same witch helping Cerberus?"

Raven shifted her gaze to the she-wolf with a grimace. "Too great for my liking. She certainly isn't finished skulking around. It would seem that she paid Carrel's mate a visit after the funeral."

"Yes," Jack ground out. "I wish we knew what she gave to Courtney. No one has seen the she-wolf since."

As soon as Jack said Courtney's name, Malinda's eyes glazed over. The witch stiffened like she was made of stone.

"Is she alright?" Silvia questioned, her eyes widening as she watched the woman beside her.

"It looks like she is having a vision," Magnus supplied.

"She is," Raven verified.

The four of them grew quiet as they waited for the sorceress to return to them. Malinda suddenly inhaled with a gasp. Blinking rapidly, her gaze darted around the space as she got her bearings. Her hands moved to grip Silvia's arm.

"River," she stressed, her gaze frighteningly wide. "We have to help River. Now!"

Chapter 15

After settling into her room, River left the manor to go for a walk. It was getting late and Roxy still had yet to return home. The she-wolf had a feeling that she knew where to find the other woman. Taking a familiar trail through the west forest, River came upon the same clearing that the gamma used for her training sessions. Sure enough, Roxy was sitting on the bank, her bare feet resting in the flowing creek. Her head was bent, with her long black and red hair shading her face, but River's heightened senses could pick up the faint smell of tears.

Lowering herself on the ground beside her friend, River gently nudged the other woman's shoulder.

"Hey," she greeted causally.

"Hey," Roxy echoed without any real feeling.

"Do you want to talk about it?"

The she-wolf shrugged. Releasing a growl, Roxy plopped onto her back and stretched out her arms.

"I can't believe that I didn't see it. How did everyone else know? I thought that he couldn't stand me."

River grimaced. "In all fairness, I thought the same thing. Crystal was the one to figure it out first and even then, she didn't tell me." Lying on her back beside Roxy, she asked, "What are you going to do?"

Roxy opened her mouth then closed it. It was rare for her not to have something to say. The two she-wolves watched the fading light filter through the canopy for a few minutes. A warm breeze was blowing and with nothing but the sound of flowing water around them, the forest was quite peaceful.

"I don't know," the dark haired woman admitted softly.

"Well, at least he's good looking. You always did want a dangerously hot mate," River teased, bringing a smile to her cousin's face.

Roxy laughed. "He certainly is that. The dangerous part," she pointed out with a smirk.

"Uh-huh."

"What?"

River shook her head and giggled, but said nothing.

"What?" Roxy insisted. Rolling onto her side, she began to tickle her friend.

As their laughter died away, the women sat up. "We should probably head back," River advised. "You know how everyone gets if we are gone for too long."

"Our parents worry a little too much, if you ask me," Roxy said flippantly.

River didn't reply. Her gaze was locked on the woods behind them. The birds had grown silent, their evening songs no longer filling the trees. Slowly, she rose to her feet as her wolf growled deeply in the back of her mind.

"Roxy, run," River encouraged, pulling her cousin to her feet.

Bristling, the dark-haired she-wolf turned her gaze towards the forest as the two of them began to back away.

Roxy, River called urgently through their mind-link. *I said run for it!*

A bright, searing light erupted from the growing darkness as a ball of flames headed straight for them. River used her power to siphon water from the creek and absorb the blast. One by one, the burning eyes of the hellhounds appeared at the edge of the trees as the beasts stepped forth from the shadows. Teeth bared, the six hounds growled at their newfound prey.

Roxy snapped back, her legs digging into the soil as she prepared to pounce.

A thick wall of ice suddenly cut off the hellhounds' frontal attack.

"Are you crazy?" River demanded, dragging her friend in the opposite direction. "We can't take that many out by ourselves."

"Says who?" the she-wolf quipped darkly. "I feel like I could take down a horde of them right now."

River didn't reply as they shifted into their wolves and continued to run at full speed. She had already linked the pack, so help was on the way. Yet with their enemy closing in upon them, River was almost certain that Roxy was about to get her wish. In a few more seconds, the hounds would be caught up to them.

Acting as bait, Roxy slowed her pace. As the fire beasts zeroed in upon her, she darted back and forth, causing them to clump closer together. Once River gave the signal, she dashed forward and leapt out of the way.

Sucking in a deep breath, River barked loudly, launching a sonic blast that flattened everything in its path as it hit four of the hounds dead on.

Ignoring their comrades, the two remaining beasts continued on their deadly path.

River twisted around, her paws pounding into the dirt as she aimed to place as much distance between her and the hounds as possible. It wouldn't take long for the other creatures to recover. Watching Roxy's form dip down out of view, River linked her with a plan.

As she approached the sharp decline, River leapt onto one of the curving tree trunks. She then created a river of ice that followed the slope down to the forest floor.

Unable to see the newly formed frozen sheet, the hounds skated all the way to the bottom and slammed into a thick buffer-like wall of ice. Flames darkening as they rose to their feet, the hellhounds jerked their heads to the left as a black and red wolf bounced out into the unmarked path. Unearthly snarls sounded from the creatures as Roxy wagged her tail tauntingly. With their eyes focused solely on the other she-wolf, the hounds didn't notice a blue wolf approaching from the rear.

Keeping her scent concealed, River called out to her power, drawing the ice beneath her foes to climb up their legs and encase their entire bodies. River knew that her prison wouldn't hold for long, but she could take at least one of the hounds out. Dashing forward, the blue wolf enhanced her claws with icicles and slashed the nearest fire beast. The creature burst into smoldering ash just as River spotted her cousin leaping onto the second creature who was beginning to thaw.

No! River cried out in her mind.

It was too late to stop Roxy's attack.

Breaking free of the ice, the hellhound twisted his head with an evil gleam as he opened his jaws to bite the dark wolf. Another form sped through the trees, landing on top of the hound and jerking his head back—right before he could chomp down.

"Finish him," Dimitri commanded as he held the growling creature pinned in a headlock.

Roxy's gaze shifted to the fire beast's exposed throat. She needed no further encouragement to jump in and tear it apart. As the black dust swirled around them, her eyes settled on the vampire. What was he doing there? Roxy couldn't very well question him in her current form, not that there was time. The four remaining hellhounds had made it to the top of the hill. Bursts of fire pounded the surrounding tree line as they unleashed their attack.

River, Roxy and Dimitri took off once more through the woods. The fire attacks ceased as they raced along. It would seem that the hounds couldn't shoot flames while they were running. A collection of brown, grey and black blurs passed by, heading in the other direction.

River knew the instant that Adrian arrived. An energy surged through her. She felt completely invigorated. Scanning the forest, she searched for her mate. The large black wolf wasn't difficult to find. River's sights locked upon him the instant that he appeared through the underbrush. When Adrian's eyes connected with hers, Crystal howled happily. River swore that the wolf was grinning as he took off to meet the hellhounds.

Bounding through the trees, Adrian zeroed in on the four remaining enemies. Nick's warriors succeeded in isolating each hound, but that didn't lessen their difficulty in defeating them. Flames scorched the wilderness causing clouds of smoke to billow up from among the trees. As Adrian was devising a way to draw their foes out to more open ground, a blast of ice extinguished the fire on his right.

River brushed past him, her fur glistening in the light. One by one, she used her powers to put out the blazes so that her comrades could focus on the battle itself.

Adrian headed towards the hound with the least warriors. Simon and Henry were engaging the third beast with another brown wolf. The hellhound leapt up, knocking Simon back as he bit into Henry's shoulder. The other warrior gripped the beast's back leg, pulling outward as he ran his claws down the extremity. Coming in from the left, Adrian wrapped his jaws around the hound's throat while Simon attacked from the opposite side. The satisfying taste of ash filled their senses as the creature disintegrated.

Are you alright? Simon asked his twin worriedly.

He barely broke the skin, Henry lied, tucking his right leg into his body to keep his weight off that side.

Take him to the doctor, Adrian instructed before peering around to study the fighting.

All of the hellhounds had been disposed of. One wolf had fallen and he could make out a few others with serious

Jay Lynn

injuries. The prince could feel Cole's anger with the loss of a
warrior. He shared that rage, but the moment he spotted
River's blue fur, his shoulders sagged with relief.

He will pay for this, came a furious female voice in his mind.
I will make him pay for this.

Adrian's ears pulled back. His mate didn't seem to know
that her thoughts were passing through their link to him.
Putting up a mental block was a little trickier in wolf form
than it was as a human.

We will stop Cerberus, Adrian told River as he nuzzled her.
We'll do it together.

Seeing her in this battle, the prince could no longer deny
his mate's fate. She wouldn't willing allow others to be hurt in
her place, and Adrian was proud of her strength of character.
He needed her to know that he would be by her side no
matter what.

River's eyes shimmered gratefully. Leaning in, she licked
the black wolf's cheek.

*Why don't you check on the others at the manor? I will meet you
there,* he suggested as Nick called for him.

River nodded, then watched both her husband and father
disappear into the trees. She had enough of battle for one
day. The only thing she wanted now was to check on her
brothers and take a long hot bath.

While Alpha Nick and his warriors were racing to River
and Roxy's aid, an explosion sounded from the opposite side
of the compound. The main gates leading to the pack house
were blown clear from the wall. A dozen werewolves and
three vampires charged forward like a raging tide. The two
wolves stationed there stood no chance as their foes piled
upon them with both teeth and claws bared.

Angry snarls drew their attention as the first wave of
reinforcements closed in from both sides. The invaders
turned their blood-stained faces one way, then the other,

before splitting their forces in half. Such a fierce and immediate response hadn't been expected.

Swift Wind wasn't known as the second strongest in the kingdom for no reason. Every wolf trained in combat and their warriors were some of the best. For each drop of blood that their adversaries spilt, Swift Wind wolves took back threefold. By the time Kyle and his men joined the fray with Blake and the second wave of fighters, five enemy wolves and one vampire had already been eliminated.

Eyes blazing crimson, the two vampires turned their attention to the incoming forces. They hissed like rabid animals, not caring about the numbers overwhelming their own. Blake's pure white wolf exchanged a quick glance with Kyle's tan form. A mind-link wasn't necessary. Both agreed that these targets were theirs. The four fighters crashed together like thunder.

Kyle leapt up on his back legs, snapping his jaws as he ripped into the vampire's arm to tear it from his body. His foe twisted with unnatural ease and ran his claws down the beta's back. Kyle spun around with a growl. Feinting to the right, he darted to the other side, aiming for the vampire's head. His foe ducked down and slammed into the beta's side at the last moment. Kyle was knocked back several feet. Digging in his back paws, he halted his slide, then raced towards the vampire without hesitation. This time aiming low, the beta struck his foe's legs, pulling him off his feet to flip him onto his back before going in for a killing blow.

Next to them, Blake and the other vampire were rolling on the ground in a tangle of paws and legs. Catching his adversary's calf in his mouth, the white wolf twisted about to toss him like a shot put. Blake gave him no time to recover as he headed right for him. Leaping high into the air, the royal wolf landed on his chest and gripped the vampire by the throat. With his next breath, he removed his enemy's head.

The wounds on his back already having healed, Kyle glanced around for Blake. The white wolf was quickly nearing his side. The two nodded to each other prior to moving towards the continuing battle. Suddenly, a pain radiated through their skulls feeling like a dozen needles. Crying out, the two wolves fell to their stomachs. Images around them blurred and sounds twisted into screams as the agony distorted all their senses.

On the edge of the forest, outside the shattered gate, was a woman shrouded in a dark cloak. A smile dominated her features as she held a hand out before her. Fingers spread wide, she bent her wrist downward as she placed more power into her spell.

"I thought I smelt a witch," Pavel observed casually from directly behind her.

Gasping, the woman spun on her heel, bringing a silver knife up to strike her foe.

His movements a blur, Pavel gripped the sorceress by the throat with one hand while his other enclosed around the thin blade. The vampire's eyes darkened like blood. A dangerous grin slowly stretched across his face. Tugging the weapon from the woman's grasp, he clicked his tongue disapprovingly.

"Not a wise witch I see. Who sent you?" Pavel questioned without loosening his hold. When he received no answer, the vampire squeezed tighter.

The woman clawed uselessly at his hand.

"I won't ask again," he informed her.

Eyes bulging from her head, the witch nodded as best she could.

Pavel waited a second before loosening his hold just enough so that she could breathe. "Do not toy with me," he warned calmly.

Coughing and wheezing, she continued to grip his hand.

"A witch," she gasped. "It was a witch."

Pavel's gaze narrowed. "Why would a witch hire another to attack a wolf pack with so few warriors?"

"I—I don't know."

The vampire pulled her closer to him. Taking a deep breath, he inhaled her scent before placing some distance between them once again.

"You're not telling me something."

The woman didn't answer as a light beckoning from the pack house lawn drew their attention. His fingers locked in place around the witch's throat, Pavel took his prisoner and headed towards the glow. As they passed through the battlefield, he purposely slowed his pace, allowing her to see that all of the rogue wolves had been eliminated.

Pain no longer coursing through their bodies, Kyle and Blake shifted back to their human forms and glared at the spellcaster. Alpha Nick and Adrian had already joined them.

"So, the cowards brought a witch as well," Adrian remarked crossly.

"I'm not surprised at this point," Nick added dryly. "Thank you for your assistance, Pavel."

"Think nothing of it," he told them before shifting his gaze to the magic circle appearing in the grass. "Are you expecting company?"

Brows lowering, Nick shook his head. "This isn't Marina's work?"

Pavel didn't respond. If it wasn't the vampire's daughter, then there was only one other possibility. In the next moment, several figures materialized in the center of the vortex spell. Among them was Malinda. As the light faded, she dropped down to her knees.

Nick and Kyle rushed forward to aid her before shifting their attention to her comrades.

"Father, what is the meaning of this?" Blake questioned the king while looking at Alpha Jack and the three witches standing beside him.

"Malinda foresaw that your brother's mate was in great danger. I couldn't get ahold of anyone on the phone so we came to warn you."

Adrian nodded grimly. "Yes, we were busy dealing with dual attacks from some rogues and hellhounds.

When the prince said the word 'hellhound', Pavel's prisoner paled.

"So you didn't know of the hounds," the vampire observed.

"Who is this?" Magnus questioned urgently.

"A witch I found hiding outside the gates. She was using her magic to attack the second prince and Beta. She claims another witch hired her."

Raven glanced at the two members of her coven standing beside her. Quickly she moved towards Pavel, her eyes never leaving his captive.

"Was this witch a middle-aged woman with blonde hair?"

When she didn't answer Pavel gave the woman a jerk.

"Yes," she growled softly.

Raven and Jack exchanged a telling glance.

"What of a blonde she-wolf named Courtney. Was she leading the attack?" Jack demanded.

"There was no she-wolf," the witch told him.

"She's lying," Malinda informed them weakly. "She knows of whom you speak."

All eyes shifted to the woman glaring at the black-haired witch as she leaned against the alpha for support.

"Has anyone seen a she-wolf not from your pack?" Jack asked, peering around.

"There was no female wolf among those who attacked us," Kyle confirmed.

Pavel's gaze was still on his prisoner. "They were a distraction," he concluded. "This witch never planned to make her presence known." His still red eyes shifted to Adrian. "Where is your mate?"

"She returned to the manor."

As the prince answered, a smirk appeared on the witch's face. His heart sunk to the pit of his stomach.

"River!" he roared, twisting around to race inside.

A cry of agony escaped the alpha's lips as he suddenly dropped to the ground. He clutched his side as a burning pain coursed through him. Looking down he saw no blood, no wound at all upon his skin.

"River," he muttered with understanding while looking at his friends and family's startled faces. He was feeling his mate's pain. River had been stabbed.

Closing the door to her room, River exhaled with a groan. She peered down at her bare feet and tried not to sigh. Her new clothes had been torn to shreds, her pack was attacked, and one of their brave warriors had lost his life. If only there was a way for her to stop the hellhounds from leaving the underworld all together. She doubted such a feat was possible. If it was, then someone would have done so already.

I don't want to lose anyone else. I should have been able to defeat them myself.

It wasn't your fault, Crystal sympathized. *Even with these powers, we are still only a single wolf. One day we will be responsible for the entire kingdom with our mate. There will always be loss, but building strong alliances will help to lessen those numbers.*

I hope so, River returned, not overly confident at the moment.

A shower should aid in lifting her spirits. Making her way over towards the walk-in closet, River's feet instantly stilled. She sniffed the air, a growl sounding in her throat. She knew that smell. It was faint, yet River would never mistake it again.

Wolfsbane, she said to Crystal.

"Show yourself," River commanded in her luna voice. She knew that whoever was there could not refuse.

A sneer on her face, Courtney strode into the space from the bathroom.

"Well isn't it Silver Fang's newest little princess," she announced snidely.

River's eyes narrowed to slits. Tracking the other woman's movements, her entire body hummed, ready to strike.

Easy, she told her wolf.

"What are you doing here?" River questioned.

Courtney shrugged mockingly. "What? Not happy to see an old friend?"

"We were never friends."

The she-wolf's eyes flashed. "I bet you think so highly of yourself. Did you use a spell to trick the prince into making you his mate after you cursed mine?" Courtney spat.

"What are you talking about?"

"Don't you dare deny it! I lost everything because of you. He should have just killed you from the start. I won't make the same mistake."

Courtney dashed forward, shifting her hand into a paw she slashed at the other woman's face.

River blocked the attack with her arm, biting back a hiss as her flesh was cut open. Twisting her right fist, she slammed it into her foe's gut, knocking her flat on her back several feet away. The wound on River's arm healed instantly. Her eyes blazed the bright blue of her wolf form as she sped across the room towards her long time enemy. Gripping Courtney by the ankles, River lifted her into the air and slammed her into the neighboring wall.

"I'm not the weakling I was when we were kids, Courtney. You're nothing but a bully," River said calmly as she watched the other woman with no feeling. "You're not going to bully anyone anymore. This is *my* home, and you're not welcome here."

With a growl, Courtney charged forward once more, plowing into River and knocking her down. The two women rolled across the carpet, fighting for control.

The door to the suite burst open. Staying in the suite across the hall, Amber's sight had seen red the moment she heard Courtney's voice. She would *never* forget the she-wolf who made her life hell. Launching off the ground in a massive leap, Amber dove into their enemy, knocking her off River. As soon as they hit the ground, she began punching Courtney in the face with every ounce of strength that she possessed.

Courtney slammed her hands into Amber's chest, sending her flying backwards.

River zipped across the space, catching her new sister before she hit the wall. Sharing a glance, the she-wolves nodded to each other, then attacked simultaneously.

Waiting until the women were within reach, Courtney removed her secret weapon. Ducking under Amber's swing, she twisted to stab River right in the side with the silver blade.

River cried out, falling to the ground.

A grin of pure ecstasy dominated Courtney's face. In that moment, she had forgotten the other wolf still in the room.

Amber grabbed hold of the blonde woman and bit down on her arm.

Screaming, Courtney dropped the knife. Taking a fist full of Amber's hair she pried her off and flipped her backwards. Retrieving the blade with her good hand, their foe set her gaze upon the brunette.

Rising to her feet, Amber spit out a mouthful of Courtney's blood. Shifting her arm into a paw, she faced her enemy straight on.

"If I'm going down, you're going with me," Amber announced coldly.

"Like hell I am!" Courtney snapped back, charging forward.

"No!" River cried, reaching out a hand towards the other she-wolf. Focusing her power, a sheet of ice appeared on the silver weapon and traveled up Courtney's arm to encase her entire body.

A sea of bodies stormed into the space just as River lowered her arm. Adrian was instantly in front of her, his hands flying to the wound on her side.

"Where is Yvette?" he shouted urgently. "Get her here now!"

Likewise, Blake was examining his mate, searching for injuries as he wiped the blood from her face.

"I'm fine," Amber insisted. "River needs help. Courtney stabbed her with a silver knife."

River's parents were already by her side. Everyone seemed to be talking all at once. As Adrian's warmth calmed River's racing heart, it struck her that her side was no longer hurting. Peering down, River slowly slid her mate's hand away and bunched up her shirt. Not one mark marred her skin.

Adrian's eyes widened. He ran his fingers over the lingering stain of blood, but saw no remaining injury.

"How is this possible? I felt her stab you."

"Interesting," Raven observed, stepping into the space with Jack. "So, what I've heard about 'Moon Blest' is true, elemental powers and an immunity to silver. I must say that I am impressed."

Frowning, River shook her head.

An immunity to silver? Is that even possible? We may be blessed, but we are still a werewolf.

How else do you explain that you are healed with no mark? Crystal questioned back.

Getting to her feet, River walked over towards Courtney's frozen form. Waving a hand, she thawed just the blade.

"What are you doing?" Adrian asked. *She can't be serious,* he said to Cole. "River this is dangerous."

"I want to see something," she told him, never taking her eyes off the gleaming blade.

Reaching out, River touched a finger to the flat side of the knife. No pain radiated from the contact. Encouraged, she placed her whole hand against the weapon. Still there was nothing.

"Wow, I guess I am immune."

"I would like to know who this is in my house and how she got a silver blade in the first place," Amanda said crossly.

"Her name is Courtney," Jack answered her unhappily. "She was Carrel's mate. We believe a witch working for Cerberus has been pulling the strings behind this whole mess. She was seen giving something to Courtney after his funeral."

"Another puppet," Nick muttered crossing his arms.

Tilting his head to the side, Pavel observed the frozen wolf thoughtfully. "His attacks are getting more aggressive. I'll send for some of my coven to help in tracking the witch."

Vaguely listening to the conversation taking place around her, River felt a strange pull calling out to her. Turning towards the small balcony off the bedroom, she walked outside and gazed at the moon.

"You won't find her," River informed them, her eyes remaining on the sky.

"Why do you say that?" her mate questioned, placing his arm around her.

"Because," River murmured. "Agatha is going to cast her spell. Tomorrow night, the Blood Moon will rise."

Chapter 16

Breathing in the lingering scent of decay, Agatha strode through the depths of the mountain like a wraith. The single candle that she carried enhanced the darkness of the shadows swirling about her. Outside, the full moon was beginning to rise in the night sky. Even the spirits knew, as she did, that the time had come.

Entering the main chamber, the witch snapped her fingers, bringing the fires lining the craggily walls to life. She made her way towards the altar without delay. Agatha reached down and sprinkled some dried herbs into the viewing mirror. Within a few moments, the three faces of her master shone on the water.

"Lord Cerberus," she greeted respectfully. "My preparations are complete. I only await your command."

The beast grinned malevolently. "Well done, witch," the middle head praised. "Begin at once."

"Yes, my lord."

Waving her hand, Agatha dispelled the image and set to work. She pulled off the cloth covering her array of ingredients to activate the curse. Some were classic staples most witches used: sage, anise seed, dandelion root. Others had a darker history. Smirking, Agatha added the wings of a bat, graveyard soil, a vampire's fang, a human's heart, the hair of a corpse and the blood of a lamb. Lastly, she turned toward the large jar carefully protected to her left.

"The time has come, my pet," she said with glee.

An eerie moaning echoed off the walls of the cave as she grasped the glass vessel. Holding it before her eyes, Agatha watched the swirling flow of the spirit inside.

"The final ingredient," Agatha told the darkness. "One soul of an alpha werewolf. I must thank you, Carrel. Without you, none of this would be possible."

Chuckling, Agatha poured his liquified spirit into the brew. Chanting softly, she watched the potion ignite. Closing her eyes, the witch could feel the twisted energy of the darkness grow stronger.

Behind her, the symbols on the arch illumined. The space between the stones shimmered, shifting into a black pit-like opening. A large clawed paw broke through to touch the cold floor of the cavern. Then, another followed as a twenty-foot-tall beast of fire with three heads appeared.

Agatha spun around with a gasp. Smiling, she stepped down from the altar and bowed deeply.

"Welcome to the mortal world, my lord."

Cerberus barely glanced at her. Stretching his shoulders, his heads lifted proudly. Fires lit on the tops of each skull, trailing down the backs of his necks and spine like a line of flaming fur. Striding forward, the beast king stomped on the altar, flattening it as he moved towards the exit. He said not a word as he traveled through the mountain with Agatha loyally following behind. When they emerged, darkness had completely fallen. Cerberus came to a halt on the edge of a cliff. Gazing upwards, he watched as the moon and earth moved into perfect alignment. Once they were in position, a red tinge shaded the moon. A pulse shot out across the lands, giving an increased power to the darkness.

Agatha could feel her body tingle from the sensation. It was electrifying, as if each cell in her body was being given a boost.

"It worked," the witch whispered, staring up at the Blood Moon now frozen in the sky. "My curse worked! Darkness will rule here forever."

Smiling brightly, Agatha laughed. No one would be able to undo her spell.

Eyes gleaming brightly, Cerberus turned to peer down at the woman standing by his side.

"You have done well," he told her. The two heads on each side of the center one, grinned with a strange light. "But there is no room for the living in my realm of darkness."

Gaze widening, Agatha's mouth gaped. She raised her arms with a scream as the hellhound attacked. Blood splattered the ground in a growing pool that dripped down the edge of the rock ledge.

Materializing from the surrounding shadows, an army of hellhounds began to appear. Cerberus raised his heads as he twisted around to face the mass.

"Go," the center head commanded in a deep voice. "Go and burn it all."

Flames brightening in the hollows of their eyes, the beasts howled excitedly. Cerberus's troops then bound out of sight. The demon looked back out at the werewolf kingdom in the distance. He sniffed, his eyes narrowing. He knew that River was still alive. The witch and his warriors might have failed, but he would not.

"I'm coming for you 'Moon Blest'."

Gazing out the window of her bedroom in Swift Wind's pack house, River crossed her arms. A worried frown was permanently etched on her features. The moon had risen and as she observed it journey through the sky, it became encased by the earth's shadow. A deep red shade colored the moon's surface as it froze in place from Agatha's curse of night.

It's begun, she said to Crystal. If Malinda's vision was correct, then Cerberus was already walking the mortal realm.

We will defeat him, spoke Adrian's determined voice through their link.

River's shoulders sagged as her mate wrapped his arms around her. She leaned back, the heaviness in her heart lifting somewhat as her sights remained skyward.

"I thought you were in my father's office," River observed.

Adrian shrugged. "I figured you needed me more."

A faint smile traced her lips. He couldn't be more correct. River did need him.

"I'm glad you came."

For a few precious moments, there was a comfortable peace. Adrian suddenly stiffened. His arms unconsciously tightened around his mate.

River twisted her head to try to peer at his face. "What's wrong?"

The prince didn't answer right away. "Shadow Claw is under attack. Cerberus is making his first move."

River gently pulled out of his grasp to gaze at his darkened eyes. She didn't need to say anything. They both knew that the battle for all of their fates had just begun.

"When do we leave?" the she-wolf questioned.

Every muscle in her body tingled with anticipation. Her heart was already increasing speed. River knew for over two years that this day would come. Now that it had, she wanted to face her demon before she lost her nerve.

"We're not going to Shadow Claw," Adrian answered firmly.

River blinked, her body freezing in place for several seconds as she just stared at him. Once her brain was able to process his words, her hands clenched and her eyes flashed.

"What do you mean we're not going? Adrian, you can't stop me from facing him. This is my destiny. You know that."

Adrian reached out and rubbed the outside of her arms. "I know," he confirmed with a frown. "And I promised you that I would be beside you. I'm not trying to stop you from facing Cerberus, River, but we have to keep in mind that he has had centuries to plan this."

Her eyes narrowed, her brows lowering to a point. Tilting her head, River waited for her mate to explain.

"Father and I have consulted with our top wolves as well as Pavel and the witches. We don't think that Cerberus will come right for you. He knows you are his weakness. These last few attacks and even Agatha's manipulations have been aimed at trying to harm you. The last thing I'm going to do is give that monster what he wants. All his plans have failed. Instead, he's going to lure you to him, so that he has the advantage. That's why we're not going to face his army...yet. Our allies are on their way to deal with this threat. You and I are going to bring Cerberus to us."

River shook her head. "That won't work. He's been around since the beginning of time. I doubt that he is going to fall into any trap that we set."

"I wouldn't be so sure of that," Adrian replied with a gleam that River was beginning to know too well. "His arrival has already been foreseen."

Hands clutching the sheets on her bed, River groaned as her head rocked back and forth on her pillow. Before her eyes, wafts of steam rose up from the ground. They billowed like earthbound clouds, distorting her vision of the surrounding area. The air was hot and humid like a sauna. It was difficult to breathe in her wolf form. Fierce growls sounded, alerting her to the presence of their enemy. River cautiously strode forward through the puddles of water covering the grass. A few shadows flittered by, but nothing appeared. River called out through her pack's mind-link. There was no answer.

Making her way to the edge of the fog, River's feet froze. She was standing on a peninsula between a cluster of three lakes. The she-wolf knew the area from the maps and photos that her father had shown her. This was the Blue Lake Pack. It was the very place where the final stand with Cerberus was to take place.

Are we having a vision? she asked Crystal. River hoped not, something told her that things were not going as her mate had planned.

It could be a dream, Crystal replied, though she didn't sound convinced.

She continued to walk along, encountering nothing other than the swirling mist. Passing by some trees, River came to the end of the peninsula. Neither of them could believe what was before their eyes.

River's father lay on the wet ground. Blood soaked his body, coloring the water surrounding him. Even without stepping closer, River knew that he was dead. Beside him, scattered across the ground were at least a dozen more corpses of her fellow pack members. River's paws shook and her breath caught in her throat as she spotted Amanda and her brothers among the fallen. Forty yards away, a single black wolf was battling a massive hellhound with three blazing armored heads.

River! Get out of here! Adrian shouted to her through their bond.

Blood was running from his left shoulder down his leg. He didn't dare turn to peer at her. Leaping out of the way, he used all of his strength to dodge one of Cerberus's heads and aim for the creature's throat. The others turned to intercept him. Cole cried out as his body dropped to the ground with a thud.

Crystal took off with every ounce of speed that she possessed towards her mate, but the gleam in Cerberus's eyes when he lifted his center head told her that she would be too late. His sights never leaving her, Cerberus's two outer heads opened their mouths with bursts of flames aimed at her injured mate. River screamed with a pain that she had never felt in all her life.

The images around her suddenly froze. A light appeared on the water behind the battle. As it dimmed, the image of a woman with long pale hair like moon light was visible. She strolled across the water and came to a halt beside the towering demon. Holding her open palm below her lips, the woman blew a long breath. Cerberus's body dissolved into dust, as did those of Adrian and her fallen pack members.

River shifted back into her human form with wide eyes. "Who are you?"

Directing her gaze upon the she-wolf, the woman smiled faintly. "You already know the answer, River."

The Moon Goddess! Crystal gasped in River's mind. Mouth moving wordlessly, she couldn't seem to speak. She could only watch as the goddess glided closer and interlaced her fingers.

"There isn't much time," she said urgently. "The longer Cerberus walks under the power of the Blood Moon, the stronger he becomes. These events here have not yet come to pass, but…" the goddess paused. "If you do not take action, then this is the future you will face."

No! That couldn't be right. If what the goddess was saying was true, then their plan to stop Cerberus was destined to fail. River couldn't stand by and allow that to happen. She had to change this course.

"What should I do? How do I save my family?"

"You must take the fight to him," the goddess instructed. Her image faded momentarily before returning. "Follow the river. Use the power inside you." The goddess's form dulled again. "Hurry!"

River bolted upright in her bed. Gripping the front of her nightgown, she sucked in rapid gasps of air. Glancing to the side, the she-wolf peered over at her sleeping mate. Watching his chest slowly rise with each deep even breath, she sighed. Slipping out from beneath the covers, River went into the bathroom and closed the door. Leaning against the far wall she slid down the tiles. Closing her eyes, River fought back tears. A sob escaped her lips. Covering her mouth with both her hands, she curled up into the fetal position and squeezed her eyes closed tighter still. Tears stained her cheeks as she quietly cried until there were no more left within her.

Lying on the cold floor, she heard her wolf calling out in her mind.

We can still save them, remember? You have to get up, Crystal urged. *It's time to fight.*

You're right, River told her, wiping the moisture away. Adrian and her family were alive and it was up to her to protect them. They had all been defending her for long enough.

Slowly opening the door, River peered out into the bedroom. The bedside clock showed one o'clock in the morning and Adrian was luckily still asleep. Zipping into her walk-in closet, River dressed for battle. If the Moon Goddess wanted her to take the fight to Cerberus, then she would. Crossing the carpet, River paused at the foot of her bed. Part of her wanted to wake her mate. However, Crystal agreed that it would only hinder their mission.

Adrian was stubborn. Since a witch foresaw Cerberus arriving in Blue Lake like they planned, he believed that everything would work out. River tried to tell him otherwise. Something told her right away that such a plan would fail, but he wouldn't listen to her. The goddess had revealed to her the *result* of the battle. Even if River could convince him to change his strategy, they would be wasting valuable time.

He will come find us, Crystal assured her. *Our bond is complete now. Wherever we go, he will follow.*

River swore that she could hear a smirk in her wolf's voice. *You sound certain of that.*

I am.

263

Nodding to herself, River snuck into the hall and made her way to her father's office. Moving towards the desk, she spread out the maps and photos that they had been using for their plans. River sorted through them until she found the one with a close-up of Shadow Claw.

What are we doing in here? Crystal asked.

River studied the area where Cerberus's hellhounds were currently attacking. Her finger tapped a blue line running through the forest.

Following the river, she replied.

Clever.

Shadow Claw's warriors had pulled back to meet up with the kingdom's reinforcements a few hours ago. The Anignah River would serve as the new battlefront. During this time of year, much of the riverbank was exposed. The water was shallow enough for wolves to easily cross, but would prove to be an obstacle for the hellhounds. For a creature of fire, water was a weakness.

"Okay," she muttered to herself. "This is where Alpha Jack and the others will be."

Tracing the blue line upriver, she followed the map. Her eyes narrowed and her hand came to a stop at a large water source.

Lake Orontein, River read to herself.

Do you think that this is what the Goddess was referring to?

I'm not sure, River admitted. *But there is a dam there. If we break it...*

Not only would the force of the water itself be a weapon against the hellhounds, it could give River the advantage she desperately needed to win this war. Scanning the rest of the map, she pressed her lips into a thin line.

What do you think, Crystal?

Her wolf was quiet for a moment. *Let's go for it,* she said confidently.

Crossing the room, River paused halfway to the door. Twisting around, she gazed at the open map left on the table. Moving back towards Nick's desk, River picked up a pen. She then circled the lake and drew an arrow along the river's path. When the others discovered her disappearance, they would need some clue as to where she went.

I'll see you on the battlefield, love.

Not wishing to delay any longer, River quietly made her way out of the pack house. She jogged towards the tree line, not wanting to let Crystal take control until they were concealed by the trees.

"Where do you think you're going?" questioned Roxy as she stepped out of the shadows.

River jumped, quickly stepping back.

"Roxy? What are you doing out here at this hour?" River returned in a hushed voice.

The she-wolf scoffed. "Seriously? Cerberus commenced with his attack. I didn't really think that you would agree to sit back and wait like your mate wanted." A smirk found it's way on her lips. "I know you better than that, River. I'm also not about to let you take on that demon by yourself." Roxy crossed her arms as Dimitri came to stand by the wolf's side. "Didn't that scroll say that you would need help from your allies?"

River felt the corners of her lips pull back. "I suppose it's a good thing that the two of you are getting along better." Her gaze darted between the pair. "Ready to face the fire?"

The she-wolf swore that their eyes glowed simultaneously.

"Bring it on," Roxy encouraged confidently.

Sunlight gleamed on the vast surface Lake Orontein spread out in the distance. Two wolves and a vampire stood on the edge of a hill studying the structure holding the water at bay. Mounds of rock and gravel spanned both sides of the walkway at the dam's crest. As a standard earth-filled dam, the structure was unmanned and unguarded.

"Let's go," River told her comrades, shifting back into her human form as she traveled the rest of the way down the hill.

Roxy and Dimitri followed behind, scanning the area for their enemy. There didn't seem to be any hellhounds in the area.

"It looks like we beat them here," Roxy observed as they made their way out into the middle of the dam. The fiery wolf leaned forward, gazing down into the serene waves. "Now what?"

River inhaled deeply and exhaled with a short hiss. Her eyes narrow as they traveled over the surface of the structure. Face scrunching up, she lightly cupped her chin.

"What did the scroll say?" she mumbled to herself.

Dimitri and Roxy glanced quietly at each other.

River didn't notice as she frowned. "Nature itself shall obey her whim..." Lifting her head, River peered at her companions. "I already control water and wind. What if there's more? Nature itself is supposed to obey me, right? What if I can manipulate earth as well?"

Roxy shifted her weight to the side. "I guess it's possible. You are still gaining new powers."

"What's your plan?" Dimitri asked, watching the she-wolves.

River straightened her shoulders. "I'm going to break the dam. The water will flood the forest where the hellhounds are attacking, wiping out Cerberus's forces. He shouldn't be able to raise a new army quickly enough to overwhelm us."

"What about our own warriors?"

"Don't worry," River told him confidently. "I'm not going to let anything happen to our people. This surprise is just for the fire demons."

The vampire didn't look convinced, though he kept his doubts to himself. No matter what, this battle would be hard fought and even harder won. His gaze shifted to his mate.

Roxy squirmed under his intense stare.

"What?" she questioned self-confidently.

"You better hold on to me," Dimitri instructed.

Her brows lifted as she watched the vampire. "What?"

"River's going to destroy the dam. She can walk on water, but you can't," he replied logically. "I can levitate us both easily."

Eyes narrowing, Roxy didn't give in. "I can take care of myself. Just because you saved me once doesn't mean that you can start ordering me around. We're not officially mated, Dimitri."

A glimmer flashed in his pale eyes. A smirk pulled at the corner of his mouth. "Not *officially*," he agreed stepping closer towards her. Holding out his arms the vampire told her, "Bridal style or piggy back? It's your choice, my little wolf."

Dimitri would have been satisfied with simply holding her hand, but Roxy's constant need to battle him made her mate want to tease her more. Vampires hated boring things. This wolf was far from mundane.

Mouth gaping, Roxy's eyes flashed at the same time that her cheeks reddened.

Go on, Rose encouraged. *We both know you want to.*

I do not, Roxy lied.

Sure, her wolf chuckled. *He is right though. We don't have any other way to ride the flow downstream. Not unless you want to run along the shore.*

Lips pressing into a line, Roxy strode behind the vampire and allowed him to pick her up. Wrapping her arms loosely about his neck she leaned in close to his ear.

"Don't be getting any ideas. Okay?"

A large grin shone on his normally somber face. Since meeting his mate, he had gotten much livelier. "No promises," he teased before shifting his gaze to River. "We're ready."

River nodded in return. Exhaling with a huff, she peered down at the earthen embankment below her feet. Her stomach churned, but she did her best to ignore it. Hopefully, her theory would prove to be correct. Otherwise, River wasn't sure how she would be completing this task. Destroying a dam wasn't as simple as it appeared. Holding out her hands, the she-wolf closed her eyes.

We can do this, she said to herself.

As with learning her skills of wind and water, it took a lot of concentration to unlock the potential of a new element. River imagined connecting with every pebble beneath her feet, right down to the tiniest molecule. Flexing her fingers, she felt them stretch and recoil with the movements of her hands. A smile appeared across her lips.

"I feel it," she told the others. "I can do it. I can control earth."

"Whoa!" Roxy exclaimed. "That is so cool."

"Vampires have powers too, you know," muttered Dimitri.

The women smirked, yet didn't add anything.

"Here we go," River declared.

Holding out her palms once more, she focused on the stones. Summoning her energy around her, River pushed forward with all of the force that she could muster. The ground below creaked, bowing outward from the lake. River pulled her hands back to her chest and repeated the motion. The stone under her suddenly slipped away. Letting out a small shriek, River almost fell with the stone until a strong hand gripped her upper arm.

Dimitri rose up several more feet out of harm's way as the weight of the water nudged against the lake side of the dam.

While the vampire kept her aloft, River used her power over water to slam its mass into the crumbling dam. The force of the liquid tore apart the rest of the stone. Dropping fifty feet on the other side, the angry waves broke loose to follow the path of the river.

"Let's go," River called, dropping down on top of the swell to surf her flood.

Jack had never seen anything like the chaos ensuing around him. The joint forces of werewolves, witches and vampires were barely holding the line across the riverbank.

Werewolves were in the front, acting as the main foot soldiers while a thin row of spellcasters created shields blocking the opposite bank. The forcefields could not hold back the sheer volume of advisories. They did however, help to lessen the number of hounds attacking. Having the least number of forces, the vampires were spread among the wolves' ranks. Their superior speed and powers made them valuable assets in defeating any foe who tried to slip through the line.

Thus far, their strategy seemed to be working. Jack just wasn't sure how much longer they would be able to hold out. A seemingly never-ending swarm of hellhounds rushed at the warriors continuously. His men were getting tired. They all were. Without aid, the line would eventually break and be overrun by the fire beasts.

A sound like thunder reached the wolf's ears. The stones of the riverbed trembled, and the water flowing around them gurgled, quickly rising with each second.

What the...? Jack muttered to Ace.

The river's flow picked up speed. When white frothy swells appeared upstream, Jack's gaze widened.

"Get out of the water," he yelled to his allies while ordering his warriors to fall back through the pack's mind-link. There wasn't a moment to lose.

Huge waves crashed down the riverbend. When the water threatened to spill over into the forest, it strangely folded in upon itself and twisted back to continue tracing the path of the stream. The thunder of the crashing water grew increasingly louder, but the hellhounds paid it no mind at first. They persisted their attack, following after the retreating warriors as the line broke. The ground on the far side of the riverbank began to rumble. Breaking free of the ground, a tall cliff shot upwards, cutting off the hellhound's strike as it carried the allies a good thirty feet into the air.

Heart racing, the old wolf could not believe his eye. A great flood crashed into Cerberus's army, wiping them out as it cleansed the forest below them. Poofs of ash fluttering into the air were the sole remainders of the demon dog's forces.

"What's going on?" questioned Isaiah, Blackwood's Alpha, as he shifted into his human form.

Morphing back as well, Jack shook his head. "I don't know. Raven?" he asked, glancing at the witch who never seemed to leave his side.

"The 'Moon Blest' has arrived," she told them simply.

"Who?" the men inquired at the same time.

In answer, Raven gracefully lifted a hand to point out at the water.

Striding across the surface was a beautiful woman with flowing blonde hair. Behind her was a black-haired she-wolf being carried by a blond vampire. The liquid rose up with a flick of her wrist as she came to stand on the cliff in front of the warriors.

"R-River?" Jack stuttered with dismay.

"Hello again, Alpha Jack," she greeted calmly.

"What are you doing here?"

"From the looks of it," she replied with a small smile, "saving you."

"Alright," Roxy demanded, cracking her knuckles. "Where is he? Where's Cerberus hiding?"

Isaiah stepped forward, offering the future queen luna a bow. "We don't know. His minions are the only ones we've seen so far."

"This flood would not have reached him," Raven enlightened. Closing her eyes, she held out a hand. Slowly moving her palm back and forth, her head tilted to one side then the other in sync with her hand. "He's by a group of outcroppings to the northwest."

"We better hurry," River said to Roxy and Dimitri. "He won't be there for much longer."

"Wait," Jack said moving towards her. "You can't be thinking of taking on Cerberus by yourselves! He's the King of Hellhounds. Let us handle this battle, Princess."

Roxy scoffed. "Like we don't already know all about Cerberus. Leave the demon to us."

"His army is going to start respawning at any moment," River observed. Swiping a hand over the flowing river, she settled the receding waves. "We best get moving."

A howl suddenly pierced the forest with its intense call. A smile appeared on River's face.

"Just in time," she whispered. "The reinforcements have arrived." The she-wolf glanced at their allies gathering near her. "This will be our one chance to defeat Cerberus before he regains his strength and destroys our world. I'm the only one who can land a killing blow, but I can't do that alone."

Jack and Isaiah exchanged a glance. The two wolves nodded.

"What do you need from us?"

"A clear path," River told them. "Can you keep his hounds off my tail long enough for me to reach him?"

"Consider it done," the Blackwood Alpha told her.

Nodding her thanks, River gazed up at the blood red moon. *We're coming for you, Cerberus.* Shifting into her blue wolf, Crystal lifted her head to release a mighty howl. In the distance, she could hear Adrian answer.

He's getting close, Crystal observed happily.

Yes, he is. Looking at Roxy's black wolf, River said, *Let's go.*

The two she-wolves leapt down from the cliff and charged across the expanding banks of the river. The sound of an army following close behind sounded in the moon blest's ears. Cerberus wasn't going to escape them. River wouldn't let him.

She raced into the damp forest without slowing her stride. From the shadows, a new army of hellhounds was beginning to emerge. The creatures rose up out of the darkness in front of her. River took a deep breath and barked, unleashing her sonic blast. The hounds were thrown into the trees without mercy. Before they could fully rise, Roxy and Dimitri pounced, tearing them apart as they had practiced in Velladona.

Just as quickly, the trio vanished from sight, racing deeper into the woods. The terrain steadily inclined the closer they ventured to the area that Raven sensed Cerberus. Pools of darkness materialized in front of River. Pausing on the next level space, she braced herself for the hellhounds attack. It would be better to defeat them face to face now than to have them gather for an ambush once she met her true objective.

Watching the beast rise up from the shadows, River opened her mouth to unleash her first attack. A flash to her right drew her attention as another hound charged at her side, ramming her hard. River's body slammed into the burned trunk of a tree with great force. She could make out Roxy and Dimitri fighting their way towards her as three more demons blocked their path. Seeing her first set of adversaries closing in, River blasted them with her ice. She rose to her feet and spun about, aiming to strike the hound who managed to land a blow.

A pale hand protruding from the front of the beast's chest had her withholding her attack. An arm wrapped around the hound's neck from behind as a vampire finished off the creature. As the corpse turned to ash, Pavel was revealed.

River's tail wagged happily. Deeper in the woods, she spotted her father's wolf along with a group of warriors helping Roxy and Dimitri.

"We got your message," the vampire said gazing about. "Don't worry. Malinda had Adrian take a different path with Blake. He'll meet you soon."

River nodded. As much as she wanted to better explain her actions, and thank everyone for coming so quickly to her aid, every moment counted. Linking Roxy, she dashed forward once again, this time with a few additional allies.

The landscape continued to rise upwards as River led the way to Cerberus. Here and there she used her ice to extinguish the burning wilderness hindering their journey. At times the smoke grew dangerously thick. In a flash, Pavel and Dimitri dispelled the nuisance with a power she didn't even know that they possessed.

I'm glad they're on our side, River quipped to Roxy.

She swore that the other she-wolf puffed out her chest proudly with a smile before proceeding.

When the smoldering tree line thinned out, River spotted a large rock outcropping in the mountainside. The ground was burned to nothing but stone and dirt. Whisps of orange and red flames simmered in the few ashen timber still laying upon the earthen floor. Standing on the peak of the boulders was the King of Hellhounds, himself.

River growled deep in her throat.

He's going down, Crystal declared confidently.

Sweeping a line of fire to block his enemies' path, Cerberus summoned a group of his warriors. A grin appeared on two of his faces.

We need to stop him before he gets away! the she-wolf announced through her pack-link.

Go, Nick instructed. *We'll hold his minions off. Roxy, back her up.*

Right, they answered simultaneously.

Both sides commenced at the same time. The warriors moved first, blocking the hellhound's path to River and Roxy, but there were too many to evade them all at once. Knowing what his mate was about to do, Dimitri appeared by Roxy's side, using his power to knock back the incoming horde.

River go! she encouraged. *We'll hold them off.*

The black and red wolf then charged forward, leaping up to sink her teeth into one of the dog's necks. She held nothing back. Ripping free, Roxy spun around, engaging her next foe before the first had even finished turning to ash.

Sliding through the opening, River raced as fast as she could towards the demon in command. The sooner she destroyed their king, then the quicker his fire army would return to the underworld. Arriving at the base of a rocky outcropping, River peered up at the beast leering at her. The she-wolf's upper lip pulled back with a snarl. He wasn't going to get away. She would make sure of that.

Eyes of flames narrowing dangerously, Cerberus leaned out over the edge of the cliff to unleash a wave of fire.

River dodged the blast, jumping up onto a nearby ledge before striking Cerberus with her own bolt of ice. Her attack froze his right head instantly. Pushing off the ground with all her strength, River leapt towards her foe. She was quick, but not nearly enough.

Cerberus twisted, moving his disabled head out of the way to give the center one the perfect line of sight to the incoming she-wolf.

Crystal cussed in River's mind. Acting on instinct, the blue wolf shot a blast of ice at the hellhound, meeting the flames he launched at her just in time. Still, her counterattack wasn't going to save her from landing right in Cerberus awaiting claws.

A black form dashed in from the right side of the cliff. Jumping onto Cerberus's back, Adrian slashed the beast down the side of his face. He quickly retreated as the frozen head broke free of his prison and the demon twisted to try and bite him in half.

As River stood by Adrian's side, the same strange energy she felt before surged through her. Her body felt lighter, stronger. A smile pulled at the corner of her mouth.

Glad you could join us, Crystal purred, keeping her eyes on the beast growling at them.

We'll discuss this later, Cole returned crossly, trying not to grin in return. He dug his claws into the rock, unable to deny the increase in power flowing through him.

It's our bond, Crystal clarified, sensing Adrian's unease with his sudden increase in strength.

There wasn't time to discuss anything further. Three sets of blazing eyes glared at the pair. Mouths opening with mixed growls, Cerberus blasted his foes once again.

River put up a shield of air in front of them, blocking the attack as her whirlwind sucked the oxygen out of his flames.

Sneaking up from the hound's flank, Blake revealed his teeth, ready to strike.

Having three heads gave the demon a great advantage: he didn't have blind spots. Once Blake moved closer, Cerberus swung his tail. A wall of ice appeared dampening the impact as Blake was hit in the side and sent flying backwards. His body slid across the rock and dropped out of sight over the edge.

No! Adrian shouted, racing towards his brother.

Laughing, Cerberus charged at them, keeping the prince from going to his brother's aid.

I'm ok, Blake said in Adrian's mind.

Eyes widening, the wolf peered around the battlefield while River leapt in front of him and created a ring of water. Jaw dropping, he watched as Blake appeared hovering above the ledge. Soon after, Dimitri joined him along with Roxy. The vampire lifted them onto the top of the rock before lowering his hands.

The calvary is here! Roxy announced proudly.

Cerberus peered at the new arrivals with irritation.

"Enough," he snapped, the line of fire on his back brightening. "No more interruptions. The 'Moon Blest' is mine!"

Pounding a mighty paw on the ground, Cerberus summoned his own ring. The flames encased the base of the outcropping, cutting off anyone else from getting close and securing his current enemies inside. None of them would be escaping him.

"You fleas aren't going anywhere," the demon's right head told them with a smirk.

"Who wants to die first?" his left questioned.

"You're the one who's going to die," Dimitri voiced for the wolves.

Cerberus turned his gaze to lock on the vampire. It didn't need to be said that he had chosen his first target. Ignoring River and the first prince, the King of Hellhounds raced across the rocks, leaping on top of some towering boulders to quickly close the distance between him and his foe. Roxy charged forward first, but the beast swatted her out of his way with the back of his paw.

Dimitri's gaze flashed red. Rising into the air, he suddenly appeared in front of the right head. Pulling a knife from his belt, the vampire thrust his enchanted weapon into Cerberus's one eye, causing black blood to spew from the wound. A set of jaws snapped closed around him, severing Dimitri's left leg below the knee.

Roxy released a pained howl as she charged at the beast.

Blake knocked her out of the way, saving her from meeting the same fate from the left head.

The look of glee on Cerberus's face didn't last long. The center head shook himself with jerky movements. His jaw slowly pulled apart, revealing Dimitri encased in his glowing aura.

Face twisted with a scowl, the vampire pulled his fists apart.

Cerberus's lower jaw snapped, dropping completely open. He reared back, his other heads howling in pain.

Moving before the beast could heal himself, the vampire fell to the ground. Roxy was by his side instantly, lowering herself just enough that he could climb on her back and dart away. Dimitri leaned against her soft fur with a smile.

"You're not getting rid of me that easily," he muttered with a huff.

Roxy whimpered in return. Glancing back at his injured leg.

Her mate threaded his fingers in her fur. "It will grow back," Dimitri assured her. "I just need a little time to heal."

While Roxy carried her mate to a safer distance, River and Adrian attacked Cerberus from his other side. Dimitri's blade was still implanted in the beast's eye, but his center head had already healed completely. River used her wind power to leap onto the hound's back. She hit him repeatedly with bolts of ice while Adrian clawed his front leg and side.

Blake moved in from the other side, striking Cerberus's other front leg at the same time.

Roaring, Cerberus spun in a circle, knocking back his opponents.

"Your attacks are useless!" he informed them with a cold laugh. "I've had enough of this game."

Pounding his paws on the ground, rings of fire lashed out.

River managed to extinguish the first few quickly enough to reach her comrades' side. Shifting back into a human, she put up an ice barrier.

"He's too strong!" River said, her eyes wide with concern. *I don't think I can defeat him.*

Adrian, Roxy and Blake morphed back as well.

"It's not over yet," her mate told her. "How's Dimitri?"

"I'm good to go," the vampire answered, rising to his feet as he stretched out his regrown leg.

"How are we going to take out *that?*" Roxy asked with a frown.

Adrian glanced at his mate as she held off Cerberus's incoming fire attacks. Sweat glistened on her made her look frighteningly pale as her limbs started to shake. She was getting worn out from the constant use of her powers. If they didn't do something quickly, she wouldn't have the energy to land a killing blow.

"Too bad your new ability won't do much good against fire," Roxy said to River as she crossed her arms. "What if I distract him while you blast him with ice again?"

"We tried that already," River pointed out. "I have to hit his heart, but his armor is blocking all of my attacks."

"What new power?" Adrian questioned watching the two she-wolves.

"Oh yeah," Roxy murmured, recalling that only she and Dimitri knew about it. "River can control earth now, too."

The prince's brows lifted thoughtfully. "Are you talking about just dirt, or can you move rocks too, Sweetheart?"

Keeping her gaze on the ice, River shook her head. "I can move rocks, but I just gained this power, so it takes a lot of time and concentration to do anything. That's why I haven't used it in this battle."

Adrian came to stand by her side. "What if we bought you some time? Could you say, control those huge boulders on the other side of the cliff?"

River's nose scrunched up as she frowned. "I think so."

The wolf nodded. Moving forward, he wrapped an arm around River's waist and leaned down with a smile.

I better recharge your powers, he teased.

River blushed, unable to reply as he kissed her. She could feel some of Adrian's strength seeping into her. The weariness of her limbs faded and her aura surrounded her with a soft glow for a few seconds.

Dimitri glanced at Roxy, but she refused to meet his eyes.

Blake scratched the back of his head with a sigh. "If you two are going to make out, then I'm going to wait outside with the demon dog."

Turning back towards the others, Adrian grinned. "All right, then here's the plan…"

Outside the dome of ice, Cerberus continued his relentless barrage of flames. His claws didn't seem to do any damage to the frozen sphere, leaving him to rely on his elemental ability. Not that the hound minded. He had a liking for burning his enemies.

Suddenly, the ice shifted into a ball of water. The new liquid erupted into a cloud of steam as his blaze obliterated it. Cerberus stiffened, his heads twisting from side to side as they sought out River and her wolves. Somehow, they had vanished. A searing pain cut into his hip. Cerberus lashed out with his tail and spun around to face his foes.

Adrian, Blake, Roxy and Dimitri kept up a constant flow of attacks striking from all sides. They couldn't give Cerberus a moment to relax, or he might realize that his greatest foe wasn't currently in the fight.

Hiding behind a rock, River had her hands out in front of her while she focused on three massive boulders on the other side of the outcropping. Moving one with her untrained ability would be difficult. Moving all three would be next to impossible.

Don't think like that, Crystal scolded in her mind. *Controlling the elementals is basically the same. Look at the way that you took out the dam. Get rid of your doubt. We can do this!*

River pressed her lips together tightly and nodded to herself. As usual, her wolf was right. Trying again, River concentrated on the large stones. Remembering how she moved the dam, she let her powers flow. The boulders slowly lifted into the air. Not allowing herself to celebrate too soon, River rose and followed as she set the rocks down and pushed them forward, using their weight to give them a massive amount of momentum.

Snapping his jaws at the fleas nipping at his feet, Cerberus growled. When were they going to acknowledge their defeat and just die already? It occurred to him that he hadn't been blasted by the chill of ice for a little while. Gazing around, the hound looked for River, but didn't see her. Where was the 'Moon Blest'? She couldn't have gotten away! He wouldn't allow it. Twisted around, Cerberus went to dive off the rocks when three massive stones crashed into him. He was knocked back and thrown onto his side by the force. Before he could recover, the boulders rolled on top of him. Cerberus thrashed about, but the stones wouldn't move. Then he saw her.

Body glowing faintly, River appeared with her arms held out before her. The she-wolf said nothing as she focused on the rocks pinning Cerberus in place.

"I will destroy you!" he shouted, clawing at the ground.

Roxy, Adrian, and Blake moved back in. Each of them striking one of his heads as Dimitri used his powers to take over the rocky prison.

River shifted back into her wolf and sped towards the hellhound. She didn't know how long Adrian's plan would last. Hopefully, it would be long enough for her to accomplish her task. With each head under attack, River was free to target the demon's armor. She raced to the first neck, using the coldest, densest freeze she had ever created to encase the metal. River then used all of her strength to smash it to pieces. One by one, she traveled over Cerberus, destroying the rings of steel holding his chest plate in place.

The demon's aura suddenly lashed out, throwing them all back across the cliff. The boulders holding Cerberus in place dissolved to dust and the armor covering him fell to the ground as he once more rose to his feet. Growling deeply, Cerberus summoned a ring of flames around River and himself, cutting the others off.

"It's time for you to die," the king stated as he glared at the pale blue wolf.

That was our line, Crystal sneered back, wishing that this time he could have heard her words.

The way his gaze narrowed dangerously made her wonder if he hadn't.

River and Cerberus charged at each other at the same time. Unable to do a thing, her mate watched through the towering dancing flames. Increasing her speed, River darted forward, zig-zagging her foe's flames and leaping into the air. She pinged back and forth between Cerberus's outside heads like a pinball, each strike backed with all the strength she could muster. Aiming for the center head, River then hit the demon under his jaw. When Cerberus's head snapped back, River kicked off his flesh, spinning about to launch a huge spear of ice straight into his chest.

A piercing roar echoed through the mountainside. Flames blasting momentarily into the air, the ring of fire surrounding Cerberus vanished. The blazes of his eyes dimmed and faded as he dropped to the ground and lay on his side.

River leapt back, watching the creature intently for any sign of movement. The others moved forward to stand by her side as they gazed at the mighty hellhound. Then, just as River had seen in her dream with the Moon Goddess, Cerberus's body turned to ash and drifted off with the wind. Below, his army disappeared as they were pulled back to the underworld. Returning to her human form, River's gaze shifted upwards at the Blood Moon. A smile stretched across her face as the red faded and the glowing orb once again slowly began to travel across the sky.

"You did it," Adrian yelled, picking her up and swinging her around in a circle.

Laughing, River peered lovingly into his eyes. "No," she corrected, her eyes quickly darting to Roxy, Dimitri and Blake. "We did it."

"That's right," Roxy agreed, dashing forward to embrace the couple.

Smiling brightly, Blake joined them while Dimitri crossed his arms, hovering on the edge of the gathering. Fighting a smirk, his mate held a hand out towards him.

"Just come here already," she encouraged.

Eyes narrowing, the vampire released an exasperated sigh. Slowly, he closed the remaining distance. Once he was within reach, Roxy yanked him the rest of the way to join in the group hug. They all remained like that for a moment before stepping back.

Images of her family lying lifeless in the damp grass of Blue Lake flashed in River's mind. Was everyone all right? Was she able to save them from the fate which the goddess had shown?

Our family, she whispered urgently to Crystal.

Turning about, the she-wolf dashed towards the edge of the cliff and quickly descended from the direction she came.

Nick? she called out through the link. *Nick? Father?*

"Over here," he shouted, waving an arm.

River appeared before him in an instant and threw her arms around his neck. "I'm so glad you're alright! I feared the worst," she sobbed in his ear.

The alpha laughed, holding her tightly. "I do believe that I should be the one saying such things. After all, you were the one battling Cerberus. I'm so proud of you, River." Lifting his gaze to take in the others making their way towards them, Nick's smile grew. "I'm proud of all of you."

"Yes, well done," Pavel praised, watching as Dimitri draped his arm across Roxy's shoulders. "Though we have not come out of this battle unscathed, there is still much to celebrate. Because of all of you, a great darkness has been defeated."

Once Roxy released her father, Adrian pulled his mate to his side. The adrenalin from battle was still pumping through his veins and his wolf wanted his other half close to his side.

"I agree," the prince declared glancing at River with a wide grin. "There is much to celebrate, for all of us. This victory was possible due to the strength and courage of our warriors and our allies. I see a great future for us, together."

"I'll second that!" Roxy yipped, causing the others to laugh.

This fight had shown her just how important it was to hold on to those you cared for. She still didn't understand why the goddess had granted her a vampire for a mate, but this fiery wolf wasn't going to let go of him for anything.

Chapter 17

"Come on, Roxy, hold still," Yvette groaned for perhaps the tenth time.

Slouching in her chair, the black-haired she-wolf hunched her shoulders and crossed her arms over her chest.

"You know that I'm not the girly type," Roxy muttered.

"It won't kill you for one day," Amanda chuckled as the two women set about fixing her hair.

Pressing her lips together, the she-wolf said nothing more. Her mother and aunt quickly went to work, twisting Roxy's red-streaked mane into an elegant knot. Pinning her hair in place, they curled the ends, leaving some of the long strands to caress her neck, then they touched up the light make-up that she had already applied.

"All done," Yvette finally gushed, some twenty minutes later. Stepping back, the two women studied their handiwork. "You look so beautiful."

"I agree," Amanda added, "Stunning."

Groaning, Roxy stood and gazed at her reflection in the mirror as both women left to finish getting dressed. The floor-length red gown highlighted the crimson in her hair perfectly. Her mother and aunt kept everything simple, while accenting her best features. If only they would let her go barefoot. Her gaze subconsciously shifted darkly to the stilettos sitting in a corner.

"Wow," exclaimed a voice from behind her. "You look incredible."

Roxy's gaze shifted to peer at River's reflection in the mirror. A smile brightened her face as she spun around to greet her cousin as she entered from an adjoining door.

"Me?" she refuted, shaking her head so forcefully that one of the pins pinged onto the floor. Ignoring both the noises of disapproval from her mother and the fact that River was trying to secure her earrings, Roxy leapt forward to lock her in a tight embrace. "You are the beautiful one. I'm so happy for you, River."

Leaning back, she took in River's whole appearance. Thin spaghetti straps held up the elegantly beaded bodice of her ivory gown. It hugged her upper body perfectly until reaching just below her hips where it flared out slightly as it fell to the ground.

"Perfect," Roxy whispered, her eyes showing the distinct shimmer of tears. "I can't believe that you're going to be Queen Luna after today."

River lifted her shoulders, offering her cousin a tentative smile. "That makes two of us."

Moisture slickened her palms as the she-wolf's heart started to hammer the inside of her chest. Her gaze connected with her reflection. River hardly recognized the elegant woman peering back at her with uneasy eyes.

This is going way too fast, she told Crystal for not the first time.

Not a month ago, she was preparing to battle Cerberus. His appearance in the mortal realm had been as violent and unexpected as a malevolent storm. Only with the help of her friends and family was their greatest enemy banished back to the underworld. Brave warriors were lost, their sacrifices mourned by all the allied packs, clans and covens. A frown etched River's brow as her thoughts turned more somber. Shadow Claw's Pack was nearly wiped out during the invasion. Yet, through the chaos, Adrian had remained a pillar of strength. Warriors from each pack were assisting with Shadow Claw's protection as new members were chosen and trained. Many residents of the Free Lands were seeking to join the packs as well for protection after the hell hounds' rampage. River had a feeling that in time, the Free Lands would be at least in part, if not completely, absorbed into the seven packs of the kingdom.

In the next few weeks, Alpha Trials would begin for Shadow Claw. The packs leading members had been killed during the attack, and their children were far too young to hold the position. In the meantime, Adrian was lending them his gamma to help rebuild and maintain order. There was much to be done. River knew that she couldn't possibly leave Adrian's side, even if she wanted to, she just hoped that she would be up to the task of ruling an entire kingdom along with her mate. And then there was still Cerberus to consider.

What is he planning next?

Everything is going to be fine, reassured a deep male voice in her mind.

Blinking several times, River's head jerked up. Looking around the space she confirmed that only Roxy and herself were present. A smile pulled at River's lips.

I thought that we had to stay apart until the ceremony, she teased.

Adrian chuckled. *Tradition says that I can't **see** you, no one said that I couldn't talk to you. Besides, Cole and I could sense your unease. We don't have to do this yet if you're not ready.*

There was a pause as River closed her eyes and sighed. Their families had put their hearts into this celebration and River knew how disappointed they would be if she cancelled it. Besides, if she was honest with herself, River knew that she didn't want to wait. Marrying Adrian wasn't the issue. River wanted to be with her mate.

What if I'm not cut out to be a queen? she asked him seriously. River swore his wolf laughed.

Humans think too much, Crystal grumbled.

Is that what's worrying you? he asked warmly. *You will be a great queen. Just look at how strong you were during the battle. Look at the way you have taken charge and helped me restore order to the land and started rebuilding. You are a born leader, River. Even I would bow down to you,* he chuckled.

Adrian! she flushed. Unable to resist, a giggle found its way past her lips. *Thank you.*

I will see you soon, sweetheart, he promised like a caress.

Nodding, River's gaze refocused back on the dark-haired she-wolf in front of her.

A smirk showed on Roxy's face as she watched her friend. "How was the pep talk?"

"Nice," River admitted. "He knew just what to say."

"Well, as your mate, I would expect no less than for him to cheer you up." Scrunching up her nose, Roxy shrugged. "And…I guess communicating through your bond isn't technically cheating. I bet it makes things easier when you need a little space," she mumbled, fighting an eye roll.

River bit her lip to keep from smiling. "Is Dimitri still shadowing you everywhere?"

"Yes," her cousin groaned. "I bet you dinner that he's standing right outside the suite's door…leaning against the wall…glaring at the wood," she said, increasing her volume as she spoken since Roxy knew perfectly well that Dimitri could hear every word.

River felt for her friend. Roxy was furiously independent, and it had to be difficult adjusting to the unique bond she shared with her mate. Vampires couldn't speak telepathically like werewolves. Roxy once told her that they could feel each other's emotion though after they marked each other.

"Have you two decided what you're going to do about the whole immortality thing yet?"

Roxy shook her head, "No." Of their own accord her eyes darted to the door. "It's not an easy decision to make," she admitted quietly. "I've accepted him as my mate, and I'm not going to change my mind, but living forever..." her voice drifted off with a pensive frown.

Impulsively, River leaned forward to wrap her in a tight embrace. Roxy was the closest thing she had to a sister. Seeing her turmoil brought her no pleasure.

"Don't worry," River told her quietly. "Take as much time as you need. No matter what, I'll always be here for you." The two women squeezed each other tightly before River drew back once more. "Now then, I have something for you before our mothers return," River informed her mischievously.

Taking her cousin by the hand, River led her across the room towards the bed. There, she removed a box hidden beneath the bedskirt. Giggling, River handed her the box.

Unable to keep from grinning, Roxy removed the lid to reveal a pair of red shoes that perfectly matched her dress. Eyes widening, she took one of the hard-soled flats in her hand. It was embroidered with metallic thread and had just the barest hint of a heel.

Lifting up her skirt a bit, River stuck her foot out to show off a pair of identical shoes tinted ivory.

"I had them made just for this occasion. Honestly, I don't how anyone expects us to walk on the grass in four-inch heels. Quickly. You better put them on while I go hide the other ones."

Laughing, Roxy shook her head. "When did you become so sneaky?" she teased as she gladly donned the more sensible shoes.

"It's not sneaky," River refuted. "It's being resourceful. Can you imagine wearing these all night?" she asked as she held up the stilettos with disdain.

"That is something that we can always agree on."

All too soon there was a knock on the door as Thomas informed them that the ceremony was ready to begin. Just as Roxy predicted, Dimitri was leaning against the opposite wall when they appeared through the threshold. The moment he spotted his mate, his lips parted soundlessly and his eyes darkened to a deep red. Roxy's cheeks warmed at his appraisal. Before the she-wolf could blink, he was by her side with his arm draped possessively over her shoulders.

River flashed her cousin one last smile before turning towards her mother. She descended the stairs in a haze, looking neither here nor there as her feet carried her closer to where her mate waited. Once outside, River froze with a gasp. She had seen the work her family was doing to prepare Swift Wind for the ceremony, but the sight greeting her in the moonlight was beyond anything she could have dreamed. Not a cloud blocked the glimmering stars which kissed the ground with their glow. A small altar had been constructed by the edge of the lake, River's favorite place in the pack. A wooden arch covered in blooming vines towered over the structure. In the center of the arch, white flowers hung down, dancing in the slight breeze like branches of willow. A path of stone was laid in the very center, leading towards the altar. Rows of white chairs tied with silver and red ribbons curved in a slight arch on either side. Along the edges were tall potted trees decorated with masses of flowers and matching ribbons.

Eyes gleaming happily, River took the bouquet offered to her by her mother.

"This looks incredible," she gushed, unable to stop smiling. "Thank you!"

"Anything for my daughter," Amanda replied sincerely, wrapping her in an embrace.

"That was going to be my line," complained Nick good-naturedly as he appeared from within the house. Moving forward, he opened his arms and River willingly hugged her father.

Now, Nick said through the pack's mind-link. *If Adrian ever gets out of line, you make sure to tell me at once. I'll put him back in his place, king or no.*

River had to bite her lip to keep from laughing. Each of her brothers had said something of the same nature to her earlier in the day. River knew that she could handle herself when it came to her mate, but still, it never hurt to have some backup, just in case.

Yes, Father.

Stepping back, River wrapped her arm around the alpha's outstretched one. Above the peace of the water came the sound of music. It was time to begin. River's Maid of Honor, Roxy, took the lead down the aisle followed by Malinda, Amber, and James's mate, Ivy. The moment that River stood beside her father and the Wedding March began, her heart started to flutter. Taking a deep breath, her feet seemed to barely touch the cool stones in front of her. River vaguely noted the faces in the crowd. Pavel and his daughter, Caleb and his sons, the alphas of the kingdom's packs...nothing else mattered to her as her eyes locked on the tall, darkly handsome man waiting for her beside his brother, beta, and gamma. Adrian was all that filled River's vision. Each step towards him wasn't enough. Crystal wanted to be with him now.

He's ours, she declared possessively inside River's mind.

The she-wolf had difficulty reining in her wolf to keep her from racing the last few yards down the aisle. Once her eyes locked with that of her mate's, just the sight of him wasn't enough. She needed to be there, by his side without a second's delay.

Calm yourself, Crystal, River urged. *He is already ours. No one can deny that. Besides, we don't want to make a scene in front the packs, do we?*

The she-wolf's answering grunt caused a smirk to pull at River's lips. Luckily, her words soothed her inner beast and Crystal was silent...for the moment. Reaching the altar, Nick stepped forward and placed River's hand in Adrian's waiting palm. The two men gazed at each other with calm determination.

"Today, I gift to you my daughter," Nick said solemnly without breaking eye contact. "Her life, happiness and protection are now in your care. Do not disappoint me."

Adrian's blue-green eyes shimmered with respect and pride. "I swear to you that I will not fail."

With a nod, Nick gave River a kiss on the cheek before taking his place by his wife's side.

A grin spreading across her face, River handed her bouquet to Roxy and allowed Adrian to escort her the last few feet to the altar. While wedding ceremonies are usually performed by a pack elder, Magnus has insisted on presiding over the matrimony service himself. Gripping Adrian's other hand, River turned to face her soon-to-be husband. The light smoldering in his eyes as he peered at her, nearly stole her breath. River didn't need a mind-link to tell her what the man was thinking. A pink color tinted her cheeks, but she didn't avert her gaze as Magnus began to speak.

"Honored guests," the retired king greeted, holding out his arms. "It is with great pleasure that we gather here today not only for the union of two people, but for the induction of a new Queen Luna. May the Moon Goddess look down upon us this night and give her divine blessing forever upon this pair."

Shifting his sights to the couple in front of him, Magnus looked fondly at his son. "Adrian Fitzwilliam Elrod, King Alpha of Silver Fang, do you take this she-wolf as your mate? To love, cherish and protect for all time? Will you guide her as she rules beside you? And in turn, listen to her guidance for the benefit of the Kingdom?"

"I swear so to do," Adrian replied in a booming, confident voice.

Nodding his head in approval, Magnus turned to River.

"River Ava Carlson," he stated, adding her true name with a friendly smirk. "Do you take this wolf as your mate? To love, cherish and protect for all time? Will you stand beside him during times of peace or strife? Will you uphold the laws of our land? And use all your strength and power for the good of the Kingdom for the rest of your days?

"I swear so to do," River announced with a bright smile.

Retrieving a small golden knife from the altar, Magnus handed the blade first to Adrian, then River. Once each of them slit their palms, the former king pressed their palms together, uniting their blood. Next, Magnus draped a red ribbon over their hands. He loosely tied it around each of their wrists, binding them together before once more addressing the crowd.

"Just as the blood of these two mates binds them to one another, from this day forth, they shall be bound to this Kingdom as Silver Fang's rightful rulers. With great pride, I present to you, King Alpha Adrian and his new queen: Queen Luna River Ava Elrod."

Magnus's words were met with a gleeful torrent of noise. Everyone present rose to their feet as the happy couple swiftly made their way back up the aisle. Disappearing around some greenery, Adrian ignored the fact that one of his hands was still bound to River's and picked her up against his chest.

"I've been waiting all day to do this," he whispered huskily against her lips before kissing her passionately.

River's brain couldn't think of a reply. Crystal was yipping happily in her mind, but it was Adrian's firm mouth moving against hers that truly held her captive. Closing her eyes, she gave into the moment. Their guests wouldn't miss them for a few minutes at least.

Once the ceremony was completed, the wedding guests made their way along a gleaming path lined with strings of lights up above in the trees' canopies. The short stroll curved along with the edge of the lake towards a large open clearing. Massive tents covered the area, their silken material thin enough to see the stars above. Inside, chandeliers hung from the ceiling, casting a soft glow on the red and silver covered table and chairs. A dance floor was constructed between the two interconnecting tents with a long restaurant-style buffet in the back.

River considered the hundreds of people chattering happily as they milled about and filled their plates. This was the largest party she had ever attended besides the Moonlight

Celebration, and even that would be nothing compared to the second wedding event they would be holding for the entire kingdom in two weeks' time. The sheer number of people coming to greet their new queen luna would be overwhelming.

"You did wonderful," Adrian said proudly, wrapping an arm around River's waist. "Soon we'll be able to sneak off for the night."

River leaned her head against his shoulder with a sigh. "I can't wait. I'm happy to have our friends and family here, yet being the center of so much attention is exhausting."

A mischievous smirk appeared on the alpha's face. "Oh? I hope not too exhausting. After all, you're the center of *my* attention," he teased.

River lightly jabbed him in the side with her elbow. "That's different and you know it."

"Come," Adrian chuckled, taking her hand in his. "Let's us make our rounds and then we should be able to call it a night."

Offering no protest, River allowed him to lead her back into the crowd. It was a good thing that she had switched her shoes or her feet would be killing her by now.

Weaving her way through a few of the tables, Malinda spotted her long-time friend, Raven, sitting at the edge of the crowd. The witch's more secluded location didn't surprise Malinda. The other woman was never one for large gatherings. Making her way over, Malinda's brow rose somewhat. Seated next to the silver-haired witch, their bodies a mere inch from touching, was Alpha Jack.

His gaze passed over her with a respectful nod. However, he simply shifted his attention back towards the other guests. Since being forced to challenge his son, the once friendly wolf had become somber and quiet. After the battle, he had begun training his beta's son to take over as the future alpha.

Malinda's gaze shifted between them for a moment. *I never thought that I would see the day that Raven would be a wolf's mate.* When her eyes locked with the other woman's, Raven's irises sparked knowingly. Had she known this would come to pass all along? A soft chuckle sounded in Malinda's throat as she joined her friend.

"Pleasant evening, is it not?" Raven greeted softly.

"Yes, quite so," she agreed. Her eyes scanned the new queen on the opposite side of the dance floor. "River certainly looks like she is ready to escape."

Raven's lips pulled back in a smile. The longer she watched the she-wolf, the more solemn her expression became until the grin faded completely.

"Let her enjoy this peace."

Malinda frowned. Turning towards the other witch, she peered at the sudden change in her expression. Her eyes darted towards the wolf's profile, stilling the words she might have spoken.

"I see I'm not the only one having visions," Malinda said carefully.

Raven glanced to the side, considering her friend for a moment.

"We have both lived long enough to know that demons are never silent for long." She watched as Malinda's gaze shifted to Jack once again. "He knows," Raven informed her. "Jack agrees that we should wait until after the celebrations to tell them."

The witch nodded her head. She had been thinking the same. "Since his mortal form was just banished to the underworld, he won't be able to act quickly. You're right, Raven, we should let them enjoy this peace while they can. There will be enough challenges to come."

Directing their conversation to a more pleasant subject, the two women continued watching the party unfold from the sideline. Over by the dance floor, Adrian clasped River's hand and guided her out of the tent. A smile stretched across his face as he led her in the opposite direction of the pack house.

"Where are we going?" River giggled as she was swiftly led away.

"You'll see," was her mate's teasing reply.

Moving down a side path, Adrian strode through the trees until a small gazebo came into view. It was nestled among the trees by the water's edge. The wood had been freshly painted white with rose brushes planted around the perimeter. A stone path led to the dark stained floor where a wide swing hovered above the ground. Candles hung from the beams around the edge of the gazebo, casting a warm, soft glow. Stepping into the structure, River's lips parted silently. The swing was deep enough for the two of them with a thick cushion. The shrubbery had all been pruned in the front, giving them a clear, private view of the lake.

"When did you do all of this?" she whispered in awe.

Leaning against the railing, Adrian loosely crossed his arms over his chest with a shrug. "While our mothers were planning the ceremony, your father and Blake helped me with this. I thought that you would like a place all your own for when we come to visit. I know leaving here isn't going to be easy for you. Do you like it?"

Turning towards her mate, River's eyes sparkled like the shimmering stars above. "I love it!" Stepping closer. She wrapped her arms around Adrian's waist. "And I love you, Adrian. As long as I have you, I can be happy anywhere."

Pulling River's body closer with one arm, Adrian's fingers lightly cupped the side of her face.

"You will always have me," he declared like a caress as his mouth slowly moved closer and closer. "I am yours, River Ava Elrod, Queen of my Heart. Forever."

As Adrian's lips connected with her own, River's heart rejoiced. In that moment, she knew that she was truly 'blest' after all.

About the Author

Creator of *The Dragon Marked Chronicles,* Jay has been a lover of the written word from an early age. She currently works a 'normal' fulltime job along with her writing. When she isn't penning her latest adventure, she enjoys reading, watching anime and spending time walking along the beach. She currently lives in Pennsylvania with her family

Printed in Great Britain
by Amazon

37829917R00172